It seemed cooler by the back door of the brick kitchen building. Aimee poured cold water into the tin wash pan, and as Dominic cautiously washed his hands, she held a clean dry towel for him.

"You don't have to do this," he said.

"I know," she said, "I want to." She didn't look up at him as she carefully dried the palms of his blistered hands.

But Dominic couldn't drag his eyes away from her, from the way the dusky light glimmered upon her black hair. He felt his body responding to her nearness, to her sweet woman's scent and the touch of her soft hands.

He gritted his teeth as she applied the salve, but it was not against the pain in his hands that he fought. He muttered something and pulled his hand out of her grasp as he took a step backward.

"I'm sorry," she said, glancing up into his face. "Did I—"

"Aimee . . ." His voice was a croak, a husky protest of warning. "If you know what's good for you . . . you'll go back into the house and let me do this alone."

Aimee's white teeth pulled at her lower lip. "I'm not sure I *ever* knew what was good for me." Her eyes were troubled and as questioning as his.

That sweet look, that moment of hesitation was all it took to break Dominic's resolve. His hands moved around her waist and in one swift movement, she was in his arms, straining against him as if she could never be close enough. . . .

ANOTHER TIME . . . ANOTHER PLACE . . . ANOTHER LOVE—
Let Pinnacle Historical Romances take you there!

LOVE'S STOLEN PROMISES (631, $5.99/$6.99)
by Sylvie F. Sommerfield
Mitchell Flannery and Whitney Clayborn are two star-crossed lovers, who defy social conventions. He's a dirt-poor farm boy, and she's a South Carolina society belle. On the eve of the Civil War, they come together joyously, and are quickly and cruelly wrenched apart. After making a suitable marriage, Whitney imagines that she will never feel the soaring heights of passion again. Then, Mitchell returns home seven years after marching away. . . .

VELVET IS THE NIGHT (598, $4.99/$5.99)
by Elizabeth Thornton
To save her family from the guillotine, Claire Devereux agrees to become the mistress of the evil, corrupt commissioner, Phillipe Duhet. She agrees to give her body to him, but she swears that her spirit will remain untouched. To her astonishment, Claire finds herself responding body and soul to Duhet's expert caresses. Little does Claire know but Duhet has been abducted and she has been falling under the spell of his American twin brother, Adam Dillon!

ALWAYS AND FOREVER (647, $4.99/$5.99)
by Gina Robins
Shipwrecked when she was a child, Candeliera Caron is unaware of her wealthy family in New Orleans. She is content with her life on the tropical island, surrounded by lush vegetation and natives who call her their princess. Suddenly, sea captain Nick Tiger sails into her life, and she blooms beneath his bold caresses. Adrift in a sea of rapture, this passionate couple longs to spend eternity under the blazing Caribbean sky.

PIRATE'S KISS (612, $4.99/$5.99)
by Diana Haviland
When Sybilla Thornton arrives at her brother's Jamaican sugar plantation, she immediately falls under the spell of Gavin Broderick. Broderick is an American pirate who is determined to claim Sybilla as forcefully as the ships he has conquered. Sybilla finds herself floating upside down in a strange land of passion, lust, and power. She willingly drowns in the heat of this pirate's kiss.

SWEET FOREVER (604, $4.99/$5.99)
by Becky Lee Weyrich
At fifteen, Julianna Doran plays with a Ouija board and catches the glimpse of a handsome sea captain Brom Vanderzee. This ghostly vision haunts her dreams for years. About to be wed, she returns to the Hudson River mansion where she first encountered this apparition. She experiences one night of actual ecstasy with her spectral swain. Afterwards, he vanishes. Julianna crosses the boundaries of her world to join him in a love that knows no end.

Available wherever paperbacks are sold, or order direct from the Publisher. Send cover price plus 50¢ per copy for mailing and handling to Pinnacle Books, Dept. 753, 475 Park Avenue South, New York, N.Y. 10016. Residents of New York and Tennessee must include sales tax. DO NOT SEND CASH. For a free Zebra/Pinnacle catalog please write to the above address.

Natchez Moon
Clara Wimberly

PINNACLE BOOKS
WINDSOR PUBLISHING CORP.

*For my family. Wayne, you really are my "inspiration."
Also to Wayne and Dawn, Mark and Carrie, Suzanne and
Doug and our latest addition—little Hannah Lee.*

PINNACLE BOOKS are published by

Windsor Publishing Corp.
475 Park Avenue South
New York, NY 10016

Copyright © 1993 by Clara Wimberly

All rights reserved. No part of this book may be reproduced in any form or by any means without the prior written consent of the Publisher, excepting brief quotes used in reviews.

If you purchased this book without a cover, you should be aware that this book is stolen property. It was reported as "unsold and destroyed" to the Publisher and neither the Author nor the Publisher has received any payment for this "stripped book."

Pinnacle and the P logo are trademarks of Windsor Publishing Corp.

First Printing: September, 1993

Printed in the United States of America

One

March 1824
Natchez, Mississippi

Pale strips of moonlight fell across the newly painted veranda and into the darkened, perfume-filled bedroom. Aimee LeBeaux restlessly pushed aside the gauzy mosquito netting and swung her bare legs over the edge of the bed. The cool broad cypress boards of the floor felt clean and soothing against the soles of her feet.

She didn't bother to light a candle; she needed the comfort of the darkness tonight. Nights in this room had always been her haven, her time alone with her husband Jim. They had selected this room purposely because it could be accessed only by the one door that led to the long, cool veranda.

Those times seemed so long ago. Now she hated the nights.

She gazed out the windows toward the huge magnolias and ancient live oaks that surrounded the plantation house. Long gray strands of Spanish moss hung from the trees, motionless, like thousands of small silent ghosts, waiting in the hot night air.

It was much too hot for March and there was no

hint of a breeze to cool the sultry darkness. The heat intensified the sweet scent of hyacinths that bloomed near the veranda and the drooping purple wisteria that hung gracefully from a nearby trellis.

Aimee jumped nervously as she caught her reflection in the long cheval mirror near the windows. Her image in the voluminous white dressing gown was faint and ghostly. The gown seemed to hang sadly on her slender, petite form.

Aimee turned quickly from the mirror, chiding herself for her nervousness. She didn't know what was wrong, except that a vague, unpleasant feeling nagged at her and wouldn't let her sleep. That and the same things that had plagued her these past few months. Too many thoughts, too many memories. Too many fears that she would never be able to make it here alone.

She pushed open the wide French doors leading to the veranda and stepped out into the fragrant Mississippi night. How she loved it here in the wild, uncivilized land along the Natchez Trace. Loved the scents, the sounds that one rarely experienced in the city.

Just beyond the veranda there was a faint glimmer of light, the moon's reflection on a bronze and marble statue that sat in the middle of a newly plowed square of lawn. Her new garden, the one she had longed for since coming here, was ready now to be planted with her favorite roses and lavender. Jim had brought the statue home from Natchez last summer and promised her a garden for it as beautiful as any in the city.

Tears formed in her eyes and she shook them away, then turned to place her hands on the low banister of the porch. She looked toward the sky, wondering how many more long, agonizing hours were left until morning.

6

The moon was full and heavy, hanging in the dark murky sky like a great splotch of orange paint. A Natchez moon, Jim called it. The kind of moon that hovered above the Mississippi River in the hot hazy days of summer and turned the night skies orange. It was different from the cool, clear wintry moon, as if the warmth of heat and humidity transformed it. This kind of moon cast its flattering light upon the white mansions along the cliffs of Natchez and even managed to make the taverns and brothels below the cliffs at the river's edge appear peaceful and benign.

"It's your Natchez moon, Jim," she whispered, unable to still the trembling of her lips.

She looked far beyond the huge trees but couldn't quite see the small plot of ground that served as the LeBeaux family cemetery. The tears came then; she could not stop them. It had been six months since Jim's death and still she could not bear to think of him without this heavy, excruciating pain upon her chest.

How many times he had teased her about his being ten years older than her. But still, he had been too young at thirty-five to die, too exciting and full of life ever to leave her.

Or so she thought.

But he had also been filled with an adventurous and daring spirit, qualities that attracted her to him from the very beginning. She'd loved that about him and even though she felt that impetuous nature had contributed to his death, she could not wish those characteristics away even now.

No one could ever know how she grieved after the duel that took his life or how many times she wished she had gone with him that cool autumn morning. She should have insisted he forget the quarrel that sent him to their neighbor's dueling field.

Afterward, Aimee's aunt Eulie, her only living relative, had begged her to move back to Natchez. But she couldn't. She couldn't leave this beautiful plantation she had restored, and she couldn't bear to leave that small silent plot of ground beyond the huge oaks.

She stood, mute and still in the shadowed moonlight, letting the tears come, letting all the pain and agony wash freely through her. She had learned that the grief would pass and so she did not try when she was alone to quell its advances upon her senses.

Dominic Valcour had ridden a long way to get to LeBeaux Plantation. As he tied his horse beneath the mossy overhang of the huge oaks he was surprised to see no lights shining forth from the house.

He smiled into the darkness. What was wrong with his old friend Jim LeBeaux? Had marriage made the rascal soft? Dominic would make the man's life miserable when he forced him to explain what he was doing in bed so early and why the house was not full of laughing, drinking travelers.

He wondered if Jim still used the old run-down plantation for an inn. He knew of Jim's plans to turn it into a cotton plantation and wondered if he had ever managed to restore the house to its former glory. But then, knowing Jim as he did, he quickly dismissed that thought. He doubted that any woman could ever tame his rowdy friend, not for long anyway. He found that as hard to imagine as Jim LeBeaux's settling down in one spot.

Dominic walked softly across the lawn toward the back of the house, thinking to use the back stairs. If his memory served correctly, the second story was where he'd find Jeanine's room.

"Ah, sweet Jeanine, " he whispered, laughing softly to himself. If he was lucky and she had no other visitor, the friendly, warm-blooded tavern wench would welcome him when he crawled into her soft bed. His three-year absence would make no difference to her.

The sounds of the forest were loud around him and the big house. Dominic didn't remember the structure being so bright in color; maybe Jim's high-class wife had at least persuaded her husband to paint it. Dominic hoped she had not made too many changes, especially since he had come to claim his half of the plantation and begin his partnership with Jim. He also hoped Jim's wife would accept him. But he wondered.

To hear Jim tell it, Aimee LeBeaux was a saint, and a beautiful one at that. Dominic had to admit he was curious about this beautiful, saintly creature he'd never met.

All he knew was that Jim had met her in Natchez three years ago. Dominic could hardly believe his adventurous friend had suddenly turned eager for marriage, ready and willing to forego his life as a soldier, couldn't believe he'd given up his wild, hell-raising ways for one woman. And a woman of the Natchez *beau monde* at that. He was even more surprised that the social creature had been willing and, if Jim was telling the truth, even eager to come to the wilderness and the badly neglected LeBeaux Plantation.

Dominic was at the back of the house. He stopped suddenly, astonished by the beautiful vision in white on the darkened lower veranda. Then he smiled.

"Jeanine. Well my little creole, you're taking the challenge away . . . and making this so very easy."

He crept across the lawn, his footsteps muffled by

9

the grass. He stepped across the banister at the end of the veranda, his soft doeskin boots making no noise on the wooden floor. The girl had her back to him and he smiled as he watched one slender arm lift the long black hair away from her neck. The perfect spot for a kiss.

Quickly he moved behind her, one strong arm going about her waist at the same moment as he bent his dark head to place his lips at the nape of her neck.

She jumped and a soft scream began in her throat. But Dominic acted quickly, whirling her around to cover her lips with his in a wild, hot kiss that muffled any further protests. Her arms were trapped against his chest and he let his hands roam freely down her back to her small waist, then down to curve over her hips.

He was a bit surprised at the feel of her; he remembered Jeanine as being soft and round, voluptuous the way a woman was meant to be. Tonight she seemed much smaller, delicate even. He also did not remember the sweet reticence of her or that she ever played games of shyness. Was it possible she had forgotten him? He would not have thought so.

Aimee's green eyes were wide open in shock, as she tried to see who held her. But in the darkness there was only his silhouette and a glimpse of dark skin and even darker hair. A rough stubble of beard scraped her skin and she thought she could hear the quiet rumble of laughter deep in his chest as she struggled and kicked at his legs. But try as she might she could not pull her lips away from his fiercely demanding mouth.

Her heart was pounding in fear. She'd always felt safe here, and thought nothing of being alone outside at night, even away from the house. But now as she

10

pushed at the hard, muscled chest and strained to free herself of the arms that bound her, she was afraid for her life. She could not break away and despite her moans of protest, the man continued his assault of ravaging kisses.

She managed to move one hand and discovered a leather scabbard at the man's waist. Her trembling fingers felt cold metal and without thinking she pulled the knife free of its binding.

Dominic was quite distracted by this new Jeanine. Something was different about her. God, the taste of her mouth, the scent of her, the feel of her soft, slender body moving against his was something he didn't remember. And the combination was making him a little crazy.

Damn, maybe he'd been in the backwoods too long. He was completely lost in the moment, in the passion that sparked between them, and it took a second for him to realize that the sharp jab of cold steel against his belly was a knife.

He stepped away from her then, his arms held out in surrender as he looked with surprise down into the face of a woman he did not know. A woman as beautiful and sultry as the Mississippi.

Black hair streamed down her shoulders, dark eyes glittered with fury in the dim moonlight as she held the knife straight out in front of her, still aimed at his stomach.

"You're not Jeanine," he said with a puzzled frown. His deep voice was soft and resonant in the enclosure of the porch.

"I certainly am not!"

He stepped back, his black eyes admiring the play of light upon her smooth skin, the shadowed curve of her lips . . . such sweet, luscious lips . . .

11

Aimee saw the glint of white teeth, his smile in the moonlight, felt his hands reach for her again. And she knew instinctively what he had in mind. She could feel it as strongly as if he'd just told her what he wanted.

She screamed then, shattering the calm of the evening and instantly causing the night sounds around them to stop. At the same time she lunged at him with the knife.

"Jesus!" he grunted, reaching to grab her wrist and twist the knife from her hand. "Do you want to wake the entire household?"

"Yes . . ." she gasped, breathless as she struggled with him. "That's . . . exactly . . . what I want."

Soon footsteps sounded at the other end of the veranda and within seconds, Dominic found himself surrounded by Negro men, some of them wielding clubs, another a heavy silver candlestick.

Candles were brought by female slaves and lamps lit, until the veranda was aglow with light. They stared with huge frightened eyes at the stranger who had dared to accost the mistress in her own home. Some of the women's eyes grew warm and curious as they moved over the handsome black-haired stranger.

Aimee stood openmouthed, her green eyes wide and questioning as she stared at the man in the light. He reminded her so much of Jim that she almost cried out.

He was taller, more slender than Jim, but just as muscular and powerful looking. But it was that wildness, that look of the brigand that captured her imagination and brought memories of her husband back with heartstopping pain.

Quickly her eyes moved over the fringed leather shirt that encased strong, wide shoulders and tapered down to a narrow waist. The worn, tan buckskins fit his muscular thighs snugly and were tucked into soft knee-high doeskin boots. He had a week's growth of beard and he looked as ruthless and cruel as any man she'd ever seen on the rugged wilderness trail that ran nearby. And she had seen many.

His long straight black hair was tied back with a leather thong and she found herself looking into the blackest eyes she'd ever seen. The devil's own eyes, she thought. Eyes that watched her now, with just the faintest hint of amusement in their ebony depths. He seemed not at all frightened or embarrassed at being caught trying to attack her.

Dominic forced himself to look away from the exquisite creature only when one of the dark-skinned men stepped toward him. He was an elderly man, with gray mingled into the black curls of his hair. He looked to have dressed quickly, but his trousers were of fine cloth, obviously those of a house servant. He lifted a lantern high in the air as he surveyed the woodsman who had come so brazenly in the middle of the night and who stared so boldly at all of them.

"Mister Dominic?" the old man whispered in disbelief. "Is that you?" He stepped closer, then turned his head slightly as if to announce to the others. "Praise de Lawd people, it's Mister Dominic!"

Dominic stared at the man a moment before his black eyes lit with recognition. Then he stepped forward to grasp the old man's shoulders and hug him fiercely.

"Amos!" Deep laughter rumbled from Dominic's throat as he clapped the servant on the back. "My God, it's good to see you. For a moment I thought I'd wandered into the wrong house." His eyes moved only briefly to the woman in the filmy white gown who

13

seemed taken aback by Amos's joyous greeting.

But Aimee recognized the name immediately; she'd heard Jim mention it enough. She should have known right away who he was. What other man could be so arrogant, so downright overbearing, or so savagely handsome as Jim's best friend—the notorious half-breed, Dominic Valcour.

"Mister Valcour." She deliberately kept her voice soft and calm as she spoke, wondering if he had felt the fearful pounding of her heart when he held her so tightly against him moments ago. "You obviously mistook me for someone else. I'm Aimee LeBeaux, Jim's wife."

He turned to her, his eyes moving slowly over her, lingering on the soft curve of her breasts above her gown. Then he looked into her eyes, noting their emerald green blaze as she interpreted his look. He smiled. She was behaving as if he'd stolen her virtue instead of having taken only a simple kiss by mistake.

"I apologize. I thought you were Jeanine." His deep voice was like a caress, obviously rehearsed for just the most flattering effect when he spoke to women.

"Jeanine no longer works here." She heard the churlish sound of her own voice and the soft laughter it brought from the servants assembled on the veranda.

Dominic bent and retrieved his knife from the floor, sliding it smoothly into the leather scabbard at his side. "Again, I apologize." He wondered why her full, beautiful lips had clamped into a thin line, why her eyes were so hard and resentful. He had said he was sorry. What else did she want? "Where is that rascal husband of yours? Don't tell me he's asleep at this time of night."

Immediately he saw the wrinkling of her brow, the

pained look on the faces of the men and women around him. He glanced quickly again at Aimee and saw the glimmer of tears that appeared in her eyes.

A sharp stab of premonition wrenched at his heart. Not Jim, he wanted to shout. She couldn't be about to tell him what he was thinking.

"Jim's dead, Mister Valcour."

"No."

His denial was a mere whisper as he frowned down at her. She had not expected a hardened man like him to react this way and for a moment she stepped forward, as if intending to comfort him.

"Would . . . would you like to come inside . . . have a drink? I'll tell you everything." She glanced at the house servants around them. This was no place to explain. And she was hardly dressed to receive guests. "Amos, take Mister Valcour to one of the guest rooms upstairs so he can refresh himself. I'll be in the front parlor as soon as I've changed." With a quick backward glance, she stepped from the veranda and through the French doors to her bedroom.

Some of the servants, the ones who knew Dominic, patted him affectionately on the back as if welcoming him home. There were softly spoken good nights and then old Amos moved beside him.

"This way, Mister Dominic. You got any bags for me to carry?"

"Those will arrive later, from Natchez." Dominic shook his head, more to clear his mind than anything. He could not believe it. Jim LeBeaux, dead. But when? How? Jim was as big and full of life as the overflowing, vibrant Mississippi; it just didn't seem possible that he was gone.

"What happened, Amos?"

"Maybe it's best you let Miz LeBeaux tell you about

it. It's a sad thing for sure . . . mighty sad. Miz Le-Beaux, she done changed from a young girl to a woman with the weight of the world on her shoulders, seems like. She's near 'bout worked herself to death, I reckon, trying to finish the house without Mister Jim. Some say she works so hard, tryin' to forget."

"Finish the house?"

"Oh, yessir. Miz Aimee done restored the plantation house, had the fields cleared. Gonna plant ol' man cotton any day now. It's a grand place now, Le-Beaux House is. Grand as any in Natchez." The pride in the old man's voice reflected his obvious approval of his mistress's changes.

"I see. That explains a great deal." Dominic glanced at the newly painted veranda and noticed again how bright the exterior of the house was.

"But where's young Lucas?" Suddenly alarm filled his black eyes and he grasped Amos's sleeve to halt him. "He's not . . . he wasn't . . . ?"

"Oh, no sir. Young Lucas is just fine. He's upstairs sound asleep. You can see for yourself in the mornin'." Amos glanced, slyly at Dominic. "Been awhile since you seen the boy. He might not remember you."

"You're right. Three years is a long time for a little boy."

Dominic breathed a deep sigh. He felt as if his whole world was coming apart and it weighed heavily on him. He might have just run a great distance for all the air that was left in his lungs. He closed his eyes and ran his hand over his face, thoughtfully stroking the dark beard of his square jaw before nodding his head at the old man.

"All right," he said. "All right, Amos. Lead the way."

Later when Aimee stepped across the threshold of the parlor, she saw Dominic Valcour waiting for her. He seemed lost in thought and didn't hear her light footstep.

She studied his face in the light of the parlor during those few moments before he noticed her. His skin, beneath the stubble of his beard, was dark and smooth, his brows and eyelashes as black as his hair. She noticed the way his long lashes lay against his cheeks as he looked down and she felt a surprising wish to see his eyes here in the light. She wondered if they were as black as she'd first thought.

He was looking down at a silver framed picture in his hand—a small painting of her and Jim on their wedding day. In the other hand Dominic held a glass which he now lifted to his lips to toss its amber contents down his throat in one quick swallow. Carefully he placed the picture back on the mantel and leaned one arm heavily against the fireplace.

"Mister Valcour?"

He looked around at her, revealing the full potency of his eyes, eyes that were shining now and filled with pain. And she saw that they were indeed as black as she remembered. He took a deep breath and cleared his throat, then the look of sadness was gone, replaced by that carefully calculated smile she had seen before.

As she walked into the room she could feel his eyes settle on her with undisguised curiosity. His quick glance took in the cream-colored silk dress she wore and its bright sash of rich tartan plaid. She guessed that he expected her to be dressed in mourning black, but she had refused to do that. Her grief was personal and private; she felt no need to display it to others.

"Won't you sit down?" she asked.

17

He took a chair across from her near the white marble fireplace. And he saw Aimee's glance of pride at the newly decorated room.

"You've made a great deal of changes here," he said, his voice casual and light.

"The idea was conceived long before Jim's death — it was something he and I planned together." She had not meant to sound so defensive, but she sensed he might think her work frivolous in the light of Jim's death. Something kept her from telling him that it was the only thing that had kept her sane these past months. She wasn't sure he would believe her anyway.

She had transformed the neglected old house into a strikingly beautiful plantation home in preparation for its new purpose. She'd found it incredible that the LeBeaux family had allowed the rich farmland to remain fallow for so many years. Even when the house was used as an inn, the fields could have been productive. But part of the land was cleared now and ready for its first planting of cotton. She thought it ironic that Dominic Valcour had chosen this particular time to visit LeBeaux, just when she was preparing a new way of life for herself.

He was watching her, waiting for her to tell him about Jim. He refilled his glass and held it casually in his long, beautifully tapered fingers. He had not changed clothes, but still wore the fringed buckskins and boots.

"Shall I pour you a drink, too?" he asked quietly. "You look as if you could use one."

"No," she said, lifting her eyes toward his. "I don't drink."

He smiled, more a quirk of his lips really than a smile, as if he did not quite believe anything she said.

She clasped her hands tightly together in her lap,

18

then nervously unclasped them again. She smoothed the skirt of her ivory silk dress, and looked into his watchful ebony eyes as she clutched her fingers together.

"I'm not sure where to begin. How long has it been since you heard from Jim?"

"I saw him last summer when he was in Natchez. He came down to the river one night and we had a drink together."

Aimee's finely sculpted eyebrows lifted slightly. She couldn't hide her disapproval of this man; she knew of his womanizing and gambling, the casual, unsavory way he had lived his thirty-two years.

"Did he mention the problems he'd been having? The altercation he had with Harold Compton?"

"Compton? He's your neighbor isn't he? No, Jim didn't say anything."

"I suppose he wouldn't. He had too much pride; always thought he could handle anything alone." She frowned, perplexed by the tears that threatened to close her throat. For some reason, she didn't want this coolly arrogant man to see her cry.

"Exactly what was the problem with Compton?"

"Land. Isn't that what all the problems in the wilderness are about? Land." Her voice was hard and bitter.

"Tell me what happened."

"Jim and I decided to use the LeBeaux land that had been idle for years. I'm sure you know that Jim's father used the plantation solely as a tavern before he died." She saw the look in his black eyes and remembered that he had come looking for the tavern wench, Jeanine. She felt her face stiffen as she answered her own question. "But what a foolish question, of course you do."

His smile was cool and amused.

"You also know I'm sure how restless Jim was; he needed something to occupy his time. It was a hard transition for him, becoming a settled landholder."

Dominic nodded. He understood exactly how Jim had felt. They had both lived the same kind of nomadic life until Jim met this woman and married her.

"Anyway, we planned to clear the land and plant our first crop of cotton. But last summer when we began to do that, Mister Compton disputed the boundaries. One day his men even went so far as to whip two of our Negroes working in the fields. They came home, bleeding . . . and begged Jim not to make them return. They said Mister Compton would kill them if they did. Jim went to Compton and there was a terrible fight. They say Jim almost killed the man."

As her emerald eyes looked into Dominic's he saw her frustration and her pain. It was hard for a woman to understand how a man's pride could lead him into something like that.

"I begged Jim to get some help, but you know how headstrong he could be."

"Oh, I know it well," he replied.

"The feud worsened. One of our barns was burned. Threats were exchanged for several weeks. Then one day last autumn, Mister Compton came here to the house—to see me this time." The tone of her voice changed and a frown wrinkled her brow as she recalled that day. When she looked up, a tear fell slowly down one cheek and she wiped it angrily away with her fingers. She took a breath and continued.

"He . . . Mister Compton asked me to . . . he . . ." She stopped, her voice hoarse and faltering.

"He made advances to you."

She was surprised at the hard edge in his voice and

the way his dark eyes glittered with anger.

"Yes."

"To provoke Jim," he said. He set his glass on a nearby table and stood suddenly. He walked to the fireplace only to turn and walk back to his chair where he stood gazing down at her. His fingers were clenched tightly around the back of the chair. "Jim should have known what the man was doing. Surely he wasn't foolish enough to let Compton provoke him into a fight?"

"I'm afraid that's exactly what he did. Jim came in just in time to see me struggling with Compton." She shuddered as if the memory chilled her. "I remember so well the look on Jim's face, the way he lit into the man so savagely. I thought he would kill him right then and there."

"He should have."

"Compton got up off the floor and smiled. He actually smiled." She looked up at Dominic, her face ashen and vulnerable with the pain of remembering.

Dominic's jaw tightened. "Go on."

"Compton challenged Jim to a duel. And the next morning . . . he was dead." She lifted trembling fingers to rub at her eyes, trying desperately to control her grief for a while longer.

Dominic wanted to go to her. He wanted to pull her up from the chair and take her in his arms. But after what had happened on the veranda he knew he dared not. Even as she told the shocking story, he'd had a hard time keeping his eyes away from her mouth, and an even harder one trying to repress the heated desire he felt every time he remembered those kisses.

He turned to stalk across the floor. "The damned fool," he muttered. His doeskin boots made only a soft swishing noise on the carpet that lay in the center

21

of the room. "Jim was always a fool when it came to fair play. He thought everyone else played by the same rules as he did."

"You knew him so well."

"We were like brothers," he replied softly.

"I'm sorry you had to find out this way. I tried to find you but . . ."

"It's all right. I can be a hard man to find. But I'm here now and I intend to set things right with this Compton."

"No," she said, her voice rising with a note of panic. "I don't want any more killings; I don't want your death on my conscience, too. Besides, I could never expect you to fight for land that isn't yours."

Dominic only stared at her, his black eyes giving nothing of his feelings away. There was nothing he could do except tell her.

"But it is," he said, his voice soft. "Didn't Jim tell you? Half of LeBeaux Plantation . . . the land, the house, the slaves . . . everything . . . is mine."

Two

"You can't be serious."

"I assure you, I'm totally serious."

She stood up quickly, stumbling slightly as she did. Dominic reached forward as if to steady her, but she pulled away angrily, her eyes shooting green fire.

"Why are you doing this? Have you come here only to cause me more grief?" She felt her face growing hot, felt the blood rush to her head. She was angry almost beyond control and she couldn't seem to help herself.

She didn't like the feelings he aroused in her, those strange, disturbing feelings that she could not understand. She didn't want him here, had known almost from the first moment she saw him that he was trouble. She'd fought so hard to maintain control after Jim's death, to keep herself sane with work on the plantation. But as much as she loved her husband, this had become her work, her own love, and she was not willing to share that with anyone. Especially not this brash, thoroughly confusing man who stood even now staring at her with those penetrating black eyes that seemed to see into her very soul.

"I'll be happy to explain if you'll listen," he said.

Dominic watched the play of emotion on her lovely

face, saw the confusion that tore at her. He should have realized it would be a shock, should have waited instead of plunging headlong into the fray as he usually did. He thought Jim would have told her by now. But then he should have known. Jim was not one to accept responsibility unless he was forced to.

Dominic had lent Jim the money last summer to pay off past debts and to buy whatever equipment he needed. He had not questioned him, nor bothered to find out his plans. And Jim had been the one who insisted on making him half owner of everything, telling him lightly that he needed to settle down himself. He'd had the papers drawn up then and there and both of them had signed them.

He could see how upset Aimee was about the news and if he was totally honest with himself, he wasn't in the mood now to discuss it either.

"It's late," he murmured. "Perhaps we should talk about this tomorrow."

"I think I would prefer that if you don't mind," she said stiffly. "It's late and I'm tired."

In truth, all Aimee really wanted was to scream at him and tell him there would be no discussion. But she remained silent, torn between doing what Jim would want and what her instincts told her to do. Did this man really expect to move into her home and become a part of all she had worked for?

She turned from him and left the room without looking back.

Later as she readied herself once again for bed, she distractedly took down her long hair and brushed it slowly until it snapped with life. She looked at her reflection in the mirror and saw the anger in her eyes.

She even resented his having seen her hair down

earlier. Her long, lustrous hair that was her one vanity and that no man had ever seen this way except Jim . . . until now.

Visions of Dominic Valcour flashed before her. The feel of his arms about her had left a surprising longing in her, a deep, physical longing. It had been so long since she'd been held, since . . .

She shook the thoughts away, but they kept returning again and again. The feel of his hard, muscular body, the way his hands moved so possessively over her, so expertly. And the memory of his mouth, the hunger in his kisses, left her trembling.

She shook her head violently as if by doing so she could dispel the visions that troubled her. She felt such guilt, and she also felt a deep, wrenching fear. She never wanted to love any man again, never wanted to feel for anyone what she'd felt for Jim. It was just too painful to take a chance on losing it.

She remembered the surprise in Dominic's eyes, the way he had looked on the veranda when he realized she was not Jeanine.

Jeanine! It hadn't taken Aimee long to send that one packing. Evidently Jim thought it perfectly all right for the woman to sell herself to any man who moved along the Natchez Trace. But inn or not, she was not about to let the woman carry on that way— not here in her own home!

For some reason it irritated her more than she could say that Dominic had come looking for the dark-haired Creole.

"Men," she muttered. Sometimes she wondered if there was an ounce of restraint in the lot of them. They all seemed to think it was their due to take anything they chose.

As she lay in bed, waiting for sleep, Aimee watched the orange moon through her window as it drifted across the sky. She felt as if she had only closed her eyes when she heard the first rooster crow.

The next morning before Aimee went into the dining room for breakfast, she'd already seen to the cook's weekly menu and given orders for the daily cleaning. Then she'd spoken to Gregory Davis, her new overseer whom she had hired only last week. She hardly knew what to tell him until she could speak further with Dominic.

But one thing had become clear to Aimee during the restless morning hours — no matter how much she wanted to deny Dominic Valcour's claim, or how she wished he had never come, she knew she had to face the possibility that he had a legal hold on LeBeaux Plantation.

She walked briskly into the dining room, pushing the already damp strands of hair back from her face. It looked as if they had another hot humid day ahead of them.

Dominic rose slowly from the table when Aimee entered the room, and there was a decided courtliness in his manner. He looked different this morning in black trousers and a cool, billowing white shirt.

Aimee took note of his clean-shaven face and as she did, she could almost feel the former rough scratchiness of it against her cheek.

Dominic's smile was wary and guarded . . . polite, as he watched her from beneath dark brows.

She nodded curtly to him and looked about the room before speaking to one of the maids who was placing a basket of bread on the table. She didn't miss the girl's sly glances at the dark-haired man, nor the way she grinned when Dominic glanced her way.

"Jezzy, where's Lucas?"

"Lordy, I don't know, ma'am," the young dark-skinned woman drawled. "I seen him out in the yard early this mornin' chasin' after that big ol' red rooster."

With a sigh, Aimee rose and walked to the hallway. "Amos? Amos . . . where is Lucas? Would you find him please and tell him to come in to breakfast?" She walked briskly back to the table. "That will be all for now, Jezzy. Just leave the coffee on the sideboard."

As Jezzy was leaving the room, she stopped, placed her hand over her mouth and sneezed loudly. She moved on to the hallway, her voice ringing back toward them. "Sneeze on Tuesday, kiss a stranger."

Dominic's dark brow lifted and he smiled crookedly toward Aimee, as if to remind her of his kiss last night.

Aimee sighed and rolled her eyes helplessly. Sometimes Jezzy's sayings and superstitions were almost more than she could take.

Dominic watched Aimee as he sipped the strong black coffee. It was evident how much respect she commanded in the household; she seemed to be very efficient for someone so young. He judged her to be a good ten or twelve years younger than Jim LeBeaux.

Almost before Aimee could settle into her chair, the boy came running into the room. But at her pointed look, he stopped suddenly, then walked more sedately to his place at the table.

Dominic smiled. It had been more than three years since he'd seen the boy and he could see that Lucas

27

didn't remember him. He and Jim had found the child wandering along the trail one day. His Cherokee mother and white trader father had both been killed in the wilderness near the natural bridge in Tennessee. Dominic and Jim had decided that the boy should stay at LeBeaux.

Dominic wondered if Aimee resented having to raise the young orphan now that she was alone.

The boy's dark eyes moved to Dominic. He frowned, then moved closer to the man.

"Who are you?" he demanded.

Dominic stood to his full height and looked down at the boy, then extended his hand. "Hello, Little Deer."

Lucas took a deep breath and his expression quietly changed into a wide grin of surprise.

"Dom? Dominic?" The black-haired boy ignored the hand and instead wrapped his arms around Dominic's waist. "Aimee, it's Dominic! And he remembered my Cherokee name!"

"Yes, so I see. Now come eat your breakfast."

Still grinning, Lucas sat at the table, but his eyes never left the tall, black-eyed man who watched him with an indulgent smile.

"You've grown, boy," he said.

"I'm ten now," Lucas said with pride. "And I'm almost as tall as Aimee."

Dominic smiled. The boy looked healthy and happy enough. But he must have been devastated by Jim's death. He had adored the man. He let his eyes wander over the boy, frowning slightly as he took in the attire he wore. His raven black hair showed evidence of having been slicked back sometime this morning. His hands looked soft, almost girlish and

28

the clothes he wore were enough to cause his Indian ancestors to rise from their hallowed burial grounds. The high-collared white shirt looked stiff and uncomfortable and the black suit seemed much too hot for this kind of weather.

Dominic's eyes shifted to Aimee and he found her watching him, a look of decided disapproval on her face. Beautiful or not, he found the woman too damned serious for his taste.

He pushed down any objections he had and continued to eat his breakfast, listening to Lucas's fast chatter and laughing heartily at the boy's enthusiasm. He seemed starved for fun. The boy was far too young to be dressed the way he was; he should be outdoors, running wild through the woods, swimming naked in the streams.

Dominic intended to make that his first order of business, though he imagined he'd have a battle on his hands with the widow LeBeaux.

As soon as breakfast was finished, Aimee sent Lucas upstairs to his lessons, leaving only her and Dominic in the dining room. The man who had come to demand his legal rights. She leaned back in her chair and stared at him, her green eyes challenging and cool.

"Well?" she asked finally. "I can see you have something you wish to say."

"You're damned right I do." His voice was hard and barely controlled. "What in God's name are you trying to do to the boy? Do you realize he's part Cherokee? What the hell do you think you're doing, dressing him up like a little monkey? Do you want to make a prissy white boy out of him?" Barely concealed fire raged in his stormy eyes.

29

She looked stunned for a moment. "I . . . I will not have you swearing in my house. . . ."

"Let's get something straight right from the beginning, Mrs. LeBeaux. I make my own decisions. I'm used to swearing whenever and wherever I please. And I don't take orders well . . . not for any reason, and never from a woman."

"Well, you're as rude and arrogant as I've been led to believe."

He waved her words away as he rested his arm on the back of the chair. He seemed bored with her assessment of him, as if what she had to say meant nothing at all.

"We were speaking of the boy," he said, his eyes cold and clear.

"All right," she said, an angry gleam in her bright eyes. "Let's talk about Lucas. I find it rather ironic that you, of all people, would remind me so arrogantly that he is part Cherokee, or that you would be so offended by his dressing like a white boy."

His eyes narrowed. Aimee decided he was downright dangerous when he looked at her that way. But she lifted her chin and waited for his verbal abuse to continue.

"It's not the same."

"Really? And why is that? You are, I believe, half Choctaw. And yet you have deliberately chosen not to return to your people since you were a boy. Instead you have drifted from one town to another, from one fight to another. You have traded your Indian heritage, it seems, for a riverboat gambling salon, and the arms of any woman who strikes your fancy. You live, I believe, exactly as the white men you seem to hold in such contempt. Shall I continue?"

"You are treading on dangerous ground, lady."

"Really? Don't come into my home and threaten me, Mister Valcour. Do you think I'm afraid of you? Or any man for that matter? Do you think I've lived here in the wilderness, along the most dangerous trail in America . . . carved a new life for myself out of nothing . . . do you think I've done that by being afraid?" She was fairly breathless with anger when she finished.

"You didn't seem so tough last night," he said, his hooded eyes raking her slender body.

She stiffened and looked him straight in the eye. "Need I remind you that I took your knife?"

Dominic found her attitude downright cocky and he felt like shaking some sense into her. He managed to restrain himself only with great effort.

"What I have done with my life is no business of yours, or anyone else's. You are Jim's widow and I will gladly give you my respect if only for that reason. But that's all. You might have had Jim under your thumb, Mrs. LeBeaux, but I'll guarantee you, it won't work with me."

His black eyes were cold, frightening even. She believed every word he said, every threat, even the ones he left unspoken.

"You flatter yourself, Mister Valcour, if you think for a moment I would even want you in such a position. Perhaps I should remind you that this is my home."

"And mine," he said with a tight little smile.

She clenched her teeth together tightly. Bright splotches of pink spread on her cheeks through her smooth olive complexion and her breasts rose and fell swiftly with her angered breathing. She was almost

31

grateful when Amos appeared suddenly.

"Miz LeBeaux, you'd better come quick. There's some trouble in the quarters."

She threw her napkin on the table and followed the old man through the house and out onto the back porch, where one of the slaves stood.

"The men, they's refusin' to go down to the bottom land, Miz Aimee. They's afraid of what old man Compton will do to 'em."

"We'll see about that," she said. "Amos, have someone bring my horse around." With a resentful glance back at Dominic, she added. "And one for Mister Valcour."

Without another word to him, she rushed to her room. Quickly she changed into a riding habit, one with a split skirt that she'd had made especially for her, against the heated protests of her Aunt Eulie. But she had little time here for worrying about fashion or proper decorum. She almost laughed at the thought of how much she had changed since coming to live with Jim in this wildly beautiful country. Life was hard here; either you learned to adapt or it would destroy you.

When Aimee returned to the back porch, Amos was holding the reins of her mare. Dominic was already astride a big black stallion that she'd never seen before. His own, she assumed. She barely looked at him as she used the porch to step up into the saddle. If Dominic was surprised at her clothes, or the way she rode, he gave nothing of his feelings away.

He rode in front and slightly away from her, giving her an opportunity to study him and to wonder about his arrogant ways. She wondered again why he had chosen to leave the Choctaw when he was young, why

32

he'd agreed to live instead with his father, a French businessman of great influence in Natchez. It was something Jim had never mentioned.

Dominic passed easily for white. His only Indian features were his straight black hair and piercing black eyes. But his skin, though dark, was the same olive tone as her own and his face had the finely sculpted, almost beautiful features of his French ancestry.

He glanced around at her, his eyes sharp and probing. It was as if he had felt her watching him, studying him. The touch of those eyes made her shiver slightly and she nudged her horse into a trot.

They had ridden from the back of the house and were now passing the small family cemetery. She looked wistfully toward Jim's grave, noting the thick grasses and vines that had finally covered the ugly scarred earth.

"Is this where Jim is buried?" Dominic asked, seeing her look.

"Yes."

The road to the slave quarters was wide and sandy, lined with giant live oaks and magnolias that dripped with Spanish moss. The woods beyond the trees were thick with cane and bamboo, making them appear dark and impenetrable. This was the one area of the plantation that always gave Aimee an uneasy tingling along her spine and as usual, she hurried past it.

The cabins of the quarters were in a clearing, one row on each side, all of them facing toward the center and the wide sandy road. She could see the glint of Gregory Davis's bright hair above the rest of the men. Her new overseer was tall, taller even than some of the

33

burly Yoruban Negroes who stood clustered around him.

She frowned as they grew nearer. Gregory Davis held a long leather whip in his hand and she wondered if he had intended to ignore her wishes. She had made it clear from the beginning that she would tolerate no whipping of LeBeaux slaves. And she was not surprised to see that Dominic had already noticed the same thing and glanced at her now with a look of intense dislike on his handsome face.

But to his credit, he held his horse back, allowing Aimee to approach the overseer and speak to him first. She hoped Dominic would not interfere; he knew nothing about her people or her land.

"What's wrong, Mister Davis?" she asked.

"Well, Mrs. LeBeaux," the tall, bronze-haired man drawled. "These boys say they ain't goin' down to the bottom land; they say Mister Compton has men waitin' there to kill them."

"Does he?"

Davis blinked, obviously not expecting her to question him.

"Why I . . . I reckon not. They're just lazy is all, don't want to work in this hot weather."

Aimee surveyed the group of young men. She knew them all by name, knew them well.

"You are mistaken, Mister Davis. None of these men are lazy; they're my strongest, my best workers. Have you sent someone to check the fields? To make certain no one is waiting there?"

"Why no. I . . . I didn't think that was necessary."

"It is necessary. I told you before that Compton has threatened them on other occasions and he was responsible for my husband's death. He's a dangerous

34

man and if we have to post guards around the edge of the fields, we will." She looked into the eyes of the black men who stood listening. "Are you men willing to work there under those conditions, with guards?"

They muttered quietly among themselves. She could still see the fear and hesitation on their faces.

"The conjure man, he seen death in the fire last night," one of them muttered.

It was then that Aimee noticed Nathaniel, one of the younger men, staring at Dominic. She watched in surprise as he stepped toward the man on the big black horse.

"Mister Dominic? It's me . . . Nathaniel . . ." he said. "I heard you was back."

Dominic reached down and shook the young man's hand, ignoring the look of disbelief on the overseer's face.

"How are you, Nathaniel?"

"Fine, suh, fine."

"Can any of you use a gun?" Dominic asked, surveying the group of men.

"What the . . . ?" the overseer sputtered. "Surely you ain't thinkin' of arming a bunch of slaves, mister?" He was looking at Dominic with disgust, as if he had lost his mind.

"Can you think of a better way to guard the workers?"

"Guard hell!" Davis snorted. "They're slaves! Let 'em work there and take their chances."

"I will make that decision, Mister Davis," Aimee replied. "Think of it in terms of their monetary value if you must." But her eyes left no mistake about what she meant. She hoped he was not one of those men who thought a woman should stay in the house and attend to her sewing and cooking. If so, their relationship would be a very short one indeed.

"Surely you ain't —"

"How many weapons do you think we'll need, Mister Valcour?" she asked, ignoring the overseer's protests.

Dominic looked at her with a slight lifting of his brows and only the smallest hint of a smile.

"Six should do it, don't you think, Nathaniel?"

"Yes, suh," the young man said, his face breaking into a prideful grin that he had been consulted on so important a matter.

"Good. We'll work with two crews, one to plow and the other to guard. We'll change shifts every three hours. Nathaniel, I'll leave it to you to pick the first crews."

"Yes, suh. Thank you, suh."

Aimee didn't know whether to feel gratitude or anger. With only a few quietly spoken words, Dominic had managed both to solve the problem and usurp her authority.

Gregory Davis watched her with narrowed eyes. He seemed to be waiting to see what she would do, waiting, she supposed, for her to override Dominic's orders. She looked the man squarely in the eye.

"Mister Valcour is half owner of LeBeaux Plantation, Mister Davis. Did I happen to mention that before?"

The man's gray eyes darted away from her, but his face grew red with anger. "No, ma'am. I don't believe you did."

"I trust that will be no problem."

"No, ma'am," he drawled, his eyes shifting from her to Dominic. "No problem at all."

36

She tugged at the reins of her mare, moving away from the group of men and out into the road between the cabins. Dominic followed and when she turned toward the bottomland, he moved up beside her, sitting silent and straight on the black stallion.

Once they were away from the quarters, she heard him chuckle and she turned with a frown to look at him.

"What's so funny?"

"You are. I could have sworn you were actually trying to defend me back there."

"I was doing no such thing—"

"Why, Mrs. LeBeaux," he said with a slow, easy smile. "I do believe you're blushing. And by the way, I accept."

"Accept what?"

"Why, your most gracious offer of a partnership. That was what you meant wasn't it . . . when you introduced me as half owner . . . that I am your new partner?" His eyes were wide with feigned innocence.

"You have given me no proof whatsoever of your claim. You haven't—"

"I have it . . . everything in writing and I'll gladly show you the papers and explain the details as soon as we get back to the house."

She stared at him for a moment, her jaws clenched. The mare skittered beneath her as Aimee's knees tightened against the animal's sides.

"All right," Aimee hissed through her teeth. *"If* you have the proof and *if* I believe you, then yes. I have no choice it seems. I will abide by Jim's wishes and . . . accept you as a partner." Her last words were rushed and barely audible; she could hardly make herself say them aloud. And she could hardly bear his smug, knowing look as she told him what he wanted to hear.

Suddenly she bent low over the mare's neck and with her riding whip, tapped the horse's rump. As they flew over the sandy ground and through the middle of the field, she could hear Dominic's soft laughter echoing across the ground, following her, branding her with humiliation because of her easy acquiescence to his demands.

"Damn the man anyway," she swore. He acted as if she actually wanted him to stay at LeBeaux Plantation.

Three

Dominic watched her go, making no move to follow or to try and stop her. His smile faded into a slight frown as he watched her disappear into the dense woods. The thought crossed his mind that he should go after her, especially since there was a possibility that Compton had men in the forest.

But he didn't, knowing how little she would appreciate his efforts. Dominic was finding the lovely Aimee LeBeaux somewhat of an enigma. Last night when he kissed her she had been so seductive, so femininely soft and beautiful in the dappled moonlight of the veranda. Not that she wasn't still beautiful. But this morning she was briskly efficient . . . cold even. And her hair, that lovely silken fall of midnight black was pulled tightly from her face and bound into a staid and unflattering bun at the back of her head. He'd found his hands itching to loosen the pins, longing to let it fall free down her back so that he could run his fingers through its soft coolness.

He laughed softly and rubbed his eyes. He was going to have to be *very* careful around this woman.

He knew she didn't want him here, even though she had finally reluctantly agreed to let him stay. And he couldn't really blame her. Hell, he hadn't been sure he wanted to stay himself. But now . . . now he wasn't so certain he wanted to go.

The big horse beneath him shifted restlessly and jerked at the reins in Dominic's hands. He was anxious, and wanted to follow where the other horse and rider had gone. But his master held him steady as he rested an elbow on the saddle and looked with unseeing eyes into the distance.

Dominic had come here to see his old friend, and perhaps to stay for a while. He wanted to reminisce and drink to their future, see if settling down was really something he wanted. He hadn't expected to find the warm and friendly tavern transformed back into a plantation house as grand and lovely as any along the great Mississippi.

Dominic had been raised in a house like that, in the society where Aimee LeBeaux had learned all her preconceived ideas about men like him. Some days he longed for the tranquillity, the clean, clear elegance of living that way again. But those longings didn't usually last long.

Looking about, Dominic had to admit that Aimee had done a tremendous job with the house and grounds. Could he blame her if she didn't want to share that with anyone, most certainly not an irresponsible, reputed scalawag like himself?

He couldn't expect her simply to look at him and know how he'd been feeling lately. He'd had the sense that something important was missing from his life. He'd thought at first it might be Jim's marriage, or simply the fact that he himself was getting older. But life on the river had become boring and he'd been filled with a strange restlessness that he couldn't shake. He'd hoped a trip into the wilderness would cure whatever was wrong. It hadn't.

No, he had not planned on staying here, or anywhere, very long. But didn't he owe it to Jim to stay long enough to see to the cotton planting? Owe him enough of his time to make sure his widow was safe from her greedy neighbor and from the problems of getting her first crop to market?

He nodded slowly and turned the black horse back toward the quarters. He would stay for one month. That should be long enough to fulfill his obligations and if he was lucky, long enough to convince Jim's widow that he was not the crude barbarian she thought he was.

Aimee rode as if the devil himself was after her. She stopped only when she reached the edge of a dark, slowly drifting stream that was surrounded by thick brush and huge, towering trees.

Here in the dense forest, wildlife grew in abundance. Jim said there was no other place so rich with deer and river otter, no place where white egrets waded freely and cohabited with snow geese and night herons.

She shouldn't have come so far; she knew that. But she'd wanted more than anything to run from Dominic Valcour and his all-knowing eyes, and the strong sensuous mouth that always seemed to quirk with some secret amusement.

He made her angry . . . and restless, and she didn't even know why. Had she changed so drastically since Jim's death that she had become rude and illogical? Before, she would gladly welcome Jim's friends, had done so in fact on many occasions. They were the

41

same kind of men as Dominic. It had made her happy to see Jim laughing and enjoying himself. So what made her want to withhold her hospitality from this particular man?

She sat for a while, letting the mare drink its fill from the stream. Aimee took long, shuddering breaths of the warm, damply scented air and rolled her neck slowly to dispel the headache she felt coming.

The water looked so cool, so inviting. Any other day she might have dismounted, tossed her clothes into a pile beneath one of the trees and allowed herself the luxury of a long, soothing dip in the stream. But not today. Today she had a crop to plant, a new life to begin on the lush, fertile land that she had come to love with a fierce pride, and to treasure as her own.

Moments later when she exited the woods and came out into the meadow, the sun was just peeking over the trees back toward the house. Men, women, and children were walking in lines into the misty fields as wagons followed them, carrying water, plows, and hoes.

Aimee rode toward her workers, with an eye on Gregory Davis as he spoke to the men and women. He would bear watching, she thought, until she was certain he was the man she wanted as LeBeaux's overseer.

She saw Dominic and couldn't help noting the differences in the two men and the way they sat their horses. Gregory seemed tense and irritable. His horse pranced restlessly, reflecting his rider's nervousness. Dominic, on the other hand, rode easily, as if he were born to the saddle. And despite his impatient attitude with her, he had an easy, quiet way of speaking to the

Negroes, a way that didn't push or threaten. And Aimee had to admit she liked that about him.

She guessed that some people might mistake that easy manner of his for disinterest, but Aimee's instincts told her differently. She remembered with a blush, the feel of his hard, muscled body against hers and she recalled the light pantherlike grace of his walk. He was obviously strong and fit and she pitied the man who made the mistake of thinking him easy.

She rode toward Dominic, where he sat quietly watching the workers walk past him. She noted the smiles and greetings of the men to him and the shy, sidelong glances of the women and children as they marched by. She knew the tall, handsome half-breed would most certainly be the talk of the quarters tonight.

As she came near, Dominic glanced briefly her way, but he seemed little interested in her or where she had been. That was good, she thought. The last thing she intended was to keep him informed about her comings and goings.

She called to her overseer and he rode quickly to her side.

"Mister Davis, keep the women and children on this end of the field, just until we can be certain Compton doesn't intend us any harm. Place the men and their guards near the woods."

"Yes, ma'am," he said, tipping his hat and moving away. She knew he was reluctant about arming some of the slaves as guards. But she was completely at ease with it. Most of them knew that if they worked hard for three years and if the plantation became successful, she intended to grant them their freedom. She wished she could afford to do it now. Those who wanted, after being free, would be allowed to stay and work for wages.

Jim had not liked her idea of freeing the slaves. But it was the only way she would agree to keeping them in the first place. She preferred to think of them now as her indentured servants, working to free themselves within three years. She supposed she should already have mentioned it to Dominic, but she knew it was only going to be another subject of contention between them.

Around eleven o'clock, Aimee saw Jezzy coming toward her, striding purposefully across the field. In one hand she could see the colorful flutter of a gauze scarf which was attached to a straw hat. Aimee smiled, shaking her head at the woman who was as protective as a mother, even though they were equals in age. As frustrated as she sometimes became with Jezzy, she loved her and tried to listen to her innumerable cautions with patience, although that wasn't always easy.

"Best put on this hat, missy." Jezzy stood on the ground looking up at her mistress. A sheen of perspiration glistened on her black skin and her teeth were a dazzling white in the sunlight. She was a pretty woman — Aimee had always thought so. But she could certainly be a handful at times.

"Thank you, Jezzy. Did you bring our dinner?"

"Yes'm, I sure did. Amos drove me out in the wagon. But it's such a pretty day that I got out and walked. He's comin'." She pointed back at the small cloud of dust that was moving toward them. "Put on your hat now, Miz Aimee. Don't wants to bake your brains."

"Yes, Jezzy," Aimee said with an exasperated, but

44

indulgent shake of her head.

Dominic sat nearby, watching and listening to the two women. He moved the black horse closer and addressed Jezzy. "I'm happy to see that you take such good care of Mrs. LeBeaux, Jezzy."

Jezzy was all smiles as she looked up at him on his impressive horse. She turned her head and preened as brazenly as any peacock.

Aimee pursed her lips and could not help smiling wryly at the girl's attempts at flirtation. When she wasn't such a pest, she was a true delight to be around. Her sparkle and sense of humor had helped Aimee through many a long, lonely winter evening.

"Yes, sir," Jezzy said, still smiling and moving her shoulders in a funny, coy little manner. "I try to, suh."

"Jezzy is an odd name," he said. "Does it mean something special?"

Suddenly the girl's smile was gone and Aimee almost laughed aloud. This was a subject that was not dear to Jezzy's heart.

"My ma named me Jezebel! Can you 'magine that? I reckon she must have hated me somethin' awful to name a poor chile such a thing. 'Course I was her thirteenth young'un and by then I guess she was just sick to death of babies. She run away right after."

"She ran away?" he asked with a lift of his brows. He was trying very hard to hide his smile. "Why, that's terrible, Jezzy."

"Didn't make no never mind to me," she said with a sniff. "My sisters raised me right good. And soon as I was old enough to hear the preacher preach on that old Jezebel, why I changed my name to Jezzy. Ain't goin' through life bein' called by no harlot name. When I cross over to the other side, don't want Saint

45

Peter confusin' me with that woman! Well, got to go. Gotta help Amos unload the food." She turned with a serious nod toward Aimee. "And you come eat now, missy. You're fairly wastin' away. A man likes a woman what's plump and sassy, ain't that right, Mister Dominic?" With a sly grin back at them, she skipped across the open ground toward the approaching wagon.

Aimee laughed out loud as she watched Jezzy. She placed the bonnet on her head and tied the blue gauze scarf beneath her chin.

"Don't mind Jezzy," she said to Dominic. "She's a chatterbox, but she's sweet and has a heart as big as the Mississippi."

"I can see that," he said, his voice quiet as he watched her.

The hat shaded her face and threw her eyes into shadow. He liked her eyes; they reminded him of the stormy and changeable sea. One moment they were clear and aqua-colored, the next a tumultuous green, dark with all the elements of a storm-tossed ocean.

The gauze ribbon from the hat blew raggedly in the wind, whipping across Aimee's face. Without thinking, Dominic reached across the short distance between them. His dark, slender fingers touched the veil-like material, pulling it back away from her cheek.

Aimee felt the touch of his hand against her skin like the warmth of sunshine on a cold day . . . moving slowly across her face, and slightly grazing her lips. Her eyes came alive then and she pulled away from him, frowning into his face with a frightened look of puzzlement.

"Let's take Jezzy's advice," he said in a husky voice,

46

"and go get something to eat." He reached toward her and despite her softly uttered protest, took the reins from her hand, and pulled her horse nearer to his before returning the bridle to her trembling fingers. He was close now, very close as he whispered softly across to her.

"Not that I think she's right you know. There's absolutely nothing wrong with your figure."

His words and his look brought last night back to her with a jolt. The way she'd felt when he kissed her, the trembling that began deep within her when his strong, hard hands had caressed her body. Her face grew hot and her heart began to pound wildly in her chest. She nudged the mare's sides, urging her away from him and hoping the wind would soon cool her burning cheeks.

Aimee managed to eat a few morsels of food despite Dominic's disturbing presence. The afternoon passed quickly with no incidents and no sign of Compton's men.

Back at the house that evening, as Aimee bathed, she worriedly contemplated dinner with Dominic, her new partner, as he liked to call himself. Today had convinced her that he was serious in his desire to stay and to help. But still she wanted to see his proof of ownership, and she was burning with curiosity to know why Jim had taken such drastic action without telling her.

Lucas's presence at the dinner table brought a lightness and gaiety that otherwise surely would have been missing. Aimee enjoyed it, watching Lucas and Dominic as they teased and joked with one another.

47

She should be happy Dominic had come, for Lucas's sake if nothing else. The boy had been so lost and alone after Jim's death and she had not been able to reach into that dark, mysterious shell he had built around himself.

After devouring his dessert of spiced peaches with cream, Lucas settled himself in to stay and chat. Aimee knew instinctively that the boy could hardly bear to tear himself away from his new hero and champion. But this conversation was not one he needed to hear and so she sent him away.

"But Aimee, " Lucas protested.

"It's all right, Luke," Dominic said. "As soon as we're finished here, you and I will talk some more."

"Promise?" Lucas's dark eyes were bright and hopeful, as if he dared not let himself think Dominic's words could be true.

"I promise," Dominic said with a laugh. His deep rich voice made Aimee remember how it had been before. How pleasant a man's voice in the house could make a woman feel . . . and how secure.

After Lucas was gone, Dominic reached inside the dark jacket he wore and pulled a worn and wrinkled envelope free. Looking at her from beneath dark brows, he carefully reached across the table and laid the packet before her.

"Perhaps this will answer your questions."

Aimee tried to keep her hands steady as she opened the envelope and pulled out the folded piece of paper. Her heart skittered wildly as she moved her eyes quickly down the length of the paper to the two signatures at the bottom of the page. There they were— Dominic Valcour and Jim LeBeaux. She glanced up briefly to find Dominic watching her as he twirled the stem of his wineglass between his thumb and fingers.

She felt sick as she read, almost gasping for air when she saw the huge amount of money Jim had borrowed from Dominic. She shook her head and continued to read. Everything was as Dominic had told her and it was dated last summer, June 1823. She knew it was Jim's signature and she was certain the document was genuine. What she couldn't understand, the thing that filled her insides with a quivering uncertainty, was why Jim had done this and never told her. And why had he borrowed so much money; the amount was staggering. It was enough to restore Le-Beaux house and several more like it.

She looked up from the paper, still holding it in her hand, and frowned at Dominic. "I . . . I don't understand."

He hesitated, looking down at the wineglass that his dark fingers caressed. "What exactly don't you understand?"

"I understand that you lent Jim the money and I understand that in return, he wanted to make you half owner of LeBeaux Plantation. That much is made very clear in the letter. But the amount . . ." She shrugged her shoulders, bewilderment showing in her wrinkled brow and the uncertainty of her jade green eyes.

Dominic sighed. He had hoped she would not ask him about Jim's personal affairs, for he himself could never understand Jim's easy way with money. He cursed quietly beneath his breath. What had the man been thinking, taking even the slightest chance of hurting this woman?

"Aimee, I'm sorry—"

"Tell me."

49

"I can't . . . because I don't know." He shrugged his broad shoulders. "Jim . . . hell, you know how he was." He waved his hand as if searching for answers, then let it drop to the table. "Let's just say he owed a lot of money, probably things he didn't want to worry you with. Most of the loan went to pay off those debts."

Her lips thinned and she shook her head slowly. "They must have been very substantial debts."

He shrugged, unable to tell her any more than he already had.

She stuffed the letter back into the envelope and handed it across the table to Dominic. "It doesn't matter," she said. "It's done. There seems to be no question that you have a legal right to half of all I possess." Without another word, she rose from the table and left the room.

Half of all she possessed . . .

The words seemed to echo in the room long after Aimee had gone. Dominic poured more wine into the small crystal glass and downed it in one swallow. He poured another and sat looking into the clear red depths of the liquid, his eyes dark and troubled. What the hell was he getting himself into here?

The next few days were hectic ones, each filled with dark, cloudy skies, the ever-present heat and the threat of rain. Aimee spent her time between the house and the fields, keeping herself busy and managing to avoid Dominic as much as possible. But once the fields were plowed and the seeds planted, there seemed to be a tremendous amount of relief among the Negroes. It built higher and higher during the long hot afternoon and by evening a celebration seemed imminent. The gaiety spilled from the quarters and among the household servants as well.

Even Dominic and Lucas seemed caught up in the gaiety. So much so that Aimee felt positively left out at dinner. Afterward, when the two left the house together, they seemed to share some sort of secret. Aimee rose from the table and wandered aimlessly about the beautiful dining room letting her eyes take in the mural wallpaper and dark shining mahogany furniture.

She could hear Jezzy down the hallway, laughing and joking with one of the other girls. Amos's laughter rang from the back veranda and in the distance toward the slave quarters the quiet beat of drums had begun.

Aimee walked out onto the veranda. The smell of rain was heavy in the air and its mixture with the fragrance of wild azaleas and cherry blossoms was potent and enticing. But it also brought an emptiness, a loneliness stronger than any she had experienced in months. She longed so much for Jim, for someone to talk to. She felt tonight as if she were the only person on the plantation who had no one with whom to share the spirit and fun of the celebration. No one who really understood what the week's work and the end of planting meant to her.

She stepped down from the porch, admiring her newly planted garden just beyond the veranda. She lifted the skirt of her pale pink muslin dress out of the dust and walked across the lawn toward the cemetery. Breathing deeply, she let the fragrance of the coming storm soothe her with its clean, familiar scent.

She grew nearer to the sound of the beating drums

and could now hear the rhythm of other instruments along with the quiet lift of the deep Negro voices as they sang and welcomed the coming rain. She was caught up in the sounds all around her and the smells of the rich Mississippi earth.

Suddenly she stopped, startled by the shadowed outline of two people in the cemetery. She frowned as she recognized Dominic and Lucas, then stepped back out of sight behind a tree. Aimee knew Lucas had not been to the cemetery since Jim's death and she didn't want to spoil his moment with Dominic. Perhaps with him, Lucas had come to say goodbye to Jim.

But as her eyes adjusted to the gloom and shadows beneath the tall mossy trees, she saw with alarm that both of them were shirtless and the skin of their faces and down across their chests was painted in vivid streaks of yellow and red.

Her heart skipped a beat at seeing their obviously clandestine visit, meant for no one else and undoubtedly the reason for the secrecy they had shared at dinner.

Why . . . they looked like two wild savages. She felt the anger growing in her as the blood rushed and roared in her ears.

How dare Dominic Valcour do such a thing! She felt an urge to scream at him or to pound her fists into something.

She held herself back, watching, spellbound as Dominic raised a long, feathered spear in both arms toward the darkening sky. His bronzed, muscular chest rippled and gleamed in the waning sunlight, the painted streaks on his dark skin bright and bizarre. He looked up toward the sky in a gesture almost of surrender. Lucas watched him and followed his every movement exactly.

Aimee shuddered. She thought Dominic looked ferocious and uncivilized, a wild, untamed barbarian. And it sickened her to see that Lucas emulated him down to the minutest detail.

Was this heathen behavior what he meant when he said he wanted the boy to learn his people's ways?

Suddenly Dominic's arms came down, bringing the lance across his knee with a loud crack and breaking it into two pieces. Fiercely he thrust the two broken pieces into the ground at the foot of Jim's tomb. Aimee gasped in horror as Lucas committed the same sacrilege.

She stared incredulously at the feathers that dangled from the broken lances, and turned and twisted in the rising wind.

"What are you doing?" she shouted, finally moving from the shelter of the trees and stalking angrily toward them. "How dare you bring Lucas here and engage in some heathen ceremony over Jim's grave!"

They turned and stood waiting for her. Lucas looked up at Dominic, who placed his hand on the boy's shoulders in a steadying gesture. And that angered Aimee even further.

"Aimee . . ." Dominic began as if in explanation.

"Go to the house, Lucas."

"But Aimee," the boy protested. "We were just—"

"Now, Lucas!" She stood staring at him, commanding him to obey her, and for a moment she was afraid he would not. She felt completely out of control, and she could feel the perspiration on her forehead and at the back of her neck. And when Lucas looked toward Dominic for approval it infuriated her more than she'd ever have thought possible.

"Go ahead, son," Dominic said.

Only then did Lucas move and even then he walked past Aimee with his head down, refusing to look at her as his bare toes kicked angrily against the sand and dirt.

Aimee walked to Dominic, taking in the look of him, his disturbing nakedness and the bizarre streaks of paint across his face. Her eyes were practically spitting fire in the dusky twilight.

"What in heaven's name do you think you're doing?" she demanded. "Do you intend to make a savage of him, too? What will you teach him next—that he doesn't need the education I'm giving him . . . that it's only for white men? My God, Dominic, you of all people should know how difficult it is for an Indian to live in a white man's world."

He reached his hand forward, meaning to calm her even though his face had grown as angry as hers. She jerked away from him as if she'd been burned.

"Don't touch me. Don't you ever touch me."

His face darkened and he gritted his teeth, forcing himself to remain still instead of grabbing her and shaking her the way his instincts begged him to do.

"When Jim brought Lucas here, were you married then? Did you even know Jim?"

"No," she snapped. "But—"

"Did Jim adopt the boy legally? Did you?" His voice was soft and dangerously quiet.

"No! What does that have to do with—"

"Jim and I found Lucas together. He's as much my son as he is anyone's. The boy needs to learn about the ways of his own people . . . and about being a man. It's obvious you don't feel that's important."

"Oh!" She shook her head, staring at him in disbelief. "And you intend to teach him what it means to be a man? Then God help him, because he will end up just like you and Jim, shirking all responsibility, not to mention carousing from tavern to tavern and taking up with any woman he meets. You have no idea what being a man is about, Dominic Valcour, and I will not have you ruining what little chance Lucas has of being respectable."

"Respectable?" Dominic's eyes glinted. He was finding it difficult to control himself where she was concerned. Could any man satisfy this woman?

But when he spoke, his voice was purposely calm and controlled. "You are the one who's ruining the boy, Aimee. Can't you see that? He's ten years old and he knows nothing of life; he's still a baby in too many ways."

"Stay away from him, Dominic. I'm warning you."

He took one ominous step toward her. Her breath was ragged and Dominic could feel it against his naked chest, could feel the soft flutter of her skirt where it blew against his legs. And as angry as she made him, strangely he wanted nothing more than to sweep her into his arms and make love to her. Right here, right now, like the savage she thought he was.

"I can't do that," he said. He stood very proud, his black eyes furious as he stared down at her. "You know I can't. I want him to continue his education—I'm not a fool. I know he must make his way in the white man's world and I also know how hard it will be. But you're blind to what he really needs, Aimee. And from now on I think it will be best if Lucas is under my guardianship." He ignored her mutter of protest and continued. "I will teach him, not only of the white man's ways, but of the Indian's as well. And you won't interfere." His eyes held an unspoken threat.

He didn't wait for her to reply, but turned away. His hard, bronzed arm scraped roughly against her, pushing her back as he walked past. He strode from the cemetery, his black hair streaming across his shoulders. The soft boots he wore made no sound and with only a few long, silent strides, he had disappeared like a swamp cat into the night.

Aimee felt such an uncontrollable well of grief sweep over her, such utter helplessness, that it seemed to press her down with a physical weight. She reeled from it. Her body began to shake and she sank slowly to the ground at Jim's grave.

She was losing everything and there was nothing she could do. First Jim, then the plantation, and now Lucas.

The wind began to whisper in the towering trees above her as the rush of rain finally began to fall upon the hot dry Mississippi earth. Aimee fell to the ground, stretching her arms across the vine-covered grave. She was indifferent to the elements as she sobbed with loud, wrenching cries, no longer able to defend herself against the cruel, hateful grief that descended upon her.

Four

By the time Aimee managed to stop crying and drag herself back to the house, her hair and clothing were soaked from the heavy rain. As she ran up the back steps onto the covered veranda, she was thinking of the slaves in the quarters. Their drums still beat, even louder now and wilder, it seemed. And she wondered what strange rituals they engaged in. She knew whatever it was, they were out in the downpour, and she shivered at the thought of the dark, voodoo ceremonies that she'd heard about all her life in whispered conversations. It was what had come to her mind when she saw Dominic and Lucas with their paint and broken lances. There was a darkness, a primitiveness to it—a mystery that white people could never understand. Even Jim would not go to the quarters when the strange, mysterious sound of the drums and chanting filled the dark Mississippi nights.

"Lord have mercy, Miz Aimee!"

Aimee jumped at the sound of Jezzy's voice.

"Where you been? You wants to catch your death? Come in this house and change outta them wet things." Jezzy had come onto the veranda so quietly that Aimee hadn't heard her. And now the girl's black eyes were huge, shining in the light from the open doorway as she stared at her mistress.

"I'm fine, Jezzy," Aimee said, not bothering to hide her face from the woman. She knew Jezzy had probably already seen her red, swollen eyes. Besides, the choked sound of tears still clouded her voice when she spoke. "You go on with what you were doing. Were you going out to the quarters to join the festivities?" Aimee nodded toward the distant primitive sounds in the darkness.

"Lordy, no. I done waited too long. The haints is done gathered in the darkness and you know how they loves the rain."

Aimee sighed and turned toward her room. She did not want to hear Jezzy's superstitious prattle . . . not tonight.

"Good night, Jezzy."

"Why you goin' to bed so early? You and that handsome Mister Dominic have words?"

Aimee jerked about, staring into Jezzy's innocent, open face.

"Why would you ask such a thing?"

"Well, it's plain to see somethin' done got you both upset. He come stormin' in like a thundercloud while ago. And here you are, wanderin' in the rain and cryin' your poor little heart out."

"I wasn't wandering in the rain." Aimee clamped her teeth together.

"Um-hum. And I guess you're gonna tell me next that you ain't cryin' neither."

Aimee took a deep breath and her hands went to her waist as she turned on the girl. "Jezzy, you take too much upon yourself sometimes. Has anyone ever told you that?"

"Yes'm. Sho, they have. Mister Jim told me that all the time and I do believe I heard it from you a time or

58

two." The girl shrugged as if Aimee's scolding did not offend her at all. "Still, I knows you better'n anybody . . . better even than old Amos. And it's my job to look after you. Mister Jim, he said—"

"Jezzy, please . . . not tonight. I'm wet, I'm tired, and I have a headache. I just want to take a bath, change my clothes, and go to bed." Aimee's smile toward Jezzy was weak. "Besides, I don't need you to take care of me. I'm perfectly capable of taking care of myself."

"No, you ain't. But I won't argue about it. I just wish you'd listen to me sometimes. Like tonight . . . goin' out on a dark rainy night. Ain't I done told you how the haints like such nights?" Jezzy looked out into the rainy darkness and shivered. "Why if I wasn't so scart we could look over our left shoulders right this minute. I bet we'd be able to see 'em dancin' around out there in the rain."

Finally Aimee had to laugh. She shook her head and turned toward the French doors that led to her room.

"Good night, Jezzy."

"I'll have one of the boys bring your bath water right away, missy."

"A cool bath, please. Thank you, Jezzy." Aimee merely waved her hand over her shoulder as she walked away. If she encouraged the girl they'd be there on the veranda all night discussing haints and other ghostly apparitions of the night.

Aimee drew the shutters across the windows in her bedroom; she didn't bother to light a lamp. She could not bear to see herself in the mirror, not if she looked as horrible as she felt. She dropped her clothes onto the floor and began to unlace her corset and the ribbons of her camisole. Once she was completely naked, she wrapped a long pink dressing gown around her, then sat in the dark near the cold empty fireplace as she waited for her bath water.

She huddled in the chair, her feet drawn up beneath her as she tried to bring some warmth to her bare skin. Through the slats of the wooden shutters she could see the flicker of lightning and hear the heavy rumble of thunder in the distance. She glanced worriedly toward the windows, wondering if the heavy rains would be harmful so soon after planting the cotton. Knowing very little about cotton, she had no idea.

But even the thought of her new cotton crop could not occupy her thoughts for long. Not when Dominic's dark painted face kept appearing before her, not when she kept seeing the flicker of pain in his midnight eyes.

"Damn him," she whispered, leaning her head back against the chair and closing her eyes, hoping to banish the sight of him.

She took a long deep breath, hoping the pounding in her head would soon go away. Her eyes were still closed when she heard the light tap at her door.

She went quickly to open it, thankful that the servants had finally arrived and hoping the cool water would chase away her throbbing headache. But it wasn't one of the house servants and she gasped as she looked once again up into the eyes of Dominic Valcour.

His damp black hair was tied back neatly again and he was dressed casually in dark trousers and a cool billowing white shirt. She pressed her lips together, noting that the heathenish war paint had been removed from his face.

As she stared at him, her head began to pound even more furiously than before. With a perplexed frown, she reached for the door, intending to close it in his face.

"Go away. I have nothing further to say to you."

Dominic's hand held the door open and he stepped into the room, moving her aside as easily as one might move a child.

"I have something to say to you." He turned from the room to face her as she still stood at the French doors silhouetted in the lamplights from the veranda. His expressive eyes moved quickly over her, then back again to her face.

Aimee frowned, feeling the touch of his eyes on her and very much aware of her nakedness beneath the robe. Why was it that everything he did, everything he said, upset her so?

"Very well," she said, trying to sound calm. "Say what you have to say, then leave. I'm preparing to go to bed." She walked into the room, deliberately leaving the French doors open. She welcomed the hint of dampness and the rain's cool breeze that rushed into the room and caressed her hot, flushed cheeks.

"This is not something to be said quickly, Aimee. This is something we need to sit down and discuss."

She was trembling, shaking from head to toe as she faced him.

"No, I can't do that. Please, just leave my room. Or do I have to summon one of the men to remove you?" She lifted her chin and her green eyes sparkled with rage as she stared up at him.

Dominic smiled then and shook his head. Had he ever met a more stubborn female?

"Who will you *summon,* Aimee . . . Amos? Jezzy perhaps, or one of the children? Go ahead . . . yell your head off. It will be your embarrassment, not mine."

She whirled back toward the door and took a long, deep breath, preparing to scream. Then she sighed heavily and turned back to face his smug, arrogant smile.

"Please," she whispered. "Can't this wait until morning? My head is pounding so that I can't think straight right now."

Dominic frowned, seeing the genuine pain across her beautiful face. He supposed that was what drew him a step closer to her . . . closer than he knew he should dare to be.

Aimee's eyes grew large when he came nearer and she wondered what he intended. She watched, unable to move as his hand came forward and his dark fingers touched her hair. She couldn't suppress the shiver that started at her neck and ran the entire length of her body.

"It's no wonder your head aches." His voice was deep, strangely intimate in the gloomy confines of her room. The rain outside seemed to isolate them, seemed to enclose them there at the end of the house in complete seclusion.

Aimee stood helplessly as she felt his fingers pull the pins from her hair. She knew she should move away from him and his too intimate touch, but she couldn't seem to make her body obey.

"These pins . . . must be painful." His voice was low and husky as he stared down at her. "Why do you bind your hair so tightly . . ." As her mass of black curls was released, it tumbled heavily across her shoulders and down her back. "It's much too beautiful for that."

Dominic felt the cool, silky curls fall against his hand and he couldn't suppress the low murmur of pleasure that seemed to come involuntarily from the very deepest part of him.

"Don't . . ." she whispered, still not moving. "You shouldn't; it isn't proper that —" She frowned, unable to put into words what she meant, and unable to step away from him.

62

Aimee was acutely aware of his rasp of indrawn breath and she looked up quickly to see the glint that leapt suddenly into his black eyes. But he did as she asked, and stepped away from her, making her feel strangely bereft when he did.

They stood in the darkness, staring silently at one another, with only the flicker of lightning through the doorway to illuminate the room.

"You . . . you should go," she whispered. "I don't want to talk about anything tonight."

"I can't go, Aimee, until I've explained . . . what you saw earlier—I meant no disrespect to you or to Jim."

Aimee frowned. As distressed as she had been, he had made her forget about her anger. In fact, she seemed to forget everything except him and how he made her feel whenever he was near. And that disturbed her even more than the heathen ceremony she had witnessed.

"Tomorrow," she said. Her voice was emotionless now, her eyes cold and uncaring. She simply could not let him see how deeply he affected her.

Dominic's brow wrinkled and for a moment, Aimee thought he might refuse to leave. But just then she heard two of the boys clattering across the veranda with her copper tub and pails of water. They stopped at the doorway, peering into the darkness.

"Miz Aimee . . . you in here?"

"Yes," she said, turning to them. "I'm here. I . . . I just haven't lit the lamps yet." She refused to look at Dominic as she went quickly to the oil lamp and took up the tinder box, sending for the first time a small shaft of light into the room.

Self-consciously, she pulled the pink robe more tightly around her as she turned toward Dominic. He

63

was watching her, his black eyes narrow and unreadable as they scanned quickly down her body.

"Is there anything else, Mister Valcour?" she said, her voice cold.

"No . . . nothing. I suppose it will have to wait until morning."

"Good."

She saw the tightening of his jaw and watched as he turned and strode from the room. His broad shoulders were held stiffly and his chin was lifted as if she had angered him again. She didn't care if she had; it was her own survival she was worried about now.

Later, Dominic paced the railed porch that ran along the second story. The house in the back was L-shaped and he had been given the room at the very end of the house just opposite from Aimee's. From here he could see across the garden and onto the end of the veranda near her room.

He watched now as shadows flickered against the shuttered windows of Aimee's bedroom. And he tried to make his mind think of something else. But how could he? Not when he could see her movements in the play of lights across the windows, when all he could envision were her green eyes and the heavy fall of silken black hair that had touched his hand and made him tremble like a young, inexperienced boy?

She had been wearing nothing beneath the dressing gown, he was certain of that. When she'd lit the lamp, his eyes had taken in all of her, the appealing, seductive picture she made there in the dimness of the fragrant bedroom. Her green eyes were so defiant and her hair tumbled about her shoulders in a sensuous cloud. He'd seen the outline of her breasts, her nipples taut and clearly visible beneath the silky material.

Dominic took a long, slow breath and blew the air out of his lungs as his fists clutched the low railing of the porch.

"Damn," he muttered, shaking his head.

Even now as he thought of her, he could feel the tightening of his body, could feel the heated rush of desire that swept over him like wildfire.

"Damn," he said again, shaking his head in disbelief. How long had it been since any woman had gotten to him this way? How long since he'd let anyone affect him the way this woman did . . . this woman who had been the wife of his best friend.

It didn't help any that the distant pulsing of drums seemed to quicken his blood. Or that the rain and wind made the night seem made for love.

Impulsively he walked to the end of the porch and thrust his head out away from the roof's overhang. He let the cool rain wash freely over his face and neck, then shook himself and leaned back against the walls of the house as his thoughts turned again to Aimee LeBeaux.

"Well, what the hell are you going to do now, Valcour?" he muttered aloud in self-derision. "This woman is not one of your riverboat dancers, or one of the pleasure girls from Natchez Under-the-Hill. She's a respectable woman . . . the widow of your best friend, for God's sake. You can't just go barging into her bedroom, making demands that way."

He ran his hand over his wet hair and closed his eyes, trying to shut out the vision of her there in the darkened bedroom. Trying to tell himself she was no different from any other woman, that these things he was feeling had more to do with his being away from civilization for weeks on end. He had expected to find a little pleasure with Jeanine, damn it. That's all it was. Expectation and disappointment . . . frustration. As simple as that.

But he was a grown man; he could handle it. It wouldn't be the first time he'd spent a night in frustration, wishing for a woman's soft body beneath his. Hell, sometimes, even having a woman wasn't enough. It was never the right woman. Hadn't been in a long time.

He must be getting old. Was this what happened to a man—what made him want to settle down and get married? Wanting a respectable woman with such hot desire and knowing the only way you could have her was through the civility of a wedding ceremony? He snorted softly, smiling at himself in the darkness.

"This is business, Valcour," he whispered. *"She's* business. Nothing more than that . . . nothing more."

But before he went into his bedroom, Dominic allowed himself one last long look across the garden to the room at the end of the veranda. One last reminder of those eyes and hair and the soft, slim body concealed so enticingly beneath a pink wrapper.

Five

For all Aimee's weariness that night, she found herself unable to sleep. She told herself it was the storm that kept her awake, the storm that made her toss and turn so restlessly in the huge tester bed.

Once during the night she pushed the mosquito netting aside and walked to the French doors to look out at the still pouring rain. The house was dark and quiet and her eyes moved almost of their own will past the roof of the veranda and up to the room at the second floor. It was dark, too.

She turned and went back to the bed, crawling in between the lace-trimmed sheets like a weary child. Then she sat propped up against the pillows, finally admitting to herself she would get no rest that night.

She allowed her mind to wander, thinking of everything that had happened. Of Jim's death and her almost frantic need to rebuild the house and turn the estate into a successful working plantation. She thought of the long backbreaking days of work and the even longer nights of loneliness. And just recently, for the first time she had begun to see hope for her future, had begun to see the land come to life and reveal its rich fertile soil that was hungry for new seed.

67

This was what she wanted now, more than anything, and she wasn't going to let Dominic Valcour interfere with that, or with her peace of mind.

And when her mind turned to him, she ignored the quick flutter of her heart. She listened to her mind instead.

He was handsome, she had to admit. And he could be charming, probably irresistible to most women. But the sparks that passed between them were more likely caused by friction than passion; they were just too different for anything else. Besides, Aimee had no intention of ever letting anyone touch her heart again the way Jim had. Certainly not his best, most trusted friend . . . never a wild renegade who scorned convention, like Dominic Valcour.

It must have been nearing daybreak when Aimee finally drifted off to sleep. She could hear a mockingbird somewhere high in the trees, singing the sun up. And as she felt the sweet drowsiness of sleep, she smiled, assuring herself she was still in control of LeBeaux Plantation. And she was still in control of her own heart and destiny.

She slept late the next morning. And when Jezzy finally came in around eleven o'clock, Aimee heard the quiet sound of rain still splattering against the house.

"Oh, I didn't intend to sleep so late," she said, stretching her arms over her head.

Jezzy pushed the mosquito netting back away from the bed, tying it with satin ribbons against the tall bedposts.

"You needs to sleep late. 'Sides, it's still rainin', can't do nothin' outdoors today. Now, how 'bout I bring your breakfast in here this mornin? What would you like? Cilla's cooked up some fine ham, just like you like. And there's plenty of biscuits and grits to go with it."

Aimee felt her stomach churn a little at Jezzy's mention of the rich, hot food. She frowned; she wasn't usually so picky about what she ate, but somehow this morning she could not face a large plantation breakfast.

"Just tea, Jezzy, and some toast. And I believe I will eat in my room. Where's Lucas?"

"Oh, he's gone with Mister Dominic already. They rode down to the bottoms to check the cotton crop and make sure the rain ain't beat the seed out of the ground. You looks tired this mornin'. Didn't have no bad dreams now did you?"

Aimee shook her head, not really listening to anything Jezzy said except that Lucas had gone with Dominic. "I . . . I suppose I did dream," she answered distractedly. "Why did they go out in this pouring rain?" Aimee swept the bed linens away from her legs and slid out of bed, looking anxiously toward the windows and the gloomy grayness of the weather outside. "Lucas will be sick getting wet so early in the spring this way. I have to go after him."

Jezzy stopped what she was doing and turned to face her mistress. Her black eyes sparkled with life and her full lips were drawn into a little bow.

"Now you'll do no such thing. Do you think Mister Dominic would take the boy out in the rain and let him get sick? My goodness alive. Why, he's as bad as you are. The poor chile had to practically beg to be took along. Then Mister Dominic made him wear a long rain cape that covered him from head to toes. Ain't no chance that boy gonna get wet—not today. Huh-uh. Now you just settle yourself right back

69

down. It's outta your hands, and I say it's about time you had somebody to help with all your 'sponsibilities."

Aimee felt an odd blend of relief and irritability. Out of her hands, indeed. Dominic Valcour had come to her home just like the storm that struck last night — unbidden and unwanted. And just as she was uncertain about the effects of the storm on her land, she was uncertain about how this man would change everything in her quiet, well-planned life.

Aimee was dressed when Jezzy returned with her tea and toast. The storm had turned the air cool and she chose a plain cream-colored cambric morning dress with a high neck and short train since she would most likely be indoors all day. The dress's only concession to fashion was several rows of green ribbon trimming around the full skirt and a row of glittering gold buttons from the neck to the tight-fitting waist. And despite her headache the night before, she again twisted her heavy hair back and pinned it behind her head, thinking with satisfaction that at least she would not allow Dominic to dictate how she wore her hair.

She sipped the sweet hot tea and watched Jezzy put her room in order. She thought the girl seemed unusually quiet this morning.

"You're awfully quiet this morning, Jezzy."

Jezzy turned and smiled. "Got lots on my mind is all."

"Like what?" Aimee dipped her head to look up into the girl's face. "Is anything wrong?"

"No," Jezzy said quickly. "No, ain't nothin' wrong. I'm just worried about Nathaniel is all."

"Nathaniel?" Aimee frowned. "Is he sick or —"

"Oh no . . . Nathaniel is a strong, healthy man." Jezzy's eyes lit with a strange little glow before she looked away from Aimee.

"Oh," Aimee said with a soft smile "Yes, he is. And quite handsome, too, isn't he?"

Jezzy actually seemed embarrassed for once and Aimee could not help laughing as she watched the girl pound at the pillows and continue to straighten the bed's coverlet even though it was already perfectly neat and smooth.

Then Jezzy turned suddenly and came to Aimee. There was a small straight wrinkle between her brows and a look of fear in her dusty black eyes.

"It's that Mister Davis, Miz Aimee. Nathaniel made me promise not to tell, but I can't sit by and let somethin' happen to him . . . I just can't." Her voice was almost a wail as her eyes pled with Aimee.

"Jezzy . . ." Aimee reached up for the girl's hand and pulled her into the chair across the small tea table from her. "Sit down. And tell me exactly what you're talking about."

"But I promised him I wouldn't. I promised I wouldn't say a word to you. And here I am with my big mouth. He's gonna be mad at me and ain't never gonna speak to me again. I just know it."

"Jezzy . . . calm down. I won't let anything happen to Nathaniel and I won't let anything happen to you either. Now tell me what this is all about."

"Well . . . that new overseer, Mister Davis, he didn't like the way Nathaniel took up with Mister Dominic. Said he was a uppity nigra and if he didn't watch his step, he'd be in trouble. Said he'd whip him, Miz Aimee." Jezzy's eyes were huge with fright as she stared into Aimee's startled face.

71

Aimee gritted her teeth; she could feel a flush of anger warming her skin from her neck to her forehead.

"Mister Davis will not lay a whip to any LeBeaux slaves, I can promise you that."

Jezzy's eyes grew even larger and rounder as she saw and heard her mistress's anger.

"You ain't gonna tell him Nathaniel told it, are you?"

"No, Jezzy. No, I'm not going to tell Mister Davis anything as a matter of fact. And if I were you, I wouldn't mention this conversation to Nathaniel either. I know how stubborn men can be when their pride is involved. He won't take kindly to a woman's interference, Jezzy, you know that."

"Yes'm, I know."

"Well . . ." Aimee patted Jezzy's hand and smiled at her, even though she was so angry she didn't feel at all like smiling. "Don't you worry about this. I promise I'll take care of it, and I promise I'll be discreet, both with Mister Davis and with Nathaniel. Mister Davis will leave LeBeaux before I ever allow him to touch Nathaniel or anyone else. But I do need you to keep me informed, Jezzy. Can you do that . . . tell me if anything else happens?"

"Yes'm," she said, her eyes bright now and more cheerful. "I sho' can."

"Good."

Aimee watched affectionately as the girl rose from the chair and headed for the door. She didn't know what made the dream she'd had last night come to mind at just that moment, but it did.

"Oh, Jezzy, I just remembered my dream. What does it mean, according to your African culture when one dreams of flowers . . ." Aimee looked off into the distance, trying to remember. "And a hill. A very large hill, covered with all kinds of beautiful flowers."

Jezzy smiled broadly and lifted her eyebrows in a knowing look. "Means success, Miz Aimee. Means you gonna have money and good luck, that's what."

"Oh." Aimee smiled and turned her head in a self-satisfied gesture. "Well, that's wonderful. I'm pleased."

Jezzy hesitated a moment at the door, then grinned slyly. "Weren't no man on that hill with you was there? Maybe a tall, broad-shouldered man with purty long black hair?"

Aimee's lips quirked in good humor as she gave Jezzy a long, dry look. "No, Miss Jezzy. There was no man in my dream at all. I was completely alone — and that's exactly how I intend to remain. And I know very well who you're talking about, you know. So don't go getting any ideas about me and Dominic Valcour. Some of you here may view him as some kind of hero, come to save the day, but believe me, he's nothing to me except a business partner."

"Oh. Yes'm. Business." Jezzy shrugged her shoulders and grinned, then turned and left the room.

Aimee finished her tea and toast. Rain or not, there was enough that needed to be done inside today. There was plenty of work in her office and besides, she needed to do some last-minute planning for the dinner this coming weekend. It would be the first time she'd had formal guests since Jim's death. And even now she made sure that those invited were very close friends who would understand her lack of formal mourning. She wanted someone close to help her celebrate the rebirth of LeBeaux Plantation. Besides her

Aunt Eulie, she had invited Jenny, her very dearest friend, whose father owned the plantation adjoining LeBeaux on the side toward Natchez.

Jenny DeVaull's family home was just on the edge of the wilderness, not far from Natchez. Both the LeBeaux and DeVaull holdings were so large that they occupied most of the territory between her troubling neighbor, Compton, and the city of Natchez. And she knew that Compton would consider it quite an accomplishment if he could manage to get his hands on both LeBeaux and the DeVaull plantations. And he wasn't the kind of man who cared how he accomplished it either.

"But that's not going to happen," Aimee said to herself as she rose and moved toward the veranda. "Not if I can help it."

She spent most of the day in her office, mulling over receipts and tax notices. If she had known before Jim's death that their capital assets were so low, she would never have ordered all the lovely and expensive Seignouret furniture from New Orleans.

Aimee shook her head and leaned back in the chair, wondering for the thousandth time why Jim had continued to let her believe the estate was doing so well and that they had money to spare. It was only after his death, when she'd had to plunge into the records in his office, that she discovered just how bad the situation was. In fact, as much as she hated to admit it, she was probably lucky Dominic Valcour came when he did. When he had told her he had money of his own, she had stubbornly refused to accept his help, or even to talk about it. Still, it was good to know that if the worst happened . . .

But now, with careful planning, and if nothing serious went wrong, she thought LeBeaux could make it.

The rain stopped in the afternoon and with the appearance of the sun, summer seemed to have arrived as well. Aimee hoped it meant a good sign for the crops.

Aimee managed, after their confrontation on that rainy stormy night, to avoid Dominic for the next few days. And she wondered if he was avoiding her as well. He usually rose early and was in the field or down where the slaves were clearing new acreage by the time Aimee arrived for breakfast.

But with the coming dinner party, she knew she should speak to him soon. She couldn't have him appearing unexpectedly in some heathenish costume. Besides, if she intended being practical, she knew they needed to sit down together and discuss the plantation. They simply could not go on avoiding each other forever. If she really meant it when she agreed to accept him as full partner and if she expected to be successful, they needed to agree on the course they would take. And while she was at it, she intended to find out exactly what he had in mind for Lucas.

Six

That evening at dinner, Aimee was surprised at the twinge of disappointment she felt when once again Dominic did not appear in the small family dining room.

As Amos served her light meal of chicken stewed with vegetables in a cream sauce, she glanced at him oddly.

"Amos, have you seen Lucas?"

"Oh, he went with Mister Dominic, ma'am."

"With Dominic? But where?" She glanced worriedly toward the windows, noting the play of gray and purple shadows upon the trees. "It going to be dark soon."

Amos chuckled and his wide smile at her was almost indulgent.

"They gone possum huntin'. Been gone a long time now. Lucas begged Cilla for a supper they could take with 'em down to Sandy Creek. He was fit to be tied, that boy was. Yes, sir. Mister Dominic done put the spark back in that chile's eyes."

Amos straightened from the table and looked at Aimee. But when he saw the look of disapproval on her face, his eyes widened and the grin on his lips faded.

"He won't let nothin' happen to young Lucas, Miz Aimee, if that's what's botherin' you. Why anybody

76

can see that the man fairly dotes on the boy."

Aimee pushed her plate away and stood up. She felt an energy building up within her that made her want to run, made her want to scream with frustration.

Since his arrival at LeBeaux, it was Dominic this and Dominic that, always Dominic. Even Amos and Jezzy, Nathaniel . . . Cilla, all the people who had been loyal to her since her first day at LeBeaux Plantation—even they praised him at every turn.

Well, what could she expect? They were innocents, all of them. She couldn't really expect them to see through his façade of sophistication and feigned interest. But she knew, as soon as he grew tired of the plantation, as soon as he grew weary of having a ten-year-old boy tag around behind him everywhere he went, Dominic Valcour would move on to other, more exciting pursuits.

"Miz Aimee? Somethin' wrong with your supper? Wants me to have Cilla send somethin' else in from the kitchen?"

"No, Amos," she said. She had almost forgotten he was there. "It's all right. The supper is fine—I guess I'm just not very hungry." She smiled at the old man, wanting to assure him that her anger was not with him. "Why don't you go ahead and have your supper? I have some more work to do in my office."

Amos picked up the plate as he watched Aimee walk from the dining room. His black eyes were round and worried as they followed her. Then he shook his head and slowly placed the untouched food back on a cart and wheeled it from the room.

Aimee paced the broad cypress floors in her office. She walked to the French cylinder desk, shuffling a few papers that lay on the surface, then walked away

77

again. Without thinking, her hand moved to the back of her head as she rubbed the tight pins.

It was that gesture that seemed to summon Dominic's face. He appeared suddenly, as he'd looked that night in her room. And with the vision she thought she could almost hear the sound of his seductive voice. It seemed even now to fill her office until Aimee sighed and quickly moved her hand away from her tightly bound hair.

She moved across the room to a small mahogany cabinet and opened the glass doors. Her lips were clamped tightly together as she lifted out a crystal decanter and a delicate crystal glass. The sherry splashed into the glass in a quiet amber gurgle as the scent of the wine rose toward Aimee's face. It smelled much better than it tasted, she thought. Then she lifted the glass, closed her eyes and forced herself to swallow. The liquid burned her throat slightly and she could feel its warmth all the way down to her empty stomach. Almost defiantly she poured another glass, drank it, then shivered at the taste as she placed the decanter back into the cabinet.

Perhaps at least it would insure her a little sleep tonight.

But tomorrow . . . tomorrow, she would speak to Dominic, no matter how hard he tried to avoid her. She would be up at daybreak if necessary.

Next morning, just as she'd planned, Aimee was dressed and in her office well before breakfast. She told Amos to be sure that Dominic knew she wanted to see him before he left for the morning. And she felt even more frustration when Amos gave her a baleful look from his dark drooping eyes and informed her that Mr. Dominic would not be leaving, but would be

78

in to breakfast as usual.

Everything the man did seemed to have her on the defensive.

Later as Aimee waited in the dining room for Lucas and Dominic, she walked about, gazing with pleasure at all the fine things she'd added to the house. It had taken weeks to clean and restore the Italian marble fireplaces in the house. She lifted her brows as she remembered the stains on the lovely marble and the black spots on the cypress floor from burning coals.

Some of the men who traveled the Trace and who stayed in this house were hardly more than savages, she thought. They couldn't have cared less where their tobacco spit landed and were even less considerate of the lovely golden cypress floors. They had been badly pitted and scratched before Aimee had them restored.

She smiled as she ran her hand down the lemon-colored watered satin draperies at the long windows. The handmade rugs that covered the center of the floor also had splashes of lemon color as well as tan and pale orange. This room had fairly come to life with the bright colors. Even the darkness, caused by the shade of the huge live oaks and magnolias outside, could not dim the light that flooded the dining room now.

The dining-room door was opened onto the wide hallway that ran from the front of the house to the back veranda, and the doors at both ends of the house were also open. Aimee stopped to listen to the pleasant sound of birdsong that drifted in through the open doors on the light morning breeze. On days like this, she thought she might actually be happy again. She turned toward the door at the sound of voices in the hallway. She could hear Jezzy's spontaneous laughter and Lucas's echoing voice. His voice was loud and full of childish enthusiasm.

Aimee was watching the doorway when Dominic's tall form appeared. He paused for a moment as he nodded and murmured a quiet greeting. "Good morning."

"Good morning," she answered, hoping she sounded pleasant, hoping the resentment she felt toward him did not show.

Lucas came bounding in behind Dominic. Seeing Aimee, he stopped, straightened his shoulders and walked more sedately to his chair at the long shining table.

"Good morning, Lucas," Aimee said, smiling as she watched him brush a wisp of dark hair back from his eyes. "Are you hungry?"

"Yes, ma'am. Starved." His glance found Dominic and the smile he bestowed on the man was one of companionship. The kind of smile that only men share, Aimee thought.

But this morning, she wasn't going to let that bother her.

Jezzy came bustling into the room. Her face was already shining from the warmth of the morning and undoubtedly a hurried trip from the kitchen. She stood very close to Dominic where he was seated at the table, as she poured steaming black coffee into the delicate cup near his elbow.

"Here's your coffee, Mister Dominic. Hot and black . . . just the way you like it." Jezzy's voice was high and giggly.

Aimee couldn't help the small frown that appeared between her brows and narrowed green eyes. But she took a deep breath and placed her napkin in her lap.

Dominic's deep chuckle seemed to grate on Aimee's ears as did his slow easy reply to Jezzy.

"Well, Jezzy, you certainly know how to start a man's day off right. You're going to make someone a fine wife one of these days."

"Oh. Go on with you now, Mister Dominic," Jezzy said with another trill of laughter.

"Jezzy," Aimee said in a deliberately slow, calming voice. "You may bring in the breakfast now. Just leave the coffee on the sideboard."

Jezzy's eyes flashed toward her mistress and her hand went up to hide the grin still on her lips. "Yes'm."

"Well, Lucas," Aimee said, turning toward the boy. "I understand you went possum hunting last night. Did you enjoy yourself?"

Lucas set his cup of hot chocolate down, in his enthusiasm splashing a bit out into the delicate saucer. But he hardly noticed.

"Oh, Aimee. You should have come with us. We built a fire down on Sandy Creek. And Dominic told me stories about the Choctaw and about when he and Jim were in the wilderness. And he told me all about when they found me. He's going to teach me to use a bow and arrow, too." Lucas turned often toward Dominic as he spoke and the look in his dark eyes was practically worshipful.

All the while Dominic sat sipping the hot coffee, gazing at Lucas affectionately and letting his potent black-eyed gaze turn at times toward Aimee with a steady, uncanny stare.

Aimee smiled at Lucas's enthusiasm. She knew Dominic was probably waiting for her disapproval. But she had no intention of hurting the boy, or of

81

drawing him into the battle between herself and his new hero. Whatever she had to say to Dominic, she would wait and say in private. Besides, she thought, she'd not seen Lucas this happy in a long while, certainly not since Jim's death. And she had to admit that even the casual way he was dressed seemed more appropriate and made him look healthy and boyish.

Jim had also disapproved of her one-sided education of Lucas and the way she dressed him. But he had given over to Aimee on that. In fact, Dominic's stubbornness and his domineering ways made her realize just how much responsibility Jim had turned over to her, not only with Lucas but with the house and land as well. Perhaps that was why she was having such a hard time now dealing with this man. He was as used to having his own way as she was hers.

Aimee allowed her gaze, beneath her lowered lashes, to wander for a moment over the man who sat across the table from her. This morning he was clean shaven and his raven black hair was tied neatly back just at the collar of his shirt. His long slender fingers looked dark, almost foreign against the delicate pale cup that he held, and she wondered at his ease in seemingly any situation. He was as much at home in the drawing room as he was on a horse.

"I'm happy to see you enjoying yourself, Luke," she said, her voice soft and sincere. "One day, when you're not busy, I'd like you to help me in the new rose garden. I have most of the roses planted and I'd like to have a brick walkway as well."

"Sure," he said. "I can do it today if you'd like." He glanced at Dominic who nodded slowly and winked at the boy as if with approval.

"Good," Aimee said. "That would be good. I'd like

82

to have it done before our dinner party this weekend. But first, this morning I'd like to ride down to the cotton fields. The new sprouts should be coming up any day now."

"I'll come with you," Dominic said, his voice low and steady.

"And me, too?" Lucas asked, his black eyes bright with excitement.

"Of course, you, too," she said, nodding at him. She was pleased that he was not still angry about the confrontation at the cemetery that stormy night.

Breakfast turned out to be a surprisingly pleasant affair. Aimee felt a twinge of guilt at Lucas's joyous response to Dominic. His happiness was so sweet, almost desperately so, and she realized for the first time how sad and lonely he had been without a man in his life, without someone to guide him and make him feel important and needed.

Jezzy hurried back and forth, bringing more biscuits, pouring coffee for Dominic. Her smile was happy and positive, too, until Aimee found herself being pulled into their enthusiasm against her will.

They were almost finished with breakfast when Aimee heard a loud thump at the front of the house, then the sound of hurried footsteps in the wide hallway. She heard Jezzy's low murmur, then a higher pitched voice that seemed alarmed.

Aimee frowned and rose from her chair, intending to see what was wrong when Amos came hurrying into the room.

"Miz Aimee, it's Mister Compton and his men. They's comin' up the drive now, comin' right straight up to the front porch, looks like."

Dominic started to rise from the table, but Aimee

turned to him, her look haughty and firm.

"Let me handle this please. This is my problem, made long before you came. I'll talk to him."

Lucas's dark eyes gazed up at her, worried and fearful, and she knew he was remembering Jim's death.

"I'll come with you," he offered.

But Aimee was already on her way out of the dining room. She hardly glanced back at Dominic who stood watching her, or at Lucas who gazed hopefully from the table.

"No, Lucas, you're too young to be involved in this. You stay here with Dominic."

She was gone before she could see the flush that crept over the boy's face, or the look of dejection that wiped the hope from his eyes. Dominic walked to Lucas and placed a hand on his shoulders.

"She's afraid for you son, that's all. Sometimes it's hard for a woman to understand. It's a woman's nature to mother and sometimes that keeps them from seeing that a man, no matter how young, needs to protect his family and his home. Aimee has a lot on her mind now with the crops and the new clearing; she hasn't realized yet that you're growing into a young man. But she will soon . . . she will."

The boy shrugged and rose silently from the table.

Dominic turned to leave the room. "Stay in the back of the house with Amos, son. I might need you."

Lucas nodded solemnly, but his dark eyed brightened at Dominic's words.

Outside on the long front porch, Aimee waited, her hand above her eyes as she shaded the glare of the morning sun and watched the men approaching on horseback.

Compton was in the lead and he rode his sand-colored horse slowly and arrogantly, leaning back in the saddle as if he owned the world. Aimee watched as they came up the long, sandy, tree-lined drive, as they rode beneath the towering oaks and stirred the hanging moss into motion with their passing.

There were three men behind Compton, all of them wearing guns low on their hips and all of them looking rough . . . barely civilized with their unkempt beards and worn, dust-stained clothes.

Compton was within fifty feet of the house when Aimee stepped to the front of the porch.

"That's far enough, Mister Compton. You're not welcome here; I shouldn't have to tell you that."

Compton pulled his horse to a stop and leaned one arm insolently across the saddle horn as he gazed up at Aimee LeBeaux. He wore a light-colored straw planter's hat that shaded his eyes from her. But the dappled spring sunlight played across the lower half of his face revealing the slight smirk on his full lips. He looked lean and fit for a man in his fifties. The hat he wore hid the shock of gray hair and the pale, cold blue eyes that Aimee remembered so well, the eyes that darted sometimes like a snake's and had hardly warmed even when he'd tried to force himself on her that terrible day last fall. She shivered now just thinking about it and she wished she had not been so hasty in refusing Dominic's help a few moments ago.

"I'm sorry to hear that, Mrs. LeBeaux," Compton drawled, smiling at her from across the yard. "I'd just like to step down and talk to you for a moment. I hope you know that your husband's death has weighed heavily on me these past months." He spread his hand above the horse's neck and smiled slyly toward her. "But I had no choice; the man threatened to

85

kill me and came of his own will to my home. What else could I do?"

"Get off my property, Mister Compton. Before I have you thrown off."

He laughed then, his white teeth flashing in the morning light.

"Surely not, Mrs. LeBeaux. Not before I've had a chance to tell you how stunning you look this morning in that lovely dress. It surely is a waste of womanly beauty, someone like you here in this big house, night after night . . ." His voice dipped suggestively. ". . . so young, so alone." He lifted his brows and laughed then, the sound ugly and insinuating.

The men behind him shifted in their saddles and glanced about at one another, laughing and enjoying the sport as they lounged so easily, waiting for their boss to finish.

"Your words are an insult to me, sir. And if I were a man I'd—"

He laughed again. "You'd what? Challenge me to a duel perhaps, the way your ungainly lout of a husband did? I think not, my dear. I think before long, this plantation is going to run you into the ground. And I hate to see that happen, especially to someone, as I said, who is so beautiful . . . so desirable as yourself. Now, I'll be glad to help you out, ma'am, with the work . . . or with the nights . . . just anytime you say the word. Isn't that right, men?" He turned slightly toward his men and smirked.

Aimee felt her face growing warm with frustration. She wished she had brought a gun with her; she'd like to see his face when she pointed it right between his eyes.

Compton turned toward her again and leaned forward in the saddle as if he meant to get down from his horse. Aimee felt her heart lurch and she took a step backward on the porch, wondering if Amos was inside the door, hoping desperately that he'd had the sense to bring a pistol into the hallway.

But just then a deep, drawling voice sounded in the still morning air.

"I wouldn't step down off that horse, Mister Compton, if I were you. I believe Mrs. LeBeaux has made her feelings perfectly clear where you're concerned. You're not welcome here and neither are your loutish friends."

Aimee gasped at the sound of Dominic's deep voice. She could tell he was standing on the second-floor balcony just above her. She could see Compton's eyes dart upward in a look of surprise and she could see the anger that crept slowly over his men's faces at Dominic's intentional insult.

Compton's jaw clenched angrily and his gaze fell once again on Aimee.

"Well, what have we here?" Compton drawled. "Have you resorted to buying yourself a hired gun, Mrs. LeBeaux? I assure you it would be much more pleasant if we could sit down and discuss this matter calmly. I'd make a fair offer on this place, just as a friendly neighborly gesture. I'm willing to help you, willing even to bow to any demands you might make. I would not even be averse to combining our landholdings through a mutual marriage agreement. A very pleasant prospect, I might add."

His smirk was almost more than Aimee could bear. She wanted to throw herself at him and slap his ugly, leering face.

But even as she thought it, the shot that echoed

loudly through the air surprised her and made her body jerk involuntarily. She saw Compton's straw hat go sailing through the air, saw his stunned expression and the blatant look of fear that washed across his face.

"The next shot will be lower, Compton," Dominic drawled. "Now, you and your men might want to turn tail before I count to five. This pistol has a very delicate, very touchy trigger, and I find myself growing really impatient with this conversation."

Compton's face was beet red as he jerked at his horse's reins. He stared up at Dominic, then back at Aimee.

She placed her hands at her waist and smiled at him.

"Oh, by the way, Mister Compton . . . before you go. Allow me to introduce you to my late husband's best friend—Dominic Valcour. And since you've expressed such neighborly concern for me, you'll be pleased to know that I don't need your help. Mister Valcour is also my new partner and half owner of Le-Beaux Plantation."

Compton's odd blue eyes darted from her, back up to the man on the upper balcony.

Aimee heard the click of Dominic's pistol and she held her breath as Compton turned the horse about quickly and rode away.

"Goodbye, Mister Compton," Dominic called loudly from the balcony. "Have a pleasant day."

Compton turned back and shouted toward the house.

"You'll regret this, Valcour. Both of you will regret it!"

Seven

Aimee stepped to the edge of the porch and glanced up toward the second-floor balcony. Dominic stood straight and perfectly still, his black eyes watchful and cold as he stared after the retreating figures of Compton and his men. She could see the muscles of his jaw flexing beneath his dark skin and she shivered at the look on his face. She watched, mesmerized, as the thumb of his right hand moved very slowly to lower the hammer of the pistol. Aimee saw now that the fingers of his left hand rested lightly on the barrel of a shotgun that was propped against the balcony railing.

Just then Dominic's black eyes turned downward toward her and she was a little stunned by the look in those eyes, so fierce, almost animal-like in their watchfulness. Then with a lift of his dark brow, he nodded and deftly placed the pistol back into a leather holster that was strapped across the top of his lean hips.

She took a deep breath and turned to cross the porch and go back into the house. She wasn't so certain that the man who occupied her home, the man whom she had so arrogantly introduced as her partner, wasn't more dangerous than the men who'd just threatened them.

Dominic was walking down the curving staircase

when Aimee entered the cool hallway. His eyes, still cold and dangerous, stared into hers, waiting arrogantly for her disapproval.

"We need to talk," she said.

"I know." Dominic glanced at Amos who stood near the doorway to the back veranda. In the old man's hand was a broad-bladed carving knife from the kitchen. Dominic smiled and placed a hand on the man's stooped, slender shoulders. "Thank you, Amos. Would you tell Master Lucas that Aimee and I will be ready to go out to the fields in a few minutes? Tell him to wait."

"Yes, suh." Amos's look was proud as he straightened his frail shoulders and smiled up at Dominic.

Aimee glanced at Dominic, at the gun that rode so easily . . . so intimately against his thigh. It seemed almost a part of his body and she guessed that was because he had worn it . . . and used it, so often in the past.

Without speaking she turned toward her office and he followed. She stood at the door as Dominic entered. And as she closed the door she thought how small his presence made the room seem. And when he turned to her, so close there in the small enclosure, her breath caught in her throat at the look from those black stormy eyes.

"Have a seat," she said, turning from him . . . from those eyes. She sat at the desk, motioning him toward a nearby chair.

But instead of sitting, he moved to the fireplace and stood resting his elbow against the elaborately carved mantel, and waited for her to speak.

"I could have handled Compton on my own," she said.

Dominic's eyes opened wide before a disbelieving smirk flickered across his mouth.

"Really?" he drawled. "From where I was standing you didn't seem to be handling anything."

Aimee gritted her teeth before she continued. His reaction was exactly what she expected.

"There was no need for guns. I have no idea why the first idea that enters a man's head is to pull a gun, shoot or threaten, then think about it later at his leisure, preferably as I understand, over a bottle of whiskey." Dark spots of color stung her cheeks as she stared at him defiantly.

Dominic's reaction was quick. As he turned his body, his hand came down so hard on the mantelpiece that the glass vases sitting there shook and rattled.

"Jesus, lady! What did you expect me to do . . . invite him in for lemonade? The man was ready to come up on the porch and drag you away with him. He—"

"Oh, I hardly think Mister Compton was going to drag me anywhere. Amos was in the hallway with a knife and—"

"My God, do you really expect a seventy-year-old man to defend you, and a Negro at that? Where in hell have you been all your life?"

He took a threatening step toward her, staring at her as if she'd lost her mind. "This is the man who killed your husband, damn it. Or doesn't that mean anything to a woman of your circumstances?"

Aimee leapt from the chair and stood facing him, shoulders back and chin forward. "How dare you say that to me. Do you think I've forgotten what an evil man he is, or that he's the one who took Jim

91

from me? Oh . . ." She whirled away in frustration, only to turn to face him again. "Can't you see? Your reaction is exactly the same as Jim's. All fire and lightning . . . you handled it just the way Jim would have and you see where it got him."

"First of all," he said slowly. "I'm not Jim, and for all our friendship, I'm nothing like Jim Le-Beaux. And I don't think I need to remind you that I was defending more here than just your reputation." His eyes were cold and hard and they never left her face. "I have a stake in this place now and by God I'm not about to stand by and let the likes of Compton take it away without a fight. And furthermore, I don't intend to take orders about my habits from you or anyone else! Now either I'm a full partner here, or you can sell your share of Le-Beaux and move back to the more civilized confines of Natchez, which I'm sure would suit you much better."

Aimee took a deep breath and her green eyes shot fiery resentment at the tall, dark-haired man whose stance was so fiercely arrogant. He had no more intention of listening to her than Jim had. And he probably would end up exactly the same way. And why that thought should bring such unexpected pain to her heart, she couldn't quite understand.

"I don't intend ever going back to Natchez." Her eyes flashed at him. "So I suppose then, this is something about which we must simply agree to disagree," she said, her lips stiff and unyielding.

His brows lifted haughtily as he stared down at her, his look just as unyielding.

"You've got that much right."

"Fine." She returned his haughty gaze for a moment, before finally pulling her gaze away.

"Well, I do feel that I should say . . . that I should . . . uh, thank you." Aimee felt as if the words of gratitude rushed from her throat almost soundlessly.

Dominic's dark eyebrow quirked upward and a slow easy smile replaced the frown on his handsome face.

"Pardon me?"

Aimee's lips tightened and her green eyes practically glittered at him from across the room.

"I said thank you . . . for helping me, regardless of your tactics." She cleared her throat and forced herself to look directly into his dark eyes. "I admit I underestimated Compton; I should have known, with Jim dead, that he would try something exactly like this." Her words came out in a tumble, as if she could hardly wait to have them said and done.

"Next time you might want to have a weapon nearby, just in case. But you handled it well enough . . . for a woman." His dark eyes were full of mischief. He ignored her flashing eyes and her look of resentment as he continued. "But we haven't seen the last of him, you know."

"I know," she whispered with a nod of her head.

"I think your neighbor is a very dangerous man, Aimee. I think he'll stop at nothing to get what he wants." He dipped his head slightly to gaze at her. "And I think he wants you."

She shook her head and looked away, feeling suddenly shy and uncomfortable. "He wants LeBeaux Plantation," she said.

He shrugged, his eyes narrowing as he saw how uncomfortable the subject made her.

The way Dominic stood, so tall and restless by the fireplace, made her feel very small and insignificant. But she plunged ahead to tell him what she'd intended to say all along.

"As you said, you are a full partner." Her cheeks were bright with color as she forced herself to say the words. "And I apologize if I sometimes forget that. There are things you need to know about the plantation, about the plans I had already made for the future before you came."

"Such as?"

"First of all, as you've probably already guessed, I had no idea that LeBeaux Plantation was practically penniless." She turned suddenly and walked to the window that looked out on the south side of the yard. This was not a subject that was easy for her. As a doctor's daughter, she had grown up knowing the value of a dollar; it wasn't as if they'd been wealthy or she had ever been afforded the luxury of being a spendthrift. But she had been foolishly ignorant about Jim's financial affairs. "I never would have spent so much money on this house if I'd known." She turned back to him, seeing the look in his eyes, the quiet patience as he waited for her to say what she needed to say. If he thought her indulgent and extravagant, he was not going to say so.

She laughed softly. "You might not have gotten yourself such a bargain here at that," she said.

"I wasn't looking for a bargain," he replied, his deep voice a rumble in the small room.

"Then . . . what were you looking for . . . exactly?"

He pursed his lips and looked down toward the toe of his boot. Long black lashes lay against his dark skin. Then his eyes flicked upward again to look at her.

"Something more meaningful I guess." He glanced up at the ceiling, his eyes roaming about the beautifully decorated room. "A home maybe."

She frowned. This was hardly what she had expected him to say. She had expected him to say he was here to make a profit — anything except the soft, almost poignant words he had just spoken. She pushed ahead, brushing aside the rush of tenderness that had come so suddenly to her heart.

"I should tell you that I planned to free all Le-Beaux slaves within three to five years. Those who wish to stay here afterward will be paid a fair wage."

His brows lifted and he pursed his lips thoughtfully.

"That's a fairly ambitious plan."

"Do you disapprove?" Defiantly, she lifted her chin, waiting for him to tell her all the reasons, as Jim had, why her plan was foolish and unwarranted.

"No," he said. "Not at all. As long as you know how difficult it will be . . . and the consequences it might bring. Your fellow Mississippians won't exactly welcome such radical ideas. They'll probably blame it on the fact that you're a flighty, liberalminded female. But if it's what you want, then I have no intention of standing in your way."

"But you . . . you don't think I'm foolish for wanting to do such a thing? You're not even going to tell me how much it will cost us? This is going to affect you, too, you know — don't you even want to know why?"

His hand lifted in a gesture of dismissal and he

smiled. "Oh, I think I already know why. For all your independence and bravado, Mrs. LeBeaux, I think you're a very kind, very compassionate woman. And I would imagine that the buying and selling of another human being is very distasteful to you, just as it is to me." His formal use of her married name was light, teasing even, meant to make the moment easier. But that didn't detract at all from his serious, insightful words.

Her cheeks grew warm and rosy as she stared into his knowing eyes. Those black eyes that had grown so warm that she had to look away from them.

"Well," she said, turning again toward the window. "You're a more perceptive man than I would have thought."

"A necessary quality for a gambler, I'm afraid," he said.

She turned and stared at him. He was trying to be kind and to smooth over their disagreement. Why couldn't she just accept that? Why couldn't she make herself feel at ease with him?

"The estate books are all here . . . feel free to look over them anytime you wish. And I need to give you a key to this desk. There's a false compartment here, behind the book shelves." She took a key from one of the desk drawers and handed it to him, making sure her fingers did not touch his when he took it. "There's a little over fifteen hundred dollars in the compartment . . . all the money LeBeaux has left in the world. But if something happens to me . . . you should know where it is."

He slipped the key into his pocket and nodded, his black eyes clear and unquestioning.

"Do you know a great deal about cotton?" she

asked, looking suddenly up at him without trying to hide the hope in her eyes.

He grinned and shook his head. "Afraid not. I haven't had much experience with farming."

She sighed. "Then I suppose that makes two of us." She had never admitted to a single soul that she hardly knew the first thing about growing cotton.

"Well," he said with a crooked grin. "Nathaniel and some of the others seem to know all that needs knowing. You and I . . . we'll learn together."

She blushed again, uncomfortable with his provocative lowering of his voice when he said the words, "You and I."

"Yes," she said, turning quickly to the desk as if searching for something. "And I also wanted to tell you that . . . that I think Lucas might benefit from being with you. Up to a certain point." She turned to look at him, wanting to make herself clear. "I still want him to receive a good education."

"So do I."

"And I want him to learn to be a gentleman. . . ."

"I agree."

"Oh. Well, I'm glad we agree . . . on that at least."

"It's a start," he said, smiling.

"I . . . I can't think of anything else I need to tell you. Except that we're having a dinner party this weekend. Just a few neighbors who knew Jim very well and my Aunt Eulie from Natchez. They'll be spending the night here at LeBeaux."

"I'll try and be on my best behavior," he said with a slight, mocking bow.

She smiled at him, unable to resist his potent charm. And she decided right at that moment that

97

for all his reckless, wild reputation, his irresistible charm might just be the most dangerous thing about Dominic Valcour.

"Then I . . . I guess that's all." She hesitated, then turned as if to leave the room.

She felt his hand on her arm and she stopped, unable to move, unable even to breathe.

"No, that's not all, Aimee. There's something I wanted to say to you as well."

She turned, looking up into his face, knowing she should step away from him as she waited for him to continue.

"That night in the cemetery—"

Dominic saw the closed look cross her face, saw the flash of her green eyes and he knew how strongly she still disapproved. Her anger on that subject had not abated in the least it seemed. She moved toward the door as if she had not heard a word he said.

His hand clamped around her arm, halting her instantly.

"Listen to me, damn it," he growled softly. "Has it ever crossed that stubborn little mind of yours that you don't know everything . . . that maybe what you see is not always necessarily what it appears to be?"

"And what exactly does that mean?"

"I wanted Lucas to have something . . . some gesture that a child could understand, some way for him to tell Jim goodbye and of knowing that his death was not a casual thing . . . not to me at least."

She frowned, her look at him incredulous.

"What are you saying? That you think it was to

me?"

"No . . . no, that's not what I mean at all. I know you loved Jim; it's in your eyes, I can hear it in your voice whenever you say his name." Dominic saw the trembling of her soft lips and took a long, slow breath. He released her arm and stepped away from her. Away from the sweet, provocative fragrance of her and the look of pain in those deep green eyes. "But Lucas is just a kid, Aimee. Children can't always see beneath the surface, can't always decipher what we adults have learned so well to hide. He needed to know that Jim's death was not meaningless."

"And what exactly did that . . . that savage ritual have to do with anything?"

Dominic's jaw clenched as he tried to remain patient with her stubborn dismissal of everything he was trying to say. Damn it, sometimes he wanted to shake her. For all the vulnerability he thought he saw hidden deep inside her, she could be as stubborn and closed-minded as a mule.

"That savage ritual, as you call it, was a religious ceremony, at least to the Choctaw and I suspect, to Lucas's people as well. The offering of a broken lance at the grave of a fallen warrior means that he died too young—it's the symbol of a death not meant to be." His expressive black eyes stared into hers as he tried to make her understand.

Aimee felt chills along her spine at his words, felt stunned when the armor she had erected simply fell away as she heard the truth in his voice. That was exactly the way to describe such grief—a death not meant to be. Her brow wrinkled and she took a deep breath and stepped away from him as if he'd struck her. Tears came suddenly to her eyes, and quickly spilled over to fall down her cheeks. She shook her head, staring silently at him and wondering at the beauty of his words, even as she felt the pain in her heart.

"I . . . I didn't know," she said through trembling lips. "I'm sorry, I thought . . ."

Dominic frowned and reached his hand forward. She felt the brush of his warm fingers against her cheek, saw the hurt in his own eyes as well and she had to stiffen her muscles to keep from falling into his arms and weeping against his chest.

"I know," he murmured. "I know what you thought."

She stepped away from him and turned her back so that he could not see the tears that still streamed down her face.

"Oh, God," she whispered, her hands going to her flushed cheeks. "Lucas . . . poor sweet, dear Lucas. How he must have felt when I came storming into the cemetery and . . . I am so sorry, Dominic. Sometimes I can be such a fool."

Quickly she turned and ran from the room, away from the dark eyes that looked at her with such understanding. She didn't want his understanding — she didn't! She thought she could hardly bear to have him look at her that way. It confused her and made her forget all her vows. And it frightened her more than anything had since Jim's death, until all she could think of at that moment was to run.

Eight

Aimee ran into the center hallway and out toward the back veranda, going quickly to her room and locking the door behind her. She didn't even bother to see who was outside near the brick kitchen building. She just ran.

Her heart was aching with sadness as she flung herself across the big bed. She was crying so hard she could barely breathe and her sobs caught raggedly in her throat.

Moments later she heard a light tap on the door, but she ignored it. After a moment's hesitation, she heard the knock again and Jezzy's quiet voice.

"Miz Aimee? Miz Aimee, you all right? Please let me in, missy."

Aimee sat up in the bed, wiping the tears from her face with the palms of her hands. She looked toward the door, feeling foolish and wishing at that moment that she could be anywhere else but here. She was too soft, too sentimental and emotional to ever be able to run this plantation. When she tried to be hard and practical, it all just turned out wrong anyway.

She scooted down from the bed until her toes touched the floor and walked slowly across the room, turning the lock and opening the door. Jezzy had seen her cry before. She'd seen her in much worse situations than this.

Jezzy's eyes were round and wondering as she stood looking at Aimee. The smooth mahogany skin of her brow wrinkled and she turned her head to one side.

"Missy, you look mighty objected. What on earth is wrong?"

Aimee smiled and shook her head, standing aside and motioning for Jezzy to come into the room. "I think you mean *dejected,* Jezzy. And yes, I suppose I do look pretty dejected at that. And frankly, I'm feeling very foolish and guilty about something I did."

Jezzy stood in the middle of the room and for once she seemed to be at a loss for words.

"Mister Dominic said for me to see was you all right. He said him and Lucas will be waiting at the stables whenever you're ready to go down to the cotton fields. And he say for you to take your time."

Aimee frowned again, feeling the tears welling, feeling the ache in her heart that would not seem to go away. She would rather Dominic scream and rail at her than to be so kind and understanding.

"If you're worried about the cotton, missy, they ain't no need. The conjure man, he done seen the flying horses in the air. Means a good crop, don't you know."

Aimee smiled and touched Jezzy's smooth cheek.

"Oh, Jezzy," she whispered. "You are good for me. You always know just the right thing to say."

Jezzy smiled broadly. "And you better now?"

"Yes, Jezzy. Much better. If Mister Dominic is still in the house, you may tell him that I'll be along

102

in a few minutes."

After Jezzy left, Aimee turned quickly back to the room. She went to the washstand and splashed cool water on her face and her burning eyes, then ran her hands against her hair, smoothing the strands that had fallen about her face. She quickly unfastened her skirt and petticoats and pulled on her riding skirt. Before going out the door, she grabbed a wide-brimmed yellow straw hat with a swath of white gauze veil that would come down far enough to cover her red, swollen eyes.

As she walked toward the stables, Aimee could hear the whinny of the horses. The long pasture behind the stables was a brilliant green now and several of the mares pranced and frolicked, some with new colts and some looking big bellied and ready any day to give birth to their own foals.

Suddenly, she could hardly wait to begin her ride.

Dominic and Lucas were outside the stables. The horses were saddled and stood nearby as Dominic spoke to one of the young black boys who worked with the horses.

Lucas saw her first and gave her a sweet, almost shy smile as she approached.

When Dominic turned, his dark eyes moved over her in a look that held concern and worry, making her glad for the hat and gauze veil.

"Sorry to keep you waiting," she said.

Dominic said nothing, but simply walked to her mare and untied the reins, handing them to her as one of the stable boys moved to help her up onto the horse. Aimee noted that Dominic still wore the pistol strapped around his hips, but she said nothing, not wanting to spoil the tentative truce between them.

The three of them rode slowly away from the stables. Lucas was chattering constantly, pointing out things to Dominic, proudly showing him all the beauty of his home. Aimee's gaze went to Lucas several times and she smiled softly at his enthusiasm.

Before long, Lucas was far ahead of them. His boyish laughter could hardly be contained any longer. And when he turned to Dominic for his usual approval, his gaze turned also to Aimee.

She smiled and waved, encouraging his pleasure. And that was all it took. Lucas nudged the sides of his horse, directing him into a trot that sent sandy clods of dirt flying behind them.

Aimee's laughter was spontaneous, and when she heard herself, she realized how long it had been since she had laughed aloud. She wasn't even worried about Compton or his threats. And if she tried to put a name to her frame of mind, she thought it would have to be that she felt safe. That was it . . . safe.

She glanced toward Dominic who lounged easily in the saddle and found him watching her.

"Are you all right?" he asked. She knew he was referring to their earlier conversation.

"Yes." She nodded, feeling too shy to look into his eyes, but wanting so much to tell him how she felt—about her misunderstanding of the broken lance ceremony. But she simply couldn't find the words.

Nathaniel saw them as they passed by the houses in the quarters. He came out of a shed and walked alongside Dominic's horse.

"Goin' down to the cotton fields, suh?"

"We thought we'd see if any of the plants are up."

"They ain't. I done looked." Nathaniel's smile showed teeth that were very white against his dark skin. And his black eyes fairly twinkled in the sunlight. Aimee smiled, thinking of Jezzy's concern for the young man. And she wondered if Gregory Davis was still causing trouble.

"I think we'll ride down there anyway," Dominic said.

Nathaniel patted Dominic's horse lightly. "Yes, suh. Nice mornin' for a ride. Mighty nice." But Nathaniel continued to walk along beside them. "I hear you done have yourself some visitors this mornin, Mister Dominic."

Aimee's eyes widened. News certainly traveled fast between the house and the quarters.

"Compton and his men," Dominic said. "You might want to keep an eye out down here, Nathaniel. Just in case he decides to come back."

"I'll do that, suh." The young man nodded, his eyes going for a moment to Aimee as he nodded respectfully toward her as well.

The rich fertile soil of the cotton fields stretched far away in the distance. Lucas returned to where Aimee and Dominic were.

"Nothing's up yet," he said.

"So I see, Lucas," Dominic said with a smile. He stepped easily down from the saddle, his long legs making the transition look simple. He walked into the field, the toes of his boots kicking clods of earth out of the way as he moved. He bent at one of the rows and flicked at the soil with his fingers. There, just beneath the surface was a pale green sprout, ready to burst from the ground and begin its stretch toward the sun.

Dominic turned and smiled, pointing toward the ground. "Well, at least the seeds weren't washed away."

Aimee moved her horse nearer and saw what he meant. She took a deep breath and looked upward as if in prayer. "Thank goodness."

She smiled at Dominic and for a moment it was as if they were completely alone. She could almost have believed there was no one, or nothing else in the entire world except the two of them in this wide fertile field with the heat of the Mississippi sun beating down on their shoulders.

"I guess we're going to have to learn about cotton now, Mister Valcour," she said. "Whether we're ready or not."

"I guess you're right." He laughed and walked back to his horse.

The morning was beautiful despite the heat of the sun and neither of them really wanted to go back to the house so soon.

Dominic turned his big black horse toward the woods and with a grin back at Aimee and Lucas said, "We might as well check the new clearing while we're here."

Lucas let out a yelp and leaned over his horse's neck, digging his heels against the animal's sides as they took off. He rode skillfully along the edge of the cotton field, but at times the horse's hooves landed in the soft plowed soil, throwing dirt toward Dominic and Aimee.

"Out of the cotton," Dominic yelled with a grin.

Lucas only threw up his hand and turned his

horse farther away from the field.

Dominic and Aimee laughed together.

"I've never seen Lucas behave this way," Aimee murmured, her eyes glowing as she watched the boy ride.

"What do you mean?"

"Well, he's always been a bit reserved, even with Jim. He just seems so . . . so carefree now." She turned to Dominic and frowned slightly. "But we really do need to find another tutor for him. His studies have been sadly lacking recently."

Dominic smiled and nodded. "I'll take care of it next time I'm in Natchez."

The shade of the woods was pleasantly cool after being in the hot sun so long. Aimee took off her hat and waved it for a moment in front of her face. They emerged a short time later on the other side of the narrow strip of trees. The smaller field beyond the trees was like a beehive. They could see Gregory Davis astride his horse as he moved between the rows where the slaves worked. He looked up as they approached and turned his horse toward them.

"Mornin'," he said, his ruddy face stern, his smile forced.

"I'm amazed at how much work has been done here," Aimee said, looking at the field that only months ago had been covered with brush and vines.

"Oh, I can get the work out of these people. I could get even more work if I laid a whip to their backs every now and then." The man was not even looking at Aimee when he spoke, but had turned lazily as he lounged on his horse, to look at the workers in the field.

"If they're working well, I can't understand why

107

you'd think that necessary, Mister Davis."

He turned and the smile on his face was one of arrogance and pride. "Beggin' your pardon, ma'am. Guess I can't expect a woman like yourself to understand these nigras. They're naturally lazy; the only thing they respect is a white man with a whip in his hand. Now if I was runnin' this place, I'd—"

"But you're not running this place, Mister Davis," Aimee said, her face feeling tight with anger. She was aware of Dominic sitting quietly, watching and listening. "And as long as that's the case, you will do as I say. And I told you when you came that I would tolerate no whipping of LeBeaux slaves. In fact"—she nodded toward the coiled whip on his saddle horn—"I'd prefer that you give me that whip you carry. I don't even want to see one on my property."

Gregory Davis's pale gray eyes narrowed as he turned to her. His mouth opened for a moment before he clamped his jaws together and stared hard at her. "You ain't serious."

"Oh yes, Mister Davis, I assure you, I'm entirely serious." Aimee's small gloved hand reached forward, palm up as she waited for him to hand her the whip.

The overseer looked at Dominic. "You got nothin' to say about this, Mister Valcour?" There was a sneer on his face as if he'd like to make an insult of Dominic's silence.

Dominic smiled slowly, a smile that did not quite reach his glittering black eyes. "Mrs. LeBeaux and I are in agreement here, Mister Davis. So I suggest you hand over the whip as the lady asked."

There was no mistaking the deadly threat in his

voice, and for a moment Aimee held her breath. Her eyes darted toward the gun he wore on his hip, but his hands made no move toward it.

Davis muttered something beneath his breath and turned to spit on the ground. Then he jerked the whip from around the pommel of his saddle and silently handed it toward Dominic.

"You're makin' a mighty big mistake here. The day will come when you'll wish you'd let me discipline these heathen. Show 'em a little mercy and you'll soon have an uprisin' on your hands. They don't understand the meanin' of the word loyalty, and if you think they care about you just because you're soft on 'em, then you two got another think comin'!" He jerked at his horse's reins and rode away from them, waving his arms and shouting at the Negroes who worked with hoes and rakes to smooth the soil.

Lucas sat nearby, taking it all in. His eyes were round as he turned toward Dominic and Aimee.

"I don't like him."

"Neither do I," Aimee said, sighing.

"Then why'd you hire him?" Lucas' voice was high pitched and accusatory, his dark eyes questioning.

She could sense Dominic's eyes on her as well.

"I didn't have much choice, Luke. Most plantations have an overseer long before spring. I felt lucky to get anyone on such short notice."

"Did someone recommend him to you?" Dominic asked.

"No, actually, he came to the house one day. He said he heard that LeBeaux needed an overseer. He told me he had worked on the Haywood Plantation in Wilkinson County for five years and before that he worked for Mister Benoist at Claiborne." She shrugged her shoulders, not knowing anything else she could have done about the man.

Dominic nodded, his eyes solemn and thoughtful. "Don't worry about it. I think Mister Davis understands now, and if he doesn't, we'll find another overseer. You did the best you could." He turned toward Lucas to make sure the boy understood his meaning.

"I hope so," Aimee said softly. "I really do hope so."

They rode back toward the house past the section of tangled forest that always made Aimee uneasy. She didn't know what urged her to turn and look into the thick stand of canes and bamboo. But when she did, just for a fraction of a second she thought she saw someone in the dense undergrowth, thought she saw the shadow of a man sitting on a horse, watching them.

She frowned and nudged her mare forward, closer to Dominic. Then she lifted the white veil of her hat and peered back toward the woods. But there was no one there, nothing to disturb the quiet stillness except the trill of birds and the raucous cawing of crows in the trees.

She said nothing to Dominic. It was probably only her imagination. But still the incident made the hair at the back of her neck bristle and caused a shiver to travel down her spine. She turned to look again, then shrugged her shoulders and tried to dismiss it from her mind.

Nine

There remained a quiet truce the next few days between Aimee and Dominic. She had decided that a businesslike attitude was best even though she had to admit to herself that was not going to be easy with such a man.

Dominic's presence in the house was electric; he was like a human lightning rod, drawing everyone to him. Jezzy and Amos adored him, and when Lucas was not with him, he was constantly singing his praises. It was hard for Aimee not to feel resentful at the easy way he had come into her home and made himself a part of it. And she was finding it even more difficult to be near him every day and not give in to the same reactions as the rest of the household.

Early on Friday, the morning before her dinner party, Aimee wandered out to the back veranda to admire her new garden. The brick walkways were in place now and there were fragrant blooms on many of the tall, stately rose bushes. She'd had rose-colored camellias planted at the four corners of the garden and all the pathways led from there to the center, to the lovely statue that Jim had brought from Natchez.

But when she looked again toward the garden, she

stopped, stunned as she saw two large cows contentedly munching away at her plants.

"No!" she shouted as she gathered her skirts and began to run down the steps toward the garden. "Shoo . . . get out . . . get out of here!"

The cows turned huge brown eyes her way and one of them made a low mooing sound as it watched her. Aimee turned about several times looking for a stick, a rock . . . anything to chase the cows away from her roses.

But after several minutes of screaming and waving at the animals, she still had not persuaded them to move an inch.

"Oh no," she muttered. "Amos! Jezzy! Come help me," she shouted back at the house.

She heard them coming across the veranda behind her and she also heard the low, quiet chuckle of Dominic's voice.

She turned to see him and Lucas watching from near the kitchen. Dominic's arms were across his chest and one hand was lifted to stroke his chin as he shook his head and watched with great amusement.

"Well . . . don't just stand there. Help me! I won't have a rose left if . . . we . . . don't . . . Oh, get out of my garden . . . get!"

When she turned back toward the house, she saw Dominic nudge Lucas and they both headed toward the garden.

Later, Amos and Lucas herded the cows back out toward the pasture while Aimee stood with Dominic surveying the damage.

"Those damned cows," Aimee fumed. "Every summer they manage to get out of the fence somehow and when they do they head straight for my roses."

Dominic smiled down at her, watching the play of sun across her nose, the way her smooth olive skin dimpled just at the corners of her mouth. He frowned and looked away, trying to keep his mind on what she was saying.

"Jim bought fencing boards last summer, but . . ."

Her words seemed to bring Dominic out of his reverie. He shrugged his broad shoulders, wishing the sight of her fingers moving thoughtfully across her lips did not bother him so. Wishing that the image of her on that rainy night did not come so quickly to mind, or the remembrance of her soft slender body outlined beneath the pink wrapper.

"If you already have the boarding, Lucas and I could probably build the fence in a day . . . if that's what you want." He lifted his arm and pointed at the side of the garden away from the house. "We'd only need to build two sides; we could run it from the kitchen across the end of the garden, then have this side join with the corner of the back veranda there."

Aimee's green eyes were bright in the morning sunlight as she turned to look up at him with surprise. Somehow she had not expected him to take any interest in such tame domestic things as a rose garden or fencing. But seeing the way his brow puckered with thought, she knew he was interested.

"Could you? It . . . it wouldn't be too much trouble—you wouldn't mind?"

That slow easy smile she'd come to know, moved across his dark face. "Of course I wouldn't mind.

I'll get Nathaniel to help . . . that should please Jezzy." He laughed and nodded toward the young woman who was sweeping the porch. "We'll have it done in no time . . . in time to show off to your guests at the dinner party tomorrow."

Aimee bounced on her toes for a moment before reminding herself of her age. And she didn't even stop to think before reaching forward to put her hand on Dominic's arm.

"That would be wonderful. . . ."

The warning flash of his dark eyes was immediate and powerful. Aimee felt the hard flex of muscles beneath the material of his shirt and for a moment she froze, staring up at him in surprise. The warmth of his body seemed to flow directly from his skin into her fingers and for a second she was lost. Lost in the feel of a man's hard body beneath her hand and lost in the glitter of black eyes that had suddenly turned as dark as midnight and much, much more dangerous.

She jerked her hand away from him as if she'd been burned and turned back toward the garden, trying to pretend that nothing had happened. Trying to convince herself that this man did not make her knees turn as weak as a new kitten's, or that the feel of him, the spicy scent of him did not make her head reel or her stomach coil with warm, sensuous longing.

"Well . . ." Aimee began, gazing at him from the corner of her eye. "I . . . I guess I should get back inside and . . . I have several things to do before tomorrow."

"We'll have your garden fenced before nightfall." His voice was warm and appealing, like the summer morning breeze.

Aimee turned to go, staring for a moment at him before pulling her eyes from his steady black gaze. Then she hurried toward the steps of the veranda and breezed past Jezzy, who was humming beneath her breath. She smiled toward Aimee as if she knew a secret.

"Beautiful mornin', ain't it, missy?"

"Yes," Aimee said, not even bothering, in her flight, to look at the girl. "Beautiful."

Several times that day Aimee wandered from her office to stand at the open doorway to the veranda. Each time she could see the progress being made on the picket fence. And she thought as she heard the low pleasant murmur of Nathaniel and Dominic's deep voices that they were enjoying their work in the sun and working with their hands.

The day had grown very hot and by late afternoon, the sun looked heavy in the western sky as it made ready to dip below the line of trees on the horizon. There was no hint of a breeze and the heat made everything seem still and sultry. Aimee felt a film of perspiration on her brow and upper lip and she looked toward the sky, wishing for a cool breeze or a quick sprinkle of rain to cool the evening.

She moved her hand upward to shade her eyes and as she looked toward the garden, her breath caught in her throat. During the heat of the day, Dominic had removed his shirt and he stood now with his back toward her as he dug the hole for the last fence post. Her heart skittered crazily and suddenly her mouth felt as dry as the dust of the cotton fields.

She watched the play of fading sunlight on his

115

bronzed skin, watched the ripple of muscles across his smooth broad back and shoulders as his arms came up and plunged the digger back into the ground. Each powerful motion held her mesmerized, breathless with some long hidden emotion she could not even name.

She was aware of holding her breath as she watched, aware that she could not quench her curiosity about his body, even when she told herself she should not stand and watch him so brazenly. The tingle that ran through her own body seemed to stop in the pit of her stomach where it changed into a warm curl of rhythm . . . beating . . . spreading a languid tingle to her chest and throat.

She swallowed hard and tried to shake herself out of her stupor.

"God . . ." she whispered, still unable to take her eyes away from his very powerful, masculine body.

"Hey, Aimee!"

Aimee jumped at the sound of Lucas's voice and she turned her eyes away from Dominic toward the boy. She smiled weakly and waved at him. He and Nathaniel were gathering up their tools and moving toward the barn. They had been on the other side of the fence and she hadn't even noticed. But then, Aimee thought wryly, she probably wouldn't have seen them if they'd been standing right in front of her.

She turned back toward Dominic then, the admitted reason for her distraction. At Lucas's shout, he had turned and looked at Aimee with a quiet smile. He continued to work, glancing at Aimee from time to time as he put the last post in place and tamped at the loose soil around the base of it. She watched him from the veranda until he had nailed the last

116

section of fencing to the post and turned to survey his handiwork.

Only then did she move down the steps toward him, hardly aware of her feet touching the ground, hardly aware of breathing.

He was leaning on the fence post, waiting as she approached. And as she grew nearer, he reached for his shirt that hung on the fence and pushed his arms into the sleeves.

Aimee felt an almost uncontrollable urge to reach for the strong brown fingers that buttoned the shirt. She felt the oddest need to still his hands, to push the material of the shirt back away from the smooth dark skin of his muscled chest.

How would he feel beneath the curve of her hands . . . how would his skin taste beneath her lips?

With a start, she looked up into his eyes, dragging her gaze away from his chest, stunned by her thoughts and her inability to control the direction they were taking. Dominic had grown very still, his hand quiet and unmoving above the buttons of his shirt. And when their eyes met Aimee felt a pain strike at her heart like the sharp stab of a knife.

Dominic thought, as Aimee stood looking at him, her eyes so openly curious, that he had never seen a woman more beautiful, or more desirable. For once her eyes held a surprising honesty and as she stared at his naked body, the look in those emerald depths made him feel as if his heart might actually stop. And oddly enough, he felt like laughing. He couldn't even use the defense of making himself remember that she was Jim's widow, or that she detested men like himself. All he knew was that her

117

eyes were beautiful, the deepest emerald he'd ever seen. The way she walked was unaffected and natural . . . she moved the way a woman should when she was not ashamed of her body or of a man's admiring glance.

He had been in every kind of situation imaginable in his thirty-two years of living. He had wrestled with the toughest keelboatmen on the Mississippi; he had outfought and outmaneuvered frontier Indians in their own territory. He'd been shot, slashed with a knife, and almost lynched. But nothing . . . nothing had ever made him feel the way this woman made him feel. This stubborn, prideful woman who had belonged to his best friend. And he didn't know what the hell to do about it.

How could he keep these growing feelings of desire secret, when he lived in the same house with her?

Aimee stopped and lifted her face toward his.

"How does it look?" he asked, his voice slow and quiet.

"What . . . ?"

He smiled. "How does the fence look? Do you approve?" He began to button his shirt but did not bother to tuck it into his trousers.

Aimee's eyes darted quickly to his covered chest and down his flat stomach, and she felt a strange little twinge of disappointment.

"Yes . . . very much. It looks splendid. I think it makes the entire garden look complete. I love it; thank you." She smiled at him, feeling her legs begin to tremble even now.

All she knew was that she needed to get away from him before she did something completely irrational, like reaching up to wipe the smudge of dirt from his cheek, or smooth his sweat-dampened black hair away from his forehead.

Dominic began to put the work tools aside and noticed the burning, raw skin of his hands. He glanced down at his open palms and shrugged his shoulders impatiently.

Aimee saw his look and moved forward to take one of his hands in hers.

"Oh, Dominic . . . your hands—you should have stopped long ago, before . . ." She looked up into his eyes, feeling the tingle that began where their hands touched. But this time she didn't pull away. She couldn't.

"I've grown soft," he said with a quiet laugh. "Jim would really ride me if he could see this. He'd tell me I've been too long in the gambling saloons and too long away from the trail."

"Don't you know how dangerous blisters can be in hot weather? What were you thinking? You could get very sick." The look in her eyes was one of genuine concern and Dominic smiled.

"I didn't notice I guess."

"Didn't notice? We should do something about this right away." She turned to go, then turned back to him with an impatient gesture. "Well, come on. We must find some salve for those hands. I'll swear, you're as bad as Lucas."

Dominic smiled and followed Aimee to the kitchen. They could feel the heat coming from the open doorway, but it didn't seem to affect Cilla and Jezzy who were preparing the supper dishes. The fire in the huge fireplace had been out for hours, but the heat still lingered in the long, low ceilinged room. But Cilla and Jezzy were laughing and talking without seeming to notice.

"Cilla, Mister Dominic has blisters on his hands. Do you have any of that herbal salve in here?"

The cook turned toward her, smiling broadly first at Aimee, then at Dominic.

"I sho do, Miz Aimee."

Her dark face was shiny with perspiration. She was a big woman, both in girth and height, and Aimee often thought she would be a match for any man at almost any chore she set her mind to. She was one of the few slaves who did not have a husband and she seemed perfectly content to cook and take care of her kitchen and the herb garden that lay just outside the back door, near her own room.

Cilla walked to Dominic, who grinned and turned the palms of his hands up for her to see.

"My, my," she said, shaking her head with disapproval. "Better go out to the back porch and wash that real good 'fore you put on the salve. Won't do no good puttin' it on over all that dirt and grime." She handed the small jar of medicine to Aimee, as her black eyes rolled. She motioned them toward the back door.

"Thank you." Aimee turned to go. "We'll be just a few minutes. We'll be ready for dinner as soon as we're finished."

It seemed cooler by the back door of the brick kitchen building. The sun had gone behind the trees now and there was a slight breeze that wafted over the small squares of green herbs and filled the air with a spicy, pungent scent.

Aimee poured cold water into a tin wash pan, and as Dominic cautiously washed his hands, she held a clean dry towel for him.

"You don't have to do this," he said.

"I know," she said. "I want to." She didn't look up at him as she carefully dried the palms of his hands with the dry cloth.

But Dominic couldn't drag his eyes away from her, the way the dusky light glimmered upon her black hair, making it sparkle as if it had a life of its own. He felt his body responding to her nearness, to her sweet woman's scent and the touch of her soft hands upon the raw nerves of his skin.

He gritted his teeth as she applied the salve, but it was not against the pain in his hands that he fought. He muttered something and pulled his hands out of her grasp as he took a step backward on the small sheltered porch.

"I'm sorry," she said, glancing up into his face. "Did I —"

"Aimee . . ." His voice was a croak, a husky protest of warning.

She frowned and reached for his hand again, but was stopped by the look in his eyes as she realized what was happening. Could he possibly be as drawn to her as she was to him? She would never have thought that possible, not with a man like Dominic Valcour.

"I can manage on my own now, thanks."

She looked away from his searching black eyes, those eyes that held so many questions.

"You can't possibly bandage your hands yourself. You —"

"Aimee," he growled, interrupting her words. "If you know what's good for you . . . you'll go back to the house and let me do this alone."

Aimee's white teeth pulled at her lower lip and her green eyes looked up at him as if she were searching for some long, lost secret.

"I'm not sure I *ever* knew what was good for me." Her eyes were troubled and as questioning as his.

That sweet look, that moment of hesitation was all it took to break Dominic's resolve. With a soft murmur he took one step toward her, bringing their bodies dangerously close. His hands moved around her waist and in one swift movement, she was in his arms, straining against him as if she could never be close enough.

"Aimee . . ."

His mouth on hers was hot, searching, and her lips answered his just as passionately, just as impulsively. Her hands went to the hard muscled surface of his chest, moving beneath his shirt to touch and explore as she had wanted to do this afternoon when she saw him standing so gloriously bare in the fading sunlight. His hungry kisses, the feel of his body against hers, made her feel completely lost and out of control.

Dominic's hands moved up to grasp the front of her dress, roughly pulling the buttons aside until his lips could touch the smooth, warm skin of her breasts.

Aimee gasped, and fell against him as she closed her eyes against the pleasurable assault. She took his head in her hands and pulled his face back up so that she could taste his lips again. She felt the searching rasp of his tongue as his lips plundered hers. And she thought for a moment she might actually faint from the rush of heat that swept over her. She could only cling to him, feeling as if she could not get enough . . . that if she lived a hundred years, she would never get enough of his kisses, his taste, or the feel of his strong arms around her.

She felt him moving her back against the wall, felt the hard thrust of his body against hers and for the first time, her mind cried out in alarm, even while her body urged her to go on.

"Dom . . . Dominic . . ." she whispered, trying to move from the steely grip of his arms, trying to arouse her own conscience somehow before it was too late.

"Shhh," he whispered. "Don't talk . . . don't say anything. Just let me—"

"No, Dominic . . . I can't . . . we can't." But his kiss took her breath and smothered the protest she tried to make. And once again, she felt herself melting into sweet acquiescence at his touch, and the hot persuasive kisses that made her head spin.

At her frightened moan, he lifted his head; his black eyes were deep and opaque, the look that of someone she hardly knew. She thought he looked fierce and savage and for a moment her heart turned over in her desperate need of him. But she couldn't, she kept telling herself—she needed time to reason everything out before she made a mistake she might regret forever. It was too soon . . . there were still people around—Lucas and Nathaniel could come walking past them at any moment.

"Dominic . . . please," she whispered, her hand moving up to touch his face. She felt the rasp of whiskers as he turned his head and took her fingers into his mouth. "Oh, God," she moaned, closing her eyes with a gasp and feeling her resistance melting away. "Please . . . we can't do this."

Using all the strength of will she possessed, she moved away from him, pushing at his hard chest, and dodging beneath his arms and around him. When he turned to face her, his eyes were stormy and troubled and his breath had become ragged and coarse.

"Yes, Aimee," he said, stepping toward her again. "We can. It would be so easy—"

She held a hand up, placing it against his chest and looking into his eyes. And it was the look in her eyes that stopped Dominic in his tracks. He knew she wanted him; he could feel it, had already seen it in her beautiful emerald eyes. But now he could see something else there as well. Fear, maybe. Guilt . . . doubt.

He stepped away then, away from her hands, and took a long, deep breath.

"It's too soon for you," he whispered, his eyes never leaving her face.

"I still love Jim, Dominic."

"Jim's dead, Aimee."

She turned from him, shaking her head in denial as her hand moved to her trembling lips.

"Not for me, he isn't. He'll never be dead in my heart."

"Jesus," he moaned, throwing his head back and raking his hand through his black hair.

"Are you sure it's your love for Jim that's stopping you, Aimee. Is it love . . . or guilt?"

She frowned, her eyes glittering now with unshed tears.

"How can you say that? How can you ask me such a thing?" She turned from him, then whirled

124

back around, anger and confusion sparkling in her eyes. "You were his best friend! If Jim were here—"

Dominic grabbed her arms and pulled her hard against his body. "But Jim isn't here, damn it. And he will never be here again. You have to stop using Jim as an excuse, Aimee; you have to let him go."

"No."

"You can't deny what's between us, what has been between us from that first night when I stepped onto the veranda and kissed you there in the moonlight."

She pushed at him angrily, the tears spilling over onto her ashen cheeks. "Are you sure it's me you want?" she asked, her voice trembling with confusion. "Or do you just need someone, need the same thing that all men—"

"I want *you*," he growled. His jaw clenched and he tightened his grip on her arms. His eyes were steely as he pulled her hand toward him and downward, placing it roughly against his body as if for proof.

Like a punishment, Aimee thought, as she jerked her hand away.

"And you want me," he whispered. "Just as much."

Her eyes wavered beneath his for a moment before she pushed him away and stepped off the porch.

"You're right, you know," she hissed. "I do want you. I want you the way I've never wanted a man in my life . . . not even my own husband. But—"

"But what, Aimee? Is that really it? You feel guilty because you never felt this way with Jim? Or are you just afraid that I'll turn out to be just like him? That I'll make love to you and you won't be able to let me go?"

"You're cruel," she cried. "Cruel and unfeeling and—"

"No," he whispered. "I'm not. And you know it. You're afraid, angel . . . scared to death of what's happening between us. You have your life all arranged here at LeBeaux . . . everything laid out in a neat little package and now I've come to shake everything loose and—"

"No," she cried. "That's not it. I'm afraid I'll care too much, damn you." Her voice broke as she backed away from him and from his searching black eyes. "I'm afraid I'll love you, can't you see that? And I know that you are not the kind of man to accept love from a woman like me . . . or to ever give it in return."

She ran from him, into the coming darkness and Dominic took a step back into the shadows of the porch. He felt as if he'd been kicked in the stomach. And for a moment, a thought crossed his mind such as he'd never had before about any other woman.

He actually considered running after her, grabbing her and kissing her into submission, then dragging her away to make love to her, whether she wanted it or not.

"Damn," he whispered, raking his hand through his hair. He leaned his head back against the wall and closed his eyes.

He had never wanted a woman so desperately that he would even consider such an ungodly thing. And it shook him, and made him doubt himself, more than anything ever had in his life.

Ten

Aimee ran almost the entire length of the long kitchen building, stopping only when she reached the open doorway where Cilla and Jezzy worked. And just as she expected, a curious Jezzy glanced toward the door when Aimee passed.

"You all be ready for supper now, Miz Aimee?" she asked with a bright smile on her face.

"Oh. Jezzy, I think I'll just take something light . . . in my room, please. I'm feeling a little . . . tired tonight." With a wave of dismissal, Aimee hurried past the kitchen and up across the veranda.

With a lift of her fine brows, Jezzy turned to Cilla who stood at a nearby table. The expression on the big woman's face was just as baffled as Jezzy's as they stared at one another. Jezzy moved toward the door of the kitchen, stepped out and looked toward the back of the building.

Then, moving quickly back inside, she turned to Cilla with a wide-eyed look of curiosity.

"What is it?" Cilla asked in a whisper.

"I ain't sure. I 'spect it's that Mister Dominic what upset the mistress so. She don't even know yet what hit her, if you ask me. And she still tryin' to pretend that man ain't the handsomest thing come

127

down the Mississippi in a long time."

"Ah, you jokin' me," Cilla said, waving a spoon toward the younger girl. "Miz Aimee was done heartbroke when Mister Jim died."

"Ain't jokin'," Jezzy said with a shake of her head. "When I stepped out the door just now?" She was nodding her head and her eyes were wide with interest. "Who did I see but the man hisself. Mister Dominic standin' there at the corner of the buildin', watchin' Miz Aimee. And the look on that man's face. Hmm, hmm, hmm. I ain't jokin' about that, no, ma'am. I ain't jokin'.."

"Well, what do you know about that," Cilla said with a smile. "You think somethin' goin' on 'tween the missy and Mister Dominic?"

"Oh, somethin' goin' on all right. But at the present, it be only in the hatchin' stages." Jezzy laughed aloud then, her eyes bright with mischief. "Yes'm, only in the hatchin' stages."

Aimee felt foolish, hiding in her room like a child, and for a moment, she wished she hadn't told Jezzy to bring her supper there. It would only make it harder to face Dominic tomorrow. She walked across the room to the large mirror and stared at herself for long minutes. Jezzy had already lit the oil lamps in the room and they glowed softly behind Aimee.

She moved her hands upward to her face, trying to see if the evidence of what she felt was there for everyone to see. She rubbed the back of her neck where her muscles felt stiff, then she closed her eyes and shook her head in despair.

What was she going to do? Life here was hard enough without having to fight Dominic along with it. And the trouble was, she didn't want to fight . . . not him and not the intense emotions she felt every time he was near. And now, knowing his kiss, his touch . . . dear God, she didn't know what she would do.

When Jezzy brought her supper, for once the girl was very quiet. She only stared oddly at Aimee, with those big black eyes as she backed out the door.

After Jezzy left, Aimee walked back and forth across the floor, thinking. Dominic was right about one thing. She felt such guilt about Jim that it was tearing her apart.

She thought that when Jim died she would never love another man . . . couldn't imagine it. She intended to dedicate her life to the work at LeBeaux and live out her existence alone . . . peaceful in the house she loved. And in her grief she had thought naively that she would always feel that way.

But she never planned on meeting anyone like Dominic.

Never planned on feeling this way, as if her nerves were raw and exposed. He made her tremble with an intensity she had never experienced before.

And he was right about her—she *was* afraid.

"Oh, Jim," she said, closing her eyes against the vision of Dominic's face. "I *do* still love you, and I don't know what to do. I don't want to forget you or what we had; no one can ever take your place, my darling. No one."

As she walked, she repeated that phrase in her mind over and over until she grew calmer and her heart slowed from its furious pounding. She was a strong woman, she told herself. She would simply steel herself against Dominic Valcour and the intense emotions that his masculinity aroused in her.

She took a long, slow breath and sat down at the small table where her cold supper waited.

"Now," she said aloud. "That's all there is to it. When . . . *if* I ever do want another man, he won't be anything like Dominic Valcour. He'll be settled and quiet, a businessman perhaps from Natchez who will understand my need for independence, a man who does not have such . . . intensity. . . ." Her eyes darkened and she swallowed as she thought of Dominic's hot, persuasive kisses. Then she shook her head and continued with her fevered recitation.

". . . a gentleman, in every way. Yes, that's what he'll be . . . a gentleman."

Early the next morning Aimee was in the rose garden. She had donned a faded cotton work dress and a pair of gloves and had set about clipping the roses. When Jezzy pushed a straw hat toward her, Aimee shook her head.

"It's early, and I won't be in the sun long."

"You'll be as speckled as a guinea hen if you don't wear it."

But Aimee ignored her until Jezzy finally gave up and went back into the house. As she pruned away the damaged limbs and blossoms, Aimee glanced from time to time up toward the house's second-story veranda. There was no sign of movement in Dominic's room, and although Aimee was dying of curiosity, she dared not ask Jezzy or Amos where he was. They were entirely too inquisitive about her and Dominic as it was.

She hadn't been working long when she heard the sound of hoofbeats. She glanced up, realizing the sound came from the front of the house and wondered who could be coming to LeBeaux at such an early hour.

Thinking of Compton, she felt a tingle of alarm and she glanced back toward the house, wondering if she should call for Dominic. But when she saw the rider come around the house and past the garden, she felt a mixed feeling of surprise and relief.

Dominic rode recklessly, just the way he did so many other things. His body was flush against the neck of the huge black horse as he dipped beneath the low hanging limbs of the live oaks and raked through the strands of gray moss.

Aimee felt her heart stirring as she watched him ride toward the stables. His black hair was untied, just the way it had been in the cemetery that night. And again, he wore the soft buckskin clothes of a frontiersman and the fringed knee boots of the Indians. She thought he looked as wild and untamed as the dangerous Natchez Trace that lay no more than half a mile from her home.

The sun was just touching the top of the huge old trees and as Aimee turned to watch Dominic, she shaded her eyes against the light, thinking she had never seen anyone ride the way he did.

She frowned, remembering his heritage, remembering the stories Jim had told her about Dominic's past. He wanted nothing to do with the Choctaw, Jim had said. And yet now, whenever he was troubled or angry, he always seemed to resort to their ways and to their dress. And she wondered why. Could it be he missed his family and their way of life more than he would admit . . . more even than he himself knew?

Aimee continued to work, glancing now and then toward the stables until she saw Dominic's tall form heading toward the house. His long legs carried him swiftly across the ground, his straight black hair carelessly flying in the wind.

Looking at him, Aimee shivered. She felt today as if she hardly knew him and yet yesterday she had been willing . . . no, more than willing, to let him make love to her. This fierce, enigmatic man whom she did not understand and whom she was not even certain she liked. And she frowned as she experienced the familiar flutter in her stomach and felt the agitated beating of her heart against her ribs. She knew if she were honest with herself, that she wanted him even now. Nothing had changed. Despite her talk with herself last night, it took only one glance for her to feel the same intense longing as before.

She still wanted him — wanted was hardly even an apt description for what she felt when she saw him this way — so intensely masculine and proud.

Dominic did not hesitate when he reached the new gate he had built into the picket fence. One hand pushed it open as he strode through to the brick walkway, letting the gate slam hard behind him. As he walked past Aimee, his black eyes turned toward her, cool and accusing. His mouth was set in a straight, stubborn line and he did not speak. She thought he looked tired and his eyes red-rimmed.

Aimee turned, her body and eyes following him as he strode silently past her, through the garden and onto the porch where Jezzy had ceased her

132

sweeping to stare at him as well.

"Jezzy, have Amos bring up some hot water . . . and a bottle of bourbon."

Jezzy's eyes darted toward Aimee. There was a look of doubt in her big brown eyes and her mouth flew open soundlessly.

"*Now*, Jezzy!" Dominic was already past the girl, and for all his angry strides, his footsteps across the porch were eerily quiet in the doeskin boots.

"Yes, suh, Mister Dominic. I go tell Amos right away." Again she glanced at Aimee before hurrying into the house to find him.

Aimee felt her stomach tighten anxiously. What on earth did Dominic intend? Was he the kind of man who drank himself into a stupor when he was angry or upset?

She'd known men like that, men who preferred drinking to talking. Some of her father's patients had been that way and she could still remember her father shaking his head in dismay when he tried to help them and couldn't.

"A man who drinks too much loves the bottle more than he can ever love another human," her papa would say. "And that is what, in the end, ultimately destroys him and sometimes those he loves."

Aimee shivered. She could envision Dominic alone and brooding. And she could imagine him being very angry, dangerous even. But for all his fierceness and unpredictability, she could not imagine him ever hurting her or Lucas.

She hoped she was not wrong about that, not today when her guests would be arriving soon.

She groaned, thinking about it as she went back to the roses. This evening was something she had looked forward to for so long. And she desperately hoped Dominic did not come downstairs like a storm and embarrass her.

Later as Aimee surveyed her work in the garden, she thought the damage from the cattle was hardly noticeable. In fact, she thought the garden looked quite lovely. And she had to admit that the new fencing contributed greatly to that. She stood for a moment, remembering Dominic's hard work, remembering the blisters on his hands and the look of chagrin on his face when she scolded him. He had been like a boy, a very sweet and vulnerable boy and just thinking of it made her heart feel soft and tender, made her insides turn shaky and weak.

She hurried into the house, pleased with the scent of cleaning and the lovely splashes of color from the fresh flowers that filled every corner. She'd had several of the girls come to the house from the quarters and she smiled now as she heard their laughter and watched them work.

Jezzy was placing the newly polished silver epergne in the middle of the dining-room table. Later the tiered crystal dishes would be filled with nuts and candied fruit, perhaps even some of Cilla's delicious marzipan. Aimee's mouth watered just thinking of the delicious confection of crushed almonds, sugar, and egg whites.

Later Aimee was in her room getting dressed when Jezzy came breathlessly to announce the arrival of her guests.

"Carriages comin', Miz Aimee. Carriages comin' up the drive right now."

"Show them in, Jezzy," Aimee whispered as she turned toward the dress that lay spread upon her

134

bed. "I'll call one of the other girls in to help me into my dress. Please seat our guests on the front veranda and serve the ladies lemonade and the gentlemen mint juleps. Tell them I'll be out momentarily."

"Yes'm . . . mo-men-tarly," Jezzy said, rolling her eyes in delight as she savored the sound of the word. "I sho will," she said, obviously pleased with herself. "I tell them you be there mo-men-tarly."

Aimee laughed as she dipped her head to look at her hair in the mirror. She still wore it pulled back into a tight chignon, but today she had loosened some of the curls about her face and forehead.

"Oh, and Jezzy," she said, turning to catch the girl before she went out the door. "Where's Mister Dominic? Has he come downstairs yet?"

"No, ma'am," Jezzy said with a wide-eyed look. "We ain't seen hide nor hair of him since he went stormin' up to his room this mornin'."

"Oh dear," Aimee muttered beneath her breath.

"What's that, missy?"

"Nothing, Jezzy . . . nothing. You go tend to our guests and make sure Lucas looks presentable. I'll be right there."

"Mo-men-tarly," Jezzy said again with a lift of her brows. She looked toward Aimee as if for approval, making sure she had the new word just right.

"Yes," Aimee said laughing. "Momentarily."

Eleven

Aimee turned toward the long mirror and held out the skirt of her gown. The girl who had come to help her dress stood nearby, her eyes wide with admiration and delight.

"You is a picture, Miz Aimee," she said in a soft drawl.

Aimee smiled at her. "Thank you, Delilah." She watched the girl as she turned to leave. Delilah was Nathaniel's sister and at fourteen, she already had the creamy golden brown skin and almond-shaped eyes of a woman.

Aimee turned for one last look at herself in the mirror. As a gesture of respect for Jim, she had decided at the last moment to dress in black to-night. She knew her friends would understand if she had chosen another, brighter color and she frowned as another thought entered her mind. If Dominic saw her, he would probably think she was only doing this in an attempt to keep Jim's image alive between them.

"I'm not," she whispered fiercely.

The dress was not entirely mournful looking, she told herself. The low puffed sleeves fell just off her shoulders and the full black satin skirt was

136

overlaid with delicate blonde gauze material that was sprigged with tiny pink roses. She wore no jewelry except a pair of exquisite black onyx and diamond earrings that Jim had given her on their wedding day.

Taking a long deep breath, Aimee slipped out the door and went quickly toward the main hallway. From the front veranda she could hear the sound of laughter as it filtered down the hallway on the warm afternoon breeze.

When Aimee moved through the wide doorway to the porch, she smiled and turned toward the group of people seated at the end of the long front veranda. Her smile faded for only a second, not long enough for anyone to notice, she hoped. She had wondered about Dominic all day, but she had hardly expected him to be here laughing and entertaining her friends. She wasn't surprised though to see Lucas right beside him, listening adoringly to his every word.

Dominic's black eyes turned toward her, and they moved languidly down her figure, taking in the black satin dress she wore, then returning once again to her fashionable, but staid hair style. And only Aimee saw the look of amusement in those smoky black eyes. She hoped sincerely that no one else saw the flush that flew to her cheeks.

Dominic stood slowly, his eyes warm and watchful as he waited for her. Jenny's father, Stanley DeVaull, also stood and smiled, stretching his hand forth to take Aimee's in his. And Aimee was happy to see that Jenny's cousin Theodore had also made the trip.

Among all the greetings, Jenny stepped forward

and took Aimee in her arms. She was a tall girl, taller than Aimee, and her figure was slender, even frail looking. Aimee had always thought that the girl's pale creamy skin contributed to that look, even though her thick golden brown hair which fell like a cloud to her shoulders had somehow just the opposite effect.

"You look wonderful, Aimee," Jenny murmured softly.

Aimee smiled into the girl's brown eyes, knowing how she had worried about her since Jim's death. Then her eyes moved toward the other woman who stood waiting . . . Jenny's mother.

Aimee loved Rebecca DeVaull. She had become a second mother to Aimee after her own parents' death from yellow fever. And anyone looking at the woman could immediately see where Jenny received her delicate good looks.

" 'Becca," Aimee said, going to embrace the woman. She smiled down into Rebecca DeVaull's green eyes, thinking that she looked older than when she'd seen her last, not that it diminished her mature loveliness.

Jenny's cousin Theodore stepped forward then and took Aimee's hand, bending low as he placed a soft kiss on her skin.

"I'm so glad you could come, Teddy." She looked up into Teddy's face. His skin was almost as smooth as a girl's and the mustache he tried so desperately to grow looked thin and ragged. But he was not as boyish as he appeared; Aimee knew he was near her own age.

"You grow more beautiful every time I see you, Aimee."

Aimee glanced at Jenny and they both grinned. Theodore Ridley was a well-known flirt who liked nothing more than to find a woman gullible enough to believe every flattering little lie he told.

"Why, thank you, Teddy," Aimee said, her voice demure and innocent.

She moved past Lucas, her hand going of its own will to smooth down his dark hair. She was taken by surprise when he pulled away and looked at her with sheepish embarrassment.

Aimee took a seat in one of the high-backed wicker chairs and wished that she did not have to look directly across the small veranda table at Dominic. His eyes seemed to bore right through her skin, seemed to be able to strip away all the façade of social amenities and make her remember every word they had spoken . . . every touch . . .

She glanced away from him, vowing she would not allow him to spoil this evening for her.

"I wonder where Aunt Eulie is," she said.

"Oh, you know your aunt," Rebecca DeVaull said. "Always late. Why, no doubt Eulie Dunbar will be late for her own funeral." But she smiled fondly as did everyone else. Eulie was well loved, despite her self-centered little habits.

"I was just telling Mister Valcour here, how pleased I am that he's come to LeBeaux Plantation. We were very worried about you, you know . . . here virtually all alone in the wilderness." Mr. DeVaull's glance toward Aimee was kind and protective.

"I'm wasn't alone . . . not really." Aimee smiled, knowing Mr. DeVaull meant his remarks with good intention. "I had Amos and Jezzy, not to mention

139

five hundred slaves who would come to my defense if need be."

"Oh, my darling. Surely you wouldn't expect slaves to do such a thing?" Rebecca DeVaull's eyes were wide and troubled. "Why if they ever turned their hand against a white man, they'd be strung up from the nearest tree."

"And they know that . . . that's why they would never come to your defense in the first place," Theodore drawled.

Aimee's lips thinned. It always angered her when the slave argument came up. That was one of the reasons she preferred not discussing it, especially on social occasions. She glanced toward Dominic, thinking he should at least come to her defense. But he said nothing, his black eyes watchful and enigmatic.

And she didn't miss the way Lucas's eyes darted about the small group of people as he apparently wondered what would happen next.

"Well, Mister Valcour *is* here now," Aimee said, hoping to end the conversation. She also intended to turn the tables on the man who seemed to be trying to make her uncomfortable with his steady glances. "And now that he's come, we all feel tremendously safe and secure." She doubted that anyone caught the sarcasm in her voice except Dominic. And his eyes were cool, even though there was the slightest twitch of a smile at the corner of his mouth.

Aimee swallowed and forced her eyes away from his lips. Perhaps she was the only one here who was *not* safe, she thought.

"I imagine you do," Mr. DeVaull said, glancing

with open admiration toward Dominic. "We heard about his altercation with Compton and his men. I understand your new partner here handled it very well indeed."

"You should have seen it, Mister DeVaull," Lucas said quickly. "Dominic shot old man Compton's hat right off his head and he looked scared enough to—"

"Lucas," Aimee warned with a frown. She glanced toward Dominic as if he was responsible for Lucas's outburst.

"As Lucas said," Aimee replied, meeting Dominic's glance across the table. "He handled it very well. I'm afraid I might have been in serious trouble without him."

Why did she feel so breathless? And why did the sight of him in his dark jacket and buff-colored trousers make her heart feel so strange. She had often called him a savage heathen. And yet today he looked every bit the part of a gentried plantation owner, with his splendid white waistcoat and white silk stock, tied just so beneath his square chin. His tight-fitting trousers were tucked into gleaming black knee-length boots. And she wondered where he had obtained such fine, stylish clothes.

Aimee dragged her eyes away from him, trying to listen to the conversation that had drifted away from her.

"There's big money to be made in cotton now," Mr. DeVaull was saying. "You mark my words, son, if this first crop from LeBeaux is a good one, you will be on your way to being very wealthy . . . both of you. Yes indeed . . . very wealthy.

The conversation was interrupted by the sound of a carriage rattling down the sandy road between the line of trees.

Aimee smiled and stood up. "It's Aunt Eulie." Lucas followed her to the edge of the porch to wait for the carriage to pull around the small circled drive. When its passenger emerged, Lucas hung back as Aimee walked down the steps to take her aunt's arm and lead her toward the house.

"Where have you been?" she asked. "I was worried about you."

"No need to worry about me, my dear. George is an excellent driver . . . excellent." The woman glanced back at the dark-skinned man who sat grinning on the high seat of the carriage. He nodded down toward Aimee.

"Afternoon, Miz Aimee," he said.

"Good afternoon, George. It's good to see you. After you've unharnessed your horse at the carriage house, you're welcome to go to the kitchen if you're hungry."

He tipped his tall black hat and grinned. "Thank you, Miz Aimee."

"Can I go with him, Aimee . . . please?" Lucas's face was full of expectation. Aimee knew he was probably bored with the adult conversation. But she worried that he spent too much time with the slaves and not enough with his studies.

"*May* I go, Lucas, darling," Eulie corrected with an indulgent smile.

The boy grinned and shuffled his feet restlessly as he gazed up at Aimee.

"Yes," Aimee said. "I suppose, but stay out of

trouble and don't get in George's way."

She laughed at the sound of his whoop of glee as he climbed up onto the seat beside George.

Aimee walked with her aunt back up the steps and glanced sideways at the tall woman. Her aunt's dress, as always, was the picture of sophistication, and she usually walked with her head up and her eyebrows lifted in a haughty little look of condescension. Today she wore a wide-brimmed bonnet of brown watered silk that matched her very stylish gown. The ostrich feathers that sat pertly atop the hat ruffled in the breeze as she walked.

Aimee was hardly surprised at her aunt's complete dismissal of everyone present on the veranda . . . everyone that is except Dominic Valcour. She went directly to him, taking his hand in a bold manner as he stood, and assessing him from head to toe. Aimee knew how curious her Aunt Eulie was about him and probably disapproving as well. That was why she had deliberately waited until last week to send a letter to her aunt explaining about Dominic's presence at LeBeaux.

"Well," Aunt Eulie was saying. "This is certainly a surprise to me. Of course I've heard Jim speak of you often, Mister Valcour. But I was more than surprised to hear that you had moved into Le-Beaux house . . . lock, stock, and barrel."

Dominic bowed and gave Aunt Eulie a look that fairly smoldered with flirtatiousness.

"And I have heard much about you as well, Mrs. Dunbar. But I'm afraid none of the accounts could possibly surpass the pleasure of seeing you in person."

143

Aunt Eulie stood very still, staring skeptically at the man who stood before her. But when he smiled down at her, her head moved slightly, nodding to one side and then she giggled ever so softly.

Aimee stared at the woman, and almost laughed aloud. In her entire life she didn't think she could remember ever hearing her aunt giggle, and certainly not in the presence of company.

"Well, you do have a way about you, I'll admit," her aunt said. "But don't think to flatter me with your glib tongue, young man. You and I must have a very serious chat before I leave for home tomorrow. Yes indeed, very serious."

"At your pleasure, ma'am," Dominic said smoothly with just the hint of a smile.

The entire gathering was smiling as they watched the sparring between Dominic and Aimee's sometimes overbearing aunt. Indeed, their meeting seemed to set the tone for the evening, which turned out to be delightful and full of spirited chatter and laughter.

At dinner, Aunt Eulie insisted on being seated next to Dominic. And during the meal, she questioned and watched him with her flashing brown eyes, seeming to make mental notes.

Aimee was astounded at Dominic's ease with her aunt. She had found him to be intensely private and yet here he was, sitting in her elegant dining room, chatting with her Aunt Eulie and making no effort to dodge any of her blatantly personal questions. Indeed, he seemed to find her as charming as she obviously found him.

Aimee shrugged and turned toward Jenny and

was surprised to find her watching her.

"He *is* a very handsome man, *chère,*" she whispered. "Exciting and intense . . . if I were you I might not find it so easy to remain only business partners with a man like that."

"Why, Jenny," Aimee said, her eyes widening.

"Oh, don't look so surprised," Jenny said with an easy laugh. "Just because I'm an old spinster of twenty-two doesn't mean that I haven't thought about such things."

"Well, Jenny DeVaull," Aimee said, glancing at Dominic. "You do surprise me."

"Don't tell me you haven't noticed the way he looks."

"Well . . . no," Aimee said, reaching for her glass of wine and lifting it to her suddenly dry lips. "He is . . . attractive, I'll admit . . . if you like that kind of man. But it's just too soon, you know, for me even to notice another man besides Jim." She found that her hands were shaking when she set the glass of wine back on the table.

Jenny watched her friend carefully, seeing the flush of color on her pretty cheeks and the slight trembling of her fingers against the wineglass. But it was the troubled look in her eyes and the small frown that wrinkled her brow that made Jenny wonder. She glanced at Dominic again and saw his black gaze upon Aimee.

Jenny smiled. So, there was something between these two after all. She had suspected as much on the veranda this afternoon when the two seemed to be a bit at odds with one another. And she had wondered why. Normally she might be hurt that her friend had chosen not to confide such matters in her. But this time, especially after seeing the odd look on Aimee's face, Jenny thought she knew the reason.

Her friend Aimee didn't even realize herself that she was falling in love with the handsome, dark-haired gambler named Dominic Valcour.

Twelve

After the meal was finished, Aunt Eulie rose from the table and looked toward her niece.

"Tell Cilla the meal was excellent as usual, darling. No, never mind, I'll tell her myself. Besides, I want to see your new garden."

Aimee smiled and went to stand beside her aunt. "I thought perhaps we might all take a stroll in the garden. It isn't quite dark yet."

Mr. DeVaull looked toward Dominic. "Perhaps you would like to join me on the veranda, Mister Valcour. I have some excellent imported cigars. Besides, I might be able to give you a few hints about growing cotton."

Dominic nodded. "I think at this point, we can use all the help we can get."

"You, too, Theodore," Mr. DeVaull said over his shoulder as he and Dominic started toward the door.

"Thank you, Uncle, but I believe I prefer seeing the garden with Aimee . . . and the rest of the ladies of course."

Aimee caught Dominic's darkly sardonic look at her. Teddy's attention, such as it was, seemed to amuse him greatly.

147

She ignored Teddy's crooked arm and walked instead between Jenny and her mother while Aunt Eulie, independent as always, walked around the veranda and out toward the kitchen building. The windows there were aglow with lights and they could hear the women giggling as they finished their chores and cleaned the kitchen.

And far in the distance, they would also hear the beating of the drums in the slave quarters. For some reason, the sound tonight made Aimee shiver and she looked through the moss laden trees toward the setting sun.

"I'm surprised that you allow your slaves to indulge in their old voodoo culture here, Aimee." Mrs. DeVaull gazed out toward the fields as she spoke. "Heaven knows what they're saying . . . or what they're plotting."

"I don't believe they're plotting anything," Aimee said. "The songs and the chanting are simply part of their religion. I wouldn't feel right denying them that. We have many Yoruban slaves, but the majority of them come from Senegal, near the Congo River. I'm told they are well known for their easy disposition."

"Huh," the woman scoffed. "I'm not sure they know what religion is." She put her hand on Aimee's arm and stepped closer. "Heathenistic hogwash, if you ask me."

"Mother," Jenny protested.

"Well, it is!"

"How can you know that, Mother, when you have no idea even what they're saying?"

"Oh, I've overheard enough right in my own home to know what it's about. They sing about unspeakable things . . . sexual things. . . ." She whispered the last words so that Theodore, who was walking behind them could not hear.

Jenny laughed and looked across at Aimee. They both smiled at one another before Aimee began to point out her roses to Mrs. DeVaull to change the subject.

"They're lovely, dear. You've done a splendid job with the place . . . just splendid." She glanced back again at Theodore. "But do you really think it's wise to have Mister Valcour living right here in the same house with you? I mean, can you imagine what the gossips in Natchez would say about that? They'd be scandalized, simply scandalized . . . and your reputation would be ruined."

"Well, we're not in Natchez, Mother DeVaull," Aimee said. "And I hardly think there's anything scandalous about my living in one end of the house while Mister Valcour occupies the other."

"Oh, darling . . . you just don't know how some men can be . . ."

Theodore stepped forward. Obviously he had heard more of the conversation than Mrs. DeVaull intended.

"She's right, Aimee." He fell into step beside her. "I don't like the look of the man myself. Why, I heard he's a riverboat gambler and a frequent patron of the houses at Natchez-Under-the-Hill." At Mrs. DeVaull's gasp, he turned and nodded. "My apologies for being so blunt, Aunt 'Becca. But this is something I think Aimee should know."

"Yes," Mrs. DeVaull said, taking a handkerchief from her sleeve and holding it delicately to her nose. "I think you're right, Teddy. Do go on."

They all stopped now near the statue in the middle of the garden. The sun was falling behind the trees to the west, casting a pale golden light against the back of the house and the tops of the trees. But Aimee could hardly enjoy the beauty of this sunset. She found herself growing more and more irritated with her guests' interference.

"Why, I've even heard the man is a half-breed, Aimee," Theodore said, lifting his eyebrows with a look of disapproval.

"Yes he is, Teddy. His mother was a Choctaw and his father a Frenchman. But I hardly think, since he had nothing to do with it, that you can hold that against him. Besides, you know very well how I feel about such discrimination."

"Oh. Well, I mean, he has impeccable manners and all, but what's beneath it? Have you ever thought of that? He has the look of an adventurer, my dear . . . a very dangerous and unpredictable adventurer."

"Teddy . . ." Aimee began with a sigh.

"Please," he said. "Just hear me out."

Aimee glanced toward the veranda and even at this distance she could feel Dominic's black eyes upon her. He held a cigar between his fingers and a haze of smoke rose toward his face, making it impossible for her to see his eyes. But she didn't have to see to be able to tell that he was watching her. Why should it offend her that Teddy called him dangerous? She had thought the same thing about him many times herself.

"They say he killed a man in a duel at Nashville." Theodore's eyes narrowed as he gazed down at Aimee in the growing darkness.

"I know about that. Jim told me every story imaginable about Mister Valcour. Need I remind you that we live on the edge of the wilderness where men must defend themselves . . . or that Jim was also an adventurer, just like this man?"

"Ah, but Jim was not a gambler," Theodore said with a triumphant wag of his finger.

Aimee felt like laughing in his face. And she felt like shouting at him, telling him how Jim had borrowed such a great sum of money against this very plantation. Was that not gambling? In any case, it was what put her into this situation with Dominic in the first place. But she clamped her teeth together, willing herself to remain silent.

"I know about Mister Valcour, Theodore, and I'll be careful. But I appreciate your concern. Yours, too, Mother DeVaull." She glanced at Jenny, whose dark eyes held a quiet look of sympathy.

She also saw the exchange of looks between Theodore and his aunt. And heard Mrs. DeVaull's satisfied sniff as she took Theodore's arm and moved with him ahead of Aimee and Jenny.

"Are you afraid, Aimee?" Jenny asked, her eyes dark with worry. "Are you afraid of this man, Valcour?"

"No, of course not," she muttered.

"Then what?"

"Oh, Jenny . . . I don't know. It's just a feeling, I guess. I've never felt this way about anyone in my life. I'm so confused; sometimes he makes me angry and sometimes . . ."

"Yes? Sometimes?"

Aimee's voice grew softer. "Sometimes there's a sweetness in him, Jenny . . . a vulnerability that Jim never had. It's as if he's lost something precious in his life and he's afraid he'll never get it back. But I have a feeling he would never let anyone know what it is. He can be cold and hard . . . distant and unpredictable, just like Teddy says. And he abandoned his own people as a young man to make a life of his own. What kind of man would do that? And why? That's something about him that even Jim never explained to me. I . . . I guess I've just never met anyone like him before."

Jenny's eyes were sparkling as she watched her friend, but she said nothing. She thought it would be much more fun to let Aimee find out for herself.

Suddenly, as they turned to go back to the house, the quietness of the soft Mississippi night was shattered by a loud high-pitched scream.

Aimee looked toward the house. There on the end of the veranda, near her room, was Jezzy. In her agitation she was jumping about and flinging her arms wildly as she continued to scream and cry.

Aimee began to run as did Dominic toward the end of the veranda.

She heard Mrs. DeVaull's whispered gasp behind her. "What on earth . . . ?"

By the time Aimee reached the veranda, she saw her Aunt Eulie coming from the kitchen area, followed by Lucas and Cilla and two servant girls. Amos's gray head peeked out the back door of the house, his eyes wide with wonder. But he made no move to come out onto the veranda.

When Aimee reached Jezzy, she could see the girl's fear was real. There were tears in her eyes as her trembling hand pointed toward the thick stand of cane and bamboo that grew along the road to the quarters.

"Death lights," she screeched. "I seen the death lights! Oh, Lawd Jesus Christ, I done seen 'em."

"Jezzy . . . Jezzy, calm down," Aimee said, taking the girl's arms and pulling her around to face her. "What are you talking about? Just calm down and tell me exactly what you saw."

Jezzy's entire body was trembling and her eyes were huge as they darted back toward the darkness.

Aimee saw Dominic walk to the railing around the veranda and gaze out toward the area where Jezzy pointed.

"Oh, sweet Jesus," Jezzy continued to chant over and over. *"Mawa . . . mawa."* Aimee had never heard the girl speak in her own language and she glanced toward Dominic with frustration.

His dark eyes met hers over the girl's head. "It means to die," he said quietly. "Jezzy thinks someone is going to die because she's seen the death lights."

Aimee tightened her grip on Jezzy's trembling shoulders. "But . . . did you see anything just now?" she asked him.

"No, but the vision isn't supposed to be seen by everyone."

Aimee wondered how he knew such things. But she hardly had time to think about it. For just then, she felt Jezzy pull away from her and

153

watched in stunned silence as the girl fell in a heap to the floor.

Everyone else on the porch seemed just as stunned for a moment as they stood in a circle, staring down at the girl.

"Jezzy . . ." Aimee said, reaching down for her.

Jezzy continued to cry as she writhed about on the floor. Her eyes were shut tight and she seemed to be holding her breath. And for some unexplained reason, she had her fingers in her ears.

"What is she doing?" Aimee glanced around toward Cilla, hoping she could explain. But the cook's eyes were large with fright, too, and she lifted her hand as if to shield her eyes from the side of the house where the lights had been seen.

"For heaven's sake, child," Aunt Eulie said, stepping forward. "Get up off this floor and stop acting like some wild African."

That command seemed to be the only thing that reached through to Jezzy. She stopped writhing and looked up skeptically, staring at the people above her. "Is they gone?" she asked. She looked again out into the darkness and as she rose, she waved a hand in that direction. *"Quende . . . Quende ona."*

Aimee sighed and shook her head, feeling frustrated that she could not understand Jezzy's words. She turned to Dominic, hoping he could explain and she noticed how Lucas had come very close and how his eyes were alive with curiosity as he looked up at Dominic.

"She's telling the spirits to go . . . to go on and leave her alone," he explained.

Aimee saw old Amos nod in agreement. And all

154

of the blacks were staring toward the canes where Jezzy had supposedly seen the death lights.

"Here, Jezzy," she said, pulling the girl around and putting an arm around her shoulders. "You go with Cilla now . . . she's going to fix you a nice cool glass of lemonade and let you rest a while until you're feeling better." Aimee glanced pointedly toward Cilla and the woman stepped forward, taking Jezzy and turning her back toward the house.

"Oh, Big Cilla," Jezzy whispered, resting her head against the woman's bosom. "It was the demon from hell, come to carry little Jezzy away. I seen him once before when my brother died. When you see the lights you gets this un'splainable notion to follow it, you know. But you can't follow, cause if'n you do, old demon lead you straight to hell. You has to close your eyes and ears and lay on the floor to scare old demon away."

"I know, Jezzy," Cilla murmured. "You come with Big Cilla now. You done your duty . . . you warned us all. Now we has to wait."

Aimee glanced at Amos, but he looked away. Then one by one the servants moved on, going silently back to their duties or their rooms.

"Well, I've never heard such gibberish in all my life," Eulie scoffed. "You only encourage the girl by being kind to her, my darling."

"A firm hand is what she needs," Theodore growled in agreement.

"It's the voodoo, just like I told you earlier, Aimee," Mrs. DeVaull said. "You must put a stop to this foolishness before it gets started in earnest. If they ever get their heads full of that nonsense,

155

death and destruction will surely follow."

"Oh, now, Mother," Mr. DeVaull said. "Don't you think you're being a bit melodramatic? Let's stop this talk of death and uprisings."

"Yes, why don't we?" Aimee said, impatient with the conversation. "Jezzy just tends to get a little carried away with herself, that's all. But she's a very sweet girl, and I assure you, completely harmless. Now, if you will all go into the parlor, I'll have one of the girls bring in coffee and dessert. Lucas, honey, would you see to that for me?" She didn't miss the look of disappointment on the boy's face. She was sure he wanted to wait and see what else happened.

"Go on, son," Dominic said.

Just as Aimee hoped he would, Dominic remained on the veranda as the others went back into the house, murmuring in low voices about what had happened. Once they were out of sight, she turned to him, almost in a gesture of desperation.

"Dominic . . . what on earth does all this mean? Demon lights and this talk of death? And what did Cilla mean when she said that now we have to wait?"

"Well, she obviously took Jezzy's words seriously and she meant we would have to wait to see who dies. It's voodoo, just as Mrs. DeVaull said. But it's also mostly superstition, even though there's no doubt Jezzy believes she saw something." He glanced with a frown into the darkness. "But I don't think there's much we can do about it."

"But . . . you . . . you don't believe it . . . do you?"

She suddenly remembered him as he'd looked that night in the cemetery, his bronzed chest painted, his black hair straight and free. Was that why he could interpret Jezzy's words, because it was so much like his own culture?

He looked at her for a long time, his lips quirked in an odd smile.

"What if I do believe it?" he asked. "Would that surprise you . . . frighten you?"

"No," she said quickly.

"No?" he asked, leaning close to her. "Maybe that's what frightened you away last night. Does the thought of making love to an Indian . . . a man who believes in all kinds of strange, barbaric practices, frighten you, Aimee?"

Aimee stepped backward at the fierceness of his words. A line appeared between her eyes as she stared up at him.

He stepped close, reaching out to touch her cheek and trail his fingers down toward her opened lips.

"Or is that what excites you, angel?"

She could only watch in stunned silence as he brushed past her and walked casually back across the veranda and into the house. He never even looked back.

Thirteen

The next morning at breakfast, there was more talk about Jezzy's "spell" as Mrs. DeVaull preferred to call it.

"I hope you had a talk with Jezzy, my dear," Aunt Eulie said. "You have a plantation to run now and you simply cannot allow your house servants to behave in such an unseemly manner."

"I will, Aunt Eulie," Aimee said with a quiet sigh.

Aimee noticed that when Jezzy came into the dining room to bring more hot biscuits or to pour coffee, the conversation stopped almost immediately. Aimee was only glad that the girl was too naive to notice. She acted as if nothing at all had happened.

"Jezzy, where is Lucas this morning?"

"He gone with Nathaniel, ma'am, to shoe young master's horse."

Aimee nodded and sighed. Lucas was as restless as a young colt himself and Dominic seemed to think his wanderings were perfectly all right.

"How are you feeling this morning, Jezzy?" Dominic asked.

Aimee flashed a look his way, wishing he would just let the incident die.

"Oh, I feelin' fine, Mister Dominic," the girl said with a wide grin. She reached inside the bosom of her dress and drew out a leather thong that was tied about her neck. Her fingers went to the end, displaying a small burlap sack tied at the top and bulging with some unknown content. "Got me a *gris-gris. Tigewala* made it for me . . . to keep them old demons away."

"That will be enough, Jezzy," Aimee said, more sharply than she intended.

"But Miz—"

"I said that will be all, Jezzy. Please take these empty dishes back to the kitchen." Aimee glanced resentfully at Dominic and saw the spark of amusement in his black eyes. Then slowly, his dark lashes lowered as if in dismissal. He sipped from his coffee cup as though nothing more important than a mosquito buzzed about his head.

"That girl is going to be trouble, Aimee," Mrs. DeVaull said, shaking her head. "You would do well to find someone else for the house."

Aimee pushed pieces of food about her plate, but she said nothing.

"I think, Mother, that you should leave such household matters to Aimee. This is *her* home." Mr. DeVaull's voice was soft, meant to appease.

Aimee had looked forward to their visit so much. And now everything seemed to have gone wrong. She found herself anxious for them all to be gone and for her life at LeBeaux to return to normal.

She stood up from the table, forcing a smile to her lips that she did not feel. "I thought we might all take a ride this morning if you're feeling up to it."

"Splendid," Theodore said. "Just what is needed, I think."

159

Aimee smiled at him, grateful that someone had come to her rescue.

When they all met later at the stables, the talk of Jezzy and what happened last night seemed finally to have evaporated. There was too much to see, too much beauty surrounding the beautiful house to dwell on the dark, frightening events of the night.

They had already heard from Nathaniel that the cotton plants were up. But as Aimee sat on her horse, gazing out across the rows of green she felt her heart swell in an unbelievable feeling of pride and possession such as she had never experienced before. It seemed to renew her and to give her optimism about the success of LeBeaux.

And strangely it was Dominic whom she wanted to share that feeling with. After all, they had begun the planting together.

He was sitting near her, the big black horse beneath him restless, pawing at the ground. Dominic seemed as entranced by the sight of the new plants as Aimee.

"It's beautiful, isn't it?" Aimee asked, her voice soft with awe.

Dominic turned and smiled. And for a moment, there seemed to be a truce between them, an unspoken sense of sharing that erased all their past disagreements.

"So far so good," he said with a crooked grin.

"You have a fine piece of land here, Aimee," Mr. DeVaull said. "Rich and fertile . . . perfect for growing cotton. If you can get it to the picking stages and have it ginned properly . . . well, you two will be well on your way. What did you plant?"

"Plain Gulf cotton," Dominic said.

"We hope to try a small acreage of Sea Island cotton next year," Aimee added.

Mr. DeVaull nodded. "Sea Island probably won't do well here. But then, I'm sure you know that. But if your intention is to try a small plot just for experimentation, I don't see that you have anything to lose."

Aimee smiled at Dominic. Mr. DeVaull was a very successful businessman and his good opinion meant a great deal to her.

It was near noon when they all arrived back at the house. The sun was high and brilliant in a cloudless cerulean sky. A light breeze stirred the trees and the hanging moss, carrying the faint honeyed scent of roses from the garden. Suddenly Aimee felt like opening her arms to the skies, felt like dancing and laughing like a child. Life seemed glorious and the events of the night had faded into the distance.

As they walked through the garden onto the veranda, Jenny came and caught Aimee's arm in hers.

"Oh, Aimee. This is such a beautiful place. I only hope that someday I'll have a home as beautiful."

"Thank you," Aimee whispered, glancing about. "I had no idea one could love a piece of land so possessively. But I do. And I hope the same thing for you, too, Jenny."

"And a handsome, exciting man like Dominic to share it with," Jenny continued, her voice wistful and soft.

Aimee stopped, turning to stare at Jenny.

"Dominic and I . . . we aren't sharing a home . . . I mean, you make it sound as if we . . . as if—"

"As if what?" Jenny's dark eyes were dancing with

161

mischief.

"Dominic was Jim's best friend and now he is half owner of LeBeaux. But that's as far as it goes, Jenny. There is nothing between us—absolutely nothing."

Jenny eyes were wide with innocence. "Oh, of course. I didn't mean to imply that there was. I was only speaking personally when I said I hope to find a man like that." Suddenly Jenny spread her arms and gathered the skirt of her riding habit, dancing one full turn before stopping with a laugh. "I want someone who is exciting, Aimee, maybe even a bit dangerous. A man who makes me feel all warm and . . . and stimulated."

"Oh, my Lord, your mother would have a fit if she heard you talk that way."

Jenny laughed, the sound ringing like glass bells through the roses.

"Did Jim make you feel that way, Aimee?" Jenny's eyes were serious now, dark with wonder. "I've never asked you before about what it's like being married . . . being with a man."

Aimee took a long, deep breath as she gazed into her friend's curious eyes. "Jim made me feel very special and loved. He made me feel secure."

Jenny frowned. "But . . . was it exciting? Did you feel as if you would die from the glorious excitement of it all?"

"Well . . . Jim was an exciting man, yes. But . . ."

"But?"

Aimee waved her hand in the air and walked away. "Oh, Jenny. This is just too complicated to talk about casually in the middle of a rose garden. Why don't you come back one day soon—we'll sit

162

on the veranda and I'll tell you everything you want to know about men and marriage. At least what I know."

Aimee was relieved when her answer seemed to satisfy Jenny. But the conversation left her with a strange, nagging feeling. Almost as if she had deceived Jenny.

But she hadn't lied. She *had* loved Jim. And she *had* felt excitement at times. Hadn't she?

A small still voice whispered to her, making comparisons between Jim and Dominic . . . forbidden comparisons that Aimee did not want to hear. Goading her with the power of Dominic's fascinating masculinity, with the unspoken allure of his eyes that pulled her to him sometimes against her will. He was a mystery to her, a man who seduced with his eyes and challenged everything she ever thought she knew about herself.

Aimee shook her head, pushing away her unwanted thoughts and linking arms again with Jenny as they went into the house.

After a very pleasant noon meal on the front veranda, the house grew quiet as everyone went to his or her room and rested in preparation for their trips home. But Aimee paced the floor of her own bedroom, restless without even knowing why.

She glanced out the long windows that faced the back veranda. Her green eyes narrowed when she saw her Aunt Eulie walking in the garden arm in arm with Dominic. His dark head was lowered as he listened to the matronly woman beside him. And from time to time he would nod seriously or look down at her with a quiet, thoughtful smile.

Aimee was not familiar with this side of him and

she frowned. What on earth did they find to talk about? Aunt Eulie seemed so serious. But then, she was also always volatile and always opinionated. Aimee wondered why watching them gave her such an uneasy feeling. Were they talking about her?

The two stopped in the garden and Aunt Eulie turned to face Dominic. Her hands were in constant motion as she talked to him. He listened thoughtfully, his hands clasped behind his back as he stood, leaning toward her just the slightest bit.

Aimee thought she had never seen him look more handsome as he was in his buff-colored riding breeches and high-topped boots. She could even see the effect of a breeze as it played against the soft material of his shirt and his black hair.

She continued to watch until Aunt Eulie seemed to finish her speech, then stepped forward to put her hand on Dominic's forearm in an intimate gesture that surprised Aimee. It was as if their conversation had been satisfactory to her aunt. Dominic took the woman's gloved hand and brought it to his lips, placing a kiss there as he bowed with a courtly gesture.

When her aunt turned and walked back to the house, Aimee's eyes remained on the tall, dark-haired man in the garden. He seemed lost in thought as he strolled slowly along the bricked walkways, glancing toward the sky or sometimes at the flowers that grew along the walk.

What on earth had Aunt Eulie said to him?

Dominic thought he had never felt so much pleasure in a home and its surrounding acreage before. He didn't know what it was about LeBeaux. It was beautiful; there was no doubt about that, especially

164

since Aimee had restored the lustrous cypress floors and filled the interior with elegant furniture. But there was something more here than beauty.

He glanced around at the garden she had planted. Then he glanced down at the palms of his hands. They were still sore, but the blisters were healing already and beginning to form calluses. He walked to the garden fence, placing his hands on the whitewashed railing.

Dominic couldn't remember ever feeling such satisfaction with something he'd done. And he felt the same thing this morning looking at the green rows of cotton.

He couldn't explain it. He felt at peace here . . . at home. And that was something he had not felt in a long, long while.

He frowned, turning to go back toward the house. Aimee's guests would be leaving soon and he wanted to say goodbye to them. He grunted softly, amused with himself. He never thought to see the day when he would be playing host, or making an effort to be polite and hospitable.

He remembered the conversation with Aimee's aunt and his lips pursed thoughtfully.

"My niece is vulnerable right now, Mister Valcour," she had said. "And I will not have her hurt. You are too charming by far . . . much too charming and handsome to be here alone and unchaperoned with her. Now, I'm not saying you should turn your back on your responsibilities here—I find your loyalty quite admirable. But if you care anything about Aimee's reputation you will make arrangements for other living quarters as soon as possible. Do you understand my meaning?"

Dominic had not protested. How could he? He knew she was right. It was something he had considered when he first came, but he had dismissed it, telling himself he would be gone in a month. And now he found himself wanting to stay, wanting this place to be his home . . . wanting to be near Aimee.

A month would not be enough time, not nearly enough. One month with a woman like Aimee Le-Beaux? That would be like one small breath of air in a man's entire lifetime.

He shook his head, wishing away his thoughts. Was Aimee as vulnerable and helpless as Aunt Eulie imagined? Somehow he had not thought so, except where her guilt about Jim was concerned. No, he had found her to be stubborn, willful, and very ambitious. He thought she was more aware of what she wanted in life than any woman he'd ever met.

But he was afraid that what Aimee wanted and what he wanted were two entirely different things. His dark eyes grew clouded as he remembered the feel of her in his arms, the hungry search of her lips beneath his.

Aimee LeBeaux was no virginal innocent, unaware of what she was doing or what her kisses did to a man. She was a woman in every way . . . a woman whose desire seemed to match his own.

But why had she pulled away that night? Did it really have anything to do with Jim? Dominic didn't think Aimee was the kind of woman to play games, to tease a man just to see if she could arouse him. No, he was not so easily fooled; she had been driven by needs just as hotly compelling as his, he was sure of that.

He thought . . . hoped that the only thing holding

her back was her conscience, her misguided idea that she was betraying Jim somehow if she gave in to her feelings.

Dominic's glance moved toward Aimee's room as he stepped up onto the veranda.

She would probably laugh if she knew that he was almost as afraid and uncertain as she was. What he felt when he was with Aimee was powerful, almost overwhelming at times. And the idea of trying to keep that power under control was almost too much for him sometimes. He had been with scores of women, but never had any of them made him feel this way. Never.

And the question remained, one that haunted him and kept him awake at night. What was he to do if he actually found himself falling in love with this unpredictable woman ... this exciting, beautiful woman who could cause his heart to behave strangely with just one look from those emerald green eyes.

Fourteen

Despite the pleasant ride that morning and a delicious late lunch, Aimee still felt a wave of relief as she watched the carriages drive down the tree-shaded lane. She had barely turned to go back into the house when Lucas came scampering around the side of the house and halted at the bottom of the steps.

"Aimee . . . Aimee. Dominic says I can go fishing with him if it's all right with you. Can I?" His eyes were bright and filled with such anticipation that she did not have the heart to correct him again and certainly she couldn't deny him.

"Of course, as long as you'll be careful and do as Dominic says."

The boy turned immediately to go.

"Lucas," Aimee said, laughing.

He turned back, his weight shifting impatiently as he waited.

"Have you eaten anything? Why don't you ask Cilla to make a basket for you and Dominic . . . in case you don't get back before supper."

"Thanks, Aimee."

His eyes lit as he ran impulsively up the steps and placed a quick kiss on Aimee's cheek. She stepped back, a bit startled by his actions; Lucas was not usually so demonstrative with her. But she could not

168

resist a smile as she watched him race back around the corner of the house.

That day seemed to mark the beginning of a change in Lucas. He seemed hardly able to contain himself in the mornings long enough to eat breakfast. He was much too anxious to be out with Dominic or Nathaniel. He didn't even complain about the chores that Aimee gave him. In fact, he didn't complain about anything unless for some reason he was not allowed to be with Dominic.

But it was a busy week and Aimee hardly had time to wonder about the boy, except to remind herself about getting him a new tutor.

Since the first appearance of the small green plants in the cotton fields, they grew so rapidly that their growth could almost be marked on a daily basis. The slaves were already busy chopping out the rows, leaving only the strongest and most healthy plants growing. Then mounds of dirt were raked into hills around the surviving plants.

Aimee was pleased that Dominic spent so much time in the fields. She knew he wanted to learn as much as possible about the whole process of raising cotton. But she also suspected he was there to keep an eye on Gregory Davis.

The incident with Jezzy's "spell" seemed almost forgotten, although the girl still wore the *gris-gris* around her neck. In the evenings, she would scurry to her room before dark, glancing out toward the canebrake as if at any time the demon lights might appear once again.

One late afternoon as Aimee rode home from the fields, her eyes darted to the same stand of cane and bamboo. She didn't like to think that this was the same place where she thought she'd seen someone before. But now, every time she passed, she could not keep her eyes from moving cautiously to the dense undergrowth. And Jezzy's declaration of seeing demon lights there had not helped her nervousness. But on this particular afternoon, when her eyes sought the long shaded areas through the bamboo, she was certain she saw something move in the shadows.

Her hands tightened on the reins, causing the mare to move sideways nervously. And this time, Aimee was sure—there *was* a man there . . . an Indian. He stood straight and tall, his dark eyes watchful as she moved along the roadway, and he seemed to be making no effort to hide himself.

She reined her horse to a stop. "Who are you?" she shouted. "What do you want?"

She was so close that she could see the faint smile on the man's face. He was a young man, probably no older than Dominic. His chest was bare and the leggings he wore looked similar to those she had seen Dominic wear.

Suddenly, the man's eyes darted past Aimee and he turned, moving away into the dense growth of brush and palmettos. He had not made a sound; it was as if he had not been there at all.

"What's wrong?" Dominic called from behind her.

Aimee had been so preoccupied with the man in the canes that she had not even heard Dominic approaching.

"I . . . I saw someone . . . there where the canes and bamboo are growing." She pointed where the man had been, but of course there was no evidence to prove that what she said was true.

170

Dominic stared at her, then at the area where she pointed, before getting off his horse and walking across the road to peer into the growing darkness.

A shiver trailed down Aimee's arms, making her wonder what or who she had seen. Or if she had seen anyone at all.

She closed her eyes and shook her head to clear her mind. Could it have been her imagination . . . a daydream of some kind? For some reason she couldn't explain, Cilla's words came back to haunt her . . . "now we has to wait."

She watched Dominic, almost holding her breath as he pushed his way slowly through the canes, gazing down at the ground. He knelt to pick up something, then came back to where she still sat on her horse.

"What is it?"

"Nothing," he said, holding the twig in his hand toward her. "Whoever it was was very careful not to leave anything, except perhaps this very small broken twig. What did he look like . . . do you think it could have been one of Compton's men?"

A strange, eerie sensation tugged at Aimee's chest. There had been someone there; she hadn't imagined it after all.

"No, I don't think so. Dominic . . . I . . . I think he was an Indian. He was tall . . ." She glanced at him as he placed his foot in the stirrup and pulled himself easily up into the saddle. "Maybe not as tall as you. And he was bare chested. . . ."

Dominic's eyes moved back toward the canes, his brows together as he scanned the darkening brush.

"Was he wearing any paint . . . have any feathers or adornments in his hair?"

171

"I . . . I don't know. It was dark and it all happened so fast. . . ." She shrugged her shoulders, wishing she could remember more.

Dominic frowned and rubbed his chin. "Let me take you to the house, then I'll go back and talk to Davis and Nathaniel. See if they've seen anyone hanging around lately. Maybe it's just someone who wandered off the Trace and is looking for a meal."

Aimee nodded, but his answer had not satisfied her. The man she saw was not some hungry vagabond. He had been muscular and well built, and looked perfectly capable of taking care of himself and she thought that certainly would include finding food whenever he needed it.

The eerie feeling within her persisted as they moved slowly back toward the stables and the house. She felt as if there were millions of eyes behind her, watching her . . . waiting.

It was almost dark outside the stables when they arrived. Dominic stepped down from his horse and came to stand beside Aimee's mount. She glanced down at him, wondering for a moment at his actions as his hands reached up for her.

She gave in to the feelings that made her want to throw herself in his arms, at least in a small way, as she allowed him to help her down from the horse. And when he did not immediately step away from her, she did not protest.

Seeing the man in the brush had made her more frightened than she'd been in ages. And oddly it made her long for a man's arms around her . . . and if she were truly honest she'd have to admit that it was not just any man's arms that she sought.

"Dominic . . ."

"Are you all right? You seem tired. Shall I see to your horse before I go or—"

"No . . . no, I'm sure one of the boys is inside. I can see to that much on my own."

"Then what is it?" He stood very near, his head bent as he looked intently at her.

Aimee had the feeling that any moment his hands would reach for her. She could feel the tension in the air between them, almost as if an invisible cord drew them toward each other, pulling them closer and closer. The feeling was so strong that it was incredible. . . .

"I . . . I don't know. Just this terrible feeling I have," she said. "I'm afraid, Dominic . . . and I don't really know why." Her voice broke and her eyes shifted toward him in an almost pleading way.

One corner of his mouth lifted as he continued gazing down at her. "Now you're beginning to sound like our Jezzy."

"Don't laugh at me."

"I'm not," he whispered. "Believe me, I'm not laughing."

A tingle shot through her entire body, making her feel strangely weak, causing her stomach to curl with warm anticipation. She took a long, slow breath, still staring into his eyes. She wanted him to touch her . . . dear God, how she wanted to feel his strong hands on her body, taste the heated sweetness of his mouth.

"Aimee?"

"Yes, I'm fine." she replied softly, moving slightly away from the tantalizing warmth of his body. "I . . . I should go. But please, be careful. Do . . . do you know where Lucas is? We should tell him to come inside and—"

His hand moved to brush a strand of hair from her face, stopping her words, and making her breath catch in her throat.

"I'll find Lucas, Aimee. I'll take care of everything. I don't want you to worry." His voice was soft and warm with concern.

When his hand moved downward to cup her chin, Aimee couldn't keep her body from straining toward him . . . waiting . . . wanting.

When Dominic turned abruptly and pulled himself back on his horse, Aimee actually felt as if she might fall without him to steady her. She stood looking up at him, frowning and wondering why he didn't stay. Couldn't he see what she was feeling? Didn't he feel it, too?

"Wait for me on the veranda; I'll tell you everything when I get back."

She frowned as she watched him ride away. She actually felt sick with longing as her eyes squinted into the darkness. How had this happened . . . this almost overpowering need she felt for Dominic to make love to her?

It had happened so suddenly, in just one moment it seemed, with just one look from those steady black eyes.

But as she walked in bemusement to the house, she admitted it had not been one moment and it had not happened suddenly. This sexual awareness between them had been building from the first moment they met. Just as Dominic said, it had begun with that strange, disturbing encounter on the veranda the first night he came to claim LeBeaux.

He might as well have claimed her then, too, she

174

thought. It was just as inevitable.

As Aimee bathed quickly and changed her dress, the excitement within her built, heating her skin and making her heart pulse with a strange new rhythm. And later as she waited on the porch, the tension in her breasts and legs was almost unbearable, making it impossible for her to sit still.

Finally she heard the sound of hooves coming from the quarters. She stood quickly, brushing her hair back and smoothing the skirt of her summer white muslin dress.

Tonight, she would let Dominic know . . . somehow she would find the courage to tell him how she felt. She had to; she simply could not bear another moment of this bittersweet torture that wrenched at her body and filled her mind with such desperate longing.

As she stood, looking toward the rider's sound, she clasped her hands to her breasts, trying to quell the tension of her body, trying to make her hands stop their trembling.

The gunshot that rang through the darkness was like an explosion making the silence that followed seem eerie and unreal. It was as if the whole world erupted. The night sounds stopped, then closed in around her again, louder than ever.

Aimee's clasped hands flew apart and she gasped. Her heart began to pound, beating loudly in her ears and against her throat. In that split second she seemed unable to move.

Then she began to run.

"Dominic . . ." she whispered. "No . . ."

175

Fifteen

The big black horse stood pawing the ground, its saddle empty.

Dominic was lying in the road near the canebrake, his body still and lifeless. When Aimee saw him, her footsteps faltered as she closed her eyes and fought against the sick fear that threatened to stop her breathing. Then she began to run again.

"No . . . please," she whispered. "Not Dominic. Please God, not Dominic, too." She was gasping for air as she ran.

Aimee saw Lucas and Nathaniel running toward her; both of them held lanterns in their hands and ran awkwardly as they held them away from their bodies. There were others behind them. But Aimee had eyes for no one except the man who lay so still on the ground.

"Dominic," she whispered as she threw herself to her knees beside him.

His long shining black hair had come unbound and strands of it splayed across his face and neck.

With trembling fingers Aimee touched him, pushing back his hair and taking his face in her hands to turn it toward her. She gasped when she saw the blood and dirt that streaked his face.

She heard Lucas's quiet cry behind her, felt his presence very close to her.

"He's dead," she heard him cry. And she heard the scuffling sound of struggles and glanced back to see Nathaniel holding the boy away from her and Dominic.

"Dominic," she whispered again, feeling the slow rise and fall of his chest beneath her hand. "Please . . . please don't leave me. You can't leave me . . . not now." Her voice was a sob, muffled as she leaned closer to his chest. Her hands moved over his body, searching for broken bones or other wounds. But there seemed to be only the one to his head.

Her heart skittered as the thought penetrated her mind. A gunshot to the head . . . how many people had she ever known who survived such a thing?

"Help me," she said, turning to Nathaniel and the others. "Lucas, you can help, too . . . get a wagon from the stables, sweetheart. We have to get him to the house and see how badly he's hurt."

"Then he's not . . . he's not . . . ?" She could see that Lucas did not really believe her, but stood stiff legged, staring down at her, his eyes filled with incredible pain and disbelief.

"No," she snapped. "But I need you to hurry, Lucas. I really need you to hurry."

As she waited for Lucas to return with a wagon, she moved closer to Dominic, putting her arm beneath his head and lifting him toward her so that she could cradle his head in her lap. She held him very still, caressing his face and whispering words to him that the others could not hear, desperate words she did not even know she said.

The faintest whisper of his breath against her hair

177

encouraged her and frightened her all at once. Was his breathing strong enough? Did it waver just now, perhaps even stop for a moment?

She felt the touch of someone's hand on her shoulder and turned to look up into Nathaniel's face.

"Ma'am? Miz Aimee . . . do you know what happened? After Mister Dominic left us, we came along behind. Did he fall off'n that big black horse? We thought we might have heard a gunshot."

"Yes," she said, shaking her head and trying to stop the loud buzzing noise in her ears. "A gunshot. There was a gunshot. I heard it from the porch." Her eyes flickered, then widened. "Oh, Nathaniel, earlier I saw someone . . ." Her eyes sought the thicket of canes which was now black and murky. ". . . in the canes." Her hand pointed toward the place where she'd seen the Indian. "There was a man there, just watching."

Nathaniel's dark eyes also peered into the darkness, his stance wary and guarded. "Mister Dominic told us someone was lurkin' around. What did this man look like, ma'am?"

"I . . . I'm not sure," she said. Something made her reluctant to tell Nathaniel and the others that the man she'd seen was an Indian.

Gregory Davis stepped forward then. "I'll take some of the men and have a look."

"Thank you," she whispered, distracted by the weight of Dominic's body against hers, worried by the sound of his shallow breathing. Her eyes scanned the darkness toward the stables, wondering where Lucas could be.

Just then they heard the rattle of the wagon and

178

the sound of Lucas's voice as he urged the mules on into the night.

Within minutes the workers had lifted Dominic from the ground and placed him in the wagon. Aimee ignored her overseer's outstretched hand as he offered to help her up onto the seat. Instead, she lifted her skirt and climbed into the back of the wagon with Dominic where she again positioned herself close and cradled his head against her body.

They left the others standing in the road and when the darkness obliterated the wagon, Aimee whispered again to Dominic.

"Please . . . just a few more minutes . . . we'll be home in a moment." Her fingers trembled as they touched his lips and she began to cry.

Those lips had kissed her so passionately; he had made her feel desired in a way she'd never felt before. There was no holding back in this man, no unnecessary concern for her feminine sensitivity, as Jim liked to call it. Dominic had made her feel like a woman in every way . . . a real and equal partner in the heated passion that always surged between them.

And now, if he died, she would never know what it was like to love him.

As they approached the house, she pushed away the pangs of regret that stabbed at her heart. Lucas pulled the wagon around past the kitchen so they could enter the veranda without going through the garden.

Jezzy, Amos, and the others were waiting for them. And once again, Aimee watched as dark hands reached for Dominic and carefully cradled his lifeless body to carry him up the back stairs toward

179

his room.

Lamps were lit, illuminating the massive oak bed that dominated the room. Quickly Jezzy went to the bed and grasped the covers to fling them back out of the way so they could place Dominic's body there. Then she took Lucas's arm and pulled him with her to stand back out of the way. Aimee gasped as the light illuminated the blood on Dominic's face and neck. And her dress was soaked with it. Her hands went to still her trembling lips as she watched Cilla begin to clean the wound.

Aimee turned and saw several of the household servants standing in the doorway. For a moment she felt impatient with them . . . until she saw the look in their eyes, saw how they could not take their eyes away from the man lying on the tall four-poster bed.

"Amos . . . why don't you take the others downstairs. And bring back some tea. I'll let all of you know just as soon as I can, how he is."

"Yes'm," he said with a nod. But his dark, sad eyes never moved away from Dominic until he turned to leave the room.

"How is he?" Aimee asked, turning again to Cilla.

Cilla had washed the blood from Dominic's face and now the big woman was cutting away the bloodied, dirt-stained shirt.

"Not bad as he looks, thank the good Lawd."

Aimee's heart fluttered with a hope she was almost afraid to feel. "He's . . . he's not?" She stepped closer and placed her hand on Dominic's bare arm.

"Lookee here," Cilla said, pushing Dominic's dark hair away from the long straight wound at his temple. "That bullet been a bit closer, Mister Dominic be dead now. Yes'm . . . be dead for sho." The woman straightened and shook her head, gazing down at the bare-chested man on the bed.

"But why is he still unconscious?"

Aimee felt Lucas as he came to stand beside her and she turned to him. Without looking she placed her arm around him, pulling him closer to the bed. "He's all right, son. See . . . you can see for yourself; it's just as Cilla says, he's not hurt as badly as it seemed."

"But why *is* he still asleep, Cilla?" Lucas asked.

Cilla was placing a bandage around Dominic's head and she turned with a smile. "Well, that old bullet whapped him real good, boy. Knocked Mister Dominic right into heaven for a while, I reckon." Cilla smiled as she wiped her hands on her white apron. The light from the oil lamps reflected on her white teeth and sparkling black eyes.

"And if'n he was on that big old black horse of his when he was shot, well—goodness sakes, chile, that fall be enough to knock the sense right out of a man." Cilla smiled at Lucas and patted his shoulder. "But he gonna be all right, Master Luke. Mister Dominic's a big strong man and he gonna be just fine."

"Are you sure?" Aimee asked, gazing down at him. He looked so still and his usually dark skin seemed very pale.

"Sho 'nuff. That is if somethin' drasticated don't happen during the night."

Aimee glanced over into the corner where Jezzy stood. She thought she'd never seen the girl so still. Only her hands were moving as her fingers nervously twisted the *gris-gris* that hung around her

181

neck and muttered words that Aimee only partially heard.

"Lawd, Lawd, help him," Jezzy whispered. "Have mercy, Jesus . . . pray, sister, pray."

"Jezzy?" Aimee asked. "Are you all right?"

She looked up as if seeing Aimee for the first time. "What? Oh, yes ma'am. Just prayin' Miz Aimee . . . prayin' for poor Mister Dominic."

"You heard Cilla, didn't you? She says he's going to be fine."

"Seen the death lights," she muttered. "Seen the death lights."

"Jezzy, I want you to stop that, right this minute! Now, Cilla said he's going to be all right and he is."

But Aimee saw the doubt in Jezzy's eyes. And the fright she saw there made her afraid as well.

"Do you hear me, Jezzy?"

"Yes'm . . . yes'm, I heard."

Jezzy hurried across the room, glancing back once at Dominic before leaving.

Aimee turned to Cilla with a sigh of relief. "Thank you, Cilla. I'll stay here with him now."

"Me, too," Lucas said.

Aimee turned to the boy, intending to deny his wish, intending to tell him he'd be better off in his own room. But the look on his face was stubborn and closed, as if he knew exactly what she was about to say.

She sighed and smiled at him. "Of course, Lucas, you, too." She turned to the black woman. "Cilla, tell Amos to bring Master Lucas something up to eat when he comes, and a glass of milk."

"Coffee," Lucas said with a determined look in his eyes. "I want coffee . . . hot and black, the way

182

Dominic drinks his."

Cilla's eyes flew open wide and she propped her hands on her broad hips as she grinned and looked to Aimee for approval.

Seeing the determined, almost angry look in Lucas's eye, Aimee sighed and closed her eyes for a moment.

"All right," she said. "Black coffee, Cilla."

Long after Lucas had eaten, Aimee sat silently beside the bed, sipping tea, her eyes never wavering from Dominic's face. She glanced over now at the other side of the bed and saw Lucas's eyes beginning to droop tiredly. Before long he was sound asleep, slumped in the chair with his head tilted at an uncomfortable-looking angle.

Aimee tiptoed to the armoire and pulled out a quilt, then lightly draped it over Lucas's arms and across his legs.

Dominic had grown restless during the last thirty minutes. And Aimee thought that was a good sign; perhaps he would be awake soon. She went back to him now, adjusting the sheets and letting her hand linger on the warmth of his muscular chest. Her eyes went to his face, wondering what on earth he would think if he woke suddenly and found her caressing his dark smooth skin so intimately.

She watched, mesmerized, as his lips moved and he turned his head restlessly from side to side on the pillow. She bent closer, touching his shoulder and waiting.

"Dominic?" she said. "Can you hear me?"

He was murmuring something beneath his breath and now she could see a faint beading of perspiration on his brow. Aimee reached for a damp cloth

183

and carefully wiped his forehead and face.

Suddenly, Dominic's hand shot forward, grasping her arm in a hold that threatened to snap the delicate bones of her wrist. Aimee gave a low moan of protest, but stopped struggling immediately when she saw the lift of his long dark lashes. His eyes stared into hers, unseeing and wild with some deep primitive fear.

"Where is she?" he demanded, his voice deep and hoarse. "Tell me, damn you!" He shook Aimee's wrist and pulled her closer to him.

"Dominic . . . it's me . . . it's Aimee."

"Yes," he whispered, frowning, his eyes suddenly filled with an unbearable pain.

"Dominic . . . ?"

"Ma," he said, his eyes growing blank as if he had willed away the pain that had been there before. *"Tichou mingo . . . tichou mingo."*

Aimee felt his strong hands slowly releasing her wrist, and with disbelief she watched as tears filled those black, sightless eyes, watched as he lifted his chin in a defiant gesture.

"Choctaw siah," he whispered fiercely. *"Choctaw siah."*

Then his eyes closed again.

Sixteen

Aimee sat for a long while, hearing Dominic's strange words in her head and trying to imagine what they meant. Although she didn't know exactly where she'd learned it, she thought the word *ma* meant yes in the eastern Indian dialect. But the other words, she had no idea.

His last words, *Choctaw siah,* had been spoken proudly with a familiar defiance that didn't surprise Aimee. What had surprised her, stunned her even, was the glitter of tears in his black eyes, tears that shook her to her very soul as nothing else he had ever done. But she had a very distinct feeling this was not something she should mention to him when he woke. This was something very private to him, she thought . . . and painful.

She didn't know how late it was, but finally she drifted off to sleep, waking only when the birds began to sing in the trees outside the house. The room felt cool when she opened her eyes and glanced at the faint strips of light at the windows.

Then quickly, almost having forgotten where she was, she turned toward Dominic, moving forward in her chair so that she could touch him and make sure he was all right.

She put her hand on his chest, feeling the steady rhythm of his heartbeat and the slow, even rise and fall of his breathing. She let her hand remain there as she turned her gaze across the bed to Lucas. The boy still slept soundly, seemingly undisturbed by the uncomfortable chair. She smiled, thinking how easily children adapt to situations.

She felt Dominic's warm hand close over hers and her eyes swung immediately back to him, surprised to see him awake and watching her with an odd look on his face.

"How are you feeling?" she asked.

He frowned and glanced around the room. When he tried to lift his head he groaned and lowered it gingerly back onto the pillow.

"God," he murmured. "I feel like I've been kicked in the head by a mule." Dominic's fingers moved to his head, cautiously touching the white gauze bandage. He licked his dry lips and frowned at her with a puzzled look on his face.

She smiled, pleased beyond words to hear his voice and to hear the old familiar sarcasm in his voice.

"Someone shot you," she said, her face now reflecting the seriousness of her words.

"I don't remember," he said, still frowning.

"It's all right; there will be plenty of time to remember later. Right now, I just want you to get well. Are you hungry . . . thirsty?"

"Thirsty . . . very," he said with a smile.

He winced when he turned his head slightly to one side toward Lucas. "Is the boy all right?"

"Yes," she whispered, quick to assure him. "He was just a little worried, that's all, and he insisted

186

on staying here with you. But he's fine I think. He even managed to sleep through most of the night in that awkward position."

Dominic smiled and turned back to her.

"And you . . . did you stay here in my room all night?" Even as weak and ill as he'd been, he was still able to make his question sound provocative and intimate.

"Yes," she said, rising quickly and going to pour him a glass of water.

"Well," he drawled. "Perhaps I should have been wounded a long time ago."

"Dominic," she scolded, frowning at him as she walked back to the bed. "Don't say that; it's not funny. I was worried sick about you. I was so afraid that . . ." She stopped, seeing the questioning arch of his brow.

"Yes?" he said. "Afraid of what?"

She sat down and put one hand beneath his head to lift his lips toward the glass of water. "Here . . . drink this."

"I don't think I like this very much," he muttered after he'd finished.

"Oh? And what exactly don't you like?"

"Other than feeling as if my head might explode at any minute, I don't like being helpless, and I don't like being waited on by a—"

"If you're going to say that you don't like being waited on by a female, just don't bother. You will notice that most of the caretakers in this house are women."

He looked at her for a long while, his gaze searching and filled with just a hint of amusement. "I was going to say that it's rather disturbing being attended to so . . . intimately"—his eyes moved to her lips—"by a beautiful woman. Especially when that beautiful woman has removed my shirt." He looked down toward his bare chest with an innocent grin.

"You're awfully clever, Mister Valcour, for a man in such a helpless position. But for your information, it was Cilla who removed your shirt last night. And it was also Cilla who tended your wounds and bandaged your head."

"Ah," he said with a conciliatory lift of his brows.

"Now, if you have no other complaints, I'm going to find Amos. And if you feel up to it, he can help you bathe and dress." She waited for his answer, with a smug look of satisfaction on her face.

"I do."

"Good, then I'll bring up something for your breakfast." She glanced across the bed and saw Lucas begin to stir.

"Lucas . . . look who's awake."

Lucas opened his eyes, scooting forward in his chair as if he'd just stumbled down the stairs on Christmas morning.

"Dom!"

"Come around here boy, so I can see you," Dominic said with a grin.

Aimee thought the look on both their faces was wonderful to see and as Lucas hurried around the bed, she slowly tiptoed out of the room.

Aimee came back about an hour later, carrying Dominic's breakfast. She was surprised to find him alone, sitting up in bed.

"Where's Lucas?" she asked.

"He left with Amos. I expect he'll be back soon."

He was freshly shaven and had on a clean white shirt and a new pair of buckskin breeches. His color was much better now and except for the bandage that slanted rakishly around his head and brow, he looked perfectly normal.

As she placed the silver tray on a table beside his bed, Aimee glanced with a puzzled look around the room. Candles flickered everywhere, from every table and piece of furniture and even across the mantelpiece of the fireplace. She turned back to Dominic and saw him watching her with a decided look of amusement.

"What's this all about?" she asked, waving her hand around the room toward the candles.

"Jezzy. Need you ask?"

"Oh my. Don't tell me it's some sort of voodoo protection . . . for you."

"Exactly," he said with a wry grin. "Candles will protect me from danger . . . her words." He lifted his arm from beneath the covers. "And she even made an amulet for me to wear when I'm away from the candles' protective light, I assume." He chuckled as he turned his arm back and forth so that Aimee might get a better look at the piece of beaten copper around his wrist.

"Oh dear. I'm sorry, Dominic, if she disturbed you this morning with her nonsense. I—"

"She didn't disturb me," he said. "Jezzy is a delight, for all her peculiarities. And there's no need to apologize for that. Besides, you sound as if I'm your guest here, as if I'm not aware of Jezzy's quirks, or any other curiosities of this household."

189

"I'm sorry . . . really, of course I didn't mean to imply that."

Aimee busied herself with Dominic's breakfast but she could sense him watching her. Finally he reached for her hand and pulled her toward the bed.

"Aimee . . . sit down." His voice was quiet and patient as he continued to look at her. "Why do you keep apologizing? God, I'm not sure I'm ready for this new, deferential Aimee. Am I dying or some such horror that you haven't told me about?"

She grimaced, then smiled as she sat in the chair beside his bed. She took a cloth napkin and placed it against his chest, then moved the tray onto his lap.

"Here . . . eat," she said with a mock scowl.

"That's much better," he said, laughing at her.

Aimee could not keep from laughing with him. It was so good to see him well and behaving more like his old, arrogant self. A tingle jabbed at her chest as she recalled the way he had looked last night . . . so pale and still, his black eyes closed against her pleading words.

"Now," he said, turning more serious. "Tell me what happened last night."

Those black eyes watched her carefully as he ate the scrambled eggs and biscuits that Aimee had brought. There was no humor in his look now and Aimee could see how hard it was for him to maintain his patience as he asked about who shot him.

They could hear the sound of voices outside, men's voices, slightly raised and agitated. Aimee frowned and went to the window, gazing down past the garden. She saw her overseer standing in the road just past the house and with him she saw Nathaniel and Amos, as well as two of the stable boys and Lucas. One of the young boys seemed agitated as he gestured and pointed at the canebrake out past the stables.

Aimee continued to watch as Gregory Davis and the others followed Lucas and the two boys, then she turned back toward the bed.

"What is it?" Dominic asked.

Aimee shrugged, then went to sit in the chair again. "I'm not sure. Mister Davis and some of the men were in the roadway talking. Lucas is with them, too."

"Oh. I thought maybe you were trying to find some excuse not to talk about what happened last night."

"No, of course not. Why would I do that?"

"Maybe you thought I'd forgotten that it was an Indian you saw in the canes just before I was shot."

"No. I didn't think you would forget." She watched him, seeing the bitterness in his eyes and the confusion. He didn't want to believe it was the Indian who had shot him, that one of his own people would do such a thing. And now she wondered if the words he had mumbled in his unconsciousness had anything to do with his doubts.

"I don't think it was the Indian who shot you, Dominic."

"Why?" His dark eyes narrowed and he pushed his breakfast away from him as if he suddenly had no patience with eating.

She shrugged. "I . . . I don't really have a reason why. I just don't. He seemed so young . . . handsome even and—"

His response was a quiet grunt of laughter. "Oh, well, that makes perfect sense."

"You aren't listening to me," she said with a huff of exasperation. "I just had the feeling that this man . . . this Indian wanted something from me and—"

"Really?" he drawled. "I wonder what."

She leapt up from the chair and stood staring down at him, her hands on her hips. "Damn you, Dominic. Why must you always be so sarcastic and cynical? And why must you ridicule everything I say? I might be a woman and I might not be as . . . as seasoned as you, but I'm not ignorant. And if you would just listen for a moment, you might even learn something!"

Dominic's head bent forward so that all she could see was the top of his black shining hair. Aimee held her breath for a moment, then took a step toward the bed. Just as she reached for him, he looked up and she could see his shoulders shaking with laughter. He nodded his head as if in agreement with her words, but was laughing so hard he could hardly speak.

"Seasoned," he said chuckling. "Now that's a really wonderful description." He took a deep breath and leaned back against his pillow, gazing up at her through crinkled eyes that still sparkled with laughter. "Ohhh," he said, putting his hand to his head. "I'm sorry, Aimee. Please sit down again; I promise I'll listen this time."

Reluctantly she sat down, moving to the edge of her seat as if at any moment she might leap up and run away from him.

"You know," he said, still smiling and looking deep into her eyes. "You're the only person I know who stands up to me this way. Not that I'm such an ogre, but for some reason, no one has ever been quite so blunt about my impatience before."

"You should learn to listen," she said, pouting slightly.

"I know."

She was silent for a moment, as she looked haughtily at him and waited for him to become serious again. His look changed then as they stared at each other and his eyes became smoky and warm.

"I like that about you," he murmured, reaching for her hand. "That honest courage you have. I like it a lot."

Her breath caught in her throat as his fingers stroked the skin on the back of her hand. She didn't pull away, but instead gave in to the sensations he always caused when he looked at her that way, or when he touched her.

"You make me forget what I'm saying," she murmured. She found that her voice had grown hoarse and unsteady.

"I doubt that," he said, gazing into her eyes. "Not the cool, levelheaded Aimee LeBeaux who is always in control."

"What I was saying is that I believe someone else was there. I believe the Indian must have left as soon as he saw me looking at him."

For a moment, Dominic's thoughts seemed far away, as if something in his mind was triggered by her mention of the Indian.

"Dominic? What are you thinking?"

193

"Nothing important," he murmured. "Just that I wonder if . . ."

She waited for him to continue and watched as he looked thoughtfully past her.

"What?" she finally asked. "You wondered what?"

"This man you saw . . . this Indian. He was young you say . . . and good looking?"

"Yes. Very."

"Hmmm."

"Dominic . . . do you . . . do you think you might know who he is?"

"It's possible," he said, his eyes turning to meet hers. "It's entirely possible. And I think you're right." His fingers continued to move slowly over her hand. "More than likely it was one of Compton's men who did the shooting. But still, I want to know who this other man was that you saw."

"Yes, so do I." He stared into her eyes. "Then for once, we are in agreement."

"Yes," she whispered. "It seems that we are." The look in his eyes drew her, made her lean closer to him. She could not seem to take her eyes away from his mouth or the play of emotion deep within his black eyes.

When the door opened with a rattle, Aimee sprang away from Dominic and sat back in the chair. She turned to see Lucas bound through the doorway, his eyes bright with anticipation as he looked toward Dominic. She sighed and with a wry grin, caught, Dominic's own look of disappointment and frustration.

His eyes seemed to question her, to warn her silently that this interruption did not mean he was going to forget what was between them. His look was a warm promise that did not let her forget for a moment.

Seventeen

"Dominic!" Lucas ran to the bed, breathless with excitement. "They found him; they found the man who shot you!" Lucas's dark eyes glittered as he sprang against the bed.

Dominic grunted softly as the bed shook, jarring him and causing pain to flicker across his features.

"Lucas," Aimee warned, putting a hand forward as if to protect Dominic from any further disturbance.

But both of them ignored her. Dominic, despite his obvious pain, pushed himself up in the bed, leaning toward Lucas and taking his arm.

"Slow down, son," he said. "And tell me exactly what you're talking about. Who is this man and where is he?"

"I . . . I don't know who he is. But Lucien and me and Tim found him in the canebrake just a few minutes ago. Nathaniel said I should come tell you right away." Lucas could barely stand still as he spoke. "He's dead, Dominic . . . someone slit his throat from ear to ear. I never saw so much blood and . . ." Lucas stopped, remembering Aimee, and his glance toward her was apologetic.

"Uh . . . sorry," he said, acknowledging her shocked frown.

Dominic swung his long legs over the side of the bed, eliciting Aimee's murmur of protest.

"Dominic . . . no," she began.

"Get my boots, Lucas," he said as he stood up.

The boy darted away to the other side of the room as Dominic tried to steady himself. He swayed back and forth on the heels of his feet and his eyes closed as he put his hand to his forehead.

Aimee's arms went around his waist, steadying him as she looked up with worried eyes into his face. His teeth were clenched tightly together and his usually dark face seemed drawn and ashen. Aimee admired the will it took for him to remain standing, but still it angered her. Why were men so quick to action, so anxious, no matter what the circumstance, to jump into the middle of a fray? It was something she thought she'd never understand.

"Dominic Valcour," she said, her emerald eyes sparkling. "I won't have this. I will not have you rushing out of a sick bed for no good reason. You'll be—"

She felt his arm tighten around her shoulders as he leaned against her and she felt his soft grunt of breath as he fought to overcome his pain.

"I'm fine," he managed to whisper. Impatiently he pulled the bandage from around his head, revealing the ugly gash at his temple. "I'm not dying, for God's sake and I intend to have a look at the man who shot me even if I have to crawl out of this room."

Her lips clamped together and she shook her head as her cheeks grew flushed with frustration.

"You are as stubborn and pigheaded as—"

"Don't say it," he hissed. "Just don't say it. I don't

197

think at this moment I can take another comparison to Jim LeBeaux."

His words stung and she only stared up at him mutely. Was it her fault that her late husband was the only man with whom she could compare Dominic?

"All right," she muttered. "You don't have to bite my head off."

Lucas was on the floor now, helping Dominic with his boots. He looked up at them, his dark eyes darting from one to the other.

"Just help me to the door," Dominic grumbled. "Once I'm outside in the fresh air, I'll be fine."

Aimee rolled her eyes and shook her head, but she said nothing else to try to persuade him. They walked slowly with him leaning against her. He was a big man and heavy, but with each step, she could feel the strength returning to him. It was as if he simply willed himself to do it.

When they reached the door, Dominic released his grip on her shoulders and walked out alone, his head high, as if he did not want anyone to see him dependent on a woman.

Aimee was not surprised to find Amos waiting on the balcony just outside the door—the old man had been as watchful of Dominic as a mother hen. But she was surprised to see several other of the household servants waiting and watching, as well as Jezzy, who smiled broadly as Dominic walked slowly across to the steps.

"I knowed he could do it." The pride in Jezzy's voice indicated she had something to do with it. "See," she said, turning to the others. "See that charm I made for Mister Dominic's arm? It what got

198

him through the other side and back into the light."

Aimee glanced at Jezzy, but said nothing. If the girl thought she had helped Dominic recover, she supposed there was no harm in it.

Aimee watched anxiously as Dominic went down the steps and out across the garden to the men waiting in the roadway.

It was a bright sunny day, and the brilliant sunlight shone down on his black hair, making glittering streaks as he walked. She watched the long stride of his muscular legs, the way his buckskins encased his thighs and she thought what strength it took for him to appear so coolly unfazed by the bullet that had grazed his skull last night. Just thinking of that strength, she felt a warm, unsteady feeling that went straight to the pit of her stomach. And if she had not already decided that she wanted him, this moment would have made up her mind completely.

He was stubborn and untamed. He did as he pleased, without regard for anyone else's opinion. But he also possessed a quiet will and strength that she envied and that made him seem even more desirable than she'd thought before. He was not a man to be coddled and pampered, no matter how much a woman might personally enjoy doing it. No, Dominic Valcour was every inch a man . . . his own man, and as he'd told her often enough, he took orders from no one.

She watched anxiously from the top balcony, oblivious to anything or anyone except the tall, black-haired man in the group of men beyond the house. Her eyes never left him as he moved with them toward the canebrake.

Aimee gasped softly when she saw Dominic walk

to the covered figure of a man lying just beside the roadway within the shadows of the trees. It was too far for her to see clearly, but she squinted as Dominic knelt on one knee and threw back the blanket from the man's face.

She saw him sit back on his heels, and motion with his hands as he glanced up from time to time at the men gathered around him.

Aimee stared hard at the man on the ground. She didn't think it was the Indian. She was almost certain this man was not bare chested and he looked shorter and heavier than the man she had seen in the canes. But from this distance she couldn't be sure. Who was he? And the question remained: who had killed him?

She heard a giggle behind her on the balcony and turned to see Jezzy and a couple of servant girls watching her and whispering. She had been so intent on Dominic that she had forgotten they were there and now their laughter irritated her and made her speak more sharply than she normally might have.

"All right, girls," she said. "You may return to your duties now. And you, Jezzy, if you have nothing better to do than stand here and giggle, I suggest you remove all those candles from Mister Dominic's room."

Jezzy's eyes widened and rolled toward the other two girls. They soon scurried away and Jezzy headed toward Dominic's room.

But as she went she rolled her eyes toward Aimee in an exaggerated way. "Yes, ma'am," she said in her high-pitched voice. "Yes, ma'am, indeedy do."

Aimee turned back toward the men at the canebrake just in time to see them dragging the body across the ground and, then lifting it across a horse. She stepped closer to the porch railing, frowning as she wondered at Dominic's actions.

She couldn't believe her eyes, but he was walking to his horse as if he intended to ride. His hand took the reins of that big black brute of a horse he rode and now he was pulling himself up into the saddle. She stepped forward with a murmur of protest and saw him lean forward in the saddle, saw him hesitate before pulling himself up straight and tall.

"Dominic, you are a damned stubborn fool," she said to herself. Then she lifted her skirts and ran toward the steps.

When Aimee reached the garden gate, Dominic had already gone around toward the front of the house and was moving out the long drive through the tunnel of trees. He held the reins to the horse behind him, the one that carried the man's body. Gregory Davis was with him, but he was the only one.

She felt her heart sink, felt a panic that seemed to reach clear to her soul. He was going to Compton's house; she knew it, and she found herself trembling with fear and frustration.

"Nathaniel," she shouted from the garden. "Bring me a horse . . . and a rifle."

Nathaniel's dark eyes widened and his mouth opened slightly as if to protest.

"Don't argue with me, Nathaniel, I don't have time for that now. I don't intend to sit at home this time and let Compton kill someone I . . . kill Dominic, too."

Without a word Nathaniel turned and ran toward the stables as Aimee went back to the house to change clothes.

Within minutes she was on the veranda, tucking her shirt into the waistband of the breeches she wore. She'd bought them in Natchez, pretending they were for Lucas, but she'd never had the nerve to wear them before. But now, in her worry about Dominic, she didn't care. She didn't care who she shocked or what anyone thought. She just wanted to make sure she could ride quickly and easily.

She met Nathaniel at the gate beyond the garden fence and took the rifle from his hand, then placed her foot in the stirrup and swung herself up into the saddle.

"Miz Aimee," Nathaniel said, looking up at her with a worried frown. "Let me go with you."

"No," she said, pulling the reins around and moving away.

"Then let Master Lucas go," he continued.

Aimee glanced toward the roadway and saw Lucas standing there. His heart was in his eyes, pleading with her, begging her to understand his need to be involved. She remembered all too well Dominic's opinion that Lucas needed to become a man.

But she couldn't . . . she simply could not take a chance on him being hurt. If she lost Lucas . . . A sharp pain twisted in her chest at the mere thought of it.

"No," she said, ignoring Lucas's pained expression. "You stay here, Luke. If something should happen . . . if none of us return, you are to go to the DeVaull Plantation for help. Do you understand?" She glanced at him over her shoulder as she rode away, hoping he understood and praying that his trip to their nearest neighbor would not be necessary.

The horse beneath her seemed to sense her impatience. Galloping down the broad sandy drive beneath the big trees, the animal stretched out, throwing sand from its hooves behind them. Its ears were back and Aimee could almost feel the exhilaration in the horse's muscles as she gave it full rein.

Still, for all their speed, she did not see Dominic and Gregory Davis until she reached the last bend in the road just before the driveway that led to Compton's house. She reined her horse back, pulling over beneath some trees and waiting. She knew exactly how Dominic would react if he saw her and she did not intend to be sent home like a child.

She watched through the leaves as the two men disappeared down the driveway, then slowly she picked her way through the trees. She would remain in the woods near the house and watch. She reached back behind her and pulled the rifle from its saddle scabbard, laying it across her lap. She would be ready this time . . . this time Compton would not have the advantage.

The large red brick house was surrounded by trees. The yard was small and almost bare, unusual for such an elegant home. But Aimee supposed it was because Compton was unmarried and took little interest in the appearance of the exterior. She'd been told though, that the inside contained only the rarest and most unusual treasures from France and Italy.

She sat very still when she saw Dominic and her overseer approach the columned front porch. Dominic pulled the horse carrying the body up beside him. She heard him shout toward the house, then she stiffened as Compton walked casually out between the tall columns and stepped down onto the front stairs. Several men came out as well and lined

203

themselves along the porch. And Aimee's heart fluttered when she saw another man in a doorway on the second floor.

She lifted the rifle in her hands, holding it unsteadily just above her thighs so it would be ready.

She wished she could get closer. From this distance she could barely make out the voices, just enough to hear the inflection of anger in their words. But she could not understand exactly what was being said.

She saw Dominic reach across to the other horse, saw his hand whip forward and the flash of steel in the sunlight as his knife slashed through the ropes holding the dead man's body on the horse. She gasped as she watched his booted foot reach across and brutally shove the corpse off the horse and onto the ground. Then her eyes turned immediately toward the house for Compton's reaction.

The man's fists were at his hips as he stood watching Dominic. One of the men behind him took a step forward, but Compton lifted his hand, warning the man back. She could hear his voice, soft and menacing and she saw Dominic lean forward across his mount's neck as he answered. Every movement he made was a threat . . . the way he held himself as well as the softly menacing murmur of his words.

Aimee felt the muscles in her arms beginning to tremble and she shifted the position of the rifle. She realized that her thighs were tightly gripping her horse's sides, making them ache with fatigue. But still, she could not take her eyes away from the man on the porch. One move, she told herself. Just one move from any of them toward Dominic and she would have to be ready to fire.

Then suddenly, it seemed over. Dominic pulled at

the reins of his horse and wheeled around, away from the house. Gregory Davis sat for a moment, as if standing guard. Aimee saw him nod toward Compton, then he, too, turned and rode away from the house.

She continued watching to make sure none of them followed. She noted that Compton seemed little moved by the death of one of his henchmen. He spared hardly a glance at the dead man on the ground before turning and walking back into the house, leaving the men on the porch to pick up the body and carry it away toward the back of the house.

Once they were all gone and Aimee knew they had no intention of following Dominic, she heaved a sigh of relief and shoved the rifle back into its scabbard. And when she finally relaxed, her arms and legs began to tremble so badly that she was afraid she would not be able to ride. She sat for long moments, taking deep breaths of air and willing herself to stop trembling. For some strange reason, she felt an overwhelming urge to cry. But then, she clenched her teeth together and quietly moved her horse away from the house and back toward the main road.

Eighteen

When Aimee rode back up the long driveway to the house, she purposely guided her horse away from the road and toward the left. She didn't want to take a chance on seeing Dominic and having him know she had followed him.

She rode around the house to the long brick kitchen. Then, tying the reins to a rail outside, she walked to the open doorway, smiling at the familiar sounds of Cilla's singing. Stepping inside, Aimee let the warmth and the wonderful smells of cooking soothe and calm her. She was home now, she tried to tell herself. She was safe at home and so was Dominic.

"Why, how do, Miz Aimee," Cilla said, turning to her with a broad smile. "You hungry? I got some of that corn bread you like so good. Here, let me fetch you some . . ."

"No, that's all right, Cilla, maybe later. There's something I need you to do first." She looked Cilla straight in the eye, as if to make sure she knew how important it was. "And I need it done quickly."

"Sho," Cilla said, her eyes bright and curious.

"My horse is tied to the railing around behind the kitchen. Have one of the girls get Nathaniel and tell him to take the horse back to the stables; tell him and Lucas that I'm home and that everything is fine. And Cilla, whatever you do, make sure Mister Dominic doesn't know about any of this."

"Yes'm," she said with a solemn nod. "I sho take care of that right away, Miz Aimee."

"Thank you, Cilla. I'm going to my room to change."

Cilla's eyes moved downward and widened with surprise and curiosity as she took in the breeches that her young mistress wore. But she said nothing.

Aimee felt like a fugitive as she slipped away from the kitchen, pausing once on the veranda to glance out toward the stables. Then she ran quickly and silently across the porch and let herself into her room.

Once she had bathed and changed back into a dress, she walked casually out onto the porch as if she had been doing nothing more strenuous than lounging there all morning. She glanced toward the garden, thinking Dominic should be back at the house by now, and she wondered where he was.

It was then she saw Amos shuffling along the walkway toward the kitchen. He was carrying a tray which held a teapot and a cup. Aimee began walking toward him, thinking that he must have just come down the stairs from Dominic's room.

"Amos?" she said as she grew nearer.

The old man turned and stopped. His smile was gentle as he waited for Aimee to reach him.

"Yes'm? Anything I can do for you, Miz Aimee? Want I should bring you some tea?"

"No, Amos, I'm fine. But I was just wondering . . . have you seen Mister Dominic since he returned to the house?"

"Oh yes, ma'am," he said, lifting the tray in his hands as if for emphasis. "He's upstairs." The old man frowned and he leaned forward, whispering to her as if in conspiracy. "He wouldn't want nobody to know it, but that ride done give him a powerful headache. He could barely make it up them stairs." He glanced down at the tray in his hands. "Cilla sent up some willow bark tea for his fever and pain and—"

"Fever?" Aimee asked, her eyes shooting upward toward the closed door at the end of the balcony. "Oh dear," she whispered. "That man is going to kill himself with his obstinance."

"Huh?" Amos said, frowning at her.

"Never mind, Amos. Has he eaten anything?"

"No, ma'am. He was feelin' too poorly to eat I reckon."

Aimee turned to go up the stairs and Amos frowned at her. "I reckon he wouldn't want nobody to know he's took to his bed, ma'am."

"Oh no, I'm sure he wouldn't," she muttered, stalking purposefully up the steps. She gazed down at Amos. "It's all right, Amos—I promise he won't know that you told me. Would you find Master Lucas and tell him I expect him to be dressed properly and in the dining room for supper this evening? He and I have some things to discuss."

Amos's eyes twinkled up at her and he nodded. "Yes'm, I sho will."

Opening Dominic's door, Aimee stopped and gazed into the darkened room. After a moment, her eyes adjusted and she could see the outline of his body on the bed. She didn't bother opening the heavy curtains at the windows, thinking the bright

208

sunlight would only make his headache worse. Instead, she went to the bed and lit a small oil lamp on a nearby table.

Dominic turned his head on the pillow as he reached forward to grasp her arm. "Aimee," he muttered, letting go of her. Then he groaned and closed his eyes.

Aimee sat down quickly, seeing the look of anguish on his face and feeling a stab of concern at the pain she saw in those black eyes.

"Dominic?" she whispered. She reached forward and placed her hand on his forehead, noting with satisfaction that the wound was not bleeding at least.

"God," he whispered. "I've never had such a headache in my life. It even hurts to breathe."

"It's your own stubborn fault," she said, keeping her voice quiet. "You never should have ridden out of here like that; it would kill a normal man."

He opened his eyes a bit, and there was a slight quirk at his mouth when he looked at her. "I'm too stubborn to die."

"Yes, thank goodness, I believe you are." She reached to the bedside table for a cloth and dipped it into the washbowl. Wringing it free of the dripping water, she folded it and placed it gingerly on Dominic's forehead. "You have a fever again, too."

"Cilla's dreadful tea should fix that soon, the pain, too, if I'm lucky. Mmm, that feels good," he murmured, closing his eyes again.

"Dominic . . . I know you don't feel like talking just now. But—"

He smiled, although he didn't bother opening his eyes. "But you're dying of curiosity." He took a long slow breath and his eyes opened languidly as if he

209

was growing sleepy. "It was one of Compton's men in the canes, and I suppose he was the one who tried to kill me . . . something I didn't take kindly to as I told Mister Compton." His mouth was grim as he spoke. "What I don't know is who slit the man's throat."

"What . . . what did Compton say?" She hesitated, hoping he could not hear the deception in her voice.

"Said he didn't know anything about it . . . denied that he had sent the man, which is exactly what I expected him to say."

"And you . . . what did you say to Compton?"

His eyes flickered toward her and he saw the look on her face, the fear that moved in her green eyes. "I told him if anything else happened to LeBeaux Plantation . . . to its people, the buildings or the land . . . that I'd kill him." She thought she'd never seen such cold determination in anyone's eyes.

She took a long shuddering breath, exhaling slowly through her lips. And she watched Dominic with worried eyes as his eyelashes slowly lowered and his chest began to move slowly and steadily as he neared sleep.

"Oh, by the way," he said, opening those black eyes and gazing steadily at her. "I appreciate you backing me up there at Compton's. . . ."

Her mouth flew open and she started to protest, but stopped at the look in his eyes. Why should she be so surprised? She'd often thought that this man seemed to know everything. Had she really expected him not to see her there in the woods, or not to sense somehow that she was there?

"It took a lot of courage to do what you did," he

said, studying her face carefully. "I suppose you were only protecting your interests . . . weren't you?"

She stared back at him. "No," she said with a lift of her chin. "For your information, I hadn't even thought of that. I was worried about you and I didn't intend to let you end up the way Jim did if I could help it." She looked at him defiantly. "I know . . ." she said at the look in his eyes. "I know I've mentioned you and Jim together too many times, and I'm sorry if it angers you. But I never intended my remarks to be a comparison. In fact, I'm seeing more every day how very different you are."

He reached for her hand and the black eyes that met her gaze were steady and warm. He nodded and closed his eyes.

"Good," he whispered.

In only a few moments he was sleeping soundly.

"Oh, Dominic," she whispered, moving her hand from his.

She reached forward, gently turning the cold cloth on his forehead. Her fingers lingered and moved to touch the thick strands of hair that would not stay in place, but fell over his forehead. Hair so black and shining that it reminded her of a raven's wings, gleaming in the sun. It felt soft and warm beneath her fingers and for a moment she found herself actually longing to crawl into bed beside him and hold him, keep him safe as he slept. It was all she could do to remind herself of where she was and who she was.

She was a woman of substance, she told herself, a woman of some respect in the community who could live independently of a man. She could hardly allow her passion for this man to turn her into one of his easy saloon women.

She sighed and let the back of her hand move from his hair to trail slowly down his face, to the corner of his mouth. Then she bent forward, letting her lips touch the place where her fingers had lingered, letting the feel and scent of him penetrate her skin.

She didn't want to leave him and she sat by the bed for a long while, staring at the man who had come so suddenly into her life. Who had forced her to begin living again, feeling again . . . feeling oh, so many things. While he was asleep, she could look at him all she pleased, from his black shining hair, to the soft boots that he hadn't bothered to remove. Her eyes wandered over his face and the sensuous lips that fascinated her so, the closed lids that hid those incredibly disturbing black eyes.

She was practically holding her breath as she allowed her eyes to wander further, down to his broad shoulders and chest, to the lean waist and hips. She stopped and closed her eyes, feeling herself growing weak, wondering what he looked like beneath those clothes, wondering how it would feel to . . .

Her eyes flicked back to his face. She was afraid he might suddenly open his eyes, see the look on her face and know what she was thinking. Seeing that he still slept, her white teeth caught at her lower lip and she continued her heartstopping examination of him.

His arms were strong and muscular. She could remember the feel of them around her, like bands of steel. And his legs, so strong and muscular . . . powerful.

She rose suddenly, feeling warm in the small, darkened bedroom.

"Stop this," she whispered to herself. Quickly she pulled a soft quilt over Dominic's legs and turned to leave the room. She glanced back once, her look wistful. And she wondered when he would be well, when she could go to him and put her arms around him, tell him that he had been right that day behind the kitchen.

She did want him as much as he wanted her. Every bit as much.

The day passed. Aimee peeked into Dominic's room several times and found him still sleeping soundly, Cilla's tea apparently working well. In the afternoon when Aimee stepped into his room one last time, she saw that he had turned over onto his side and his boots lay on the floor.

She smiled and stepped quietly back out the door, feeling confident that he was better.

In the heat of the afternoon, she walked to the stables and asked the young stable boy, Lucien, to drive her out to the fields in one of the wagons. Lucas was still nowhere in sight and she felt a small tug of worry. She hoped he had not been so angry with her this morning that he had run away to hide. He was a strange, moody little boy at times and she was anxious to find a tutor for him, someone who could keep him busy now that she and Dominic were occupied so much of the time with the cotton crops. That was one of the things she intended to discuss at supper.

The iron wheels of the wagon clattered and rattled as they drove out the sandy road through the slave quarters. Children ran out of the houses, smiling and waving at them as they passed, some of them tagging along behind the wagon.

Once at the fields, she didn't bother getting down from the wagon, but sat on the wooden seat surveying her people as they worked. She watched Gregory Davis carefully as he moved on his horse between the rows. She saw that he had not replaced the whip she'd taken from him, and as far as she knew, there had been no more incidents of his threatening any of the slaves. Still, she did not like the man. But as Dominic told her, it was not a requirement that she like him, only that she trust him to do his job. But she wasn't sure she trusted him any more than she liked him.

The workers did not look up as they worked chopping out the weeds from the cotton. From now until June they would have to be in the fields every day, constantly cultivating the plants with shovel plows, scrapers, and what they called scooties. That would help retain moisture around the still vulnerable plants.

Aimee looked up at the sky that was as clear and blank as a sheet of paper. They needed rain. The sun was lowering in the sky, but still the heat in the fields was stifling and the soil so dry that small clouds of dust drifted around the workers' feet as they worked. She could feel the perspiration on her neck and at the base of her skull where her hair lay heavily in its tightly wound coil.

She glanced toward the woods, thinking of the clear stream and the cool shade of the magnolia and live oak trees that surrounded it. She closed her eyes for a moment and visualized the small rippling waterfalls and moss-covered rocks, and she was tempted to go there if only to stick her feet into the water for a moment. If she had been on a horse instead of in the wagon with Lucien she might have done just that.

When Aimee returned to the house, the sun lay above the line of trees to the west. Still, there was no hint that the approaching darkness would bring relief from the heat. It was as hot and still as before. Not a leaf moved on the heavy trees around the house.

She lingered for a moment, letting her fingers trail over the fragrant rose blossoms, causing a cascade of fading petals to fall at her feet. She breathed in the fragrance of the roses, feeling the poignancy of the sultry Mississippi night as the sounds and scents stirred around her.

Her eyes moved automatically to the top level of the house, searching the windows of Dominic's room for any hint of light. And as she recalled his pain, she felt an unexpected wave of tenderness toward him.

This morning he had been so fierce and coldly arrogant at Compton's house. He had seemed fearless in the face of danger, his attitude that of a man accustomed to winning. She supposed that was why it had shaken her later to find him in his room, vulnerable and in pain.

She smiled to herself in the growing darkness. Oh yes, he'd almost had her convinced that he was unconquerable, until then.

She dressed very carefully that evening, making sure the lavender gauze dress fit just so before she stepped out onto the empty veranda. She hoped that Dominic would be at dinner, hoped that somehow he had miraculously recovered enough to laugh softly at her across the table during a quiet conversation, to

215

glance at her with those sultry black eyes and make her feel beautiful and womanly. But she tried not to expect it.

Just as she stepped onto the porch she saw Lucas running toward the house and she frowned, then smiled with indulgence.

"Lucas, you haven't even bathed yet. Didn't Amos tell you that I wanted you to dress properly for dinner tonight?"

"Yes, ma'am," he said, his voice breathless. "But I didn't know it was so late."

She glanced at the sky and sighed. "You didn't know it was so late, even when you saw that it was getting dark?

He shrugged and kicked the toe of his boot against the wooden porch.

"Well, it doesn't matter now," she added. "I'll sit here on the veranda and wait for you. But hurry, darling . . . and I'd be very pleased if you would wear a nice shirt and tie."

"Yes, ma'am, I'll hurry," he said, grinning at her as he ran across the porch toward the stairs.

Her gaze followed him and she frowned, realizing that he had not even bothered to tell her where he had been.

Nineteen

The sounds of the night surrounded the house. Aimee sat quietly on the veranda in the darkness, listening to the sounds and breathing in deeply the scent of magnolia and honeysuckle. She thought there had never been anything as beautiful or as provocative as a summer night in Mississippi.

She looked up to see Jezzy coming across the porch. In her hand was a lamp which she set on a table beside Aimee.

"They's carryin' supper in right now, missy," she said. "What you doin' sittin' out here in the dark?"

"Oh . . . just admiring the night," Aimee said, her voice soft and wistful. "And waiting for Lucas. He only came home a little while ago."

"Oh, well then, you want I should have them put your supper back in the warming oven?"

"No, it doesn't matter," Aimee said. "I'm sure he'll be down shortly. Jezzy . . . have you . . . do you know if Mister Dominic is still—"

"Still in his room?" Jezzy replied saucily. "Yes'm, last time I was up that way, he was. Want me to go see 'bout him?"

"No . . . no," Aimee replied. "I don't want to disturb him."

217

She tried to push away the disappointment she felt, tried to tell herself it didn't matter—she'd see him tomorrow. But as Jezzy turned to go, Aimee wished for a moment she had told her to go and find Dominic and ask if he felt like coming down to supper.

But instead she closed her eyes and leaned her head back against the chair as she waited for Lucas.

She didn't hear the soft footsteps across the veranda, didn't hear anything until Dominic's deep quiet voice sounded very near to her.

"You look beautiful tonight, Mrs. LeBeaux."

Aimee's eyes flew open and for a moment she thought she had been dreaming. He was standing there near the railing of the veranda, so close and yet far enough away that she could not see his eyes in the shadows.

His white shirt accentuated the darkness of his skin and made his hair look like ebony. The faint breeze carried his clean masculine scent toward her and seemed to make her heart beat faster.

Aimee sat forward in the chair and her mouth moved ineffectively; she had no idea what to say to him, or how to tell him all the things she wanted to say.

"Dominic . . ." she whispered. "I'm so happy you're here . . . I mean, it's wonderful that you're feeling better and . . ." His soft laughter stopped her stammering words and she shook her head, amused by her own awkwardness. He must think she had turned into a bumbling fool.

She stood up and walked to him, looking up into his face and trying to determine if he was indeed well or if he had dragged himself from his bed again by some sheer force of will.

"Are you really all right?" she asked. "Is the headache gone?" Without thinking she reached forward to touch his face.

His hand caught her wrist and he pulled her against him, letting his arm go around her waist in an easy, unhurried manner.

"Remind me to take to my bed more often, m'lady," he said, his voice quiet and warm. Then he laughed at her murmur of protest. "I'm teasing you," he said.

As Aimee stepped into the dim light of the veranda lamp, Dominic's breath caught in his chest. Something had changed about her, something that made his pulse quicken; his heart leapt at the sight of her emerald green eyes gazing up at him that way.

He reached out, pushing a wisp of hair away from the corner of her mouth. She still insisted on wearing her hair back in a severe fashion, but she couldn't control the dark wispy strands that came loose and curled about her face.

He thought that looking at her this way was an extra torment; being near her was a sweet torture that made his heart pound and threatened his ability to reason.

Her throat and shoulders in the dim light were beautiful . . . smooth and silky. He could see the slender column of her throat and the lovely dark hollows from her collarbone. And he found himself wanting desperately to put his lips there, to taste her skin, feel her soft gasps as he held her tightly against him.

Aimee knew with an uncertain joy what was happening between them. It was a moment such as she had never experienced with anyone. And even though this was what she wanted, what she had been thinking of for days, she felt as nervous and giddy as a new lamb.

She moistened her lips with the tip of her tongue, wanting to speak and not knowing quite what to say to this man who was a stranger and yet whom she felt she knew better than anyone in her life.

Dominic's eyes darkened as he watched her mouth and the quick glimpse of her tongue.

"Aimee," he groaned, pulling her into his arms. "If you still feel the way you did before . . . if what you felt for Jim is still between us, you'd better say so now." His voice was a whispered warning against her lips. "And we'd better go in to dinner unless you want me to make love to you right here . . . right now."

His voice was a husky, throaty growl and it sent hot sparks shooting through Aimee's body. Yes, she wanted to shout. I do want you to make love to me . . . here, now . . . anywhere.

With a soft murmur, she put her fingers in his hair, feeling the soft texture of it, and pulling his head down, intending to give him an answer he would never forget.

They both heard Lucas as he clamored down the stairs at the end of the veranda. Aimee pulled herself away from Dominic, feeling bereft without his arms around her, feeling sick with disappointment and need.

God, she thought, I was almost willing to let him take me right here and now, on the veranda floor if necessary, without a thought to who was in the house. That realization stunned her and she stepped away to stare up into his eyes as if to break the spell he held over her.

Even as Lucas came bounding toward them, Aimee could not take her eyes away from the fire in Dominic's black eyes. When he looked at her that way she felt her entire body growing hot and weak. And the mere thought of his mouth, the way it moved and tasted, was enough to send shivers of longing down her spine. Her feelings completely shocked her and fascinated her at the same time.

She had known the first time she saw him that he was dangerous, that with him she might never be able to retain the memory of her husband, the only man she'd ever loved. And that was why she had run from Dominic and fought with him. But was she really ready to let go . . . to give herself up to these powerful emotions? Even now, after she had admitted she wanted him, she had not let herself think that there was more to it than sexual need. She should never have let him stay; should never have allowed his black eyes to wander over her, igniting such sweet desire in her soul. For now, it was too late . . . too late.

"Hey," Lucas said. "What are you two doing out here? It's so dark I can hardly see."

Dominic's mouth curved in the darkness and he looked down at Aimee with a wry smile.

"Just waiting for you, Little Deer," he said, ruffling Lucas's hair. "Just waiting for you." Then he turned back to Aimee, offering her his arm, the message she saw in his gaze making her breathless.

"Mrs. LeBeaux," he murmured.

Aimee hardly tasted any of the food she ate for supper. She felt awkward, absolutely senseless at

221

times when Dominic looked at her from across the table.

It certainly helped that Lucas was there and she tried to focus on him and on the things she needed to say to him.

"Lucas, I think it's past time for us to find a tutor for you. You simply cannot continue to run through the woods and swamps like a wild thing. I'm afraid your education is sadly lacking already."

Aimee glanced at Dominic, remembering the night in the cemetery when he had told her angrily that Lucas would be in his charge now. She certainly didn't want to offend him, but she felt she still had some right where the boy was concerned.

Dominic pursed his lips and nodded his approval. "Exactly what kind of person do you have in mind?"

"Oh, I don't know," Aimee said thoughtfully. "An older lady perhaps, one with experience . . . someone who can teach Lucas about the arts and—"

"Oh no," Lucas protested, his dark eyes snapping at her. "I ain't about to start drawing any girly pictures. It's bad enough I have to wear these clothes sometimes. If I have a tutor like old Miss Fossil Face—"

"His last tutor," Aimee said with a wry look toward Dominic.

". . . please, Dominic," Lucas said, turning to his mentor for help. "Explain to her about women and about how all they want is to dress you up and teach you things like dancing and piano."

It was very difficult for Dominic to hide his smile as he looked at Aimee with a lift of his brows.

"Explain about women? Do I have to remind you that Aimee is a woman and that so far she's been willing to let us experiment with other things besides dancing and music."

"Yeah, I know. But Aimee . . . Aimee's different. She's real different since you came." Lucas was intent on his food and did not see the look that passed between Aimee and Dominic, nor the blush that colored Aimee's cheeks.

"Why thank you, Lucas . . . I think," she said.

"I think I might just know the perfect tutor for Lucas," Dominic said.

"You do?"

"Yes, I do. A young kid who worked on one of the riverboats. He was smart, well educated . . . he kept records for the captain, but I think he'd be more than wiling to come to LeBeaux for a while."

"Would that suit you better, Lucas," Aimee asked. "Having a young man as a tutor?"

"Yes, ma'am!"

"But let me warn you," she said with a smile. "I still expect you to learn music and art as well as all the other social graces." She turned to Dominic. "That is, if it's acceptable to Dominic."

"Of course it is," he said.

Lucas glanced at both of them and his brow furrowed slightly. "What's wrong with you two? You look funny. And you haven't had a fight in days."

Dominic leaned his head back and laughed loudly, shaking his head at the boy. "What indeed," he said. When he finally managed to stop laughing, he looked toward Aimee with a wicked, teasing grin.

They finished their supper and sat talking quietly as they waited for Jezzy to bring dessert.

"There is another item of business we need to discuss Aimee, besides Lucas's tutor."

"Oh? What's that?"

"It's fairly obvious that this feud with Compton is only going to get worse. Who knows what the man will try next. You know we're fairly defenseless here, with myself and Davis the only white men on the plantation."

"What about me?" Lucas asked.

"And of course Lucas," Dominic agreed. "But I've been thinking about hiring several men who could serve mostly as guards, although they would be available if we needed them for other duties as well."

Aimee shrugged. It was something she had considered herself after Jim's death, although she'd had no idea how to go about hiring such men.

"I agree," she said, frowning at the thought of their having to protect themselves this way.

"Good. Then I'll go to Natchez within the week . . . talk to the young man about tutoring Lucas and see how many men I can round up."

As the evening ended, Aimee could hardly keep her eyes away from Dominic. Did he intend to continue their earlier conversation on the veranda? She didn't want to be the one to send Lucas up to bed, but she found herself growing very impatient with the way the evening was dragging.

"Dominic," Lucas said as soon as he had finished his dessert. "I wanted to show you something. You know the bow you made me? Well, I made one just like it and it works! Can you come up to see it now?"

Dominic's eyes moved to Aimee. "Lucas, wouldn't you rather wait until morning?" he asked. "We could take it down to the creekbank and—"

"No, come now," Lucas pleaded, turning toward Aimee when he saw Dominic looking at her.

The Publishers of Zebra Books Make This Special Offer to Zebra Romance Readers...

AFTER YOU HAVE READ THIS BOOK WE'D LIKE TO SEND YOU 4 MORE FOR *FREE* AN $18.00 VALUE

NO OBLIGATION!

ONLY ZEBRA HISTORICAL ROMANCES "BURN WITH THE FIRE OF HISTORY" (SEE INSIDE FOR MONEY SAVING DETAILS.)

MORE PASSION AND ADVENTURE AWAIT... YOUR TRIP TO A BIG ADVENTUROUS WORLD BEGINS WHEN YOU ACCEPT YOUR FIRST 4 NOVELS ABSOLUTELY *FREE*
(AN $18.00 VALUE)

Accept your Free gift and start to experience more of the passion and adventure you like in a historical romance novel. Each Zebra novel is filled with proud men, spirited women and tempestuous love that you'll remember long after you turn the last page.

Zebra Historical Romances are the finest novels of their kind. They are written by authors who really know how to weave tales of romance and adventure in the historical settings you love. You'll feel like you've actually gone back in time with the thrilling stories that each Zebra novel offers.

GET YOUR FREE GIFT WITH THE START OF YOUR HOME SUBSCRIPTION

Our readers tell us that these books sell out very fast in book stores and often they miss the newest titles. So Zebra has made arrangements for you to receive the four newest novels published each month.

You'll be guaranteed that you'll never miss a title, and home delivery is so convenient. And to show you just how easy it is to get Zebra Historical Romances, we'll send you your first 4 books absolutely FREE! Our gift to you just for trying our home subscription service.

BIG SAVINGS AND FREE HOME DELIVERY

Each month, you'll receive the four newest titles as soon as they are published. You'll probably receive them even before the bookstores do. What's more, you may preview these exciting novels free for 10 days. If you like them as much as we think you will, just pay the low preferred subscriber's price of just $3.75 each. *You'll save $3.00 each month off the publisher's price.* AND, your savings are even greater because there are never any shipping, handling or other hidden charges—FREE Home Delivery. Of course you can return any shipment within 10 days for full credit, no questions asked. There is no minimum number of books you must b

4 FREE BOOKS

TO GET YOUR 4 FREE BOOKS WORTH $18.00 — MAIL IN THE FREE BOOK CERTIFICATE T O D A Y

Fill in the Free Book Certificate below, and we'll send your FREE BOOKS to you as soon as we receive it.

If the certificate is missing below, write to: Zebra Home Subscription Service, Inc., P.O. Box 5214, 120 Brighton Road, Clifton, New Jersey 07015-5214.

FREE BOOK CERTIFICATE

4 FREE BOOKS

ZEBRA HOME SUBSCRIPTION SERVICE, INC.

YES! Please start my subscription to Zebra Historical Romances and send me my first 4 books absolutely FREE. I understand that each month I may preview four new Zebra Historical Romances free for 10 days. If I'm not satisfied with them, I may return the four books within 10 days and owe nothing. Otherwise, I will pay the low preferred subscriber's price of just $3.75 each; a total of $15.00, *a savings off the publisher's price of $3.00.* I may return any shipment and I may cancel this subscription at any time. There is no obligation to buy any shipment and there are no shipping, handling or other hidden charges. Regardless of what I decide, the four free books are mine to keep.

NAME

ADDRESS _____ APT

CITY _____ STATE _____ ZIP

TELEPHONE (   )

SIGNATURE _____ (if under 18, parent or guardian must sign)

Terms, offer and prices subject to change without notice. Subscription subject to acceptance by Zebra Books. Zebra Books reserves the right to reject any order or cancel any subscription.

ZB0993

GET
FOUR
FREE
BOOKS

(AN $18.00 VALUE)

ZEBRA HOME SUBSCRIPTION
SERVICE, INC.
120 BRIGHTON ROAD
P.O. Box 5214
CLIFTON, NEW JERSEY 07015-5214

AFFIX
STAMP
HERE

Aimee said nothing, although she knew the disappointment was there in her eyes for Dominic to see.

"All right." Dominic's eyes lingered for a moment on Aimee's face and he nodded toward her. "Good night then, Aimee. We'll see you in the morning."

"Good night," she whispered.

Later, Aimee wandered along the veranda, feeling restless, almost as if she could cry. She really didn't understand why she could feel such intense disappointment. It wasn't as if she'd never see him again. Even Jezzy stared at her oddly when she found Aimee at the porch steps gazing out toward the garden.

"Miz Aimee?" Jezzy asked. "You all right? You seem awful quiet this evenin'."

"I'm all right, Jezzy," she replied, without even bothering to turn around.

"Well, you don't sound all right to me," Jezzy muttered. "You want I should have the mojo man make a charm for you? You seen how good Mister Dominic's worked . . . why he was well in no time . . . up and around . . . a big strappin' ve-rile man, just like before. Yes, ma'am. But it don't have to be no sickness what calls for a charm, you know. Mojo man can make a charm for just 'bout anything . . . love sickness . . . even the repressions like you got."

Aimee closed her eyes and sighed. "I don't have the 'repressions,' Jezzy, or anything else for that matter. I'm just tired. I won't be needing a charm or a *gris-gris*, or whatever else you call them."

"Well, all right," Jezzy said with a shrug of her shoulders. "I guess you knows if you got the mully grubs or not. If you say you don't, then I guess you don't. Ain't nothin' wrong with admittin' it if—"

"Jezzy, for heaven's sake," Aimee snapped.

225

"There's nothing wrong with me, except I'd like a little peace and quiet."

"Huh," Jezzy muttered before wandering back toward the kitchen.

Aimee sighed again and went to her room at the end of the veranda. But she knew she wouldn't be able to sleep and she didn't even bother to undress. Instead she walked the floor, wishing the restlessness would leave her, wishing she could think of something . . . anything, except Dominic's eyes and his lips, the way his body felt against hers.

She walked to one of the long windows and looked through the slatted shutters out toward the garden. The moon had risen and in the heated night air, its light was a warm, golden orange. A Natchez moon . . . the same kind of magical moon that had been shining the night Dominic came to LeBeaux. That night seemed so long ago . . . so many things had changed since then . . . *she* had changed. Dominic had made her change, forced her to feel emotions she thought were dead to her forever, and she knew that now she would never be the same again.

Finally, unable to find any rest, she turned up the oil lamp and found a book of poetry to read. But the romanticism of the words, the real emotions the poetry elicited in her were simply too painful, and she put the book aside.

She had almost decided to go out into the garden again, when she heard a very light tap at her door.

Her heart fluttered for a moment before she finally commanded her legs to move and her fingers to turn the door latch.

He was there. Standing in the shadows with the moonlight at his back, Dominic looked tall and

226

daunting. He leaned toward her, resting his hand on the door frame beside her head. His softly spoken words were like the sound of a warm, sultry wind through the trees in summer.

"Aimee," he said, his voice husky and full of emotion. "I meant what I said earlier. If you still feel guilty about Jim . . . if I've misinterpreted what's been happening between us these past few days . . . then tell me now. Just tell me to go and I'll close this door and never mention it to you again."

Aimee's heart was full of wonder. How could she be feeling all these confusing emotions at the same time? He was sweet and patient with her, yet sometimes his fierce masculinity was almost frightening.

He was the most sexual, most desirable man she'd ever met; she'd never felt such overwhelming desire, not even for Jim. And she thought she *should* feel guilty about that. But beneath the heat of his gaze, she couldn't make herself feel guilt, she could feel nothing except desire, could think of nothing except how it would feel to make love to him, wanting to feel and taste and savor everything about him.

"No," she whispered, reaching forward to take his hand. "Please . . . I don't want you to go . . . not tonight . . . not ever."

Twenty

Aimee backed into her room, pulling him with her, watching the hungry look that flared in his eyes. She could feel the blood rushing through her veins like liquid fire as she realized what was happening. It was quiet in this end of the house and only the muted sounds of night creatures drifted in, or the cry of an owl far in the distance.

And now that he was here, now that her dream was becoming a reality, she felt herself begin to tremble. She was afraid of so many things . . . of being too inexperienced to please him, of not being beautiful enough in his eyes, or desirable enough. She had never made love to anyone except Jim and those experiences were all she had with which to measure and compare.

Jim . . . with his quiet soulful eyes, his look of apology as if he was afraid he might hurt her. How many nights she had wanted him to take her in his arms and fulfill all her wildly passionate longings, to love her with no regard for anything except the moment.

He was not like Dominic . . . never like this man.

She held her breath as Dominic stepped closer to her, his hands moving to caress her throat and the curve of her breasts above her dress.

"Oh," she whispered. The quiet cry that rushed from her lips surprised even her. She had not expected to feel so breathless, so completely and totally out of control.

As if he could not wait another moment to feel her in his arms, Dominic pulled her against him, crushing her mouth beneath his, kissing her with deep, hungry kisses that left her weak and breathless . . . left her longing for more.

His fingers fumbled roughly in her hair, pulling the pins free with an impatience that excited her. She heard his soft murmur of pleasure as he let the weight of her loose hair fall down her back and over his hands.

"God, Aimee," he whispered against her hair. "Do you know how many nights I've lain awake up there in that room thinking of this moment . . . being so close to you . . . wanting you and knowing you were not within my reach."

His words thrilled her and warmed her. "I know," she whispered. "I felt it, too." She let her arms slide around his waist, pulling herself closer to him and feeling with exquisite pleasure the length of his body against hers. She had told herself so many times how she would react to this moment, how she would remain in control. And when she finally admitted that she wanted him, had to have him, she had even told herself she would allow only one night with him. One night to get him out of her dreams and out of her thoughts for good. And yet now she found herself quickly losing grip on the control that she sought so desperately.

His kisses were brutally sweet, at once ravishing

229

and tender, kisses that left her weak and hungry for more. The days, the weeks of waiting, of seeing him every day, had taken their toll on her senses. Now that he was here in her arms, she could not seem to get enough of him. And she could feel his own excitement at her ready response.

His hands were at the back of her dress, moving expertly over the small buttons. But when one of them refused to give, Dominic cursed softly beneath his breath and ripped the dress free, mindless of anything else but what he sought.

For a second as the dress fell away, Dominic hesitated, stepping back from her as she stood before him in delicate silk and lace. His eyes took in every inch of her small, curvaceous body. Slowly he lifted his eyes to hers and in them she saw so many things . . . desire and wonder, admiration. And when he slipped off his jacket and began to unbutton the studs of his shirt, she stood very still watching his dark fingers, feeling a pulse begin to beat deep within her as each button revealed more of the dark, smoothly muscled chest. And then her hands reached restlessly to help him.

"In all my life," he whispered, his voice soft and husky, "I've never wanted anyone the way I want you, Aimee . . . never."

She could hear the sound of his breathing, the heavy rasp of desire in his voice, and she stepped into his arms again, anxious to feel his naked skin against hers.

They moved toward the bed, hardly conscious of their movements. Aimee could feel his fingers shaking with impatience as he untied the ribbons at her shoulders, then his lips kissed the bare skin there, and trailed lower to her breasts. Slowly, with tantalizing kisses, surely meant to drive her insane, he pushed away the lacy material and his lips followed, until finally she was trembling from head to toe and the garment fell away from her into a soft mound at her feet.

She heard Dominic's swift intake of air; he was driving her crazy . . . making her want to beg, to cry out at the sweet, torturous movements of his hands. They caressed expertly and his mouth tormented her with a promise of what was to happen next.

"Tell me what you want," he whispered as he lowered her onto the bed.

She arched against him, offering him her breasts, feeling the heat of his mouth and his hands. Her hands went to his head and she pulled the leather tie away from his black hair, letting it fall against her naked skin, then winding her fingers into the soft silky depths of it as a cry escaped her lips.

"You know what I want, Dominic," she gasped. "Now . . . oh, please . . . now."

The waiting was becoming the sweetest torture, the sensation of fire and liquid so strong that it was consuming them both. And he was deliberately making her feel things that were too much . . . too sweet . . . too threatening to her heart and soul.

"Tell me," he insisted, torturing her. "Say it, Aimee," he demanded. "God, I have to hear you say it once and for all."

His eyes stared down into hers and for a moment he was still and waiting. The deep black eyes, so heated with desire were demanding and arrogant. She had rejected him before and now he was exacting his own sweet revenge. Having her was not going to be enough; he demanded more . . . he wanted her admission that what was between them was extraordinary, that this moment was as heartstopping for her as it was for him. And he had to hear her admit it.

"I want you," she whispered, moving against him, almost wild now with an urgency to feel him inside her.

He kissed her again, his lips capturing hers in a soft, sweet kiss that promised more, laughing softly when her mouth reached for his again as he pulled away.

"Tell me," he demanded fiercely against her mouth.

"Oh, God, Dominic, please . . ." She gasped softly, reaching for his mouth, putting her arms around his neck and writhing against him. "Love me," she cried finally. "I want you to make love to me, Dominic . . . love me . . . love me."

His black eyes were triumphant as they held hers and with a soft groan he obeyed, his body finally capturing hers, and making her cry out with pleasure and fulfillment. The storm that overtook them both was wildly passionate and overpowering, surpassing all her expectations and making her forget everything except the sensations and the feel of his arms, and his powerful body.

Aimee gave herself up completely to him, and to the passion and desire that both of them were feeling. She had waited so long for this . . . all her life it seemed.

She thought she had known before what desire was, thought she had experienced everything there was about the physical love between a man and a woman. But she was wrong . . . so very wrong. His abandon excited her beyond reason, and sent a wild storm rushing through . . . a storm that made her feel reckless and completely out of control. The words he whispered in her ear were hot, untamed words of love, words that made her cling to him weakly, made her want to give him everything he asked for and more.

It was like a summer storm that rose quickly and swooped across the sky, lifting both of them higher and higher until she felt herself crying out with pleasure and surprise, until bright lights exploded behind her closed eyelids and spread in a hot rush through her entire body. And then she felt Dominic's response and heard his harsh cry of delight.

Was this death? Was this wonderful, beautiful experience of drifting away in a pleasurable storm what death was like?

"Dominic," she whispered, kissing his neck and his face. "Oh, Dominic."

She looked up into his eyes, black eyes that were quiet now and filled with such tenderness that she'd never have thought it possible. How odd to see those fierce eyes looking at her in such a way.

"You are so beautiful," he whispered, bending to kiss her lips.

She thought there was also a glimpse of pain in those eyes and for the first time she remembered how sick he had been.

"Oh, Dominic," she said, putting her fingers tenderly against his temple. "Are you all right? Is your headache—"

He smiled and took her fingers, bringing them to his lips. "I'm fine," he whispered, kissing her mouth

233

again. "More than fine." He shifted his weight away from her and pulled her into his arms, cradling her head against his chest and letting his fingers move through her long dark hair.

They lay quietly, their passion spent, the wild tension that had been between them for days finally at rest. She thought both of them slept for a few moments, but she woke first to the strange feel of a man's arms around her, of a man's naked body against hers. And she frowned at the quickening feeling of warmth and desire that rushed again to her heart.

This was not what she intended. She never meant to feel anything except relief and pleasure. She had thought she could make love to him once, and rid herself of this constant gnawing desire that she felt for him. Get it out of her heart and soul for good. But it hadn't worked that way . . . making love with him had only magnified those feelings and that was something that frightened her to death. This couldn't last . . . nothing in life as wonderful as this could possibly last.

She tried to put aside those thoughts that kept coming again and again, that had sometimes kept her awake at night. Terrible thoughts of what she would do if she lost Dominic, too.

She turned to look at his face and saw his black eyes watching her. He smiled and reached forward to kiss her, making her shiver, making her feel surprise that she wanted him again so soon.

His face was beautiful and his male nakedness breathtaking, but she found that besides the obvious, she actually liked him. For all his stubbornness and fierce pride, she had discovered him to be honest and good, a man who didn't shy away from hard work, a man with honor and character. And as she looked at him, she thought Jim had not told her everything about Dominic Valcour . . . not by half.

"What were you thinking, angel?" he asked. "Your green eyes change like the colors of the sea."

She shook her head, thinking she *should* feel shame and guilt for the unabandoned intimacy that had just passed between them. But she felt none of that; she felt free . . . and happy.

"Just thinking how beautiful you are," she whispered, letting her fingers trail down his face to his sensuous lips.

"Dear God," he groaned with a wry smile. "The girl's lost her mind."

"No," she whispered with a bemused shake of her head. "You are so . . . handsome . . . so perfect; this night with you was perfect. Oh . . . I never knew it could be this way between a man and a woman . . . never."

He smiled and pulled her closer against him. "What way?"

Aimee took a deep breath, afraid she had made a mistake. It had been good between them—breathtakingly good, and she didn't want Dominic to think that this meant he was committed to her in some way. He'd never want that and she didn't want her enthusiasm to send him away.

She snuggled against him, saying nothing, and determined not to let him see how much this night had meant to her.

Dominic relished the exquisite feel of her body against his and he sighed. He felt as if he never wanted to let her leave his arms. Not now after what had happened between them, after feeling the weight of her hair against his hands and looking into those green eyes in that first sweet, incredible moment when her body had accepted his with such sweet passion. So many times in his life, he had made love to a woman, only to find that moments later, he regretted it, and that after the heat of desire faded, there was nothing left between them.

But God, that wasn't true with this woman. And he knew it would never be true. Making love to Aimee brought an entirely different meaning to the phrase . . . and he knew that in all his wanderings, this was what he had been seeking. This place . . . Aimee, made him feel at last as if he'd come home.

He smiled down at her, watching her eyes, and seeing her mind at work as she tried to think of how to respond to his question.

"You didn't answer me," he teased. "What way?"

"You know," she said. Her voice was quiet as she struggled to find words that would not turn him away. "So wild, so exciting . . . that a woman could enjoy . . . sex with a man and feel this way without being married, without being in love."

She was so intent on explaining that she did not feel him tense beside her, did not feel the slight pulling away of his body as he stared hard at her face.

"It's the best of both worlds, don't you think?" she asked, turning to look into his eyes. "Being able to love this way . . . with no commitments . . ."

Dominic shook his head as if to try and clear her words from his mind. Without being in love? No commitments? Well, what the hell had he expected.

His smile was polite as he pulled away and swung his legs over the edge of the bed. He stood up and walked across to his clothes, not seeming at all modest about his male nakedness.

"Yeah," he muttered softly. "The best of both worlds."

Aimee watched him, letting her eyes wander over him, enjoying the sight of his lean, muscular body. She liked the way the muscles in the small of his back moved when he walked, the way he moved so quietly, with the grace of a cat. She wondered what everyone would say if they could see her now, openingly admiring a man's naked body and remembering how it had felt against hers. Would she be considered a harlot for the way she felt about this man?

Surprisingly she found that she didn't care . . . she wanted him more than she'd ever wanted anything and she was delirious with happiness that he wanted her, too. If that made her a fallen woman, she just didn't care.

Her eyes widened as she watched him dress and she felt a sharp twinge of disappointment. She had assumed they would fall asleep together, wake together in each other's arms.

"Where . . . where are you going?"

His head turned only slightly and he looked at her from the corner of his eye. "I should go back to my room, don't you think . . . for propriety's sake? After all, you have a certain reputation in the community. I wouldn't want to take a chance on damaging that."

Did he seem cold . . . distant? Was the glitter she saw now in his eyes ice instead of fire?

"But, Dominic . . ." she protested, sitting up in bed and staring at him.

He walked back to her. She thought his smile was wan and forced and she frowned at him, wondering what she had done to displease him.

"It's all right, angel," he said. "You've won. You see before you a defeated man." He spread his arms and bowed slightly with an odd teasing smile on his face.

He bent to kiss her lips lightly, then turned to go. "I'll see you in the morning."

She sat up straighter in bed, staring at him as he walked toward the door. "But, Dominic . . . wait."

The protest on her lips faded away and she was left alone in the room, in the complete and empty silence, as if he had never even been there.

"Won?" she said aloud. *"I've* won? What on earth does he mean? He stormed into my life . . . into my heart. He came into my bedroom and made me weak with desire, made me beg him to . . ." She stopped and her lips trembled as she remembered her wild desperation earlier. Her eyes closed as she gave in for a moment to the flood of emotion that rushed over her at the thought of his lovemaking. "I've lost everything, Dominic," she whispered. "Lost my reasoning, my sanity . . . I've lost my heart . . . don't you know that?"

She felt hot tears stinging her eyes as she stared at the door. His leaving made her feel abandoned and confused. It made her wonder if this night with him had been a mistake after all. Then she stepped out of bed and reached for a wrapper which she tied loosely around her naked body.

She hadn't been mistaken about his passion or his desire, she knew that instinctively. He had wanted her just as desperately as she had wanted him. Then what was it?

She was certain the look of tenderness in his eyes afterward was real . . . the sweet way his hands caressed her face, the way he looked at her.

"Dominic," she whispered, turning to the door. For a moment she actually considered going after him, going to his room and demanding to know what she had done wrong. What she had done to make him suddenly pull away and become cold and distant. But she couldn't do that . . . she couldn't beg him.

"Damn you," she muttered, trying to push away her feelings of restless desperation. "Damn you, Dominic Valcour, for what you've done to me. What else do you want from me? You made me want you; I never meant this to happen. You made me love you and now even that is not enough."

It was just as she had feared. He had come into her heart like a storm, making her love him wildly, and now he probably would be on his way, back to the life he'd had before. *He* was the one who had won. And she wondered, now that he had conquered her, was he ready to move on to the next challenge?

Twenty-one

Dominic stalked across the veranda, mindless of the sound his heavy footsteps made against the wood floor or of who might awaken and wonder where he'd been. He took the steps at the end of the veranda, two at a time, walking into his room and closing the door before flinging the jacket he carried across the room.

"Goddamn it!" he hissed between clenched teeth. "Stupid, mindless fool," he muttered, stalking the room like a caged tiger. "Did you think this night would change anything with her? Did you actually think she would simply fall into your arms and declare her undying love? God! What a fool you are . . . damned half-witted fool! The best of both worlds, my ass," he growled in self-derision.

He walked to a chair across the room and fell into it, stretching his long legs out in front of him in a restless gesture.

"Aimee LeBeaux is not the kind of woman to fall in love with a man like you," he continued softly. "A renegade half-breed . . . a gambler . . . a man with no important family connections. Hell! I could be rich as Croesus and what would it matter? Can't you see she'd never marry a man like you?"

He stopped for a moment and frowned. He had never actually used those words before. He'd never let the word *marriage* linger in his mind for more than a moment, much less said it out loud. But there it was . . . his admission of what he really wanted, of what Aimee made him want, more desperately than he'd ever wanted anything in his life. He wanted her and he wanted this plantation and Lucas. A home and family, with only one woman . . . with Aimee.

"Jesus!" he swore, coming to his feet and running his fingers restlessly through his hair. He jammed his hands into his pockets and stalked angrily across the floor.

If he had bothered to find out what she wanted before tonight, he might have prevented all this. It would have been easier just to ride away from LeBeaux and from her than to have to face this gut-wrenching reality, after knowing the sweetness of loving her.

He had thought himself past being shocked about anything. But he was stunned that Aimee considered him good enough to sleep with, yet nothing more—but she had made it perfectly clear tonight that she had no intention of it being anything more. Sex . . . without marriage . . . without love. She had said it all.

"What a laugh," he whispered. It was the way he had lived his life . . . dangerously, always on the run with no ties, no commitments. Well, the tables had certainly turned, hadn't they?

He sighed heavily and shook his head. It was too late now; it was too late to ride away from here and away from her. He was in way over his head

241

this time and he'd hardly even seen it coming, fool that he was.

And the question was, what was he going to do about it?

Quietly he opened the door and stepped out onto the balcony into the dappled moonlight, letting the sounds of the night soothe him and blot out his thoughts. He could see a faint glimmer of light through the slatted shutters of Aimee's bedroom windows. He took a long, slow breath, letting himself remember, letting the breathtaking image of her flash before his eyes. Her eyes and lips, the quiet little moans she'd made when he made love to her, the feel and texture of her beautiful black hair. There was a sweetness to her, a scent and taste that was hers . . . hers alone. And he couldn't seem to get it out of his mind.

"Lord," he whispered. He thought he could die in those eyes. Simply float away and die on that cloud of silken hair, and never make a sound of protest.

His eyes narrowed and he frowned.

He was in love . . . he was goddamned in love!

He grunted and raked his hand through his hair as he let the thought soak in.

Aimee was willing to be a part of his life, more than willing to have him make love to her it seemed. And it was ironic that he wanted more than that . . . more perhaps than she would ever be willing to give. Could he settle for that? For being with her every day as a business partner, then stealing into the darkness of her room at night when the house was quiet. Making sweet, hot love to her in secrecy?

He frowned and glanced again toward her room. Closing his eyes, he could almost feel her in his arms, could smell the scent of her perfume that still clung to his body.

"Yes damn it," he whispered to the night. If that was all he could have with her, then it would have to be enough. For God help him, he loved her, and there was no turning back as far as he was concerned . . . no leaving LeBeaux *or* its beautiful mistress.

When Aimee woke the next morning, she stretched languidly and turned over with a smile. But seeing the empty bed and the rumpled pillow, she frowned and pushed the mosquito netting back.

She had been dreaming . . . sweet, sexual dreams about Dominic and for a moment she thought he was still here beside her.

She was surprised that she had slept so soundly. Last night after he left, she could think of nothing except him and the way he'd made her feel. And she had wondered why he left so suddenly.

After taking a long, slow bath, she dressed, her mind turning again to Dominic. She found herself nervous with anticipation at seeing him again and she hoped that this morning things would miraculously be right between them again. The last few days had been tense ones, and he had been nearly killed. Perhaps they both were a little tired and that was all there was to it.

She chose a summery dress of lightweight cotton. It was going to be another hot day it seemed; the early morning air was already warm and humid. When Jezzy came to help her into the dress, Aimee turned before the long mirror, admiring the color of the gown and the way the pale pink material seemed to bring out the color in her cheeks. The skirt, featuring four flounces, fell softly to the floor and at the puffed sleeves were streamers of rose-colored ribbons that fluttered about her bare arms when she walked.

"You is a sight in that dress," Jezzy declared. "Yes, ma'am, a pure indeedy sight!"

"Why, thank you, Jezzy," Aimee said with a mock curtsy. "It's not too much is it . . . too young and little girlish?"

Jezzy's eyes widened as she took in Aimee's voluptuous breasts and tiny waist.

"Little girl ain't 'xactly what I'd call it, missy." Jezzy nodded wisely as she glanced up and down her mistress's figure. "Mister Dominic would say you is an allurin' woman."

Aimee laughed. "Oh? Is that what he tells you?"

At Aimee's teasing, Jezzy sniffed with an air of authority. "Mister Dominic is a gentleman and he has been knowed to compliment a woman."

"Oh yes," Aimee said with a sudden catch in her throat. "I'm sure he has."

Later when Aimee walked into the dining room, she stopped, seeing Dominic's dark head bent as he sat at the table talking to Lucas. Just the sight of him made her heart begin to pound, and she had to take a quick short breath to regain her composure.

Dominic looked up slowly, his eyes moving up from the flounced skirt of her dress, to the swell of her breasts. His dark lashes flickered and stopped when his eyes met hers. Then he smiled and rose from the table to come around and take her hand.

"Good morning," he said. His dark, knowing eyes gazed into hers and the sound of his sensual voice sent shivers down her spine.

"Good morning," she managed to whisper.

The touch of his hand was warm and reassuring as he walked with her to the table where she took her place beside Lucas.

"Good morning, Lucas," she said. Silently she warned herself; she sounded so breathless, almost as if she had just come immediately from her bed . . . and Dominic's arms.

Lucas was busy eating, but he managed to give her a smile and a quick wave as he continued with his meal.

"Boy," he said after he had swallowed his food. "You look really nice today, Aimee." His eyes were bright as he gazed at her. "Don't she, Dom?"

"Doesn't she," Dominic corrected. "And yes, she does look especially nice this morning." His eyes told her that he remembered last night, that he remembered everything, and she found herself blushing as she poured a cup of tea.

Inwardly, Aimee breathed a sigh of relief. Dominic seemed fine this morning; the coolness she'd seen in his eyes last night when he left her room, was gone. His look, his quiet easy conversation . . . everything about the way he acted, convinced her that she had worried unnecessarily. They were going to be fine.

And so she was a bit surprised when he left immediately after breakfast, telling her he had some business to attend. He made no mention of her going with him, and with this new, fragile relationship between them, she could not find the courage to demand what his mission was, or to ask if she might go along. She simply stood by with a small frown of disquiet as she watched him leave with Lucas at his side.

Several times that day, when Dominic and Lucas had not returned, Aimee was thankful that she had plenty in the house to occupy her time.

She had all the carpets and rugs rolled up and stored in the attic for summer, and while the golden cypress floors were being scrubbed, she set herself the task of polishing the crystal and silver epergne as well as the silver punch bowl and tea set that sat on the dining-room sideboard. She had donned a long white apron to help protect her dress and a pair of cotton gloves to keep her nails from becoming grimy and broken.

She was almost finished when she heard the sound of riders coming toward the front of the house. She walked into the wide hallway and out onto the front porch, surprised at her feeling of relief when she saw Lucas and Dominic riding up the drive. For some reason she felt today the same way she had when Dominic first came, as if he and Lucas were very close . . . a family even, and she merely an observer.

Supper that evening seemed nothing out of the ordinary. She learned that Dominic and Lucas had ridden to the DeVaull Plantation to see a new piece of equipment. And again, she felt a pang of regret that they had not included her in their plans. She would have enjoyed seeing Jenny and Mrs. De-

Vaull, sitting for a long, quiet afternoon on the shady porch of their home.

That night in her bed, she lay awake for what seemed like hours, wondering if Dominic would come to her. She had been certain at first that he would, but as the night grew on and the house became silent, she knew with a heart-wrenching disappointment that he was not coming.

The next morning he was already away from the house when she took breakfast. That day was one of the worst she could remember. She felt restless and melancholy . . . she had no energy to do anything and she found herself watching the road at the back of the house and listening for any sound of riders coming in from the fields.

What was wrong with her anyway? Had she expected what happened between her and Dominic to change things? She winced, remembering that she had been the one to say they had the best of both worlds, with no marriage and no commitments. She had intended to put him at ease with that remark and let him know that she would put no pressure on him to conform to the standards of the society that he so obviously despised.

Her heart fluttered when she remembered adding that there was no love. Had that hurt him? She hardly thought so, not a man like Dominic. She would think that love and commitment were the last things he was looking for. But she wanted him on any terms, and had already decided that was how it would have to be.

But now, she wasn't sure anymore what she expected. She was just as confused about herself and her relationship with Dominic as she'd been at the beginning.

The weather continued extremely hot and dry over the next few days. Gregory Davis told them that the young cotton plants needed plenty of moisture and sunshine while the cultivating was going on. But looking up at the relentless sun and clear, faded blue sky, Aimee was beginning to worry. The dry spell couldn't have come at a worse time, just before the plants began blooming. And Aimee was afraid that if they didn't get rain soon, there would be very few blossoms to produce the cotton bolls.

One afternoon she rode out to the fields, as much out of restlessness as anything. She still could not understand Dominic's distant behavior. He was warm and sweet, very attentive and complimentary at the house, yet still he had not come again to her room, had not even mentioned what was between them except for an occasional quiet, teasing remark. Sometimes she would catch him watching her and there would be a look in his eyes, almost a wistful, haunted look. Then he'd see her looking at him and he'd smile and the look would be gone.

And now Aimee was beginning to wonder if he regretted what had happened between them, or worse, that she had been correct in her first assessment of him as a man who took his pleasure with women wherever he could find it.

That day in the fields, Lucas was there. Dominic had insisted that he learn all he could about growing cotton and that included doing some of the work. Aimee smiled as she watched him toiling in the hot sun along with the slaves. Some of them smiled at him, too, when he grumbled or when he made numerous trips to the water bucket.

She didn't see Dominic and even though his absence made her feel empty and melancholy, she could hardly ask Gregory Davis where he was. Her eyes wandered to the woods and she smiled, thinking of the cool stream and the shade of the huge trees.

Why not, she thought. It had been a very long time since she simply sat on a creekbank with nothing more to do than dangle her feet in the cool water.

Slowly she turned her horse away from the workers, riding out to the end of the rows and across the field toward the woods. As she approached the beckoning shade, she reached behind her head and took the pins out of her hair, letting it fall down her back.

Once at the stream, she tied the horse's reins to a tree limb and sauntered casually along the sandy banks. Here the air felt damp, and moved like a warm, fragrant opiate through the trees. The smell of hot, rich soil mingled with the scent of pine-woods and magnolia blossoms. The effects caused a soft languor in Aimee that crept through her blood, and she knew that this place, this rich, Southern land was something an outsider could never understand.

They might feel its magic and admire its beauty, but only one Mississippi born and bred could truly embrace it and have such a fierce pride in its possession.

Aimee took off her shoes, neatly placed her stockings in them, and set them on the bank. She

249

stepped gingerly into the water, closing her eyes and breathing a quiet sigh of pleasure at its coolness.

The dry weather had lowered the water and most places were shallow enough to walk in. She kicked her feet as she walked, watching the dark muddy green water swirl around her legs. She stopped once, thinking she heard something ahead of her toward the small waterfalls. But after hearing nothing else, she continued on, enjoying the different wildflowers that grew along the banks and the sound of the birds high in the trees above her.

When a tiny mud turtle leapt with a splash from a rock, Aimee jumped and squealed. Then laughing, she gathered her skirts higher, noticing that much of her hem had already become darkened with water. She was still smiling when she ducked her head beneath a low hanging tree limb and looked toward the quiet spray of the falls.

"Oh!" There was a man standing in the pool at the bottom of the falls.

Dominic had turned to watch her approach, having heard her laughter. He stood waist deep in the water and his naked body glistened in the light that filtered down through the dark canopy of huge trees. Behind him the small waterfall rose no more than eight feet; its water splashed and sprayed in a glistening cascade over moss-covered rocks.

The sight of him there in the primitive setting, gloriously beautiful in his nakedness almost took Aimee's breath away.

She couldn't speak. She was entranced . . . mesmerized by the sight of him, and she could not have looked away if she wanted to. He was perfect in masculine appeal, she thought . . . perfectly formed and muscular, his skin dark and sleek from the water. And he was smiling at her with a look that made her heart skip crazily in her chest.

"I . . . I'm sorry," she stammered. "I didn't know you . . . I didn't know anyone was here."

"Why don't you join me?" he asked, his eyes sparkling with an amused challenge. "After the hot sun, the water is quite refreshing."

"Yes," she said, her voice breathless and uncertain. "I'm sure it is, but . . ."

"Come on," he urged, lifting his hand toward her.

"It's too deep," she protested, gazing down at her dress. "And my clothes . . . my dress—"

"Ah," he said, pushing his way toward her through the sparkling water. "If that's the only problem, we can fix that easily enough."

She watched him come nearer, stared at him openmouthed as he walked closer and into the more shallow water.

"No, Dominic," she said, her eyes darting down the contoured muscles of his chest and sleek, flat stomach, then lower as he continued his march toward her. "You . . . you're . . ."

He didn't seem to mind at all that he was naked; in fact, she thought he rather enjoyed it. He was smiling and on his face was a devilish look.

"Why, angel," he said, his voice soft and taunting. "You've seen me this way before." He came to stand before her, tall and imposing, beautiful and bronzed like some wild god of nature.

She could smell the water on his skin, could feel the coolness of it reaching out to her like a sweet beckoning caress.

His wet fingers moved to the buttons of her riding habit, pushing the material aside with cool determination. She pushed at his fingers and when she murmured a soft protest, he bent to stop her words with his kiss. Her took her hands, holding them away, and taking her lips in a long thorough kiss until she was breathless and trembling.

"And might I remind you, love," he whispered against her mouth, "that I've also seen every inch of your very beautiful . . . very desirable body."

Twenty-two

He continued his slow, provocative assault on her senses with his lips, with his whispered words and with cool wet fingers that expertly unbuttoned and undressed.

It was the cool water that made her tremble so, she told herself. She had long stopped protesting and instead found herself moving closer to him, placing her hands on his in silent urgency. When Dominic stepped to the bank to drape her clothes across a tree limb, Aimee closed her eyes, giving in to the liberating feeling of standing naked in the water with the warm breeze against her bare skin. She felt Dominic behind her, felt the strength of his arms as they slid around her waist and moved upward to cup her breasts and pull her back against him.

She found herself completely under his spell as he turned her in his arms to kiss her neck and leaving a sizzling trail upward across her cheek as his mouth moved toward hers. She found she had no more thought of protest, no more worries about why he had not come to her sooner. All she could think of was the moment and the wonder of being in his strong arms once again.

She laughed when he pulled her out into the water. He was watching her with those incredible black eyes, smiling at her as he pulled her closer toward the deep pool beneath the falls. Then he stepped away into the deeper water and his hands lifted, palms up to implore her silently to come to him.

She kicked her feet away from the sandy bottom, swimming toward him and gasping with surprise as the cool water sluiced over her hot skin. She came up directly in front of him, letting her hands slide up the side of his hips to his waist and feeling his fingers close around her forearms to steady her against him. There near the falls, they could feel the spray of the water as it cascaded off the rocks behind them. Its sound drowned out all other sounds of the forest and made their voices seem intimate and close, made them seem completely alone and isolated from the rest of the world.

He held her away for a moment when she wanted to move into his arms and she looked up at him with a slight frown.

"Now," he said with a slow, devilish smile. "I will teach you about being a warrior's woman."

She lifted her eyebrows and smiled.

"Oh, really?" she said. "Are you a warrior then, Mister Valcour? A fierce, savage warrior who would terrorize a poor, defenseless woman?"

"Terrorize?" he whispered, bending to kiss her wet lips. "Never, love . . . never."

"All right," she said, feigning a defeated pose. "Then I suppose you must teach me what you will."

He stood straighter in the water, looking down at

her through narrowed eyes and assuming the authoritative position of a warrior. She smiled, waiting as he removed his hands from her arms and stepped backward. Being much shorter, Aimee had to move her hands back and forth in the water to remain on her feet and she smiled at him, wondering exactly what he intended.

"When a warrior chooses a woman—"

"Have I been chosen, then?" Her voice was quiet and almost breathless as she asked the teasing question. "Am I a warrior's woman?"

"Yes," he said with a solemn nod, still keeping to the pretense. "You are the woman of Blackfox, the Choctaw warrior—Sarnee."

Her eyes widened as she looked at him standing there chest deep in the water. With his black hair sleek and wet and with the sun making gleaming streaks across his bronzed skin, she thought he looked like a warrior. And she thought the name Blackfox suited him very well. He looked as imposing as the Indian she had seen in the canes . . . and every bit as dangerous.

"Sarnee," she whispered.

"Your duty is to obey . . . in all matters," he continued, his black eyes burning into hers. He reached forward to touch her breasts, letting his fingers caress and tease. "The Choctaw warrior is ruler of his hut and of his woman . . . in all matters, even those of intimacy. I may touch you, but you . . ." He lifted his finger as a warning when she leaned toward him. ". . . you may touch . . . only on my command."

"Dominic . . ." she protested, smiling and shaking her head.

He stood straighter, feigning a fierce, haughty look until she grimaced and lowered her hands submissively into the water.

"All right." she muttered. "All right. I am yours to command."

"Now . . ." He stepped forward, dipping his hands beneath the water, smiling as she gasped and closed her eyes. His hands, warm within the coolness of the water, moved over her entire body, touching, caressing, enticing her, until she thought she would die if she could not lift her hands to touch him in return.

"Dominic," she gasped, her eyes begging him to stop the pretense.

He smiled and bent his head to kiss her, moving her hands away when they reached to touch his chest. She found the game to be a tantalizing one . . . torturous and sweetly forbidden. And his warning that she must not touch him made her almost crazy to do just that. When his hands and mouth became more demanding, she groaned and moved closer. Her skin was hot . . . hot enough, she thought to heat the cool water around them, and all she could think of, all she wanted was to touch him, to feel the smooth, muscled texture of his skin beneath her fingers.

"Dominic . . ." she whispered again. "Enough . . . please. . . ."

"Sarnee," he commanded against her mouth.

"Sar . . . Sarnee," she managed.

She felt his teeth biting at her lower lip before the kiss became deeper, all consuming, and she felt her knees buckle beneath her.

Her hands fluttered toward him and suddenly

Dominic took her wrists, putting her arms behind her back and holding her with one hand while the other arm went around to lift her from the water. She made a quiet sound of pleasure as she felt the trail of his mouth and tongue against her breasts and down her rib cage. And when his lips touched and teased down the soft curve of her belly, she groaned and tried to pull her hands free of his hard grasp.

She felt she couldn't possibly stand another moment of his sweet torment; she was going to shatter into a million pieces and float away on the silky water if she couldn't touch him soon, couldn't feel his heated skin beneath her hands.

Then just as she thought she might actually die from the overwhelming longing, she felt him release her hands as his kisses became deeper and hotter . . . all consuming. There was no more protest; the game was forgotten and she sensed he was as lost in the passion as she.

Finally she was able to put her arms around his neck and feel the cool naked skin of his body against hers in the water. She thought she had never experienced such a glorious, sensual feeling.

"You make me forget everything," he whispered against her skin. "All my discipline and power are gone when I have you in my arms."

Dominic slid his hands beneath her hips and when the buoyancy of the water lifted her she wrapped her legs around him. Her head was slightly above his, and as he looked up into her eyes her dark hair tumbled around them, shutting out the world and encasing them in its sweet, provocative scent. With a groan of pleasure, he

257

watched the play of emotion on her face as he took her there in the water.

Aimee cried out at the pleasure he gave her, at the sensuality of it all as she clung to his shoulders. There was something unreal about being there beneath the falls, with the cool water swirling and moving around their hot naked skin as they made love. It brought a wildness, a recklessness to both of them and once begun, their lovemaking was not tender or gentle.

Dominic's body was as demanding as ever, driving both of them with a hard passion that blotted out everything around them. Aimee felt almost detached from life itself as she quickly felt her body responding to the new, almost overpowering erotic emotions and Dominic's own hungry demands. In only moments, her body seemed liquid with sweet, hot passion that rose and sang through her like distant thunder, coming closer and closer until finally she cried out and the world around her seemed to go black.

Her passion excited Dominic to a point of no return until he felt the same quickening response of his own body and groaned with pleasure . . . and with regret that it was ending too soon.

Aimee reveled in the feel of Dominic's trembling body and the urgency of his arms that tightened around her, crushing her against him.

"Oh, Aimee . . . love," he whispered.

They held each other for a long while, her legs still around him as they kissed and whispered their wonder and pleasure. And slowly, very slowly, the world seemed to come back into focus.

Aimee felt her feet touch the sandy bottom of

the stream and she thought if Dominic's arms had not been around her, she might have slipped into the water and drowned. She felt weak and exhausted . . . wonderfully spent and fulfilled and completely entranced with the man who held her. She lifted her lips to Dominic and tasted his mouth again, savoring the feel and scent of him. Then remembering how desperate he had made her to touch him she let her hands wander freely over his chest and shoulders.

He kissed her again before pushing himself backward in the water, floating on his back like a sleek otter and watching her with black, triumphant eyes.

"You are the woman of Blackfox now," he teased, going back to the game.

"Oh, yes," she said with a smile. Her green eyes followed him as she splashed the water around her. "The woman of a warrior . . . a fierce and demanding Choctaw warrior who can bend me to his will and have his way with me whenever it pleases him."

"And don't you forget it," he warned, turning to swim back toward her.

"And what happens next?" she asked, waiting breathlessly for his answer.

"Next?" he asked, his black eyes growing cool and unreadable.

"Yes, is that all there is to it . . . being a warrior's woman? Is there no ceremony . . . no—"

"Oh . . . ceremony," he muttered, floating away again. His eyes were very cool and she thought she detected the slightest hint of bitterness there as well. "Don't worry, love," he said. "In Choctaw custom, it is not forbidden to take a lover, and there is no more need of commitment than there is in the white man's world."

The quick pang of disappointment she felt at his words shot clear through to her chest. Why had she asked him such a question? She had been the one to hint that their relationship would be only sexual . . . that there was no need for marriage . . . or even love.

"That is what you wanted, isn't it?" he asked, his eyes wary.

At that moment, for all her need of control, she wished he would take her in his arms again and demand everything he wanted . . . whatever that might be. He had made her want him with his tantalizing sexual domination, had practically made her beg for his love a few moments ago, and made her weak from wanting him.

She frowned, then shrugged her bare shoulders above the water. "Yes, that's . . . that's what's best for us both, isn't it? I mean, a man like you . . . and a woman like myself . . . we're as different as night and day."

His head came up in that proud stance she'd seen so often, that look of quiet dignity that indicated both his heritage and his heart.

"Of course," he murmured. "How else would it be—a man like me and a woman like you."

Aimee stared at him, knowing she had not expressed her feelings very well. But how could she change a free-spirited man like Dominic, a man used to adventure and excitement, used to taking the world into his own hands and molding it into whatever he wanted it to be. How could she expect a man who was as wild as this primitive land around them, to change . . . expect him even to speak of such things as commitment, let alone settle into the staid and relatively uneventful life of a plantation owner?

Dominic swam away from her, going to the rocks and reaching for a piece of soap he had placed there earlier. She watched him as he rubbed the soap over his body, watched the white soapy lather cover his dark skin. And when he turned toward her, he was smiling again as if nothing had changed. He reached his hand toward her, the soap in his palm.

"Soap, m'lady?"

She smiled and swam toward him, taking the soap from his hands. And soon the two of them were splashing and playing beneath the falls like two children, lost in an enchanted forest.

After they had bathed, he took her hand and pulled her back toward the bank.

"We'd better get dressed and head back to the house," he said. "Before someone grows curious about where we are and comes looking for us."

He helped her up onto the mossy creekbank. Then, using his shirt, he dried the beaded moisture from her skin, letting his hands linger at her breasts and the curve of her waist before lifting black eyes to look into hers.

"I'm glad you found me here today," he whispered, bending to kiss her.

"So am I . . . so very glad."

He helped her dress, his hands tender and gentle as he closed the buttons. Then he turned away and pulled on his clothes, not bothering to put his dampened shirt back on. She thought he looked savagely handsome in his buckskins with his dark chest bare and his black hair wet and sleek where he had pushed it behind his ears.

"Where's your horse?" he asked, untying his own black mount and pulling it along behind them. "And your shoes?" He looked at her small bare feet and smiled.

"Just down the stream."

By the time she found her shoes and brushed off her feet with the hem of her skirt, Dominic had untied the horse. He made no effort to help her into the saddle, but took the reins and led both horses behind them as he came to Aimee and put his arm around her waist.

"We'll walk through the woods as far as we can." His warm eyes surveyed the disarray of her hair and damp clothes. He thought she had the definite, but beautiful flush of a woman who had just enjoyed a heated session of lovemaking. "If we're lucky we can slip back into the house without being seen."

"I must look awful," she said, her hands going to her loose, wet hair.

"On the contrary, you look beautiful," he said, pulling her against his side as they walked.

"Hardly that," she said with a quiet laugh. "I must look like a wicked woman . . . an evil, fallen woman."

He stopped and gazed down at her, wondering if she really meant those words, if she really worried about the reputation she would gain if everyone knew they were lovers. "If you are that, love, then I'm afraid both of us are condemned to hell. And I for one, will go gladly, if that's the price I must pay for what's happened between us." He kissed her mouth lightly, before laughing and pulling her with him along the narrow trail that animals had made to the creek.

His words, even though said teasingly, made her heart ache. Everything about him, his fierce love-making, the look in his black eyes that she sometimes could not understand, the way he could be so wild and reckless, then gentle and sweet with her . . . everything about him made her want him with an aching torturous longing.

They walked quietly for a long way, enjoying the dark cool forest around them and enjoying being in each other's arms to kiss and touch as they wished. They had managed to go around the cotton fields and the slave quarters and were not far from the stables when Aimee felt Dominic stiffen at her side, felt his arm move from around her waist to push her back, slightly behind him.

She looked up, surprised and wondering, and saw a man standing there in the woods before them. She blinked, wondering if her eyes deceived her in the shadowy forest. Her heart began to pound loudly against her chest.

It was him; it was the Indian she had seen before.

She gasped, reaching toward Dominic and placing her hand on his arm.

"So," Dominic said slowly to the man. "It *is* you."

"Yes, cousin," the Indian answered. "It is good to see you again after all these years."

Dominic stepped away from Aimee and she

watched, puzzled and entranced as the two men clasped hand against forearm and stood face-to-face. The Indian was almost as tall as Dominic, and narrow hipped, though not as broad through the shoulders and chest. Still, he was a big man, and even more handsome than Aimee had first thought. His skin, smooth and sun bronzed was breathtaking, a dark golden honey color, and his hair, pulled behind his head in a braid, was as shining and black as Dominic's. The only thing that marred his manly beauty was a long white scar that slanted down across his left cheekbone.

Dominic turned then, back to Aimee.

"Aimee, this is Hawk, my cousin, and I assume the man you saw in the canebrake."

"Yes," she managed. "Yes, he's the one I saw."

"I apologize if I frightened you," the Indian said, his voice deep and as gallant as any gentleman's in Natchez. "But I had heard of your husband's death, Mrs. Lebeaux, and when my cousin returned here, I was fearful for him." He turned to Dominic with a taunting smile. "I feared he might have lost his warrior's edge since he has lived so long in the white man's world."

"You might well be worried," Dominic replied with a crooked, self-deprecating grin. "One of Compton's men tried to kill me the other night . . . almost succeeded, except for his having extremely poor aim."

The Indian grunted and moved his legs in a restless, irritable manner. "He was a cowardly little man, to hide in the cane," he said, his words erupting angrily from his lips. "You're right . . . and lucky for you he was a damned poor shot."

Aimee frowned at his words and Dominic's mouth flew open.

"You," he whispered. "You're the one who killed him. Hell, I should have known, especially when Aimee told me she'd seen someone like you around here."

The Indian's sensuous lips curved into a sneer. "He died poorly—like the sniveling little coward that he was. And you have only to say the word, Sarnee, for your neighbor Compton to meet the same fate."

Aimee shivered at his words and his proud stance, so much like Dominic's.

"No, Hawk," Dominic said, clasping the man's arm in an affectionate gesture. "I'll handle Compton in my own way. But thank you." He smiled at his cousin. "Why have you waited so long to come forward?"

"Well, knowing the way you departed from our grandfather's house, I wasn't sure how I would be accepted by you, cousin. And although I had the opportunity to speak with Mrs. LeBeaux, I felt I should approach you first." He turned and smiled at Aimee in an odd, disquieting way, his black eyes sparkling with some hidden meaning.

"That was what I had intended today when I saw you enter the woods, but later when the lady joined you . . ." His smile and the way his eyes held Aimee's left no doubt as to what he meant.

Aimee made a sound of dismay. She could feel the blood rushing to her face and she gasped. "You . . . you were in the woods . . . near the falls? But . . ." Her eyes darted to Dominic and she saw the effort he was making to keep from smiling.

"Don't worry," Hawk said. "I left soon."

"But . . . but, how soon?" she sputtered, her green eyes flashing at both of them.

"Never mind," Dominic said, his eyes still smiling at Aimee. "Come to the house with us, cousin. Have supper and spend the night."

The Indian's dark eyes moved to meet Aimee's still troubled gaze. "Only if the beautiful lady gives her permission."

His look was so intensely sweet, so hypnotic that she found she could not even remain embarrassed. He had already dismissed the subject from his mind.

"Of course," she replied. "My permission and my warmest invitation. It is Dominic's house now . . . his plantation, and you are welcome here, Hawk."

Twenty-three

Hawk nodded his agreement and stood with Dominic as Aimee began to walk away from them.

"I envy you, cousin," Hawk whispered. "Such a woman is very rare."

As they walked the rest of the way through the forest toward the stables, Dominic watched Aimee from the corner of his eye. Hawk was right—she was a rare woman. A very intelligent, spirited woman who was also beautiful and desirable. and she made him lose all sense of reason when he was with her. She made him want to forget everything except the excitement of holding her in his arms, of kissing her soft lips and hearing her heated cries that simply drove him out of his mind.

He shook his head as they walked, wondering if he would ever be able to banish her from his heart and his mind.

Her gracious response to Hawk had surprised him and made him realize that she had changed a great deal since he first met her. Today, with her hair streaming over her shoulders, she seemed young and carefree, less tense and controlled. And her easy, relaxed smile was breathtaking. He caught her eye for the briefest moment and smiled at her, wanting her to know how much it meant to him that she had accepted his cousin with such warmth and graciousness.

Aimee thought that when Dominic looked at her that way, she could simply melt into the ground. She felt as if she could actually feel her bones growing weak and languid and the feeling brought back such sharp memories she had to clamp her teeth together to keep from sighing out loud. What was she going to do about him? How on earth could she keep the plantation going when all she seemed able to think about was Dominic and the way he made her feel?

When they reached the stables, Dominic stayed behind, letting Aimee go to the house alone. Already he could see her anxiousness returning as she made ready to try and sneak back into the house without being seen. He frowned, annoyed with himself; this beautiful, refined woman should never have to sneak anywhere . . . most certainly not into her own home.

"Well, cousin . . ." Hawk's deep voice sounded behind him in the dimness of the stables. "I never thought to meet a woman who could put that look on your face."

Dominic turned, his lips lifting slightly at the corners as he faced his cousin. "What look?"

"I think you know very well what look," Hawk said with a grin. "You look like a man completely besotted to me. A man, I might add, who has more than enough sense and stubbornness to gain anything he's ever wanted. And so, I wonder at this look of wistfulness on your handsome face. That look has usually been reserved exclusively for those women left behind, waving as you ride away." Grinning, Hawk lifted his hand and make a weak, mocking wave.

Dominic grunted with amusement and turned to unsaddle the horses. "Just because you spent a couple of summers with me on the river doesn't mean you know everything about me, my friend."

Hawk laughed and his dark eyes twinkled merrily at his cousin's defensiveness. "Of course," he murmured, still smiling. "An uncivilized Indian like myself should not make such observations."

Dominic turned slowly. "Don't try and pull that uncivilized Indian routine on me, cousin." His eyes wandered over Hawk's long braided hair, down to his naked chest and the buff-colored buckskins that encased his muscular legs. Dressed that way and with the long scar across his cheek, Dominic thought he certainly looked the part anyway. "We received our education together at the same school, remember? And I also recall that your grades were much better than mine . . . as well as your prowess with women, most of them having no idea you *were* Indian."

Hawk tilted his dark head back and laughed, pleased with the camaraderie that was still between them, despite their years spent apart.

"Touché cousin . . . *touché."*

Dominic turned back to the horses, his look more serious as he spoke without looking at his cousin. "Why have you chosen to go back to the old ways, Hawk . . . even to dressing and speaking in the way of the Choctaw?"

"And why should I not?" he replied. "I am a Choctaw and proudly so. I think the more appro-

269

priate question would be, why have you not returned?"

Dominic shrugged his broad shoulders, not willing to discuss his past or his heritage.

"Grandfather speaks often of you; he misses you, Dominic."

Dominic whirled to face Hawk, and his eyes were dark with fire and bitterness. "Don't speak to me of him, and don't try to play on my sympathies by telling me how much he misses me. He is a hard, cruel man . . . the man, might I remind you, who was responsible for my mother's death." Dominic's voice faltered and he turned to pull the saddle off his horse and swing it hard over one of the stalls.

"So, you are still bitter . . . and unforgiving."

"Bitter?" Dominic growled. "My God, of course I'm bitter and you're damned right, unforgiving. How can you ask me such a question? You were there . . . you know what happened."

"Yes," Hawk said. "I do, but it was a long time ago, in another age. I thought time might have eased the pain for you since then. But I'm sorry, I didn't mean to anger you . . . not on this first day of our reunion. I will speak of it no more."

"Good."

Later when Dominic came out of the stables, Hawk was waiting for him. He was letting his eyes wander over the buildings of the plantation, noting the orderliness of everything and the beauty of the house and gardens in the distance. He turned at the feel of Dominic's hand on his shoulder and he saw the look in his cousin's eyes, the look that said their earlier conversation was forgotten.

"You have done well here, Dominic."

Dominic nodded and there was the slightest hint of a smile on his lips as he gazed about them while they walked to the house.

"It wasn't exactly in my plans," he said. "When I lent Jim a sum of money last year, I certainly never dreamed that months later he'd be gone and I'd be living in his house."

"With his wife."

Dominic turned and looked sharply at Hawk.

"It's not the way it seems. What you saw today was . . ." Dominic's words faltered and he frowned.

"Was . . . ?"

Dominic took a deep breath and continued. "This thing between Aimee and me . . . it's new, untested. I don't want you to think that I just moved in here and she came running to give herself to me. It wasn't like that. She's a good woman, a decent, respectable woman and—"

"You don't have to tell me that, cousin," Hawk said with a frown. "I know that. I have eyes and ears. Aimee LeBeaux is the kind of woman you marry . . . raise children with. Lucky for you, she happens to be beautiful in the bargain."

Again Dominic frowned. "Hell, I don't know about the marriage part. I don't think she wants to marry . . . not someone like me at least."

"Ah," Hawk said with a wry grin. "The tables have turned, no? Seems as if the most sought-after bachelor on the Mississippi has finally met his match . . . something I've been waiting for with joyful anticipation, cousin."

Dominic nudged his cousin playfully and they wrestled together like young boys, laughing and shouting as they moved toward the house.

271

"Don't gloat," Dominic said, stopping to catch his breath and put his damp shirt back on. "It will happen to you one day, my friend, and when it does, expect to see me standing somewhere in the shadows, laughing the loudest."

When they entered the garden and walked toward the veranda, Dominic saw Lucas standing on the porch, his eyes growing wide with wonder as he watched the two men walk toward him. Jezzy, too, who came out the door carrying an armload of linens, stopped and stared, then walked slowly toward the kitchen. But her eyes remained on Hawk's lean, handsome face.

The man beside Dominic laughed. "Well, I hope my presence doesn't cause an uprising in your own home, Dominic."

"Hardly," Dominic said. "If they've grown used to me, you should be no problem at all." He reached out and flicked a finger beneath Hawk's braid. "As soon as we get you cleaned up and looking civilized, that is."

They stepped up onto the porch and Hawk stood smiling down at Lucas whose mouth was still open.

"Lucas, this is my cousin, Hawk. He will be our guest for dinner and I hope he will agree to remain with us for a day or two. Would you take him upstairs to the room next to mine, then find Amos and tell him we have a guest?"

"Huh . . . yeah . . . you bet," Lucas said.

Hawk was smiling broadly at the boy. "Lucas and I have already met, cousin. I came upon him and one of the black boys on the creekbank one evening. Lucas was making a bow and I offered to help."

272

Lucas's eyes moved guiltily up to Dominic's.

"Oh, really?" Dominic said with a dry smile. "Now that makes for a very interesting story which I'm sure you meant to tell me all about, right, Lucas?"

"Huh, yes . . . yessir, I did . . . I mean I will." Finally the boy turned to the Indian. "Your room is this way, Mister Hawk."

Hawk laughed, his deep voice echoing about the low-ceilinged veranda. "Just plain Hawk will do, son."

Dominic watched them go up the stairs, smiling at Lucas's embarrassment. He'd paid a price for claiming responsibility for making the bow himself.

Dominic turned then, his eyes going to the end of the porch and Aimee's bedroom. He was still standing there, deep in thought when Jezzy came back from the kitchen onto the veranda.

"Well, who was that handsome devil, Mister Dominic? I ain't never in my life seen no man what looked like that, 'cept maybe for you when you came. Matter o' fact, you two look alike."

"Really? Perhaps that's because we're related. Hawk is my cousin—we grew up together."

"Well," she said with an interested lift of her brows. "Well, well, well."

"Where were you taking those, Jezzy?" he asked, nodding toward the clean stack of linens in her hands.

"Goin' to Miz Aimee's room," she drawled.

"Here . . . I'll take them."

She turned her head and gave him a look of skepticism, then she grinned broadly and handed the linens over to him.

273

"She might still be takin' a bath," she warned with a mischievous grin.

"Don't you have other chores to do, Jezzy? Perhaps in some other part of the house?"

"Oh," she said, her eyes wide and sparkling. "Yep . . . I sho do, Mister Dominic. I sho 'nuff do." With that she hurried away, giggling and looking back over her shoulder at him.

Dominic laughed and walked the few steps to Aimee's door. The thought of her at her bath made his breath catch in his chest and he found himself remembering the hot, watery interlude at the falls. He swallowed hard and knocked on the door.

The door opened and a soft cool breeze wafted out and seemed to wrap itself around Dominic. The scent of lavender soap and some sweet, forbidden perfume moved and teased at his senses, before drifting out to mingle with the outdoor scent of roses and magnolias. Aimee stood staring at him with such a sweet look of welcome that he almost forgot why he came. She pulled her soft wrapper around her body as a pale pink color rose to stain her olive complexion.

"Hello," she said, her voice breathless, her green eyes shining with surprised pleasure.

He handed her the linens and stood for a moment, their hands touching as he looked into her eyes.

"I just wanted to see if you were all right," he said. "And find out if you made it back to the house . . . without anyone seeing you and wondering—"

"Yes," she said, unable to take her eyes away from his face. "I made it fine and as far as I know,

274

no one saw me, thank goodness, looking the way I did."

"You looked beautiful," he said. His eyes took in the shining mass of hair piled loosely atop her head and he could not stop his fingers from moving to touch the soft tendrils that fell around her face. "You *are* beautiful," he said. "I liked your hair down the way it was today."

Her eyes grew dark as they looked up at him. He could see the leap of desire in their green depths and was amazed by it . . . pleased and amazed if she was only feeling half of what he felt.

"I'm sorry," he whispered with a quiet smile. He had to shake himself mentally and issue another silent warning. "I shouldn't be standing here in your doorway with you . . . not properly . . . dressed." He stopped and took a deep breath, stepping away from her and smiling ruefully. "I just wanted to say that today when you found me, I was so . . . pleased and so . . . I'm afraid I wasn't thinking when . . ." He paused and laughed softly at his own stammering words. "Damn! I don't even seem capable of putting a sentence together when you look at me that way. What I wanted to say is that today, when you found me, I was taken off guard, and all I could think of was kissing you and holding you. I shouldn't have put you in such a position. I—"

She stepped forward and reached up to brush her fingers against his lips, stopping his apology. "No," she whispered. "Don't ever apologize for what happened today. It was wonderful." She took a steadying breath and smiled. "*You* were wonderful and I . . . I wasn't thinking either, I was only enjoying

275

being with you. And if the entire world finds out, I don't care."

His black eyes narrowed and he waited, entranced with her and hardly able to believe her words.

"I don't care anymore what anyone says, or what anyone thinks," she said, her voice soft and breathless. "And even if I did, I don't think I could make myself stop . . . wanting you, Dominic. It's much too late for that now."

Without a word, he pushed her back into the shadows of the doorway, taking the linens from her arms and tossing them aside. He swept her up into his arms and took her parted lips in a kiss that was incredibly sweet and gentle. When he stepped away and lifted his head, it was with a reluctance that left him amused at his own actions.

"I'd better go," he said, his voice husky. "No matter how happy I am to hear you say that, I think I should at least try and act responsibly where your reputation is concerned."

She reached forward and let her fingers curl around one of the buttons on his shirt. "Responsibly . . ." she whispered, smiling up at him in a teasing way. "Do you hear yourself, Dominic? Everyone will begin to wonder what's happened to you if you continue to behave so . . . responsibly, don't you think?"

He smiled, amused by her uncharacteristic teasing, then he kissed her mouth lightly and forced himself to turn away. He glanced back at her over his shoulder and grinned.

"No more than I, love. No more than I."

Twenty-four

That evening when Aimee walked into the dining room, she found Dominic and Hawk talking while Lucas sat nearby watching and listening with expectant fervor.

Aimee's eyes briefly scanned Dominic's cousin, noting that he looked entirely different in the dark trousers and shirt and the black boots he had evidently borrowed from his cousin. She thought he wore the vestments of the white man very well indeed. Even the scar on his cheek did not detract from his rugged good looks. She thought him almost as handsome and irresistible as Dominic.

She smiled, seeing the two men turn to greet her. Both of them held small goblets of burgundy-colored wine, and as she approached them, Hawk gazed at her, his dark eyes openly admiring over the rim of the glass that he lifted to his lips.

She had chosen a deep green silk dress that was very lowcut and youthful looking. But it was summer and the night was hot. And for some reason, tonight she felt young and carefree, anything but mournful. She felt happier than she had in a very long time. And when her eyes sought Dominic's, she saw the look reflected in his own black eyes and she felt as if he knew her mind, could even see the happiness in her heart.

"Good evening," he murmured with that crooked smile that seemed to wrench all the air from her lungs.

"Good evening," she said, finally pulling her eyes from him and nodding a similar greeting to Hawk and Lucas.

"Well, Lucas," she said. "I suppose it will take us weeks to get you back to normal with such an exciting guest in the house, isn't that right?"

"He has an Indian name and a white name, Aimee, just like me and Dominic." he said, his voice loud with excitement. "His name is John . . . and he's going to stay here with us while Dominic goes to Natchez."

Aimee's look swung toward Dominic and she saw the slight perturbed shake of his head and the apology in his eyes.

"I'll tell you about it later," he said, smiling.

That evening was one of the most enjoyable Aimee had spent in a long while, even more than when her Aunt Eulie and the DeVaulls had come to visit. But tonight, the new and delicate bond between her and Dominic made it seem more like an intimate family gathering. She found that having Dominic's cousin in the house gave her a warm feeling of belonging and sharing that she had not experienced before.

Aimee was perfectly content to sit and listen, laughing with the two men as they traded stories about their childhood and watching Lucas's enjoyment. Perhaps Dominic had been right before; perhaps the boy did need to know more about his own people and their ways. Tonight with his two heroes, he was simply ecstatic.

"But where did you live?" Lucas asked.

"To the north," Hawk replied. "In Indian territory. But since my youth, more and more Indian land has been ceded to the United States through peace treaties. Soon, I'm afraid there will simply be no more land to give."

Aimee noted the exchange of dark, knowing glances between the two men.

"Did you live in a tent, Dominic?" Lucas asked guilelessly.

Dominic laughed and his eyes were warm when he looked at the boy. "Actually the Choctaw are not nomadic people, Lucas. So we had permanent homes, usually log houses, much like your people, the Cherokee. That is, we never wandered about in search of food the way some tribes do. And of course being here where it's warm all year long meant we did not need summer and winter homes. No, the Choctaw are a peaceful, stable tribe who love their land and their homes."

"But why did you leave?"

"The first time I left was to go to school. I told you that my father was French; he settled in Natchez for a while and it was he who insisted that I be educated in a white school."

"Are you white, too?" Lucas asked, turning to Hawk with wide, questioning eyes.

Hawk laughed, his dark eyes crinkling at the corner. "Not enough to tell," he said. "Although it's been said that my great grandfather was a white trader." He shrugged as if the subject did not matter much to him. "Dominic and I have the same grandfather—his mother was a Choctaw, his father a Frenchman. But both my parents are Choctaw."

Aimee noticed that Dominic had grown quiet and thoughtful, perhaps even a bit uneasy about the subject. This was the most any of them had heard about his family.

"Dominic told me before that his parents are dead, just like mine," Lucas said, his voice solemn. He turned dark, curious eyes toward Dominic. "But you didn't tell me about your grandfather, Dom. Is he dead, too?"

"No," Dominic said, his eyes narrowing as he glanced toward Hawk. "No, Grandfather is still alive and well."

"Not quite so well," Hawk corrected. "He is old now and frail, but once he was a great *mingo* to our people."

"Mingo?" Lucas asked. "What's that?"

"A chief . . . each tribe has a *mingo,* who is the leader, and he has an officer who speaks for him at various ceremonies. This man is called a *tichou mingo*—which means a servant of the chief."

Aimee's brows lifted with interest. Those were the words Dominic had uttered when he lay sick with fever after the gunshot. Had he been, in his delirium, declaring himself a servant of the chief, and of his grandfather?

She watched Dominic lift his glass toward his cousin and she thought the sarcastic look on his face was one of challenge.

"And I believe that my cousin Hawk here is now the new tribal *tichou mingo,* Lucas. He is the one who speaks for our grandfather in his old age."

Hawk's eyes glittered dangerously as he met and

held Dominic's gaze. "I am what you say," he said. "But I am also my own man, cousin, and I speak for myself in matters of the heart and soul." He touched his chest lightly and Aimee wondered at the emotional exchange between the two men and what it meant.

"How far is the village?" Lucas asked excitedly. "Maybe while Dominic is gone, you could take me there, Hawk. I could meet the old grandfather and we could—"

"No," Dominic said, his voice gruff. "No, it's too far and . . . besides, Aimee needs you here." He looked to her for support and she said nothing to contradict him, even though she could think of no reason for Lucas not to visit the village if he wished. And she was puzzled. Wasn't that what he wanted . . . for Lucas to learn Indian ways?

"But Dominic," Lucas cried.

"No, Lucas, don't argue with me. I'll be bringing back your tutor with me from Natchez; it's time you got back to your lessons. I will hear no more about it."

Lucas frowned and his chin quivered as if he might actually cry. Aimee felt her heart ache as she looked at his solemn little face and bowed head and she wondered why Dominic, usually so lenient with the boy, had spoken so harshly to him now.

But soon, Lucas's hurt feeling were forgotten and he quickly entered back into the conversation about Dominic and Hawk's boyhood. He seemed eager to soak up anything and everything about the past and about the Indians.

After supper, Hawk and Lucas strolled out to the veranda and stood at the rail talking. Dominic came across the dining room to Aimee and took her hands, holding them against his chest as he talked.

"I'm sorry . . . I should have told you first that I intended to go to Natchez tomorrow. But actually it was Hawk's being here that prompted it; I hadn't really wanted to leave you and Lucas here alone. But now—"

"It's all right," she said, smiling up at him. "It *is* a good idea, asking Hawk to stay here while you're away. I only wish I could go with you."

"So do I," he said, moving closer as his voice became hushed and quiet. "I'd love nothing better than to carry you away for a long, very slow cruise to New Orleans. And I promise that if our first cotton crop is a good one, we'll do just that."

"That sounds wonderful . . . so wonderful," she whispered.

"Hey you two . . . you comin' out or not?" Lucas yelled from the porch. "It's not so hot out here on the veranda."

Dominic's black eyes never left Aimee's as he ignored the boy's enthusiastic shouts.

"He's right," he murmured. "It is getting pretty warm in here at that."

"Very."

Dominic laughed, delighted with the look in her eyes and completely charmed by the vision of her in her green silk dress. He thought it made her eyes look like glittering emeralds. She smiled knowingly and her lips parted ever so slightly.

He groaned and stepped away from her. "Let me remind you, we are in the middle of the dining room . . . beneath many very bright, very revealing

282

lights and might I also remind you that Jezzy is bound to skip into this room any moment now, or I might — "

"Might what?" she whispered, moving closer, obviously pleased that she could arouse him so easily.

"I might rake all those beautiful, very expensive dishes off onto the floor, in which case I would most likely ruin that lovely green frock you're wearing when I made love to you right here on this table."

She laughed, delighted by his erotic teasing. His eyes left her breathless, his touch and the warmth from his body made her feel weak with longing and the very idea of what he had described made her close her eyes with a quiet little gasp.

She felt his mouth touch hers in a quick, intimate, searching kiss. Then he stepped away, still holding her arms and giving her a little shake.

"We need some fresh . . . cool air," he said with a grin. "And later tonight, after Hawk and Lucas have gone up to bed, I'll meet you in the garden, near the statue where I will court you, Mrs. LeBeaux, in a more sane and proper manner."

It was almost midnight before Aimee heard Hawk leave the veranda and go up the stairs. She peeked out the door and saw Dominic's tall form as he walked down the steps and out into the garden.

When she joined him there he was waiting, turning to catch her as she ran into his arms. His laughter in the darkness was warm and intimate and Aimee felt as if it had been a million years since he had last held her and kissed her this way.

The sultry heat of the Mississippi night seemed

to close around them, swallowing them in the hot, sweet scent of the roses as they kissed and clung to each other.

Aimee thought there was something deliciously seductive about the blended scent of the roses and the heated night which matched their own volatile passion. Their desires were quickly stimulated by the combination, provoking and kindling such white hot responses that soon they were both gasping for air, both filled with wonder at what was happening between them.

"So much for my attempt at a sane and proper courtship," he said with a soft amused groan.

They never even made it to the statue, but stumbled laughing, unable to resist touching and caressing, back up the veranda steps and toward her bedroom.

When Aimee woke early the next morning, Dominic was gone and there was only the scent of him on the pillow next to hers. She turned, smiling, and pulled the pillow to her, clasping it against her breasts and burying her face into it as she breathed in the spicy male scent. He had said goodbye early, and she'd felt like begging him to stay for only a moment longer.

She had known him for such a short time and already she could hardly bear being separated for a moment, much less three days. She was mesmerized, totally and completely under his spell. She stretched and smiled.

"And I don't care," she whispered, gleefully kicking her feet into the air. "I don't even care."

She lay for a while, hating to leave the bed and the memories that it held of last night's lovemaking. Dominic was a powerful man, strong and sensual, and yet last night he had been as tender and sweet as a young naive boy. It excited her even now, just thinking about his lips, the feel of his body, the way his muscles and hips moved beneath her hands.

They had lain in each other's arms for hours, talking and enjoying being able to touch and caress naked, warmed skin and to look into eyes that marveled with wonder. Aimee had been secretly thrilled, hearing him talk about the plantation and his plans for the future, knowing he intended to stay. And only when she had asked him about his grandfather and his past had he grown quiet and reluctant to speak.

"If it's something you'd rather not discuss . . ." she had said, feeling him pulling away from her even as she said it.

"No," he had said. But the frown still lingered on his brow as he leaned on his elbow and turned to look down at her. "I do want to talk about it . . . I want to tell you everything, one day soon. But not tonight, not now when I'm feeling more blessed and contented than I've ever felt. My past has haunted me all my life, Aimee . . . the pain and confusion I felt when my mother died, when I left the only family I'd ever known to live with a father who was cold and distant. It was a hard time for me, a bitter time that made me grow up much faster than I should have." His fingers caressed her cheek as he talked. "I suppose that's why I'm so protective of Lucas and so determined that he'll have a different kind of life. I want him to be a little boy for a while yet. I don't want him to have to grow up as quickly as I did."

"I know," she whispered. "I want that, too."

"And I want you," he said, bending to kiss her slowly and deliberately. "Do you know that I'm in danger of losing my mind when I'm with you . . . that I'm completely captivated by your eyes . . . your smile, the sound of your voice. I'm afraid I've become a complete fool for you, Aimee LeBeaux."

She smiled and reached up to encircle his neck and pull his head down toward hers. "Oh no," she whispered "You're no fool, Dominic . . . never, ever that."

Still remembering, Aimee stretched her legs, like a sleek, satisfied cat, as she smiled. She loved the way he touched her and kissed her, made her wild with a passion that swept her to the stars and back. She had never felt this way about anything or anyone, not even about Jim, the husband she had adored.

"I love him," she whispered, feeling a warm rush of astonishment sweep through her. "God help me, but I do. I'm in love with him . . . totally, heart and soul in love."

Twenty-five

Later Jezzy came in to help Aimee dress. She was quiet, her big dark eyes curious as she took in Aimee's smile and her faraway, wistful look. She was standing behind Aimee, fastening the long row of buttons on the dress, when she heard Aimee humming.

"Well," Jezzy said with a soft grunt. "You is lookin' mighty fine in this new dress, Miz Aimee. Pink sho do become you."

"Do you think so?" Aimee asked, turning before the mirror and smiling at her image. "I bought it last fall in Natchez, right off one of the barges. But after Jim died . . " She paused for a moment, and smiled wistfully before continuing. She held out the full skirt and turned around before the mirror. "It's called marguerite pink; isn't that a lovely name?"

"Huh-uh," Jezzy said, rolling her eyes at her mistress. "You is mighty chirpy this mornin', missy. Yes'm . . downright chirpy."

"Chirpy," Aimee said, turning with a broad smile to Jezzy. "Now, that's a word I think I have not heard before. But from the sound of it, it seems to mean something good and bright."

"Yes'm," Jezzy said with a wise nod. "Just like a

little bird in a tree, you are. Hummin' and dancin' about. Sometimes, missy, you are a huckleberry beyond my persimmon."

Aimee shook her head, frowning, then laughing as she stared at Jezzy's blank face.

"Lord, Jezzy. What on earth are you talking about? I swear, sometimes your language just confounds me."

"That's it . . ." Jezzy said with a grin. "You confounds me, too. Don't understand it. First you can't stand the sight of Mister Dominic . . you mope around, lookin' like the world done come to a end. And now all of a sudden, you is as alive as a spring flower sproutin' forth in the April rain. Don't understand it . . just don't. All I can figure is, if'n he caused the mopin', then he must be the reason for the chirpin', too." Her eyes were wide and she seemed pleased by her own perceptiveness.

Aimee laughed. She didn't care anymore if Jezzy knew; she didn't care if everyone in the entire world knew how she felt about him. What woman wouldn't feel this way with a man like Dominic? Aimee was happier than she'd ever been in her life and she was weary to death of holding back and pretending. And when he came home, she intended to tell him just that. She intended him to know that she loved him.

"Jezzy," she said, smiling. "Sometimes you are a very perceptive woman."

"Yes, ma'am," Jezzy said with a pleased nod. "I's a perceptive fool, that's what I is." Jezzy giggled and bent over to slap her hand against her knee.

They went out onto the veranda, both of them still laughing. Aimee saw Hawk and Lucas there and she walked over to them, still smiling at Jezzy's ways.

288

"Ladies," Hawk said. He smiled at Jezzy and the girl almost twittered with delight. And Aimee had to admit that the man's smile was quite devastating. Even the scar he bore added to his rakish good looks and gave him a look of handsome devilishness.

Oddly, at that moment, Jezzy reached inside her dress and pulled out another of her strange necklaces, obviously wanting everyone to see it.

"That's a lovely necklace you have there, Jezzy," Hawk said, accommodating her and glancing toward Aimee with good humor.

"Oh, did you notice it?" Jezzy said innocently, as if she had not just placed it for everyone to see. "It's a love charm, that's what it is. This little round cake here is made from amaranth seed and new wheat and before the next full moon, it's gonna bring me a new man."

Lucas snorted and grinned. "Huh! What happened to the 'old' man? I thought Nathaniel was your man, Jezzy."

"Nathaniel? Shoot! That boy is so slow, he don't never catch on. I done told him life is just gonna pass him by—he ain't gonna have no woman to warm his bed in his old age. I done give him his chance, but I can't help it if he be slow." Jezzy rolled her eyes at Hawk as if her words held a special message for him.

As Jezzy smiled at Hawk and walked away, swinging her hips in an exaggerated manner, Aimee could not help laughing. Jezzy was unpredictable and outrageous, but she certainly knew how to brighten the day.

"I'm sorry," Aimee said, still laughing. "But I do believe our Jezzy has her eyes on you, Hawk."

He laughed, his teeth very white against the darkness of his skin. Aimee quirked an eyebrow, sensitive to his potent male charm and thinking mischievously that if Hawk had come along before Dominic, her life might have taken an even more unusual turn. She smiled at her thoughts, feeling her heart beat a bit faster at even the remembrance of Dominic. Actually, no one could ever take his place.

"I'm complimented by her attention," he said. "Perhaps at my age, I should be thinking of getting a love charm myself."

"Hardly," she said, teasing. "I don't imagine you have anything to worry about in that regard."

"You flatter me," he said, obviously enjoying the flirtatious banter. "Dominic left early I see."

"Yes. I think Nathaniel went with him. Dominic intended to take a wagon and buy a few supplies while they're there."

"Is there anything you need this morning?" Hawk asked. "Anything I can help you with? Lucas and I planned to ride out to the fields, but we'll be back before noon."

"No, nothing," she replied. "I'm going to have a light breakfast and then there's some work I must take care of in the office."

"Good." Hawk smiled at her before turning to put an arm around Lucas's shoulders. The boy's look was adoring, his eyes shining and anxious for them to leave. "Then, we'll see you at noon."

Aimee ate breakfast, then walked for a while in the garden, taking a basket with her and snipping off several sprays of roses.

She loved the scent of roses in her bedroom. Going back to the house, she gave the basket to Amos before heading to her office.

"Amos, would you please have one of the girls put these roses in water and place them in my bedroom?"

"Yes'm, Miz Aimee," the old man said with a smile.

Aimee worked on the estate books and on her journals until almost noon. She sat back in the chair, stretching her stiff muscles and reaching her arms over her head. She was behind in her weather journal and had spent an enjoyable time making notes on what was blooming. She also recorded the number of foggy days, or especially dewy mornings, as well as the number of rains and storms. She was not certain this would ever be useful in the future, but it was interesting and something she enjoyed very much.

Putting her journals away, she noticed that the lock on the secret compartment of the desk was slightly askew and she smiled. Dominic had intended to take a small amount of money with him for supplies and had probably left it open accidentally. She opened the small door and peeked inside, then without thinking, picked up the small tin box that held the plantation's last bit of money.

She opened and box and stared inside as the smile on her face slowly faded away and was replaced by a puzzled frown. In disbelief, she turned the box upside down, then reached her hand inside the dark compartment to see if the money had fallen out somehow.

But there was no money . . . not even a coin was left in the box or the compartment.

Aimee leaned back in the chair and the sound of

her breath leaving her lungs was loud in the room
. . . a loud, ominous whisper of denial.

"It can't be," she said aloud. "Why would he take
all the money; he needed little for supplies and . . ."
She jumped up from her chair, feeling an energy
overtake her muscles that would not let her sit any
longer. She fought the images and thoughts that
dashed through her mind . . . memories of things
Jim had told her about Dominic . . . about his restlessness, his need to sleep in a different house every
night . . . and his need to be at the gaming tables.

"Dominic will never settle down," Jim often said.
"He has the river in his veins. Take him away from
the Mississippi and his gambling saloons and he'd be
lost. Poor Dominic," he had laughed. "He'll never
know what it's like to have a woman beside him, not
a respectable woman at least. And he'll never know
what joy there is in settling a place, having his own
land, his own home."

Aimee shook her head now against the images and
the words. "No," she whispered. "That's not true.
Dominic is not like that . . . he's nothing at all like
that. He's changed . . . he cares about me and Lucas, and he cares about this plantation."

But could it be true? Could she be blinded to his
faults by all that had happened between them lately?
Could she be wrong about the man who only this
morning she admitted to loving?

"Oh, Dominic," she whispered. "Please . . . don't
do this."

She paced the floor, chewing her lower lip as she
tried to reason out what she should do. Perhaps
Dominic had thought to increase their small cache of
money; perhaps he'd decided to use it to gamble only

292

in the hope of winning money for the plantation . . . for them.

"No," she muttered. Even if his intentions were good ones, he would have told her. He should have told her he was taking all of the money and why.

"What shall I do? I trust him . . . I do. But what if . . . Oh, Dominic, this is all the money we have left in the world. What if this first crop fails; it could happen very easily if we don't get rain soon. There's just too much at stake here to risk losing it all." She began to pace again as she continued talking to herself. "My Lord, what would I do; where would I go if I lost LeBeaux? There's Lucas to consider . . . and Jezzy and Amos . . . Cilla and Delilah . . . Nathaniel. I couldn't bear selling them. I just couldn't."

When a light knock sounded at her door, she whirled, flinging it open and standing there at the threshold like a woman bent on flight.

Hawk frowned at her, noting the turmoil in her eyes, and the way her smooth brow wrinkled with worry.

"Aimee . . . what's wrong?" He stepped into the room, taking her arms and pulling her toward a chair. He actually thought for a moment she might faint.

"Hawk," she whispered, turning back to the desk. She picked up the small metal box, holding it toward him and not even thinking he wouldn't know what she meant. "Dominic's taken all the money, and Jim always said he was a gambler, that the river was in his blood. But there must be some reasonable explanation, something he forgot to tell me. Dominic would never take a chance on losing the money, would he? On losing LeBeaux?"

293

"Aimee," he whispered, worried by the frantic look in her eyes. He took her arms and pushed her gently into a chair, then sat on the settee near her. "What are you talking about? Calm down and tell me exactly what's happened."

Looking into his black eyes, so much like Dominic's, Aimee took a deep breath, then began to tell him everything. She told him about Jim's death, about her fear that she could not handle the entire estate on her own, then how Dominic had come . . . their disagreements and fights. And finally she told him all the things Jim had told her about his friend.

"And I just ignored all Jim's warnings," she said, looking into his eyes with a haunted look. "I thought I saw a different man from the one my husband described . . . a good, honest man who cares about Lucas and about me, who cares about the land and the people here. I forgot everything, and I fell in love. . . ." Her voice faltered and she leaned forward as if in pain.

Hawk reached toward her, taking her wrists and pulling her up from the chair and into his arms. She fell against him, holding onto him as if he was her last hope.

"I'm in love with him, Hawk," she whispered in a desperate voice. "Maybe loving a man makes a woman see things that aren't really there, believe in things that can never be—I don't know." Her eyes were questioning as she confessed her deepest fears. "It seems that every time I begin to count on something or someone, it all ends. It just disappears right before my eyes as if it was never real to begin with."

"No, Aimee," Hawk said, smoothing his hand down her hair that she wore loose this morning. He held her away from him and looked deeply into her beautiful green eyes. Lord, he thought, but it was easy to see why Dominic had fallen so hard for this woman. "Listen to me. You're right about Dominic . . . he *is* good and honest and I think he loves you and Lucas just as much as you do him. But you have to remember the life he had before he met you." Hawk glanced around the room, waving one hand at the beauty and elegance of it, at all the expensive accoutrements of a woman like Aimee LeBeaux. "This . . . all this is something Dominic shunned, can't you see? He's been torn all his life between this kind of life . . . the life his father wanted for him . . . and the other, more simple life of our people. And in the process, he's substituted other things to help him forget . . . other people and other diversions. But that doesn't mean he can't change, or that he hasn't already changed."

She closed her eyes and leaned her forehead against his shoulder. "I don't want to doubt him." she whispered.

"Then don't. Just hold on to your feelings for him, Aimee. Listen to your heart and believe what it tells you."

She nodded, pulling away from him and smiling weakly at his handsome face. "You're right, I know you are," she said. "Dominic will be back in three or four days and everything will be fine."

Hawk nodded, but he was troubled by the look in her eyes, by the doubt he saw still lingering there in their emerald depths.

Damn Dominic anyway. What was he thinking, knowing what this woman had suffered, to take even the slightest chance of hurting or disappointing her?

And what in God's name *did* he intend doing with the money?

As much as Aimee tried, the rest of the day was lost. She couldn't seem to concentrate on anything except Dominic and with those thoughts her doubts returned . . . doubts about herself and the wisdom of some of her decisions. She had become a fool for him, letting the emotions she felt change her into a soft, caring woman who forgot all about protecting herself. She had spent months trying to rid herself of that softness, knowing what it cost her before. She had sworn never to be hurt again by the loss of someone she loved. And for Aimee, even though she didn't know it herself, that meant she simply could never love again.

But she had loved. She loved him more deeply, more completely than she'd ever thought it possible to love anyone. And she found that more than the possibility of being wrong about him, she couldn't bear the thought of losing those feelings that being in love with him gave her.

Late that evening after everyone was in bed, Aimee walked along the veranda in front of her room. She would go to the railing and stare up through the trees at the clear sky only to turn away again.

"Where are you tonight, Dominic?" she whispered, tortured by the thoughts that whirled through her mind. "What are you doing?

Finally, she walked out to the garden, hoping the fragrance would soothe her as it always did when she was troubled.

She was there when Hawk stepped to the balcony on the second story. He shook his head and walked slowly and quietly down the stairs and out toward the garden.

"Aimee," he said, keeping his voice soft so he wouldn't frighten her.

She turned, not bothering to feign modesty by pulling her wrapper to cover the swell of her breasts above her nightgown. Hawk had probably already seen more of her body than she was comfortable thinking about.

"Hello," she said. "I . . . I couldn't sleep."

"Neither could I," he said. "You're still worried about Dominic. I thought we put an end to that earlier."

She shook her head and turned away from him. "I can't. I can't help thinking about it, wondering where he is or—"

"Aimee," he said, his voice holding a soft rebuke. "Don't do this to yourself. There is a perfectly reasonable explanation for all this and I'm sure as soon as Dominic gets back he'll—"

"I can't wait that long," she said, turning back to face him. Her chin was lifted and her jaws clenched tightly together. "I've decided that first thing tomorrow morning I will ride into Natchez and find him."

"No, little one," he said. "You don't want to do that."

"There's no need to worry," she said, her look stubborn. "I only intend to find him and see for myself what he's doing." Her eyes darkened as she stared defiantly into his face. "I have to, don't you see? I have to do this. I simply can't sit here for three more days waiting and wondering."

"No, damn it, I don't see. You're only going to make things worse, Aimee. What will Dominic think when he sees you . . . when he knows you've come searching for him as if he's a dependent little boy. He's stubbornly proud, Aimee, and he'll hate it. I'm afraid I can't let you do that."

She stared at him and took a step backward. *"You* can't let me? I wasn't aware that you had anything to do with this, Hawk. I'm a grown woman, perfectly capable of making my own decisions, and tomorrow morning, whether you like it or not, I will be riding to Natchez."

He moved toward her, clamping his hand on her arm as if he intended to make her listen. "No, Aimee, you won't."

She jerked her arm from his grip and when she spoke, her voice was shaking with anger. "I will . . . and you can't stop me." She whirled away from him and left, the pale color of her robe fading into the darkness as she moved toward the house.

Hawk shook his head, staring ruefully into the darkness.

"Stubborn," he whispered with a frown. "Damned stubborn willful little wench." Then he smiled and shook his head in amused defeat. "Dominic, my cousin, I think you have met your match, and in the bargain, you have gotten yourself a spitfire . . . a beautiful little spitfire with the eyes of a wildcat and the courage of a panther. Your nights with that one will be anything but dull or boring." He laughed softly before going back toward the house.

Twenty-six

The next morning Aimee was awake very early and dressed in a royal blue riding habit, long before Jezzy would normally come to help her dress. She took a small canvas bag that contained a change of clothes and a black silk top hat with a royal blue gauze veil that matched her dress. Then she slipped quietly out of her room. At her waist hung a small, beaded black reticule which she opened as she gazed about the back veranda. She slipped a small polished steel lady's pistol into the bag, closed it, and hurried through the garden and out toward the stables.

She wanted to be away from the house before daybreak, before even the stable boys were awake, which meant she'd have to take the time to saddle her own horse. She only hoped she could manage that quickly and quietly before anyone discovered her, especially Hawk.

She had told no one in the house except Amos—he was the only one she could trust to keep quiet and not interfere. And even if his tired old eyes gazed at her with a disapproving look, Amos said nothing, but merely nodded before going back to his duties.

Finally her horse was harnessed and ready and Aimee lifted herself up onto the English sidesaddle, frowning with displeasure that she had to resort to riding this way. She only wished she'd had the seamstress make at least one riding habit with comfortable breeches. But since she was going into the city, she certainly didn't want to attract attention by riding like a hoyden, so she supposed this simply would have to do.

Riding away from the house, Aimee glanced back once to make sure no one had seen her. Now that she had made her decision and was on her way, she felt better, more hopeful. And she didn't want to chance spoiling that by having Hawk see her. Lord, but he was going to be terribly upset with her as it was. And she wouldn't even let herself imagine what Dominic would say.

Hawk stood in the shadows of the house, watching Aimee ride along the dark, tree-lined drive until he could no longer see her. With a quirk of his brow, he sighed and pulled himself up onto the horse that was tied to a nearby tree.

She hadn't listened . . . just as he'd known she wouldn't. She was one stubborn, headstrong woman and it would serve her right if he let her ride through the dark morning alone. Perhaps a few keelboat hoodlums could scare some sense into her; he certainly hadn't been able to. The little fool should have more sense than to ride alone along the Natchez Trace. But since she didn't, he supposed he owed it to Dominic to follow along behind to make sure she made it safely into the city.

Aimee had ridden almost an hour and as she gazed around at the beauty of the dark forest beyond the

300

narrow road, she was relieved that the sun finally was up. She'd heard noises and felt her horse skitter beneath her more than once in the past hour; she'd even thought she heard someone riding behind her. But in the early morning shadows, she could see nothing and finally convinced herself it was only nerves that made her see and hear things that weren't really there.

She'd be at the DeVaull Plantation soon. She planned to stop and ask Mr. DeVaull for someone to ride with her the rest of the way into Natchez. It would be foolish of her to attempt the entire ride alone—a man couldn't even be considered safe these days riding this trail. Since travel on the river was so common there were often scores of men—rough, unkempt deckhands and keelboatmen who rode south on the river as far as Natchez, helped unload their boats, then followed the Natchez Trace back upriver to Nashville or Ohio to begin the process all over again.

She breathed a little sigh of relief when she finally saw the DeVaull Plantation. She glanced down at the small gold watch pinned to the bodice of her riding habit, hoping someone in the house was awake. It was still relatively early.

The road to the house was almost twice as wide as the one leading to LeBeaux and there were no huge overhanging limbs to block the view of the mansion. Aimee nudged the sides of her horse and cantered up the lane, stopping near the long, low front porch of the brick house.

Aimee smiled, noting the beautiful camellias planted around the front porch and the thick vines of wisteria that crept up the tall, wide columns at either end of the porch. Rebecca DeVaull loved flowers and

301

her home was utterly alive with the scent and color of many different varieties.

Aimee stepped onto the flagstone surface of the porch that had no steps but lay flat on the ground. She was surprised to see the front door open and to find Jenny staring at her oddly out the small opening before stepping out to greet her.

"Aimee," she said, her dark eyes wide with surprise. "'What on earth are you doing here at this time of morning?" She glanced about, noting that Aimee was alone. "And with no escort or driver. Has something happened?"

"No," Aimee said, anxious to explain so that she could get on with her trip to Natchez. "But I do need your help."

"Yes, of course; come into the parlor. Shall I have Sally bring us some coffee?"

"That sounds wonderful." Aimee glanced back over her shoulder out toward the dense forest and the Trace. "I have the most uncanny feeling that someone has been following me."

Jenny took her arm, pulling her inside while her eyes scanned the forest. "I wouldn't be at all surprised. Mother would be scandalized if she knew you were riding at this time of morning . . . all alone."

Once inside, Aimee learned that Mr. Devaull was away for a few days and that Jenny's mother was still in bed. Then, over steaming cups of coffee, she explained quickly to Jenny why she had come.

Hawk held his horse back as he watched Aimee ride to the imposing brick house. She glanced around before stepping onto the porch, then he could see her talking to someone at the door before both of them went inside. His eyes narrowed as he watched and waited, wondering what her intentions were and why she had stopped here.

Finally, he dismounted, tied the horse's reins to a bush, and edged his way through the dense forest up toward the house. The place was quiet and there seemed to be hardly anyone stirring about. Nearing the house at the end of the long, low porch, he pushed aside a thick tangle of vines and stepped softly onto the stone-lined porch. His soft moccasin boots made not a whisper of sound as he crept low across the flagstones to one of the long, wide windows.

Gazing in at the edge of the window, he saw nothing and had decided to go back to his horse, despite his curiosity, and wait for Aimee to leave. It was then that he sensed, rather than heard someone behind him . . . someone who stole very quietly and stealthily toward him.

With a low growl, Hawk turned, seeing the soft glint of a gun barrel. Without thinking he reached forward to lift the gun and sling it out of the way where it landed with a soft swish in the bushes that surrounded the house. He heard a quiet gasp and a soft grunt of pain as his arms came back down, encasing his attacker, and pushing him back across the porch against one of the tall white columns.

"Oh."

Hawk's black eyes opened wide as he looked down into the face of his attacker. But even then, seeing that it was a young *woman*, and a very beautiful young woman at that, he did not loosen his grip. He was too angry . . . too frustrated with himself for being approached so easily, and he wasn't about to let her go now.

Jenny's eyes held surprise and anger and as she fought to free herself from the man's steely grip, she opened her mouth to scream.

"Oh, no," Hawk said, clamping his hand over her mouth and shoving her back against the column. "You aren't getting away so easily as that little wildcat. Now . . . do you want to explain to me exactly what you're doing, shoving a shotgun in my back? Did you intend to shoot me? Well? Tell me . . . did you?"

He shook her, angry with himself and even angrier with the girl who writhed and struggled against him. The feel of her firm breasts against his chest and the scent of roses that clung to her made his head reel with some heady, forbidden emotion. And he had to remind himself that this was a white woman he held in his arms, not that she was the first. But this one was a woman of wealth and substance. One had only to look around to see that. And she was different. How, he couldn't really say; he only knew that holding her and touching her, feeling her soft lips against the palm of his hand made him feel things he'd never felt before. The desire that rose quickly in him, hit like a fist and it took him completely by surprise when he found that he didn't want to fight with her at all. What he most wanted to do was kiss her.

Hawk stepped away, looking into her eyes with a silent warning as he tentatively lifted his hand away from her mouth. His eyes, black and fathomless, gazed down into brown ones that were filled now with a mixture of awe and fright.

"Well . . . answer me, girl."

But he was surprised when rather than cowering from him, she used the opportunity to spit her venom

304

at him.

"Of course I was going to shoot you . . . you . . . you heathen! And what else would you expect, sneaking around someone's front porch at this time of the morning."

Jenny stared at the man for a moment, at the way he was dressed. She could feel his naked skin practically burning her through her gauze dress and she thought the slash of scar across his cheek made him look fierce and frightening. But she didn't intend to let him know that.

"I wasn't sneaking," he said, trying to maintain his patience. "I was—"

"Oh, I know what you were doing. You thought you'd sneak here in the middle of the night—"

"The middle of the night?" He stepped back and put his hands at his hips as he stared down at her. What a wild-eyed little minx she was.

"You thought you'd just sneak in here, break into the house while everyone was asleep and then who knows what you intended." She was practically breathless with anger.

Hawk wanted to laugh. What in God's name did she think he wanted?

Jenny's tongue darted forward to wet her lips, made dry by her fear, and her eyes swept over him, taking in the broad muscular shoulders, the naked bronzed chest that tapered down to a trim waist and narrow hips. And when her eyes lifted back to his face, she found him watching her, smiling in amusement as if he could almost read her mind.

"'What exactly do you think I intended?" he asked, letting his eyes rake insultingly down her small, slender figure and back up to the shining tumble of golden brown hair. Her brown eyes glittered at him. "To find your room perhaps? Crawl through a window into your very soft, sweet-scented bed?"

"Oh! How dare you say such a thing to me! First you follow my friend and put her life in jeopardy— God knows what you intended doing with her—then you stand here on my very own porch and insult me with your vile words." Her eyes blazed with fury and she stepped toward the edge of the porch, toward where he had tossed the shotgun only moments ago.

"Jenny, no," she heard from the doorway.

She turned to see Aimee looking from her to the Indian and the look she saw on her friend's face was not fear—it was one of recognition and chagrin.

"You know this man?" Jenny asked.

"Yes," Aimee said with a weak smile and a nod. "He's Dominic's cousin, and he is staying at LeBeaux until Dominic returns from Natchez."

Hawk's eyes closed as he sighed with disgust and moved his legs restlessly. Then slowly they lifted as he stared into Jenny's surprised eyes.

"Well, I don't care who he is. He's sneaky and ruthless—"

"Ruthless?" Hawk snapped. "Look, lady—"

"He practically threw me against that column and I'm sure my arms must be bruised where he—"

"I didn't hurt you," he growled, his eyes warning her beneath his dark brows.

"You did . . . you bruised my arms and when you clamped your hand over my mouth, you . . ." Slowly her voice trailed away, as black eyes snapped and challenged, then moved languidly to her soft trembling lips.

"Jenny . . ." Aimee said. "Hawk . . . please. This is

306

all my fault; I should have guessed it was you before Jenny insisted on going around with a shotgun. If I had looked before trying to find help . . ." Aimee's eyes flashed toward Jenny. "And I should never have let you talk me into it."

Jenny lifted her chin, her cheeks flushed now as she purposefully avoided the Indian's furious eyes.

Watching the two, Aimee frowned. She saw Jenny's telltale flush and the way her eyes darted away from Hawk's intense gaze. And she also did not miss the way Hawk's black eyes moved over Jenny's figure, or the fact that his breathing was still hard and unsteady, long after the struggle had ended.

"Hawk," Aimee said with a sweet, knowing smile. "Perhaps we should start over. Let me introduce you to my dearest friend, Jennifer DeVaull. Jenny, this is Dominic's cousin, Hawk."

Hawk's eyes still watched the girl cautiously as Jenny lifted her brown eyes in a cool, haughty stare.

"Hawk who?" she asked, her voice petulant and stiff.

"Just Hawk," he said, sneering. "Or you might prefer John — if my Anglo name would make you any less hostile."

Jenny swallowed and lifted her eyes to his face, wondering how he got the scar across his cheek. Then looking into his eyes, she shivered. "No," she said, her voice still defiant and cool. "Hawk will do."

Aimee grinned, watching the two. She had not seen such blatant sparks between two people since . . . Seeing Dominic's face before hers, she shook herself, remembering her mission and knowing she needed to be on her way. And now that she knew it was only Hawk who followed her, she felt a tremendous burden lift from her shoulders.

"Hawk, I'm sorry if I worried you this morning," she said.

"I *was* worried," he said, turning to Aimee. "But knowing you, I had already guessed what you intended. If you insist on going through with this, at least let me ride into Natchez with you. Once we find Dominic, I'll go back to the plantation and make sure everything there is secure."

"All right." she agreed with a weak smile. "You might find this hard to believe, but it would really be a relief if you would go with me."

His smile was a bit skeptical. "Then it's settled," he said, his voice deep and warm. "Let me get my horse." When he turned, his eyes barely grazed the brown-haired girl who stood so still, watching and listening to him and Aimee. "Good day, Miss DeVaull, and thank you so much for your *charming* hospitality."

At his sarcastic words, Jenny's lips clamped tightly together and she clenched her fists as she watched him walk away. The fringe of his buckskins whipped against his long legs and the morning sun glistened on his black hair and bare golden skin. She thought he looked wild and untamed . . . and completely daunting.

"What an infuriating man," she said. As she turned to Aimee, her eyes practically spit fire. "I wonder how you can stand such an arrogant, beastly man."

Aimee grinned and went to put her arm around Jenny's shoulders. "Isn't he though? But attractive, too, in an arrogant, beastly kind of way, don't you think? Definitely a very masculine, very sensuous kind of man. Dangerous, too . . . just the kind of man you described to me not so long ago if I remem-

308

ber correctly."

"Oh," Jenny said. "Don't be ridiculous. I was speaking of Dominic, not this . . . this rude, insolent, arrogant man. Why . . . I could never find someone like him attractive."

"No," Aimee said, still grinning. "Of course you couldn't."

Jenny flushed and gritted her teeth, glancing again back toward the edge of the woods where the infuriating man mounted his horse. He sat straight and commanding on the horse as it pranced and pawed the ground and Jenny shivered as she felt a tingle rush from her spine up to her hairline.

"You be careful, Aimee," she said, her eyes never leaving the man on the horse. "That man is more dangerous than you realize."

Aimee laughed and kissed her friend lightly on the cheek.

"I'll stop back on my way home."

Twenty-seven

On the ride into Natchez, Aimee glanced from time to time at Hawk as he rode beside her. He seemed quiet and thoughtful and she wondered at first if he was concerned about their safety. When they neared the outskirts of the city with no problems, she turned to thank him for coming after her.

"I stopped at the DeVaull Plantation to beg an escort for the rest of the trip," she said, giving him an apologetic smile. "There was simply no one at LeBeaux who I could ask . . . you know that was one of the reasons Dominic made this trip. He had hopes of finding a crew of men to work for us."

Hawk's look was cool as he glanced her way.

"You could have asked me."

"I know," she said, her voice quiet. "But you made it perfectly clear that you didn't approve."

He grunted and looked at her with only the slightest bit of a smile. "I'm not sure you are the kind of woman who seeks anyone's approval, Aimee."

"Well, you're wrong. I'm not nearly so willful that I can ignore common sense. And whether you believe it or not, I do listen to Dominic's opinions . . . and even though I don't know you as well yet, as his friend, I value yours also."

He smiled then and shook his head, letting the matter drop. He knew better than to argue with a beautiful woman.

"Speaking of friends," he said. "How did you happen to become friends with such a hotheaded little wench as Jenny DeVaull?"

"Jenny . . . hotheaded? Well, I must confess, you've seen her in a different light than I ever did. I would never consider Jenny hotheaded."

"No? Not even when she threatens to shoot a man?"

"She was afraid, Hawk, that's all there was to it. And how was she to know who you were? Would you have us sit there until the man we saw creeping through the trees came and bashed in the door?"

"I still can't imagine that you two are friends."

"Well, we are. We met several years ago at the Planter's Cotillion. That was before I met Jim and I was very pleased when we moved out here to find that Jenny was my closest neighbor. She and I have a great deal in common."

Again Hawk frowned at her and shook his head as if he did not believe what she was saying.

"It's true," she said, her voice soft and convincing. "Jenny is a wonderful person . . . a sweet, loyal girl who would do anything for her friends. And as you already know, she's also strong-willed and courageous."

Hawk said nothing more, but Aimee could see his mind working as they rode into town. He seemed so preoccupied that he hardly realized where they were until someone shouted nearby.

"Miz Aimee . . . Miz Aimee . . ." they heard.

"Look, Hawk . . . over there by the livery . . . it's Nathaniel."

She waved at him and turned back to Hawk. "I think you should go back to LeBeaux now. Dominic is going to be angry enough with me as it is. I don't want to be responsible for causing problems between the two of you as well."

He looked skeptical for a moment, frowning toward the livery stables where Nathaniel stood near a wagon. "I suppose you're right. And if I leave now"— he glanced up at the sun which was in a position well past noon— "I'll be there before midnight. But are you sure you'll be all right? I can stay if—"

"No, I'll be fine." Her eyes were bright and already the worry seemed to have disappeared. "Dominic is here, getting supplies just as he said. I'll tell him I meant to surprise him and we'll ride home together. Besides," she said, leaning slightly toward Hawk, "it will be a wonderful opportunity for us to spend a little time alone."

"All right," he said with a quick grin. "It seems you've made up your mind and I've already learned not to argue with you when that happens."

She lowered her lashes, then opened them in a flirtatious little mannerism that made both of them laugh.

"I'll be fine. And thank you, Hawk, for caring enough to follow me this morning. I don't think I've ever been happier to see anyone. The trail was darker and more frightening than I had imagined. I guess sometimes I can be too stubborn for my own good."

He pursed his lips, letting his eyes wander over her face, noting the brilliance of her green eyes. She was happy, he thought. Just the prospect of finding Dominic had changed her outlook completely and erased all the doubt that had been there yesterday.

And he hoped his cousin was not going to disappoint her.

"I'll see you at LeBeaux then . . . in a couple of days."

"Yes," she said, smiling.

Aimee waved as Hawk rode away, then turned anxiously toward the livery stable.

"Nathaniel," she said. "I can't believe we found you so quickly. Where's Dominic?"

Nathaniel shrugged and looked up at her where she sat on the horse.

"I ain't sure, Miz Aimee. He went off early this mornin'. Said he had some business to take care of. Said if he don't come back tonight, not to worry, that he'll see me in the mornin'."

Aimee cocked her head as if she had not heard correctly. "If he doesn't come back? But where . . . ?" She stopped, frowning as she tried to think where he could be. Gone to find the young man perhaps, who would tutor Lucas? The city was small. Surely if he were here she could find him. "Nathaniel, would you take care of my horse and traveling bag? I think I'll walk about in the city . . . visit some shops. Perhaps when I return, Mister Dominic will be back."

"Yes'm," he said, his eyes watching her cautiously. Aimee could see that he didn't really think Dominic would be back, even though he didn't actually say it.

Aimee walked until her feet were tired and hot. She thought she had visited every store, every mercantile in town and still she had not seen the tall, dark-haired man she sought. Once, she even peeked into a saloon on Canal Street, but seeing only a handful of men at a card table and an old man playing songs on a piano,

313

she walked on. The scent of stale smoke and whiskey drifted out through the doors and seemed to follow her down the street. She frowned, feeling a disquiet begin to move over her as she realized there were not many more places in town where he could be. Not decent, respectable places anyway.

She recalled Dominic's words about the young man he hoped to engage as a tutor. He worked on a boat, didn't he say? She frowned, turning to look toward the wide open space that marked the Mississippi's flow past the bluffs of the city.

She knew if Dominic was there on the docks he would not welcome her unexpected visit; it was not a place frequented by ladies. She glanced down at her blue riding frock, noting the dust-covered skirt and the grimy edge of hem that had swept along the streets all afternoon. She felt as dirty and grimy as the dress and the sun that beat down relentlessly against her face and shoulders made her feel sticky and hot, made her long for nothing more than a cool bath and a very large glass of water.

She had already decided as she walked back to the livery that she would have to visit Aunt Eulie. She had not intended it — had even hoped to avoid her entirely while she was here. Her aunt would not look with approval on her jaunt into the city — an unmarried woman alone — with a man whose standing in Natchez society was questionable to say the least.

She sighed. It couldn't be helped. She could hardly spend the night in the streets or at the livery. She would go to Aunt Eulie's, enjoy a cool bath and a pleasant night's sleep on clean white sheets. In the morning, she would begin her search for Dominic again.

At the livery she found a piece of paper in her traveling bag and wrote down her aunt's address and handed it to Nathaniel.

"If Mister Dominic returns, you give him this. Tell him that I'm here . . . I'm at my aunt Eulie's and he's to come there no matter what time of night it is. Do you understand?"

"Yes, Miz Aimee."

Later, riding along the tree-lined streets, Aimee enjoyed the beauty of the houses and their landscaped gardens. As she turned the horse onto High Street, the huge white house on the hill was the first thing that greeted her eyes. Aimee looked now at the tall, stately elegance of her aunt's home with its pristine white Corinthian columns and delicate ironwork around the top balcony. Aunt Eulie's husband had purposely built the house on this small hill, everyone said, just so he could look down on all those beneath him.

Aimee smiled, remembering her uncle's snobbishness. He had been a quick-tempered, ambitious man who never seemed to sit still for a moment. And it was that ambition and his insatiable quest for power and wealth that sent him to an early grave, or so everyone said. Her aunt had never remarried, but continued to live in the huge house, surrounded by her faithful old servants, and a host of friends whom she entertained almost daily. The house was rarely free of overnight guests who were made to feel completely at home by the woman who the local society considered the Queen of Natchez elegance.

A young dark-skinned youth came immediately to help Aimee down from her horse and to lead the animal around toward the back of the house. Another young man came down the wide marble steps to take her bag.

The porch, usually filled with guests on a warm summer evening, was empty now and Aimee assumed they were preparing themselves for their evening meal.

She took off her hat and stood quietly in the cool hallway as she waited for the boy to tell her aunt she was there. Glancing around at the massive gold leaf French mirrors and bronze chandeliers, Aimee thought that this house made LeBeaux look like a country cottage and she smiled, trying to imagine Jim LeBeaux at home in a house like this. Oddly enough, she could picture Dominic at peace in this elegance . . . much more than Jim, and she realized again what an oddly diverse man he was.

She heard a clock down the hallway striking six o'clock just as her aunt appeared at the top of the stairs, paused, then hurried down the steps with her elegant silk dressing gown trailing behind her. She was the very picture of what Southern charm and lady-hood should be, Aimee thought with a wry smile.

"Aimee, my darling . . . what on earth has brought you to Natchez? Not that I am not perfectly delighted to see you, of course. But . . . well, just look at you — you look completely exhausted. Your lovely skin is positively baked and where on earth have you been to gather so much dust?" Her aunt's eyes raked over her, critically surveying and making notes. "That's a perfectly lovely gown, but my dear, don't you think royal blue is quite the bit warm for a summer afternoon?"

"I was on horseback, Aunt Eulie," Aimee said. "And I began my journey very early this morning when the air was much cooler. But yes, you're right, it is quite warm now and I'd like nothing more than a

316

cool bath and a change of clothes. I had thought to buy myself a new frock before starting the trip home, but I wasn't able to find Dominic and so—"

"Dominic? You and Dominic are here . . . together . . . alone?"

"Well, no . . . not exactly. He was already here and I came today looking for him but . . . Oh, it's a long story . . . and complicated. Could we talk about this later?"

"Well, of course, you must be quite exhausted, my darling." Aunt Eulie came to put her arm around Aimee's shoulders. "And here I stand chattering like some twittering old fool. Your room is always ready and waiting for you, my dear, you know that. And I'm certain there are enough dresses in the armoire to last a month if you wish to stay. You just go on up now . . . I'll have your bath sent right away, then you can rest awhile before dinner. We'll talk . . . whenever you feel up to it."

Aimee's smile was wan and as she turned to go up the stairs, her aunt's gaze followed her, dark with worry and concern. What on earth was going on with her young niece anyway? And why did she have such a strong feeling that Dominic Valcour had everything to do with that wistful, little lost look in the girl's eyes?

Upstairs, just as her aunt said, Aimee found there was everything she needed in the large, cool bedroom on the second floor. After she had bathed, she enjoyed the feel of silky undergarments and a light, airy, and very elegant wrapper against her skin. She stretched out on the tall four-posted rosewood bed and was soon asleep, exhausted not only by the ride from LeBeaux, but also the hot afternoon of searching for Dominic.

317

When she awakened more than an hour later, there was a slow rhythmic swishing hum in the room. Aimee glanced toward the foot of the bed to see a very small black girl pulling a rope that led to a fringed fan above the bed. As Aimee's eyes opened wider, the girl smiled. She continued pulling the rope down and up.

"Well, good evening," Aimee said, her voice still rough with sleep. "And what is your name, little miss?"

The small girl, not more than eight or nine years old, ducked her head shyly as she answered. "Tisha Ann."

"Well, Tisha Ann, you are a very pretty little girl and I thank you indeed for making my sleep more pleasant."

"Welcome, ma'am," the girl said with a curtsy.

Aimee laughed, feeling ever so much better after her rest. But seeing the darkness at the windows and feeling the growl of her empty stomach she was certain she had missed supper.

"Tisha Ann, honey, would you run downstairs to the kitchen . . . tell Cook I'd like a supper tray sent up here? Can you do that for me?"

"Yes'm," the girl said, dropping the cord and heading for the door. "I go find her right now."

Later, after a delicious meal of crispy fried chicken and fresh vegetables, Aimee felt much better. She had just finished eating when her aunt opened the door and stepped into the room.

"Well, I'm happy to see that you've eaten and rested some. You look much better, dear."

"I feel much better, Aunt Eulie—thank you."

"Oh," her aunt said with a dismissing wave of her

hand. "There's no need to thank me. This is your home, Aimee, you know that; I've told you enough. When I'm gone, it will be yours completely. I suppose that's why I don't understand why you won't leave that godforsaken plantation and come to live here now. The country is no place for a refined young woman like yourself. Besides, I worry that something will happen to you way out there in the wilderness, with no one to protect you now that Jim is gone."

"Mister Valcour is there now, Aunt. And, in fact, he's in Natchez at this very moment, finding a crew of men who will help guard the plantation. And he also is finding a tutor for Lucas. So, you can see we're becoming quite progressive at LeBeaux."

Aunt Eulie's lips tightened and she came to sit on a small, round brocade chair near the bed.

"I'm glad you brought up the subject of Mister Valcour, for he's exactly who I came to talk about."

"Aunt Eulie . . ." Aimee began.

"Now, you know I spoke to him at length when I visited you, darling, and I have no doubt he is a fine and honorable man, despite his upbringing." She did not seem aware of the slight lifting of her nose as she spoke. "But I suggested that he move out of the house and I'm quite disappointed that he has not done so."

"Oh, Aunt Eulie . . . you didn't!"

"But really, dear, you know I do not think it proper that the two of you continue living there with no chaperone or—"

"Aunt Eulie . . . we talked about this before and I told you that I—"

"Yes, I know what you told me. But now, here you are, looking quite exhausted and desperate, searching for this man on the streets of Natchez. And I want to

319

know exactly what is going on. I'm concerned about you."

Aimee sighed. She had known this would happen if she came here and it was exactly what she had hoped to avoid. For all her aunt's intentions, she could be completely exasperating where her ideas about conventional behavior were concerned.

"Nothing is going on, Aunt. Dominic had business in the city and I thought it would be the perfect opportunity for me to visit you . . . that's all."

"Hmmm," her aunt murmured, eyeing her doubtfully. "That's not the idea I received when you arrived this evening. It must have been a spur-of-the-moment idea . . . since you left home with hardly a thing to wear." Her glance turned to the small canvas bag nearby.

Aimee could feel the blood rising to her cheeks, but she refused to look away from her aunt's eyes as she replied.

"It was actually . . . a spur-of-the-moment decision, and it probably was impetuous of me at that. And I apologize, Aunt Eulie, if I've worried you by my actions; it was not what I intended."

Eulie sat for a moment watching her niece. Then she sighed and rose from the chair.

"You are very precious to me, Aimee, you know that. You are all the family I have left and I probably am a foolish old woman, but I believe you. And I expect in any case, you will do exactly as you please, despite my wishes. I will say no more about the matter."

"Thank you, Aunt Eulie," Aimee said, smiling as she lifted her cheek for her aunt's kiss.

As soon as her aunt left, Aimee slid off the bed and began rummaging through the rosewood dresser,

320

searching for stockings and a proper slip to wear beneath her gown.

Something had been nagging at her all day—a thought she had tried more than once to put out of her mind. But now, rested and no longer hungry, she felt her energy returning and she knew she had to follow through on her intuition.

She had not been able to find Dominic anywhere. Nathaniel had seemed very secretive, and she had a feeling he knew more than he was saying. He probably knew exactly where Dominic was and simply did not want to tell her. And now she thought she knew, too.

After she dressed, she slipped quietly down the stairs, making sure none of the guests on the front porch saw her. Then she inched down the hallway and out the back door to the kitchen where she found one of the young servant boys and asked him to summon a driver and a covered carriage for her right away.

Once inside the carriage, Aimee pulled the dark velvet curtains across the windows and opened the small door at the front so she could speak to the driver.

"Where to, Miz Aimee," the man said.

"Oh, George, it's you. Good. I want you to take me to Natchez-Under-the-Hill."

The man turned around on the seat to stare down into the carriage at her and there was a frown of disapproval across his dark face.

"But Miz Aimee, your aunt Eulie will have a fit—"

"My aunt Eulie is not going to know, George. She thinks I'm sound asleep in my bedroom after a long, exhausting day. And that's exactly the way I want it. Now, if you feel disloyal to my aunt or if you don't want to take me down to the river, you may step down and go on back to the house. I'm perfectly capable of

321

driving this carriage myself."

George sighed and slapped the reins against the horse's rump, causing the carriage to leap as they began to move.

"No, ma'am," he said, his voice muffled as they moved down the back drive and out onto the street. "You is as stubborn as ever you was when you was a little girl. But I reckon I can't let you drive yo'self. You don't supposed to be down in that part of town . . . least I can do is go with you."

"Thank you, George," Aimee said, smiling with satisfaction as she settled herself back against the cushions. "And you are just as sweet as you were when I was a little girl."

She heard the man's grunt and she smiled, feeling free, feeling an urgency to be at the riverfront. She wanted to clear her mind for good of the troublesome feeling that Dominic could be in one of the gambling saloons that lay at the foot of the bluffs along the Mississippi River.

Twenty-eight

They drove slowly through the streets of Natchez, past the quiet elegant homes and down Canal Street toward the river. There was a light fog that lifted from the street and spread softly around the lighted windows of the houses. The night air felt sultry and uncomfortable and in the distance Aimee thought she heard the soft rumble of thunder.

As George turned the carriage toward the river, the roadway began to turn steeply downward. And soon, even in the enclosed carriage, Aimee could hear the tinny sound of piano music and the loud boisterous laughter of the patrons in the notorious saloons and bordellos that lined the river.

Only for a moment did Aimee allow herself to have doubts. She probably should not be here, she knew that. She inched her fingers down to the beaded reticule, assuring herself that the small pistol still lay safely inside.

No decent woman would come to this part of the city, and if she had hoped she might remain in the carriage as she scanned the various barrooms, she soon discovered that was an impossibility.

The dusty street swarmed with men, many of them loud, some of them weaving unsteadily as they moved

323

from one building to another. There were carriages parked everywhere and horses stood quietly beneath large spreading trees that she could faintly see in the darkness. And here, the pungent, muddy scent of the river was almost overpowering as it blended with the nauseating stench of refuse and open latrines.

She tapped against the window, "George, pull over here. I'm going to get out."

"Miz Aimee . . . no. You can't just go wanderin' by yo'self out here—it ain't safe."

"I'll be fine, George. Besides, I'm only going to walk along the boardwalk and glance into some of the . . . uh, establishments."

Stepping down quickly from the carriage, she pulled the hood of a lightweight silk cape over her hair. Then, putting her head down, she picked up her skirts and made her way to the nearest building. Even in the darkness, she garnered instant attention as several of the passersby whistled and called out to her.

"Hey, girlie," one yelled. "I got shiny gold coins in my pocket, and a brand-new bottle of Tennessee whiskey."

She hurried on, ignoring the calls and the invitations. Luckily for her, the men she silently rejected only laughed and moved on to easier, more friendly territory.

She noted that George pulled the carriage slowly along the rutted street behind her, keeping her in sight as she went from door to door. She peeked in at the windows and slipped away from the men who reached for her. She managed to escape them all and finally came to the biggest and loudest of the saloons. A sign hanging from the edge of the roof read, SADIE'S RIVER CLUB and along the boardwalk, yellow light spilled from the wide, glass-paned windows. This was a loud, raucous place and seemed to be the most popular club along the river. From inside came the sound of masculine voices and giggling women that mingled oddly with loud music and the sound of tinkling glass.

When Aimee saw a small boy coming out the swinging doors, she stepped forward and caught his sleeve.

"Excuse me, but do you work here?"

He looked up at her in the light and grinned. His lean face was sprinkled with dark freckles and from beneath his hat stuck a thatch of dirty, reddish-blond hair.

"I works for anybody," the boy said, still grinning as his eyes scanned quickly up and down her expensive cape and dress. "Want I should do somethin' for you, lady?"

"Well, actually—I'm looking for someone . . . a man named Dominic Valcour. Do you know him?"

"Know Dom? Why o' course I know him. Everybody on the river knows Mister Valcour. He's a Cock o' the Walk, he is. He can outsmart, outfight and outshoot just about any man on the mighty Mississip', ma'am, and that's a natural-born fact."

She breathed a heady sigh of relief and bent down toward the boy, catching the unpleasant scent of unclean hair and clothes.

"Do you know where he is?"

"Shore," he said, cocking his thumb back over his shoulder. "He be playin' cards right here at Sadie's place."

Her heart sank and for a moment she thought she might actually be sick. She could feel her heart pounding against her ribs, feel the muscles tightening in her stomach as all her fears seemed to have become a reality.

"No," she whispered.

"What's that, ma'am?"

"Nothing," she said. "Nothing. Look, boy . . ." She rummaged in the small reticule, taking a few coins and holding them toward the lad. "Can you take me to him?"

The boy took the money and slipped it quickly into his ragged pockets before glancing up at her. His eyes moved over her clothes, down to the toes of her expensive shoes beneath her gown. "Beggin' yer pardon, ma'am. But I'm thinkin' you might not oughta be here in this place. And I'm thinkin' Mister Valcour might just tan my hide if'n I brung you inside."

Aimee clamped her teeth together and nodded to the boy. "You just let me worry about Mister Valcour." She handed him another coin, seeing his face light with glee before he looked up at her again. "Now . . . take me to him," she said.

"Yes, ma'am," he said, reaching his hand up toward her. "Right this way, ma'am."

Aimee swallowed and took a deep breath, then took the boy's warm, grimy hand in hers. He led her through the doors and into the loud interior of the saloon.

She kept her head low, holding the hood of her cape with her other hand as she tried to avoid attention. But it was just a matter of time in a place like Sadie's before a woman such as Aimee demanded immediate and fervent attention. She had walked into a den of animals, it seemed; men who held little respect for any woman who entered the door and even less respect for one who did not favor them with an agreea-

326

ble answer to their vulgar suggestions.

The boy glanced worriedly over his shoulder as he pulled her along through the reaching, grabbing men. She was jostled and bumped. The gaudily dressed women at the tables turned, and seeing the attention she commanded, some of them cursed at her. And for a moment, Aimee felt like bolting for the door. She was completely overwhelmed by the smells of the place and by the pawing hands and loud vulgar talk. But then, she saw him, just at the foot of a stage that covered the back of the room. There at a table full of men, their heads completely wreathed in smoke, sat Dominic, as cool and completely unconcerned as she'd ever seen him.

Dominic had heard the commotion at the front of the saloon and as the cards were being shuffled, he glanced that way to see what was happening. He saw Timmie, one of the river runners, dragging a woman through the crowd of raucous men and he frowned. What in hell was a well-dressed woman like that doing in this place? Probably one of those preachy wives looking for her husband. Then he shrugged and turned his attention back to the card game.

"Call the game, Bull," he said to a brawny, red-haired man sitting at his left.

The man grinned and rubbed his fingers over his bushy mustache. "Fours and whores is wild . . . one-eyed jacks and the man with the axe."

"Good God," one of the other men said. "You don't want to take any chances, do you?" Then he laughed as he stuck a cigar back into his mouth and surveyed the cards in his hand.

Dominic turned back toward the crowd, his eyes scanning through the smoke for the woman he'd seen just a moment before. What was it about her that seemed so familiar?

He saw the look in Timmie's eyes as the boy headed straight for their table. And he knew. In a stunned moment, his black eyes lifted to the face partially hidden in the shadows of the hooded cape and he knew.

"Aimee . . ." He immediately came to his feet just as Aimee reached the table. And just at the same moment, a drunk grabbed her from behind, raking his hand down the back of her head. His actions pulled the hood back to reveal long silky black hair that spilled and tumbled in the smoky lights of the saloon.

"Goddamn," the man said. "Look at this little beauty, won't you, boys."

Aimee screamed as the man lurched forward drunkenly and slipped his brawny arms around her waist, lifting her from the floor. "I'll bet she could warm a man's bed real good. Whadda ya say, little darlin'? How 'bout you and me goin' upstairs and gettin' right down to it."

"Get your hands off the lady," Dominic growled, reaching forward to pull Aimee away from the drunk and into the circle of his own arms. "She's with me."

"Oh yeah?" the man said, puffing out his chest and strutting forward to face Dominic. "And who says she is?"

"The name is Dominic Valcour, friend." Dominic's right hand lifted toward the light and Aimee gasped as she saw the gleam of steel from the broad-bladed knife he held. "And I'd suggest you find yourself another place to drink . . . real quick."

The big man's eyes grew large and he gritted his teeth, blanching noticeably at the sight of a blade in

Dominic's hand. Then he laughed and shook his head.

"Hell, yes," he said. "One saloon is good as another, I always say." He turned to his friends, slapping one of them on the shoulders. "Let's find us a friendlier place to drink, gents," he said, turning sheepish eyes Dominic's way. "I've heard the name often enough, though I confess I didn't know yer face. No offense, Mister Valcour."

"None taken," Dominic said softly.

But Aimee knew him better than that. Dominic wasn't about to take the man's word, no matter how sincere he seemed. She could feel the tension still in his arms, in the hard press of his thighs against her legs as he watched the men leave the saloon. And only then did his arms slowly relax. He sheathed the knife back into the scabbard at his side. As the men at the table watched in amazement, Dominic turned Aimee to face him and to see the bitter anger in his eyes.

"What in hell do you mean . . . coming to a place like this? Come on, we're getting out of here right now." He glanced at the young boy who stood nearby staring at Dominic with large, fright-filled eyes. "I'll attend to you later, river rat."

"Wait just a damned minute, Valcour." The big, red-haired man at the table came slowly to his feet. "You're up a few hands as I recall. It ain't usually your style to leave so early without givin' the rest of us a chance to recoup our losses."

Aimee watched, feeling a shiver travel down her body as she saw Dominic's clenched jaw and saw his nostrils flare in frustration and anger.

"This woman is a friend, Bull, and I think you can

see, she doesn't belong here. I'll be back as soon as I—"

"Oh hell, no," Bull said. Even at this distance Aimee could smell the liquor on his breath and see the wild look in his reddened eyes. He put his right hand to his belt where the handle of a pistol protruded. "The lady stays; hell, won't nobody in here bother her now, not as long as she's with Dominic Valcour and Bull Hadley." He turned to the other players with a grin as he nodded toward Dominic. "This son-of-a-bitch is the only man on the Mississippi ever to beat Bull Hadley in a Cock o' the Walk contest, gentlemen. He's one tough *hombre*."

Aimee was beginning to feel real fear now. "Dominic . . ." she said in a soft protesting voice. She prayed Dominic wouldn't have to engage in some crazy male ritual by fighting this brutish man. All she wanted now was to get out of this place. For him to come with her and explain exactly what he was doing here, gambling away their last penny from LeBeaux Plantation.

"Shut up," Dominic hissed beneath his breath. "Just be quiet and sit down." His hand pushed her down into the wooden chair beside his as he slowly sat down and leaned toward her. "Have you lost your mind coming here? Jesus Christ," he swore.

The men at the table rolled their eyes and nodded to one another. But when Dominic's black eyes lifted, warning them, they straightened their faces and began to pick up their cards.

Aimee was still smarting from Dominic's terse greeting and his obvious disapproval. She stared at him angrily now, wishing she were a man so she could fight him herself.

330

Bull cleared his throat, nudging Aimee with his elbow as he bellowed toward the bar. "Barkeep, bring the little lady something to drink . . . something nice and gentle."

"She doesn't drink," Dominic growled at the big man, looking at him over his hand of cards.

Aimee lifted her chin, still angry and still stinging from his overbearing manner with her.

"Yes, I do," she said. "And thank you, Mister Hadley. It's very considerate of you."

The big man smiled broadly and smoothed his bushy mustache with his fingers.

"Game's just like before," he said. "Fours and whores is wild . . . uh, beggin' your pardon, ma'am, I mean fours and queens." Then to the others, ". . . one-eyed jacks and the man with the axe. Deal the hand, dealer."

Someone came to place a drink at Aimee's elbow. Seeing Dominic's glare of disapproval, she deliberately picked up the glass and drank a long swallow, trying not to cough as the strong liquor burned her throat. She could feel the warmth of it burning all the way down her chest and into her stomach where it seemed to land with a thud that made her head spin and her arms and legs grow weak.

"Oh," she whispered, opening her eyes wide to clear her head.

"Aimee," Dominic growled. "'What's gotten into you? Put that glass down . . . now."

She straightened and stared straight into his angry black eyes. "I most certainly will not. Mister Bull bought it for me and it would hardly be polite to return it." She giggled and covered her mouth self-consciously, suddenly feeling giddy and strange. "Mister

331

Bull bought it . . ." she repeated. "Sounds like a poem, doesn't it?"

Bull smiled at her and lifted his glass in a little salute and soon the rest of the men were smiling and lifting their glasses toward Aimee. And with a silly grin, she saluted them back and took another drink.

Dominic watched the display with a disbelieving frown. He raked his hand through his hair and turned his dark eyes back to his cards, discarding one angrily on the table.

He couldn't concentrate. Hell, he hardly even knew what he was doing anymore. All he wanted to do was get out of the place and find out what in God's name had possessed her to come to Natchez, much less what she was doing in such an unsavory place as Sadie's.

He turned to her with a groan and whispered so the others wouldn't hear. "Is anything wrong? Everything all right at home?"

"Everything's fine," she said with a haughty lift of her brows as she finished the rest of her drink.

"God, Aimee, go easy on that stuff, will you? It's potent."

"I don't feel a thing," she said. "I feel good, very relaxed now, thank you very much, Mister Dominic, who knows everything, Valcour."

He sighed and growled softly before throwing down his hand of cards and watching Bull rake the money across the table toward him. At this rate, it wasn't going to take long for the big man to recoup his losses. And he found that he didn't even care; all he wanted was to get Aimee out of the place.

"You ain't lettin' me win now are you, friend?" Bull asked, almost seeming to read Dominic's mind.

"Just deal the cards, Hadley," Dominic snapped.

Dominic frowned when someone brought Aimee another drink, then another. Every man in the saloon seemed to want to buy her a drink, and she was foolish enough to turn and smile at each and every one of them.

He lost hand after hand, not even caring anymore. But he was worried that he wouldn't be able to talk Bull into working for him if the man got any drunker. It was definitely time to go.

"Last hand, boys," Dominic said gruffly. "Winner takes all."

"Fine," Aimee said, waving her hand toward him and frowning at him. "Lose it all, Dominic. I don't care . . . you don't care . . . who does care? That right, Mister Bull?"

"Anything you say, missy." the man said with a laugh. "For a high-class dame, you're all right, you know? You can belt 'em back with the best of 'em, lass."

"That's right," she said, weaving in her chair. "Hear that, Mister Valcour? Some men know how to appre . . . apprec . . . appreciate a good woman." She hiccuped loudly, then giggled.

"Jesus," Dominic muttered. "Would someone just deal this last hand and let me get her out of here?"

Dominic could hardly believe his eyes when he looked at his hand. He held three kings on the first deal and he paid little attention as Aimee swayed over toward him.

"Oh . . . Oh!" she said, waving her hands and looking at his cards. "Mister Bull," she said. "I see him . . . I see the man with the axe—does he have on a crown?"

"Aye, lassie," Bull said, throwing his big head back with a raucous laugh. "He damned sure does; he's the king." He glanced at Dominic who rolled his eyes toward the ceiling. "Kings, eh, Valcour? Guess I'll fold."

"Fold," came the resounding response around the rest of the table.

"Deal again." Dominic gritted his teeth and turned to stare at Aimee. "And this time, please, just keep your beautiful mouth shut."

With large green eyes, she looked at him as she ran her fingers across her closed lips as if she had sealed them together.

Finally, the game was over and Dominic stood up, pulling Aimee up with him. "Good night, gentlemen." he said as he held her limp body against him. He felt her hair and the cape of her hood fall softly across his arm. "Do we still have a deal, Bull?"

"Is this the little lady what owns the plantation?"

"She is."

"Damn right, then. We got us a deal. I'll bring six more stout, able-bodied men with me and we'll be the best damned plantation crew you ever bought and paid for."

"Good," Dominic said with a solemn nod. "Meet me day after tomorrow, ten o'clock at the livery."

"I'll be there," Bull said with a wink and a broad grin. "And you take care of that little lady now. She's a royal flush if ever I saw one. I'd hate to see anything or anyone harm her, that I would."

Dominic rolled his eyes and lifted Aimee into his arms. Then, followed by the young river runner, he pushed his way through the curious onlookers toward the door.

Twenty-nine

Outside, lightning slashed downward from the rolling black clouds, unleashing a deafening thunder that seemed to shake the earth.

Aimee, feeling barely awake, lifted her head and smiled as she felt herself encased securely in Dominic's arms. She felt so weary as she rested her head against his shoulder, and she frowned only slightly at his muttered curses.

"Timmie," Dominic barked. "See if you can find a carriage."

"She done got a carriage, Mister Valcour," the boy said, looking hard through the driving rain that had begun to fall. "There it is . . . over there. Hey . . ." he shouted. "Hey, driver."

Dominic began to move just as George shook himself and whipped the reins against the horse's rump. Within seconds Aimee was safely tucked into the carriage and Dominic had pulled himself inside as well. He turned and tossed a coin to Timmie and shouted through the rain's deluge. "Find yourself some place dry to sleep tonight, boy."

"Yes, sir, Mister Valcour. Thank you, sir."

The driver had already turned the carriage back toward the bluffs of the city when Dominic opened the window to speak to him.

"What's your name?"

"Name's George, suh, and I work for Miz Eulie Dunbar. She's Miz Aimee's aunt." There was a small roof over George's head, but in the storm, he had his head bent against the wind and pounding rain, making his words muffled.

"Yes, I know Mrs. Dunbar. Well, George, it looks as if we have ourselves a small dilemma here, wouldn't you agree?" He watched George nod solemnly. "Since Miss Aimee is feeling rather, uh"—he glanced back at her with a bemused smile—"poorly . . . I think it's best if we take her to Canal Street until morning . . . a house called 'Roselawn'. Do you know it?"

"Yes, suh, knows it well. Got a cousin what works there."

"Good." Dominic pushed himself back against the seat and lifted Aimee until she lay like a rag doll against him. And in the isolated shelter of the carriage, he whispered to her.

"Little angel, what do you have on your mind this time?" He frowned into the darkness as he held her. He had a feeling it was not something he really wanted to know.

When George pulled the carriage around to the back of the house known as Roselawn, Dominic looked out the window. The storm seemed to have intensified and here on the river's bluffs, the trees bent and twisted furiously. The flash of lightning over the city was constant.

Dominic managed to get Aimee across the bricked courtyard and up the wide steps to the back veranda.

George came onto the porch as well, shaking the rain from his black frock coat and gazing from Aimee to Dominic with large questioning eyes.

"You're welcome to spend the night here as well, George," Dominic said. "Looks like an unfit evening to be out."

"No, suh . . . I just has a few blocks to go before home. Besides, somebody has to tell Miz Dunbar somethin'." Again his dark eyes questioned Dominic.

Dominic shifted Aimee in his arms and started toward the back door, glancing over his shoulder at the driver.

"If Miss Aimee has not been missed tonight, George, I want you to go to Mrs. Dunbar very early tomorrow morning. Tell her that you took Aimee into town to meet with Dominic Valcour. Can you do that?"

"Yes, suh, I can. But what if she done missin' Miz Aimee tonight suh?"

Dominic eyes darkened and he turned to gaze down at the soft warm bundle in his arms. To hell with Eulie Dunbar, he wanted to shout, and to hell with all the pretentious women in this town who watched and censured with such cold, passionless eyes. Aimee Le-Beaux belonged to him now and he didn't care who the hell knew it; he felt like flaunting it before the entire world, before the stifling Natchez society that dictated all the rules . . . the same *beau monde* that had made him feel such an outcast as a young boy. And it was those feelings that made him answer as he did.

"Tell her the same thing, George," he said through clenched teeth. "Tell her that Aimee is with Dominic Valcour, that she's safe, and that there is no reason for her to worry."

337

As Dominic carried Aimee into the wide hallway that ran the length of the house, lightning flashed, lighting the dim interior for long seconds before darkness fell again. The thunder seemed right on top of them, jarring the house and setting the crystal chandeliers in the hallway into motion with a light chiming rattle.

And just as Dominic expected, it was only moments before his housekeeper appeared, carrying a lighted candle and staring at him as if she'd seen a ghost. Dominic thought she looked like an apparition herself in her voluminous white gown, with her graying hair tucked beneath a white sleeping cap.

"Mister Valcour," she said, her eyes large and curious as she glanced from him to the girl he carried.

"Nellie, this is Mrs. Aimee LeBeaux . . . Jim's widow." He did not bother to stop, but continued on to the stairway in a small alcove, taking the steps two at a time as Nellie hurried along behind him. "I'm afraid she's had a bit too much to drink; I'm taking her up to the west bedroom near the gallery."

"Ah, a nip of the spirits, eh?" Nellie said, breathless from the climb. "That'll do it every time, especially to a wee bit of a lass like this one." Her eyes were warm and sympathetic as she looked at the lifeless girl in Dominic's arms. She hurried into the high-ceilinged room and turned down the bed covers, then quickly lit an oil lamp from the wick of her candle. She stood at the doorway then as Dominic lay Aimee on the bed and slipped off her wet shoes.

Dominic turned to look at his housekeeper. "Thank you, Nellie. You can go back to bed now. I'm sorry I woke you."

The woman's eyebrows lifted only the slightest bit

338

before she made a small bob of her head and backed out the door. But going down the hallway toward the stairs, she smiled broadly.

So, the master had brought home a woman; she couldn't remember that ever happening, not since she had been working here and that was at least ten years. And evidently this was a woman he knew quite intimately, since it was obvious he intended on undressing the poor wet lass. And did he intend to crawl into the big wide bed with the girl as well?

As Nellie made her way down the steps, she grunted softly, still smiling. "Well, well, well," she muttered. "And if I wasn't mistaken, there was a hint o' concern in those black eyes of his. Yessir, downright captivated he is, unless I miss my guess."

The storm raged all night long, finally moving past the city sometime near dawn and leaving in its wake a sweet, aromatic freshness and a light cool breeze.

Aimee woke slowly, feeling groggy and weighed down. She opened her eyes, glancing at a gathered white satin half tester over her head and frowning as she tried to remember where she was.

Without lifting her head from the pillow, she turned, giving a small murmur of pleasure when she saw Dominic. He was sitting in a chair near the bed, his elbow bent and propped on the chair arm as his cheek rested against his knuckles. His black eyes were narrowed suspiciously as he watched her come awake, and now he frowned and sat up straight, rubbing his fingers over his eyes.

"How are you feeling?" he asked, his deep voice soft in the unfamiliar room.

Aimee frowned, trying to clear her mind and decide exactly where she was and why Dominic was sitting beside her in a strange bedroom.

"'Where am I?" she asked, sitting up in bed and noticing that she wore only her flimsy undergarments.

Bright lights exploded behind her eyelids and a dull, throbbing pain began to pound at the back of her head.

"Ohhh," she moaned, lowering her head gently back toward the pillow. "Dear heaven," she gasped. "What happened? Was I run over by a carriage . . . or did someone shoot me?"

Dominic's smile was slow and warm and as she looked at him it suddenly came back to her why she was here.

"Sadie's . . ." she gasped.

Dominic nodded. "I'm afraid Bull's idea of a gentle drink is not exactly what one might expect to have served at an afternoon tea."

"Bull . . ." she groaned, covering her eyes with her hands. "Oh, I think I'm going to die." She was also remembering how angry Dominic had been last night when she pushed her way into the saloon at Natchez-Under-the-Hill.

"We . . . we were at a place called Sadie's," she said with a moan.

"Yes."

"And it rained," she said, glancing toward the windows. "It finally rained."

She turned to him and he nodded. She saw the questions in his dark eyes and wished her head would stop pounding long enough for her to ask what he did with the money.

"What on earth possessed you to come to such a place, Aimee?"

"I . . ." Was there no way she could avoid this until

340

later? "I wanted to see for myself . . . the way you used to live. . . ." She glanced at him, finding it very difficult to meet the hard gaze of his black eyes this morning.

"Why don't I believe that?" he asked, his voice husky and suspicious. "Maybe it's because I know you too well. There's something else . . . something you're not telling me."

She clenched her jaws, feeling the pain beginning again. Every movement she made seemed to cause a giant explosion inside her brain.

She gritted her teeth and forced the words out. She had to confront him sooner or later.

"Did you win or lose?" she asked, looking at him from the corner of her green eyes.

"What?" he asked, frowning and shaking his head as if he didn't understand.

"The fifteen hundred dollars, Dominic. I know you took it but I don't care about the money . . . really. If you've lost it, I don't care. I . . . I thought I did. I thought I could not possibly bear to lose LeBeaux, but if—"

He stood up slowly, letting his hands rest lightly at the top of his hips as he stared down at her.

"What in hell are you talking about? I took the fifteen hundred dollars from the desk to buy some new pieces of cultivating equipment. I told you before about the one Mister DeVaull has . . ." He stopped, his voice trailing away as he stared at her with eyes grown dark and stormy and laced with pain and disbelief.

"I can't believe this," he whispered. "You actually think I'm capable of stealing . . . from you? And worse . . . gambling it away?" He turned quickly and

341

ran his fingers through his tousled black hair, walking to the windows that let in the clear blue sky.

Aimee frowned, trying to focus on exactly what he was saying. And even as she felt the leap of joy in her heart, she also felt a stab of guilt and pain that was almost overwhelming. God, she had hurt him. This time, she had really hurt him.

As he stood with his back toward her, she could hear his muttered curses, could see the disbelieving shake of his dark head.

"Dominic . . ." She forced herself to sit up in bed and swing her legs over the edge, frowning again at the unfamiliar room and the throbbing pain in her head. "Where . . . where are we?"

He did not turn from the window and his reply was low and muffled. "Roselawn."

"What?"

He turned then, marching toward her with such intensity that she almost leapt back into bed. Instead, her fingers reached behind her to clutch at the carved mahogany bedpost.

"I said we're at Roselawn . . . my home . . . Roselawn." He practically spat the words at her. "There was a violent storm last night just as we left Sadie's. Besides, you were certainly in no condition to go staggering into your aunt Eulie's home in the middle of the night."

"Oh, God," she whispered, putting her fingers to her forehead. "Aunt Eulie."

"Don't worry," he growled. "George and I have taken care of that. She knows where you are. I've had all your things brought here."

But Aimee was paying little attention. Instead, she was staring with amazement at the room . . .

342

Dominic's home. Jim had said he owned a house in Natchez, but that he did not care for it and was rarely there. But how could anyone turn their back on such a warm, beautiful home as this? She continued to stare at the beautifully appointed bedroom with the warm pine floors and rose drapes . . . at the damask settee. The ornate cornice around the top of the wall was overlaid with gold leaf and every item, from the lovely little hand-painted mantel clock to the fresh roses beside the bed . . . every item reeked of elegance and wealth. She turned her emerald eyes toward Dominic only to see him watching her with a look of disdain.

"Yes," he whispered, his voice bitter. "My home. Surprised? Did you think I lived in a tent somewhere? Perhaps I should have told you about Roselawn sooner, Aimee, but this was my father's house and it has taken me years to accept it as my own." He began to pace then, his black eyes turning every now and then to nail her to the spot as his words pierced her very soul. "I told you when I came to LeBeaux that I had money, that there was no need to worry. Do you remember? But you said no. You couldn't accept money from a savage vagabond like Dominic Valcour, could you? Do you remember that as well? I've taken more from you than I would ever take from a man, Aimee. You've made me forget every vow of independence I ever made and now it's too late. My money wasn't good enough for you, was it? Nor my heritage." He was growing more angry, his dark skin flushed with the fury of his words. "But God," he said, frowning. "I never knew you distrusted me so completely as this."

Aimee could do nothing but stand there, weakly

holding onto the bedpost as she felt the brunt of his cruel words and his pain that lashed out at her like a punishment. And secretly she knew she deserved it. Her fear of caring, of letting herself feel emotion had been selfish, and now she could see it slowly and surely destroying any hope for a future with Dominic.

He grunted in disgust, seeing her look, seeing the tears in her emerald eyes. "Oh, don't worry, angel," he said. "It was never good enough for me either. I was ashamed of being Choctaw, and ashamed to be the son of a Frenchman who cared about little else except making money. So hell, I can understand your confusion." But his sarcastic tone refuted his words.

He stepped closer, gripping her arms and pulling her toward him until she thought the bones in her arms might actually snap.

"Do you know, what I wish, Aimee? I wish I hadn't fooled myself into believing you cared. I wish I hadn't convinced myself that what you gave so sweetly and so passionately meant something to you."

For a moment Aimee flinched as he bent toward her, as his eyes searched her face and came to rest on her lips. And when he continued, his voice was rough and husky.

"And I wish I'd told you before about Roselawn and all my father's money just sitting in the vault, waiting for someone to spend it. Perhaps then you wouldn't have thought twice about my taking the money or gambling away the last vestiges of your respectability. And I could have just gone on lying to myself about us forever, couldn't I?" He shook her for emphasis before letting her go, letting her fall backward onto the bed as she placed her face in her hands and wept.

"Dominic," she cried, coming to her feet and reaching for him as he whirled and turned toward the door.

"Don't, Aimee," he warned. He turned to stare at her over his shoulder with eyes grown cold and hard. "Just don't."

Thirty

Aimee watched him leave, heard the sound of his footsteps ringing down the hallway. Then she slumped onto the bed, unable to hold back the tears any longer. The more she cried, the harder her head pounded, but she couldn't seem to stop; she just couldn't shake the feeling of despair that swept over her.

She had doubted Dominic, and now, before it ever began, she was losing him.

"Oh, Dominic," she whispered into the pillow. "Nothing came out right . . . nothing I do is right anymore and I don't know how to explain all these . . . feelings that are mixed up inside me. But I love you. How will I ever make you believe that I love you?"

"Aye, lassie, 'tis a hard thing sometimes . . . being in love, eh?"

Aimee swung around, clutching at her throbbing temples as she looked at the woman standing in the doorway. She was taller than Aimee, a big-bosomed woman with a very straight stance and uplifted chin. Her gray hair was pinned loosely on top of her head and the gray silk morning gown she wore, though

346

plain, looked expensive. Dark eyes gazed with sympathy at Aimee.

Aimee frowned, trying not to cry, but when the woman came forward and enfolded her in matronly arms, Aimee began to sob all over again.

"There, there, lass. What has you so upset? Tell old Nellie about it. Why if you're not careful, you'll be makin' yerself sick, that you will."

Even through her tears, Aimee thought the woman's quiet, accented voice was soft and lovely, soothing to her aching head.

"You've got a wee bit of a headache, I see. Why don't you let me send up a laudanum potion for your head? Then you can have a nice cool bath and a change of clothes." Nellie's eyes took in the softly voluptuous body and the lovely olive skin of Aimee's arms and shoulders. She was a beauty for sure and it was no wonder the young master had fallen head over heels. But for the life of her, she couldn't figure what had the two lovers so distraught and distant from one another.

Aimee wiped her eyes and took a deep breath, nodding her consent and murmuring her appreciation as the woman turned and hurried down the hallway.

In only moments a young woman came into the room with a glass of water and a small brown vial of liquid which she handed to Aimee with a nod and a smile.

"Miz Nellie says to give you this and she say for you to drink every drop of this here water."

Aimee smiled weakly and did as the girl asked. Later, while she waited for her bath, she wrapped her discarded silk cape around her and walked about the room, going to the windows where Dominic had stood and murmuring with pleasure when she saw the full view. The house was situated right on the bluffs of the Mississippi and this morning the river lay like a wide blue ribbon, a gleaming slash through the lush green bank of trees that lined it.

"Beautiful . . ." she murmured, letting the beauty of the view help her forget. Turning to step out into the hall, she was immediately taken with the wide, cool hallway that ran from a front gallery to a similar one at the back of the house. The effect was light and airy and even now a cool breeze swept along the hallway, blowing the white lacy curtains from the open doorway of the gallery.

The view of the river drew her. That and the cool soothing breeze that rustled and moved the tops of the lush magnolias around the big house. And soon she was standing on the gallery, letting the wind and the scent of the river sweep over her, letting all her cares and fears go, if only for a moment.

She knew this house; she had seen it often on her trips to Natchez. She thought she had even asked her aunt about it once and had been told that it belonged to the son of a French trader and that the man only visited the house on occasion.

Aimee turned, staring with amazement at the beautiful brick house with its sparkling white trim. The perfectly kept lawn and surrounding rose gardens were simply breathtaking, as were the stately old magnolias that surrounded the house. It was the most beautiful setting, the most beautiful house in Natchez. And it belonged to Dominic.

Soon she heard the giggle of the servants as they carried water upstairs for her bath. She went back inside, smiling at the girls who gazed at her with curious eyes, then turned away to hide their shy laughter.

Aimee had no idea where the lovely peach-colored dress came from that lay spread upon the bed. And she didn't care. After her cool bath and the numbing effects of the headache potion, she found herself feeling immensely better. And she couldn't wait to go downstairs and find Dominic. There were so many things she had to explain, and she prayed it wasn't too late.

Later, coming down the steps into another wide, cool hallway, Aimee glanced around the beautiful house. Just across the hall was an open door and she walked across to peek inside the room. It was a small parlor, probably a ladies parlor, judging from the musical instruments and collection of dainty hand-painted glassware about the room. The piano was rosewood, with keys that looked like mother of pearl. Nearby sat an elaborately carved golden harp.

Aimee turned when she heard someone coming in at the back door, and smiled as she recognized the woman who had visited her earlier.

"Well, dearie." Nellie looked up from her basket of flowers and let her eyes wander over Aimee's new dress with its lovely straight lines and streamers of turquoise ribbons. "And you do look a lovely sight, that's for sure. Mister Valcour was exactly right when he said the dress would look lovely with your coloring."

"Mister Valcour . . . ?" Aimee looked down at her skirt with its layers of alternating colors of tulle.

The woman set the basket of flowers on a nearby table and put her fingers to her lips in a quieting gesture. "Aye, and I guess I shouldn't be tellin' you such things, now should I? I'm sure the master won't be thankin' me for runnin' my big mouth."

"Telling me what things?" Aimee asked, very curious to know what Dominic had to do with the dress and who it belonged to.

"That he bought that dress for you yesterday," Nellie said in a conspiratorial whisper. "And that he intended bringin' it home to LeBeaux Plantation . . . as a surprise."

"You . . . you know about LeBeaux . . . and about me?"

"Oh yes, indeedy," Nellie said with a quick grin. "We're like family here, we are. Not that Mister Valcour is here that often. But he could hardly keep himself from talking about you, lassie, or the beautiful plantation that the two of you own together now. He's as proud as anything about that place. And I knew your husband, too, you know; he's been in this house a time or two."

"Oh," Aimee said, feeling the despair sweep over her again at her own stupid distrust. Dominic had been excited about LeBeaux, excited about her as well. And while he was in Natchez, thinking of her, buying her this beautiful dress, she had been doubting him and worrying about money. Money which she thought he had used for gambling.

She felt like a fool. And worse than that, she felt heartache for what Dominic must be thinking.

"Where is he?" she asked. "Mister Valcour . . ."

"Oh, he's gone down to the river again . . . to see a lad about becoming a tutor, I do believe."

"Oh . . . yes." The disappointment Aimee felt was almost physical and for a moment she placed her hand at her stomach, hoping she wasn't going to be sick again.

"Oh dear," Nellie said. "Here 'tis past noon and you haven't eaten a thing have you, poor lass? Would you like to sit in the courtyard while I fetch something? Or would you prefer the back parlor here?" She motioned toward the music room Aimee had seen.

"The parlor will be fine," Aimee said. "But I'm not really very hungry."

"Oh, posh," the woman said with a wave of her hand. "Nothing heavy, mind you, but when you have a taste of Cook's spiced applesauce and cream, you'll agree it's just the thing for a queasy stomach."

Aimee wandered about the room, letting her fingers trail over the lovely furniture, and stopping to admire hand-painted French vases and a huge gilded French mirror that made the room look much larger than it actually was.

It wasn't long before Nellie returned, carrying a tray which contained applesauce and a small pitcher of cream that glistened with moisture. There was also a wooden bread board that held a loaf of crusty, buttered bread. Nellie set the tray before Aimee and stood back to admire the cook's handiwork.

"And here's a glass of cold milk as well, lass," the woman said.

Aimee smiled as she drank the milk, thinking nothing had ever tasted quite so good or quite so cool to her burning stomach.

She spent the afternoon going from room to room in the large, airy house, noting with breathless awe the beautiful furnishings, the expensive carpets and draperies. Later, she walked outside where she strolled through the lovely formal garden and breathed in the scent of the roses. Finally she walked to the edge of the yard that looked down upon the river and stood enjoying the cool breeze. She leaned on the rail fence along the bluff, watching the wheeling gulls dip and soar above the water, listening to a mockingbird that serenaded her from a nearby magnolia. The sun fell lower across the river, dipping into a long stretch of clouds and turning them to breathtaking hues of pink and gold.

She hardly heard the footsteps in the grass behind her.

"Nellie asked me to tell you that dinner is almost ready."

It was Dominic. And turning to look up into his black eyes, she thought her heart would stop. His eyes, so filled with fury this morning, were now cool and unreadable. He gazed at her as if she were a stranger.

With her heart in her eyes, Aimee took a step toward him, reaching her hand forward as if to touch him. But he moved away, going to the rail fence and gazing out at the river and the darkening rose-colored sky.

"Do you like Roselawn's view?" he asked.

She sensed his need to pretend that everything was all right between them. He didn't want to talk about her distrust again and perhaps it was easier for both of them if they pretended.

"It's beautiful," she said, turning back to the fence to stand beside him. She glanced up at him; she couldn't seem to bring herself to stop looking at him. "I don't think God could possibly have made a place more beautiful than this," she whispered. "I envy you." Her voice was soft as she gazed far to the north where the wide river stretched, making a silver pathway through the green trees and gleaming now with the colors of the sunset.

Aimee felt Dominic's gaze on her and looked up into his eyes . . . black cynical eyes filled with cool disbelief. Then he turned and walked away, leaving her heart in shreds and making her feel as if her world had grown as dark as the evening skies.

She followed him back to the house, gathering her peach-colored skirts as she walked up the wide steps to the porch. There was a servant to open the door for her, and another just inside the hall who handed her a cool, rose-scented cloth which felt refreshing to her face and hands.

Dominic stopped at the door to the dining room and turned to wait for her. He watched her with no expression at all and she could hardly believe this was the same man who had kissed her so passionately . . . the man who had pulled her into the water at the falls with such sweet, slow determination.

The man she loved.

Boldly she looked up, meeting his eyes as she entered the room, seeing the hurt and bitterness that still lay deep in them. And she knew then that she would do anything, promise him anything, if only she could wipe away the past few days and make things the way they had been before.

She was surprised to see a young man in the dining room and as she turned to question Dominic, he placed his hand beneath her elbow and lead her forward for an introduction.

"Aimee, this is the young man I told you about before, the man I've hired to tutor Lucas . . . Tucker Bryan. Tucker, this is Mrs. Aimee LeBeaux."

"Pleased to meet you, Mrs. LeBeaux," the man said with a low bow over her hand.

"Call me Aimee, please," she said, smiling at the young man.

She thought he looked not much older than Lucas. He was barely taller than she, with dark blond hair and sparkling blue eyes. A handsome young man, though she wondered with his slight build how he ever managed to survive the rigors of life on the river.

As they took their places at the long gleaming table, Aimee glanced about the room. She had only peeked into the dining room previously and now she let her eyes wander over the gold drapes and matching gold cornice, the elaborate silver tea service on the sideboard. And she thought the sparkling crystal epergne that graced the center of the table was one of the loveliest she'd ever seen.

Aimee smiled when Nellie came into the room, helping the servants place the food on the sideboard. The woman glanced at Aimee as she busied about.

"This is a very light meal this evening, Mrs. Le-Beaux, and we decided to let you serve yourselves. Mister Valcour said you wouldn't mind something less formal."

Aimee glanced at Dominic. "Not at all," she said. "That suits me perfectly. Why don't you stay and dine with us, Nellie?"

She could feel Dominic's gaze on her and turning to him, she was surprised to see a hint of warm approval in his black eyes.

"Oh, no . . . no," Nellie said, still moving dishes and arranging the sideboard exactly the way she wanted it. "Tonight is my sewing circle night. I like to get out of the house on occasion. And we'll be eatin' a meal there." Having finished with the dishes, she turned to Aimee with a warm smile. "But thank you,

Mrs. LeBeaux. It's very nice of you to think of me." Then with a smile and a nod to Dominic, she left the room.

Aimee was surprised and pleased at how well the evening went. If she had not known of Dominic's anger, if she had not been aware of the barrier between them, she would have thought it a perfectly normal, even pleasant dinner.

She especially enjoyed Tucker Bryan. His conversation was spirited and lively, and she discerned intelligence in his responses to her questions. She thought his blue eyes were alive with curiosity. He was just the kind of young man she would have chosen herself for Lucas's tutor and companion.

After the meal, the awkwardness between Aimee and Dominic seemed to return. She hardly knew what to do or what to say.

Tucker stood up first, turning to her with a slightly stiff, formal bow. "If you'll excuse me, Mrs . . . I mean, Aimee . . . I think I'll have a cigar out in the courtyard before turning in."

Aimee nodded and smiled as he left the room, thinking he hardly seemed old enough for cigars. Then she turned to Dominic who was watching her.

"So . . ." he said. "You seemed to like the boy."

"Yes, I do," she replied. "Very much. I think he'll be perfect for Lucas."

"Good," he said, his voice clipped and distant. "I'll feel much better, knowing Tucker is at LeBeaux." He stood and turned as if to leave the room.

Aimee frowned at him, wondering at his words and not liking the way they made her feel.

"Wait . . ." she said, jumping up to run into the hallway after him. Two young servant girls stood in the hall, just on either side of the door. Aimee supposed they were waiting to begin cleaning the table and sideboard. Seeing them, she slowed and made herself walk more sedately beside Dominic as he turned to go upstairs.

She glanced back at the girls who were grinning broadly at them.

"What do you mean?" she asked as she followed Dominic up the staircase. "You said you'd feel better; you sound as if you might not be there."

"I won't be." His eyes were dark as he gazed down at her, but he did not slow his steps.

They were in the upper hallway now and apparently alone. Aimee clutched at Dominic's sleeve, forcing him to turn around, forcing him to face her with his bitterness.

"You can't do this," she said, her voice shaking. "You can't let what's happened between us cause you to lose LeBeaux. I know you love it, Dominic, I can see it in your eyes when we're there, when you look over the fields. You love the land and the people just as much as I do and I—"

"That's not the point," he said, clenching his jaw tightly.

He started to walk on, but she came around in front of him, blocking his way as her emerald eyes blazed up at him.

"Then what is the point?" she asked, staring with pleading eyes up into his face. "You haven't even let me explain . . . you won't listen to my apology. God, Dominic, how are we ever going to get through this if you turn away from me every time I—"

Suddenly his hands shot forward to her shoulders, closing around her arms so painfully that she stopped

356

speaking. The anger he had been holding back seemed too much for him now and in the face of her words, he seemed to explode.

"I'll tell you what the point is," he shouted, then lowered his voice a bit. "I don't understand how a woman can take a man into her bed"—his voice was husky, his face so close she could see her reflection in his black eyes—"and yet not trust him. A man would have to be a fool to love a woman like that, wouldn't he?"

"But I . . . I—"

"How could such a woman make a man feel loved, as he's never been loved before, when she doesn't even trust him? Can you tell me that, Aimee? I never even knew what it was to need someone until I met you. Did you know that? Never knew that a man could want a woman so badly that she was like a requirement for living, that he had to have her every bit as much as he had to have air to breathe. Do you have any idea how much I had begun to want you, Aimee . . . to need you? Do you?" His voice rang with anger and his hands bit into the flesh of her arms as he shook her. Then, looking into her eyes, he pushed her away and started to walk around her toward the bedroom just across the hall from hers. "You never even noticed what was happening, did you, Aimee? You were too concerned with your precious land . . . your precious plantation!"

"No," she said, feeling the anger rising in her at his unfair words. She wasn't going to let him do this. She simply would not go meekly to her room to grieve while the best thing that had ever happened to her walked away. "Damn you, Dominic," she shouted, clutching at the back of his jacket. "Don't you do this

. . . don't you accuse me and then walk away without even hearing my explanation." There were tears in her eyes now and her throat felt tight and closed. But still she continued, clutching at him until he had to turn to her with an irritable sigh.

"Don't worry, I'll stay until the crop is in," he said, his voice cool. "After all, that is the most important thing, isn't it?"

"No, damn you, it isn't," she said, tears streaming down her face. "What do you want me to say? Do you want me to say I'm sorry? Because I am. Do you want me to say I was afraid to trust you . . . that I was afraid to commit my heart to someone after Jim. . . ." She lowered her head, hiding her tears and trembling lips from him. "God, Dominic, what do you want from me?"

"I want *you*," he whispered, his voice a quiet threat above her. "That's all. Not the land or the plantation . . . not the money. Jesus, since I met you I don't want to spend another night anywhere except in your arms. No river, no gambling saloon could ever offer me what you have, Aimee LeBeaux. And all I ever wanted in return for the surrendering of my heart was you. Isn't that a laugh? I was even willing to settle for second best, thinking you'd see sooner or later that you and I were meant to be together."

"We are, Dominic," she pleaded, looking up into his black eyes. Black eyes, grown soft with hurt, that sparkled now in the dim light of the hallway.

"No," he whispered, reaching forward to touch her tear-stained cheek. "I would gladly die for you, love. But one thing I won't do anymore is live in the same house with you, wanting you, making love to you . . . not if I can't have it all, angel. Not if I can't have your

358

heart."

"Dominic . . ." The word was a sob, a plaintive cry for his forgiveness. "Please," she said. "I love you!" She clutched at his sleeve for emphasis and stepped closer, hoping he would take her in his arms.

But he smiled sadly and stepped back from her.

"No, love," he whispered, letting his fingers touch her hair. "You don't love me. You need me and you want me . . . and while that's flattering and exciting, it's not enough, not when what I really want is heaven and beyond. You're afraid to really let yourself fall in love, Aimee. And I can't stand having only part of you. I have to have it all . . . your faith and your trust . . . I have to have your heart, angel, or nothing at all."

Thirty-one

It was the most miserable night of Aimee's life. Dominic had shut her out of his bedroom and it seemed, out of his heart. And with every tick of the clock through the long, dark night, Aimee felt the sorrow inching its way deeper and deeper into her heart and soul.

He didn't believe she loved him. And why should he? What had she ever done to prove it, except to give herself to him physically. And as Dominic said, that was easy; loving from the heart was much harder. But it was that kind of love she really wanted, she had known that all along. What she hadn't known was how to go about getting it. And she wasn't even sure she knew how to do that now. Dominic made her see what was missing from her life and from their relationship, and she intended to prove to him that she loved him, even if it took forever.

It was only the finalizing of those thoughts that let her sleep, that and the effects of the night before. Otherwise, she might never have been able to sleep just across the hall from Dominic. So near and yet so far away from him.

The next morning, when she gazed out at the bright sunlit skies, she smiled. She loved Dominic's home on the bluffs of the Mississippi and she could only pray that she would be back one day . . . she and Dominic together. But for now, she was anxious to go home, back to LeBeaux and the people waiting there for them.

She would send Aunt Eulie a note of apology for leaving without saying a proper goodbye. She just couldn't face her right now.

She could hardly wait to see Lucas. And the prospect of having Hawk to confide in made her feel hopeful. After all, he knew Dominic's mind better than anyone.

When she saw Dominic that morning for the first time, she thought he looked as tired as she felt. There was a frown line between his brows and his eyes looked red and weary. Last night he had been so confident, so sure of what he wanted, certain that he was not willing to settle for less. But Aimee thought perhaps those very words had kept him awake for most of the night, just as they had her.

Even as they prepared to leave, Aimee's eyes would meet his now and then. She could not help gazing deeply into those black, shuttered eyes, could not help trying to express how very much she loved him, if only with a look. But Dominic was silent and would hardly look at her.

As Bull Hadley promised, he and his men were at the livery stables promptly at ten o'clock. Aimee thought she'd never seen a more dangerous-looking group of men. She eyed them suspiciously, vowing silently to stay out of their way. But the red-haired Bull remembered her with a broad smile and a tip of his hat. Aimee thought that the gesture and her blush even brought a flicker of a smile to Dominic's serious face.

The new equipment had been loaded onto the long wagon and Dominic drove with Nathaniel beside him. And even though the young Tucker Bryan seemed conspicuously out of place with Bull's rowdy gang, he apparently did not feel that way. He rode among them with ease, laughing and talking, sometimes joking with the loud men, and Aimee could see that they liked and respected the young man.

As for her, she kept her horse well on the other side of the wagon, staying close to Dominic as she glanced from time to time at the loud, rowdy gang of men.

They stopped along the road to rest and have a meal. Aimee felt her heart ache every time Dominic walked away from her, every time he avoided her searching eyes. And each time she determined within herself to make him see that she could change, that she did love him. But she knew for now that she simply had to give him a little time.

It was a slow trip because of the heavy load they were carrying on the wagon. And so it was late afternoon when they passed the DeVaull Plantation. Aimee explained quickly to Dominic and rode toward the house to tell Jenny that she was safe and that she had found Dominic.

"Is everything all right, then?" Jenny asked, her brown eyes showing flecks of green in the afternoon light.

"Hardly," Aimee said, glancing back toward the road. "But it's a very long story, one I promise to tell you all about soon."

"I will hold you to that," Jenny shouted, as Aimee rode away.

They were more than a mile from LeBeaux when one of the men glanced into the darkening sky and shouted. "Hey, Mister Valcour, looks like a fire some-where up ahead."

Aimee's heart fluttered, then seemed to stop as she glanced toward the western sky. Here on the Trace, the view was often blocked by the dense vegetation and tall trees. But as they progressed, they could see the evening sky lit with a dull, orange glow.

"Give me your horse, Aimee," Dominic said, jump-ing down from the wagon and coming to take the reins from her hands.

Without protesting, she stepped onto the wagon and settled herself into the seat beside Nathaniel.

"Is it LeBeaux, Dominic?" she asked, breathless with fear.

"I can't tell," he said. He pulled the sidesaddle off the horse and into the wagon, then swung his leg over the horse's bare back.

She thought he looked at ease riding bareback, with his legs tightly pressed against the animal's sides. The horse was skittish, unused to being ridden this way, but Dominic held the reins firmly while the horse pranced and bucked until finally it had to submit.

Dominic turned and raced the horse down the nar-row Trace road as the rest of the men took off behind him. Aimee felt an urgent need to follow and as she glanced at Nathaniel, she could see those same feel-ings reflected on his face as he looked anxiously at the sky.

"It's LeBeaux, Nathaniel . . . I know it is," she said. "Dear God, I can't believe Compton has burned the house." Again her eyes moved to the reins in Na-thaniel's hands. "Can't we go any faster?"

He didn't look at her, but kept the wagon moving at a steady pace. "Not with the equipment in the back, missy. Fire or no fire, if I was to wreck this wagon and ruin that 'spensive piece of equipment, Mister Dom would have my head."

Aimee clamped her lips together, trying to keep from saying anything else. She knew Nathaniel was right and he was going as fast as possible. But as she glanced back at the wooden crates that held the cultivators, she wondered if they would ever have the opportunity to use them.

Nearing the long drive to the house, Aimee sat forward in her seat, straining to see through the trees and darkness. The entire sky above them seemed lit now from the flames and they could smell the scent of burning wood. Gray ashes drifted in the air around them and clung to the tree limbs and hanging moss. Bright sparks flickered here and there in the tops of trees and Aimee held her breath praying that the ashes would not set anything else aflame.

Her hands were clasped so tightly together that they felt numb and as soon as she saw the house still standing, saw that the glow of the fire was beyond there, she breathed a sigh of relief even though her heart still pounded furiously at her throat.

"Where is it?" she whispered. "Nathaniel . . . can you see?"

"I'd say the stables, ma'am," he said, frowning up at the sky as they approached the house.

"Oh, no." Not the beautiful stables with its hand-hewn rafters and brick exterior. Then she gasped, her hand reaching toward Nathaniel. "Oh, Nathaniel . . . the horses . . . the carriages." She held her breath as they turned the corner past the house and saw the flames shooting high in the air above what was once the stables. In the distance she could see the dark shapes of people running back and forth, silhouetted against the burning building. And even at this distance, they could hear the horrible, sickening scream of the horses still trapped inside.

Aimee felt a chill run from her neck down her spine, felt the skin of her arms and legs tingle as she realized what was happening. She couldn't sit on the wagon seat a moment longer, and jumped down to the ground, shouting back at Nathaniel as she ran.

"Leave the wagon here, Nathaniel. Come on, we have to help."

She could feel the heat from the fire long before she reached the men. And when she saw two men carrying someone toward her, she stopped, her hand at her throat as she waited to see who it was.

She ran to them, catching a glimpse of dark hair and long muscular legs. And as she gazed down at the man whose entire chest was covered with blood, she gasped and took his lifeless hand in hers.

"Hawk," she whispered. She glanced into the faces of the men carrying him, pleading silently with them to tell her he was not dead.

They didn't stop, but continued carrying him toward the house as one of them shook his head and shrugged his shoulders.

"It looks bad, ma'am . . . real bad," was all he said.

Aimee turned completely around, torn between going with Hawk and finding Dominic. "Find the woman called Cilla," she yelled after the men. "She'll take care of him . . . and tell her I'll be there as soon as I can."

She ran then, lungs bursting, heart pounding furiously, until she saw Dominic, until she could be certain that he was safe. When she saw him, she stopped, then walked on.

"Oh, Dominic . . . thank God," she said when she reached him. "Hawk's been shot."

"I know." The muscles of his jaw flexed beneath his skin and she could see the bitter anger in his eyes. "I told the men to take him to the house; there's something I have to do."

"It's all right," she said. "Cilla will take care of him. And so will I. Come to the house as soon as you can."

He nodded and she saw the relief in his eyes. He turned without a word and walked back toward the burning building. The roof had already collapsed and the fire still burned brightly enough for her to see him looking at a bulky form on the ground. And silhouetted as he was against the flames, she saw the dejected slump of his shoulders, the way his hand came up in a familiar gesture as his fingers raked through his hair. Then slowly, as if in a dream, his right arm lifted and Aimee saw the outline of a pistol in his hand as he aimed toward the object on the ground.

Her hand went to her lips, closing off her anguished cry as the gunshot exploded through the night air and echoed around them. Then Dominic turned and walked slowly away.

Aimee knew without even having to look that the object on the ground was the big black horse Dominic loved so well, the one that seemed almost a part of him from the day he first came. Dominic loved the animal—had been so proud of the horse and kept it groomed until its black coat glistened in the sunlight. They were alike, the two of them . . . dark and proud . . . strong. Dominic had told her once that the horse had the heart of a lion and the courage as well.

"Oh, Dominic," she whispered, her heart aching for

366

him. She could not even see him now for the tears that blurred her vision. "Oh, my darling . . ."

Angrily, she wiped at her eyes, but she couldn't see Dominic any longer; he had disappeared into the darkness. She turned to go back to the house, knowing that he was safe at least and knowing that he would not welcome her presence. She understood his need to be alone.

She ran back toward the house, wiping her eyes as she went and praying that Lucas was safe.

The men had carried Hawk into the front parlor and placed him on a sofa. The room was warm from the heat of the lamps and the scent of burning beeswax candles seemed suffocating. The atmosphere was chaotic with everyone milling about trying to help. She breathed a sigh of relief, seeing Cilla's steady hands cutting away Hawk's bloodied shirt. And that was also when she saw Lucas, his eyes bright with tears as he stood at the foot of the sofa looking down at Hawk.

"Lucas," she said, going to put an arm around his shoulders. "Oh, thank God, you're all right."

"They shot him, Aimee," he whispered through trembling lips. "They came out of nowhere, shooting and screaming . . . and all of a sudden, there was fire everywhere. He was so brave. . . ." Lucas looked up at Aimee and there were tears in his eyes as he faltered on the words he was trying to say.

"I know, Lucas," she said. "Shhh, I know."

"Hawk fought hard, Aimee . . . you should have seen him," Lucas's eyes were filled with awe for the man's courage. "But there was just too many. They shot him . . . they would have killed him. I tried to help, but one of them held me . . . and he laughed."

Lucas's dark eyes glittered and he gritted his teeth as he remembered the humiliation. "They were going to drag Hawk behind one of their horses, and they would have, if the Indians hadn't come."

"Indians? What are you talking about, Lucas?"

There was a hint of guilt in his eyes, a hint of defiance, too, she thought, as he stared up at her.

"The Choctaw," he said with a proud lift of his chin. "Hawk and Dominic's family. I know Dominic didn't want me to go, but Hawk thought he was wrong . . ."

"So, you went anyway . . . to their village. You met the family; you met Dominic's grandfather?"

"Yeah," he said, his voice quiet as he glanced back down at Hawk. "And they came here today to visit. I guess when they were going home maybe they saw Compton's men coming or something and turned back." His black eyes pleaded with Aimee to understand. "Can't you see, Aimee . . . it was Hawk's destiny for them to come back. If they hadn't come here today, if they hadn't come back, he'd be dead now. So that must mean he's going to be all right . . . doesn't it? He wouldn't be saved just so he could die now, would he?"

Aimee frowned and pulled him against her as she brushed a kiss against his hair. "I hope you're right, Lucas. I really hope you're right." She smiled as she held him, thinking how much he had grown, how much he had learned, not only from Dominic, but now from Hawk as well. It was good . . . his learning the Indians' ways was good; he was growing up and if he became half the man that Dominic and Hawk were, she'd be very proud indeed.

Lucas pulled away and looked up at her again and

368

there was fear in his dark eyes. "Where's Dominic? He's all right, isn't he? He didn't try to go after them or anything? His horse, Aimee, we couldn't . . ."

"I know, son," she said, smoothing his tousled black hair back from his forehead. "But Dominic's fine. I saw him just before I came into the house . . . he's fine. And we're all going to be all right."

She smiled at him as he nodded and straightened his shoulders.

"Open the windows," she ordered, moving away from Lucas and going to kneel beside Hawk. Cilla had already ripped away the shirt and was cleaning the wound.

"Is it bad?" she whispered, seeing the ragged wound in his shoulder and the black bruised flesh around it.

Cilla's black eyes flashed at her. "Well, it ain't good. Lord, Miz Aimee, I sho' am glad you all is back. It was awful . . . just awful."

Aimee nodded and looked down at Hawk's ashen face. She and Dominic had left him with a big responsibility, one that wasn't even his, and yet he had fought with his own life.

"You can't die, Hawk," she whispered. "You can't." Not now, when he and Dominic were so close and when he meant so much to Lucas . . . to all of them.

"Tell me what you want me to do, Cilla," she said.

"We need to get him upstairs to a bed and I need to see if that bullet be still in there. Then we just wait, missy. That's all we can do, is just wait."

Thirty-two

The men carried Hawk out onto the veranda and toward the stairs to the second floor. Following, Aimee saw Jezzy sitting in one of the porch rockers.

Aimee stopped, staring at the young black woman who rocked and sang in a breathy little whisper.

"Jezzy . . . ?"

She might as well have been speaking to the wind, for Jezzy did not even glance up, but kept rocking as if with some great purpose while she hummed and sang phrases of a song.

"Jezzy," Aimee said, speaking louder.

The woman turned to look at her and in the dimly lit veranda, Aimee could see the whites of her eyes as she stared with terror at her mistress.

"Death and destruction," Jezzy muttered, still rocking. "Death and destruction done come to this house, missy. Better get out . . . better get out." Her words were in rhythm with the rocking of her chair.

Aimee sighed and shook her head, feeling too much anger and frustration to deal with Jezzy's superstitions, too.

"Just stop it, Jezzy. Stop this nonsense right this minute. Do you hear me? I want you to get up from that chair and find something constructive to do.

Cilla needs help upstairs; go up and ask what she needs and then you help her. Do you understand?"

Jezzy only stared at her and continued rocking. "The spirits is gatherin'," she moaned, looking around with huge frightened eyes. "Can't you feel it, Miz Aimee? Can't you feel their breath in the warm air ablowin' across this house? I can. I can feel them breathin' on us right now." She began to wail and to rock faster, leaning forward to cover her face with her hands. "Oh Lawd, have mercy on this poor black chile," she cried. "Miz Aimee," she wailed. "You gots to place a dish of salt on poor Mister Hawk's chest, ma'am. Spirits won't bother nobody else in the house if you leave the salt for them on the dead body. . . ." her voice faltered as she stared up into Aimee's eyes.

Despite Aimee's anger and frustration with the girl, chills ran down her arms at Jezzy's crazed rantings. And even though she knew that the girl always cried about death and destruction and that it meant little, tonight Aimee felt defenseless against it.

Suddenly she reached forward, grabbing Jezzy by the arm and jerking her out of the chair, turning her about and shaking her hard.

"Listen to me, Jezzy. If the spirits are coming for me and my home, they'd better hurry — I've little time or patience for their mischief tonight."

Jezzy's eyes flew open as if her mistress had committed blasphemy and she tried to pull away from her hard grip.

"Hawk is not dead yet, do you hear me?" Aimee found that she could barely contain her fury as she gripped Jezzy's arms and shook her again. "And I don't give a damn about the spirits or what they

371

want. Next time you see one, you'd better tell him for me to stay away from LeBeaux Plantation and away from the people I love. For so help me God, nothing is going to harm any one else in this house. Do you hear me? *Nothing!*"

Jezzy nodded silently, frightened and surprised by her mistress's violent flare of anger.

"Now you get yourself upstairs and help Cilla and if I hear any more of your nonsense, I'll have you lashed until you can't walk. I'll whip you myself. Now, get!"

As Jezzy hurried along the veranda and up the stairs, Aimee stood alone, trembling from head to toe. She hardly knew what had come over her, but she was mad . . . madder than she'd ever been in her life. Mad enough to fight to the death for her home and the people she loved. She went to the porch railing, lifting her face to the cooling night breeze and taking deep breaths to calm herself.

"Poor Jezzy," she whispered finally, remembering the girl's frightened little face. She shouldn't have said she'd have the girl whipped—she couldn't even imagine why she'd said it.

She took one last breath of fresh air and turned to go upstairs to Hawk's room. When she reached the top balcony, she heard the sound of hoofbeats coming from the area where the fire had been and she turned with a start to gaze out toward the road. She could hear the shouts of riders and see the torches some of them carried high above their heads as they rode past the house. And she prayed that Dominic was not with them, for she knew instinctively that their destination was the Compton Plantation.

It was nearly midnight when Cilla finally declared that she had done all she could for Hawk.

"The bullet done passed on through Mister Hawk's shoulder, praise de Lawd. When I swabbed out the wound he roused a bit, the pain was so bad." Cilla smiled and shook her head with admiration. "He some man, that one. Didn't even make a sound and I know it musta hurt somethin' fierce. He asked about you and Lucas, then he asked if Mister Dominic was all right. Then, poor man, passed dead away again. Ummm ummm." Cilla shook her head in sympathy.

"Do you think he'll be all right, Cilla?" Aimee asked.

"Can't say," she said. "I seen men die wasn't hurt nigh so bad as this one. But he's a tough one all right . . . stubborn and strong-willed just like our Mister Dominic. If'n I was to guess, I'd say he will be."

After Cilla left, Aimee sighed and sank into a chair, gazing toward the man lying on the bed. Lucas was sitting in a chair near the bed and his eyes hardly moved from Hawk's face.

Aimee rose again and walked to him and placed her hand on his hair, pulling his head against her side as she caressed his face.

"Cilla says he's very strong, son . . . and courageous. And I have a feeling he's going to be all right."

She felt Lucas's nod of agreement against her hand, but he said nothing. She bent to kiss his cheek, then knelt beside the bed, taking Hawk's hand in hers and holding it against her breast.

"We need you, Hawk," she whispered. "You're

part of our family now . . . we love you and need you. Don't leave us . . . you can't leave us now." She thought he looked so young lying there . . . so handsome and vital and too full of life to die.

But then, she'd thought the same thing about Jim, hadn't she?

Impulsively she leaned forward and kissed his lips, then whispered into his ear. "Please, Hawk . . . don't die."

She left Lucas in the room with the wounded man, knowing it was useless to try and persuade him to leave. She wanted nothing more than a cool bath and to change from her grimy clothes. And she wanted desperately to know what was happening at Compton's house.

Long past midnight, Aimee sat on the veranda, waiting. The night air was cool and the heavy scent of rain lingered sweetly in the stillness, even overpowering the ugly smell of smoke.

She couldn't sleep, knowing that Hawk lay upstairs near death, knowing that Dominic must have gone with the riders earlier. And now all she could do was wait; if it took all night, she intended to be here when Dominic came home.

Several times she heard noises and stood up to walk to the end of the veranda. Once she saw a raccoon shuffling out of the bushes to saunter across the sandy road. She walked through the quiet house, going out onto the front porch to wait for a while. She was there when she heard the distant drumming of hoofbeats and came to her feet, walking to the front steps and gazing hard into the darkness.

As the riders rode past the house and around the back, Aimee picked up her skirts and dashed through the hallway and out onto the back veranda. She was waiting when she saw Dominic's tall form come through the garden toward the steps and she turned to lift a lantern so he could see.

"Dominic . . . I was so worried about you. What happened? Did you go to Compton's? Was he the one who—"

"Which question do you want answered first?" he asked wearily, coming up onto the veranda.

Every movement he made, every gesture reflected his disgust and his weariness. His face was darkened with soot and streaked by sweat. His clothes still held the smoky scent of the fire.

"You must be tired and I know you're anxious to have a bath and go to bed, but please . . . just a few moments."

He leaned his hand against the porch railing and gazed down into her face. She had never seen him this way and it frightened her. He was hard and cold; there was not a flicker of feeling in his dark eyes and she wondered if he had even an ounce of compassion left in him. Until he spoke.

"Tell me about Hawk," he said, his voice breaking with emotion.

She could see the dread in his eyes as he spoke and she knew he thought his cousin was already dead.

"He's hurt badly, but he's alive. Cilla seems to think he's going to be all right. She said he was stubborn and strong . . . just like you."

Dominic made a small noise of disgust and turned away from her, slamming his hand against the post that supported the roof.

"I should never have asked him to stay here,

knowing what Compton is capable of doing."

"You couldn't have known, Dominic. None of us could know what would happen."

"No, but I had a damned good idea. The bastard." The black eyes that gazed out into the dark night were cold and filled with some sense of satisfaction.

"What did you do? Did you go to his house . . . confront him?"

"Let's just put it this way: Mister Compton no longer has a tobacco barn, and his cornfield won't be yielding anything this year."

"Dominic . . ." she whispered, staring at him with disbelief. "You . . . you burned his barn? I can't believe—"

"Yes, by God, we burned his barn," he said, whirling to stare at her. "An eye for an eye—isn't that what the white man's bible says? The only way to deal with scum like Compton is to meet every challenge he gives you, head-on. He knows now that whatever he destroys here will be met twofold on Compton land and perhaps he won't be so anxious next time. And I swear . . ." His voice cracked and his fist crashed against the post. "I swear on my mother's grave, if Hawk dies, that bastard will learn what true agony means. He'll beg me for death before I'm through with him!"

Aimee shuddered at his words as he turned and stalked across the veranda and up the stairs. His fury left her speechless and she found herself trembling at the intensity of his threats. She had no doubt he meant every one of them.

Dominic Valcour was a man to be reckoned with and if she had not known that before with certainty, she did now.

The next morning was gray and the clouds seemed to hang just above the rooftop of the big house. Aimee was on her way upstairs to see Hawk when she heard a scream and saw Jezzy running from the kitchen to the back porch. She had seen Aimee and was pointing out past the garden.

"Miz Aimee . . . Miz Aimeee . . . they's here . . . they's here."

"For heaven's sake, Jezzy. What is it now?"

A thick dense fog drifted just above the ground and as it moved and shifted, Aimee saw them. There near the canebrake were at least a dozen men on horseback—Indians. In the mists they looked like apparitions that changed and wavered before her eyes as they sat silently staring at the house.

"Dominic!" she cried, going to pound at his door.

He obviously had already heard Jezzy's screams for the door opened immediately and he emerged, still buttoning his shirt and frowning down at her with sleep-dimmed eyes. "What is it? Is it Compton?"

"No." She pointed silently toward the Indians and Dominic frowned, then walked slowly down the steps. She watched him as he went through the garden, his stance straight and proud, his long legs carrying him quickly across the clearing to the men on horseback.

She watched, not wanting to take her eyes away from them as they talked and gestured. And finally Dominic, with an outstretched arm, motioned back toward the house and the men began to move forward on their horses.

Aimee hurried down the steps to the lower ve-

randa and as she waited, she watched the Indians—
the family of the man she loved. She was curious
about them and about the way they lived. Some
were dressed no differently than a white farmer
might dress and some of them wore the fringed
buckskins and soft boots that Dominic and Hawk
favored. Several of the younger men were bare
chested and wore necklaces and amulets on their upper arms. They were handsome people, tall, magnificent warriors, and again, seeing them brought to
mind the phrase Dominic had used when he lay ill
and unconscious.

"Choctaw siah," she whispered to herself as a reminder.

As they approached the house, she saw Dominic
motion them away from the garden gate and toward
the entrance by the kitchen. Then she saw that behind one of the horses was a small wooden cart and
in the cart lay a man.

She and Jezzy waited while the men were out of
sight behind the kitchen. Then she saw Dominic
leading some of them past the brick building toward
the house. One of them, a large, muscular man,
carried a very old man wrapped in blankets. With a
quick intake of air, Aimee knew this must be
Dominic's grandfather and that he had come to see
his wounded grandson, Hawk. She could hardly believe he was here, or that Dominic was taking his arrival so calmly.

She glanced toward Jezzy and saw the girl clutching at her dress with a nervous mannerism. The Indians all glanced their way as several of them went
up the steps and the rest waited at the bottom as if
standing guard.

"Jezzy," she said in a low voice. "Go to the kitchen and tell Cilla to send refreshments for our guests."

Jezzy hesitated, her eyes wide and apprehensive as she stared at the dark strangers whose faces were so solemn.

"Go on, Jezzy," Aimee said. "They won't hurt you."

When Jezzy scurried past the men on the porch, she only glanced at them from the corner of her eye. One of them smiled broadly at the girl and the rest simply nodded their heads in a grave, dignified greeting.

Aimee was restless with curiosity. She wanted nothing more than to go upstairs and see what was happening. She hoped desperately that Hawk was better and that he would know his grandfather was there. And more than that, she wondered how Dominic was responding to the old man's presence. He had seemed so bitter about him before.

The Indians stayed for three days. Three days in which Aimee and the rest of the household came to know the men and learn about them. Surprisingly enough, they found that the Indians were not much different from them. Some of them even spoke a few words of English and before they left, Jezzy and Amos, Cilla and Delilah had taught them even more. Aimee could not hide her laughter at the thought of the Indians learning some of Jezzy's language, but nevertheless, they seemed to enjoy it and that was all that mattered.

The plantation had gone from a relatively quiet place to one that rang with the sound of male voices, and the sound of laughter. Even the rough keelboatmen who Dominic had hired seemed to enjoy getting to know the Indians. And Lucas and young Tucker were in their heaven.

On the last day that the Indians were at LeBeaux, Aimee sat on the veranda with her sewing basket nearby, and watched Lucas and Tucker with the Indians. She glanced around just in time to see Dominic coming down the stairs and she called to him.

"How is Hawk this morning?"

Dominic smiled and walked over to her and sat on the porch railing. "He's as irritable as a bear."

Aimee laughed, delighted that the handsome man was recuperating so rapidly. "That's good. That means he's getting well."

Dominic nodded and glanced out toward Lucas and Tucker.

"They seem to be getting along well enough."

"Yes," she said. "Everything's good." She glanced up at him from beneath her lashes. "Almost everything."

For a moment he looked into her eyes and she saw a hint of the sweet emotion that had been between them before. It surged like a warm summer breeze, touching both of them with a bittersweet hand. Aimee wanted more than anything to stand up and go to him, put her arms around him and feel his lips on hers. And she could see in his eyes that he wanted it, too.

When he stood up and walked away, Aimee's smile was wistful, but oddly, instead of her usual sadness when she saw Dominic, she felt a glimmer of hope.

Later, Jezzy was taking a tray up to the grandfather's room, when Aimee stepped forward and took it from her hands. "I'll do that," she said. "And you take something up for Hawk."

Aimee had wanted an opportunity to speak with Dominic's grandfather before. But he had been quite ill since coming to LeBeaux and was often sleeping or simply too weak to talk for any length of time. She had seen Dominic coming out of the room several times and each time his dark head would be bent as if he were lost in thought.

When she went into his room that last day, the elderly man was sitting up in bed and as she entered the room, he smiled at her.

"Are you hungry?" she asked, going to the bed and setting the tray on a table.

"Yes," he said, his deep voice weary and scratchy.

She thought he must once have been as handsome as his two grandsons, with his deep-set black eyes and rather hawkish nose. She could imagine him as a young man, tall and proud, just like Dominic and Hawk. But now he was withered and every breath he took seemed labored and hard.

She sat down beside him, noticing that despite his saying he was hungry, he ate only a few bites of food before setting it aside.

"I'm sorry you must leave," she said, hoping he was not too tired to talk.

He nodded. "It is time. My grandson Hawk grows strong and I must go. Blackfox has a good home now," he said, looking around the room with satisfaction. "And a good woman." His eyes twinkled as he looked into Aimee's. "But I wish to die in my own house, beneath my own blanket."

She frowned and reached forward for his gnarled

381

hand. It felt cold beneath hers.

"Don't say that," she said.

His smile was filled with a sweet wistfulness that made Aimee frown.

"Death is a friend, child," he said. "An old friend whom I have met along the way. He has always let me pass before, but now I can feel him near me. He waits in the night sky for this old warrior."

Finally she nodded, trying to accept his words. "I've wondered about something . . ."

He leaned his head forward as if trying to catch her words.

"I've wondered about Dominic and . . . and if he has made peace with you."

"It is what you wish for him, is it not?"

"Yes," she whispered. "Yes, I do. I want him to be happy, to be free of whatever haunts him in his past so that he can enjoy his life."

"It is what I want for him as well," he sighed. "I have tried. I have told him I was wrong. Sometimes a man is harsh with those he loves; sometimes he says things he does not mean and they live to haunt him for the rest of his days. I sent my daughter away, banished her from the family. She had disgraced us once by taking a white husband and Blackfox was the result of that marriage. I forgave her then because I loved the boy so. But she disgraced us all the second time by taking the son of my greatest enemy into her bed. Blackfox was but a young boy who loved his mother and he did not care and he did not understand."

"But, if all you did was send her away . . . why would that make Dominic so bitter?"

The old man stared into space past Aimee's head

as his eyes sparkled with unshed tears.

"She was not a bad person . . . in her disgrace and sorrow, my daughter . . ." He hesitated and sighed heavily. "My only daughter, Blackfox's mother, took her own life."

"Oh." She felt her heart aching for the young boy that Dominic had been. Neglected by a cold, ambitious father, confused about his home and heritage, he'd had to suffer the tragic loss of his mother as well. She could understand his bitterness toward this man, even though now, in his old age, he had admitted his actions were wrong, committed because of the same stubbornness and pride that Dominic had inherited.

"So you see why my grandson cannot forgive his grandfather. He could not forgive me . . . and I could not forgive myself."

"I do understand," she said. "But I also think that he has taken a great step by having you here, and by talking with you."

"Yes," he said with a wise nod of his gray head. "He has listened to my heart at last."

"Good," she said. "I'm glad."

She could see that he was growing weary but there was one last question she had to ask.

"*Mingo*," she said respectfully. "Would you tell me what something means?"

The old man nodded. "If I can."

"When Dominic was ill, he spoke two words that I have wondered about, although I never asked him what they meant. I had a feeling they were words from his past, from when he lived with you. I felt almost as if I had overheard something I should not have." The Indian nodded again and she continued.

"He said the words, *"Choctaw siah."*

The old man's eyes lit and she thought the smile that trembled on his lips was wonderful to see.

"He has not forgotten," he whispered in a husky, emotion-filled voice. "My grandson has not forgotten."

"What?" she asked gently. "What does it mean?"

When he looked at her there were tears in his dark, weary eyes. "They are the words of a warrior. The warrior's proudest boast is *Choctaw siah — I am a Choctaw.*"

Thirty-three

The next morning when the Indians left, Aimee stood with Dominic, watching them go. She also watched Dominic as he waved, saw the look in his eyes; she thought there was sadness there as well.

"Your grandfather loves you, Dominic," she said, not knowing how he would react to her interference.

"And I love him."

"Then you told him that . . . that you love him?"

"Yes, I told him." He gazed after the Indians and his mouth was clamped into a hard line. "As much as I've hated him, I couldn't let him die without telling him that I forgave him and that I love him."

"And have you? Forgiven him?" Watching him, Aimee thought she didn't see much forgiveness in those eyes.

"I'm trying," he said, turning to look down into her face. "But the meek old man that you met is not the one I knew before, Aimee. My grandfather was hard and cold; he could shut you out with just a glance. And he could be extremely cruel and unforgiving at times."

385

"Oh," she said, looking deep into his eyes. "Then I know all too well how you must have felt." She turned then and walked away from him.

Dominic watched Aimee leave and he frowned. He wasn't like his grandfather . . . he couldn't be, not with Aimee, never with her. It was all he could do to maintain the distance he had chosen to put between them. But he shook his head, wondering at the look in her eyes and the sadness he'd seen on her face since coming back from Natchez. As he walked away from the house, his eyes were puzzled, and he could not seem to help the rush of emotion he felt, remembering her, wanting her still as quickly and deeply as ever. He could not stop himself from remembering the feel of her in his arms, her warm accepting body beneath his, and the sweet murmur of her words in his ear.

The next few weeks were filled with such activity on the plantation that Aimee hardly saw Dominic. She was with him and Lucas when they told Hawk goodbye and watched him climb onto his horse, looking normal and healthy except for the ugly new scar on his shoulder.

"I won't be far away, cousin," Hawk said. "If you need me."

"I'll remember," Dominic said with a smile.

"And Lucas, my little warrior," Hawk said, turning to the boy. "Remember your promise to come visit me soon."

"I will," Lucas said, his voice highpitched with excitement. "Me and Tucker both will come."

"Good."

Hawk turned his dark eyes toward Aimee and she stepped forward as if he had spoken her name aloud. He reached down for her hand and leaned over on his horse so that his words could be heard only by her.

"I think it was your sweet kiss that saved me, Aimee."

"What?" Her emerald eyes opened wide as she stared up into his and her lips parted in surprise. "Why Hawk . . . you devil. How did you . . . ? I thought you were unconscious . . ." She practically stammered as she felt her face growing flushed and warm beneath his intense gaze.

He chuckled and bent to kiss her hand. "Ah, but your kiss, little one, could awaken a dead man." His eyes twinkled mischievously at her. "Take care of my stubborn cousin," he said. "I'll be back."

As Hawk rode away, Dominic stepped toward Aimee, his black eyes alive with curiosity. She even thought she saw a glint of jealousy there as well.

"What exactly was that all about?" he asked.

She smiled and shook her head. "I don't think you want to know."

The weather had grown almost unbearably hot. The only thing it seemed good for was cotton. The fields were alive with the plants that rustled in the hot wind. They had watched the blossoms change from creamy white to pink and then to a purplish blue before they dropped off and the bolls began to form. In only a few weeks, if nothing untoward happened, the bolls would burst forth, revealing the white cotton inside and Le-Beaux would see its first successful crop.

Despite the coolness between her and Dominic, Aimee found herself almost giddy with excitement and she was caught up in the work in the fields and house. The kitchen buzzed with activity as Cilla and her girls cooked and preserved the bounty of the garden and orchard. The air was filled with the ever-present scent of drying peaches or simmering blackberry jelly.

The days were good and Aimee thought the only thing that could make her life perfect was for Dominic to forgive her. And she knew it would take only one word from him for her to welcome him back into her arms and into her bed.

One afternoon, just before dinner, they heard the sound of riders coming up the front drive. When Aimee saw who it was, she clapped her hands together, as excited as a child and ran to find Dominic. He was upstairs in his room preparing for dinner and when he answered the door, he frowned, then smiled at her obvious excitement.

"What is it, angel?" he asked before he thought. "You're as excited as Jezzy."

"You have to come with me, Dominic. Hurry." She took his arm, even though his shirt was not quite buttoned, and pulled him toward the stairs.

Out past the garden, Dominic saw their neighbor, Mr. DeVaull, leading a prancing stallion, whose black coat gleamed in the hot afternoon sun.

There was a slight frown between Dominic's eyes as he allowed Aimee to pull him through the garden and out to where Mr. DeVaull sat smiling down at them.

"Good afternoon, Mister DeVaull. That's a beautiful animal you have there."

"Ah," Mr. DeVaull said, smiling at Aimee. "I see you haven't told him yet."

Dominic turned to her, frowning at the look in her eyes and the way her teeth chewed at her lower lip. She looked like a child who had done something wrong and was wondering if she would be punished.

He frowned and shook his head. "What?" he asked. Then he turned again to the horse that snorted and pranced as if he knew his worth and knew what a beautiful specimen he was. He had spirit and heart, Dominic could see that right away, much like the one he'd lost in the fire.

With a soft murmur, he turned to Aimee, the realization dawning in his black eyes.

"The horse . . . ?"

"Is yours," she said. "I hope you don't mind. Perhaps you would have preferred finding one on your own. But he's a fine horse, Dominic . . . well bred and—"

"Aimee," he said as a slow smile moved across his lips. He shook his head again, unable to believe what she had done. He couldn't remember anyone ever doing such a thing for him.

"Here you go, son," Mr. DeVaull said, handing the reins to Dominic. "He's all yours."

Dominic took the reins and walked up close to the animal. Its ears pricked up and its nostrils flared, but as soon as Dominic placed his hand on the stallion's nose, it quieted. Dominic murmured softly to the horse, moving away to rub his hand down its neck and chest and front legs.

"He's beautiful," he said, still not turning around.

"Mister DeVaull," Aimee said. "Won't you come in and join us for dinner?"

"I'd love nothing better, my dear. But I promised Mrs. DeVaull that I'd be home before nightfall. She's still a bit uneasy, being in the wilderness, even after all our years of living here. And I don't like her to be frightened if I can help it."

"I understand," Aimee said, smiling up at him. She nodded toward Dominic who seemed enchanted with the black stallion. "And thank you, Mister DeVaull, for bringing the animal," she said.

"It was my pleasure. The horse is going to make a fine stallion if you ever decide to try breeding racehorses. And remember, the first foal is mine." Mr. DeVaull winked at Aimee and turned with a wave of his hand to ride away.

She looked at Dominic and found him watching her as he stood with his hand on the stallion's neck.

"I can't believe you did this," he said.

"Why? You're not . . . you're not angry with me are you? Because if you are, if you don't want him—"

"No, no," he said, frowning at her with an odd look in his black eyes. "I'm not angry, or displeased . . . I'm just . . . dumbfounded that you thought to do such a thing for me."

Aimee frowned and put her hands on her hips, staring at him with a funny little look on her face. Her green eyes flashed.

390

"You're a very strange man, Dominic," she said. "How else would you expect a woman to treat the man she loved."

Aimee held her breath as she turned and walked away. She wanted to leave before he had a chance to protest, before he took the opportunity to tell her that he didn't want her love or her gift of a horse. But as she neared the house, she turned to look over her shoulder and saw Dominic still standing there, staring after her.

Dominic avoided her for the next few days. But she saw him riding the great black stallion and she thought they were made for each other. One afternoon, Dominic had been working with the men rebuilding the stables. He was wearing no shirt and when he climbed on the horse for a quick ride to the fields, she thought he looked like some splendid warrior, with the wind tugging at his black hair and the afternoon sun glinting on his dark skin.

As he disappeared into the distance, she sighed and walked back into the house.

That evening after dinner, Tucker and Lucas went into the parlor for a game of cards and Aimee wandered out into the garden, hoping to escape the heat for a while.

She was surprised when Dominic joined her there.

"Your garden has flourished," he said, running his hand lightly along the rose blossoms. "It suits the place well."

"Yes," she said, glancing at him from the corner of her eye and wondering why he had come. "I think so, too."

"Aimee," he began.

She thought his voice was as soft and seductive as the warm Mississippi night.

"Aimee," he repeated, as if trying to gather his thoughts. "I . . . I never thanked you properly for the stallion."

She turned to look at him, at the depth of emotion on his face and in his dark gaze.

"You don't have to thank me—"

"I do . . . need to thank you. He's a beautiful animal and it was very kind of you."

"Kind?" she said with a lift of her brow. "I didn't do it to be kind, Dominic," she whispered, looking up into his face. "I saw how hurt you were when your horse died in the fire and I simply wanted you to feel better. I wanted to see your face when you saw this stallion, and knew he was yours. It wasn't kindness, Dominic. I suppose, if anything, it was actually selfish . . . because I wanted to see you smile again."

"Aimee," he said, frowning at her and warning her with his dark eyes that she was treading too close to a subject he intended to avoid.

"Don't," she said, moving closer to him. She placed her hands on his flat stomach and felt his muscles tensing beneath her fingers. "Don't ask me not to care, Dominic. And don't expect me to be distant and cold. Because I can't . . . not with you. I want you, more than I've ever wanted anything in my life. And I need you, just as you said that night at Roselawn." She heard his quick intake of breath and felt the warmth of his skin beneath her hand as it moved upward to his chest. "But more than that, I love you." Her voice broke then, and she reached up to touch his lips with her own.

Suddenly she was in his arms, in the sweet familiar constriction of his embrace as he returned her kiss with a soft, reluctant groan. And for all his denial, his mouth was hungry and searching and she felt the quick flash of heat rush through both of them before she pulled away and looked up into his eyes as she tried to catch her breath.

"Don't keep your anger and bitterness between us like a shield, Dominic," she pleaded softly. "Forgive me . . . and love me if you can. For I love you, my darling . . . with all my heart."

Dominic took a long deep breath of air as he watched her walk away from him and out of the garden. He stood very still and watched until she had gone into her room, until his eyes began to burn from staring so intently into the darkness. Then he rubbed his fingers over his face and turned wearily to go up to his room.

Sometime during the night, Aimee woke, hearing the distant rumble of thunder. She got out of bed and walked to the shuttered windows, looking outside and noting how the wind whipped the flowers and bushes near the porch. Her eyes moved upward, to Dominic's room and she was surprised to see a glint of light through the closed curtains.

And even after she went back to bed, that glint of light made her wonder, and kept her awake until morning when the rain finally began to fall.

It was a long, slow, lazy day as the wind and rain kept them all indoors. The slaves would have a day of rest. Luckily, the roof had already been built on the new stables so that Bull and his crew could work indoors. Aimee was glad that Dominic had thought to include a long building attached to the back of the stables for Bull and his men. It looked as if there was enough work to keep them here for a long time, and who could tell what the future might bring if this first crop was a good one.

During that long, rainy day, Aimee would catch Dominic's dark gaze on her. Once he was coming from the stables, and as he took off his hat on the veranda, he glanced over at her. She met his glance, challenging him with her smile and feeling a rush of exhilaration when he frowned.

She knew that puzzled frown, the one that came when he found himself wanting her, she thought. And she knew that he was disturbed by being closed in today, by the rain that seemed to throw them together at every corner of the big house. And she gloried in the heat in his black eyes that silently warned her to stay out of his way.

At dinner that evening, Dominic was very quiet, even though Aimee caught him staring at her several times. She deliberately wore an emerald green dress that he liked and left her dark hair down to fall loose and free around her shoulders. She smiled at him over the candles, not caring that he could probably see her heart in her eyes, or that Lucas and Tucker might wonder what was going on between them. She didn't care; she loved Dominic and she didn't care—she wanted to be able to tell the entire world how much she adored him.

After dinner, when Dominic immediately left the

dining room without a word, she felt disappointed. And hours later when she was in her room, she was surprised to find him standing at her door with a look of purpose in his dark eyes.

"Come in," she said, her voice barely audible above the rain.

The wind whipped across the veranda, bringing the sweet scent of rain to mingle with her perfume. The soft material of her emerald skirt swirled around her, reaching out and wrapping intimately around his booted legs as if to urge him into the room.

He had tried to stay away from her and he had failed. And as he looked down into those jade eyes, he knew he was lost forever.

He took her arms then, pulling her with him as he walked into her bedroom, but holding her away as his eyes blazed down at her in the dim light of the oil lamps.

"I don't know if I can ever be the man you want me to be, Aimee," he said, his voice hoarse and urgent. "I'm stubborn, and overbearing; sometimes I have this need to be alone, often for days. I have a tendency to keep things to myself at times and I can't stand having someone tell me what to do, even when I'm wrong. . . ."

She smiled up at him, her lips trembling as she began to realize what he had come to say.

"I'm all the things you've accused me of being . . . bossy and arrogant, dictatorial . . . and sometimes I shut people out when they get too close. But never . . ." he whispered, shaking her gently. "Never does any of that mean I don't love you or want you or need you. I'm sorry." He pulled her against him. "Sorry that I hurt you and pushed you away and failed to see that you were confused and grieving. Because I love you, Aimee . . . I love you."

She was crying now and trembling in his arms. "I hurt you, too, and I'm sorry, darling . . . so sorry."

Her words were lost as he found he could not resist her lips for another moment.

The breath caught in Aimee's throat as his arms tightened around her waist and she felt herself being held close against his long muscular body.

"Dominic," she whispered, putting her arms around his neck and standing on her toes so that she could be even closer.

The rainy sounds of the night seemed to enclose them there in her room as the heat of their desire blazed higher and higher. Aimee could feel her legs begin to tremble as he kicked the door closed and scooped her up in his arms to carry her to the bed.

She could hardly believe he was here at last, that the distance between them had finally been travelled. She gloried in the feel of his hands as he undressed her, in the scent of his heated sun-bronzed skin.

She opened her eyes as his hands moved down to her waist, his fingers spanning her narrow width easily. They moved caressingly down to the curve of her hips, pulling her against him and letting her know how very much he wanted her.

Aimee gasped, feeling as if he was already making love to her, hot with excitement and oblivious to the sound of the rain that pounded on the rooftop.

Her fingers moved to his shirt, unbuttoning it

396

while she looked into his eyes and accepted his heated kisses. She spread her fingers across his chest, feeling the heat of his skin and unable to stop herself from touching her lips there.

"It's hot," she whispered. "I feel so hot."

Her eyes moved over his face as he quickly discarded his clothes and moved back into bed on top of her. She couldn't get enough of seeing his beautiful skin, the chiseled features of his face, and always those black eyes that simply took her breath away with their intensity. Shadows from the oil lamp played across his face, across his white teeth and sensuous lips that were parted with his heavy breathing.

The way he looked at her made her tremble. He moved his body provocatively against hers until she was aching for him to make love to her. And still he caressed her, and tortured her with his kisses.

He took her hands and moved them over her head, holding both of her wrists in one hand as he touched her breasts, then dipped his head to replace his warm fingers with soft, hot kisses.

At the feel of his lips and his tongue against her skin, she arched against him, moaning and closing her eyes as the heat spread and warmed, as she felt her body seeming to melt into his.

"I want to love you, Aimee," his warm, husky voice murmured against her ear. "Love you and touch you this way forever."

"Yes," she whispered. She could feel the sweet overwhelming power of his words beginning to take their toll on her body, could feel the excitement moving lower and making her wild with longing and need.

Her hands fluttered as she whispered to him and when he released her hands and quickly entered her, she felt the fierce pulsating of her own body, felt the almost unbearable spiral of ecstasy wash over her until she cried out against his chest.

"Yes," she whispered fiercely, feeling the power of him, feeling the incredible excitement of his lovemaking. "Yes . . . yes."

She held onto him, crying out his name as her body responded wildly, then slowly relaxed. She heard his soft laughter and opened her eyes to look up into his face. She saw the warmth of his eyes and the undeniable love as he smiled knowingly down at her. She reached for his mouth, kissing him and urging him to love her.

He began to move against her again, slowly, erotically, making love to her now with sweet, insistent purpose. He whispered to her, words of love, phrases that she didn't even understand. Until both of them were frantic once again and she felt herself quickly at the edge of that incredible feeling. Dominic's hands slid beneath her hips, pulling her closer until it began for both of them, the delicious, overwhelming wave of ecstasy that came closer and closer and finally erupted into an explosion of unbelievable pleasure.

"Aimee," he whispered, clasping her against him until she could barely breathe. "Aimee, love . . . my love."

She held him close, glorying in the wonderful sensations, in the response of his body and wrapping her arms around him as she kissed his face and neck with delight. As reality returned for both of them, Aimee became aware of the heated room and the sound of rain outside and she sighed. Had anything ever been so wonderful as this? This loving and being loved?

Dominic loved her. Never had any realization made her so happy, and she knew that after this night, nothing would ever be the same for either of them.

She belonged to him now, truly and totally, and he to her. He had given himself to her tonight, not only in body, but in spirit as well. She knew it, had felt it in her soul—that wonderful, unbelievable feeling when lovers give themselves completely.

And finally tonight, they both had opened wide their battered hearts and let each other in.

She was his now, body and soul; she was the woman of the handsome Choctaw half-breed known as Blackfox. And she knew now what magnificence it was to belong to a warrior.

Thirty-four

Those were the happiest days of Aimee's life. The plantation seemed to thrive and everywhere she looked were smiling faces and the sound of laughter. And she knew that many of those smiles were directed at her and the new master, as some had begun to call Dominic.

Lucas had actually taken quite well to his lessons and she knew that Tucker's youthful enthusiasm was part of the reason. He was a companion to Lucas as well as a teacher, and they began to see the boy lose his almost frenzied dependence on Dominic. She asked him about it one day.

"Does it bother you, Dominic?" she asked. "Seeing Lucas so totally involved with Tucker that he doesn't run to you with every question?"

He smiled down at her. "On the contrary," he murmured, bending to kiss her lips. "I'm ecstatic that he's happy. It gives me much more time to spend with you."

"Hmm, you seem to always know just exactly what to say to me."

"And what to do?" he said, nipping at her ear with his teeth and laughing at her soft gasp.

Some days it was all she could do not to throw

her arms around him in front of whoever might happen to be nearby. She'd look into his eyes and see that look meant especially for her and she thought she could not bear another moment without feeling his touch.

Their days were spent working hard and enjoying the progress that was being made at LeBeaux. And the nights . . . oh, she thought the nights with him were worth any price she could name.

Sometimes they came together with a love that was sweet and gentle, warmed by a day working side by side and seeing their dreams becoming reality. Other nights, the sultry darkness and the Natchez moon seemed to drive them wild and they could hardly undress fast enough to give in to their overwhelming desires. They would tumble onto the bed, gasping together at the pleasure they gave one another and engaging in quick, hot sex that left them exhausted and laughing with joyous disbelief.

"I never want to spend another minute away from you," Dominic told her. "I want to love you this way forever."

"It's what I want, too," she whispered.

"Marry me, angel, and let me hold you in my arms this way every night for the rest of our lives."

"Yes," she replied. "I think that's what I wanted from the first moment I saw you . . . for you to be mine."

"You could have fooled me," he said, laughing softly. "I am yours, Aimee," he whispered, growing more serious. "And I want everyone to know that I've captured Aimee LeBeaux, the most beautiful, most desirable woman on the Mississippi."

She laughed, delighted at his possessiveness. "I think everyone knows," she said, teasing him with her smile. "In case you haven't noticed, the entire plantation seemed to be watching our love affair with great interest."

"Let them," he said. "Let them watch . . . and envy me."

Aimee thought life was perfect. As soon as the cotton crop was in and sold in Natchez, they would be married. The only thing hanging over them was the possibility of Compton's further interference. And although things had been relatively quiet since the fire, there had been reports from the slaves, of men lurking about the edge of the forest, watching them as they worked in the cotton fields.

Finally, Gregory Davis declared the cotton ready to be picked.

"We have to work fast now, Mister Valcour," he said. He seemed to have grown used to addressing Dominic with the respect due the new master of LeBeaux. And since there had been no trouble from the slaves, he had even grudgingly given his respect on that matter as well. "The cotton has to be picked as soon as it ripens so it won't be damaged by rain or wind . . . even dust can harm a crop. If we're lucky we should be able to pick these fields three times before the first frost. And that's good. In case the first crop does go bad, we'll have the second and third ones to depend on."

"Good," Dominic said, turning to Aimee with a smile of satisfaction. "We've made it this far and we want to make sure nothing happens to harm the crop now. You just tell us what you want, Mister Davis, and we'll do everything we can to make sure you get it."

The hands began picking the cotton the next morning. And even though some of the slaves had never picked cotton, they learned quickly. Aimee watched them move through the bushy rows, a burlap bag around their neck or hung at their waist. They needed both hands free to pick. As soon as the bags were full they were emptied into huge baskets that sat on a long, flat-bed wagon. As soon as the first picking was finished, they would take the cotton into Natchez to be ginned and sold.

Aimee and Dominic sat on their horses that first day, watching the slaves move over the field. Mr. Davis came over to sit with them.

"How does the cotton look?" Dominic asked.

"Looks fair to middlin' in the half grade," Davis said, gazing out toward the field. "Hard to tell with a first crop like this. We have to be careful to keep it dry and keep the sand out of it. And we need to have it ginned properly, otherwise, it won't be worth a hill of beans."

Finally after several days, the bolls were stripped clean and the baskets of cotton stored in the dry shed. They would take the cotton to Natchez next day if the weather remained dry and clear. Aimee planned to go along, and Dominic had told Amos and Nathaniel they could go as well.

She knew Dominic was still worried about Compton and that he wanted Bull to stay with the men and make sure nothing happened at the plantation while they were gone. And he, Amos, and Nathaniel would stay on the docks that night with the cotton until the next morning when it would be inspected and sold. And at the last minute, he even allowed Lucas and Tucker to go along with them.

The trip was pleasant and the weather cooperative, at least for the time being.

Aimee looked forward to being at Roselawn again and planned to spend the night there. But once in Natchez, she did make a trip to her aunt Eulie's to let her know she was in town. She spent most of the afternoon explaining her last trip to Natchez, finally telling her aunt that she was in love with Dominic.

"We plan to be married soon, Aunt Eulie," she said, watching her aunt's face for her certain disapproval.

"Well," the woman said. "It's about time. It was plain as the nose on your face that the two of you were in love when I visited your home in the early summer."

Aimee laughed, delighted and surprised with her aunt's approval. "Well, I guess it wasn't so obvious to us until later."

"I'm delighted for you, darling . . . simply delighted. You look happier and more beautiful than I've ever seen you."

"I am happy, Aunt Eulie. To tell the truth, I'm so happy that it scares me."

That evening when Aimee had to say goodbye to Dominic, she felt only a twinge of disappointment. She had known beforehand that he planned to spend the night on the docks and she was prepared for it. And after tonight, everything would be perfect for them.

She stood on the porch as he and the others left Roselawn. She watched them ride to the crest of the bluffs and disappear down the winding road that led to the river.

And that night after a very pleasant meal with Nellie, she went upstairs to the bedroom where Dominic had brought her that stormy night. As she drifted off to sleep, her mind was filled only with the bittersweet memories of that time when she realized what a complicated man Dominic was and how much she really loved him.

She slept soundly and when she woke near dawn she was so happy and contented that she thought little of the noise she heard downstairs. She sat up in bed, thinking she'd heard the slamming of a door. When she heard voices in the hallway downstairs, she quickly got out of bed and grabbed her robe. But before she reached the stair landing, she saw Lucas coming up the stairs two at a time, his young face wrinkled with worry and concern.

Her heart seemed to stop.

"Lucas," she cried. "What's wrong? What are you doing here at this time of morning?"

"It's Compton, Aimee," he said, panting as he tried to regain his breath. "They came in the early morning hours, out of nowhere it seemed."

Aimee held her breath as she saw the panic in his eyes.

"They were shooting and yelling. Nathaniel was wounded and . . . and Amos . . . they shot Amos." His face crumpled and she saw tears well up in his dark eyes. "He's dead, Aimee . . . poor old Amos is dead."

Fear and grief stabbed at her chest at his words. "Amos . . . ?" she whispered. "Dead?" She couldn't speak, couldn't dare put into words the fear in her heart. She reached out and took the boy's arms, running her hands down them as if to convince herself he was whole.

"They burned the cotton . . . all of it, then they took off into the night."

"Is Nathaniel all right? Where is he?"

"There were other men on the docks. They said they'd take him to a doctor's house. Nathaniel said for me not to worry about him. He said I had to come and find you right away and tell you what happened."

"Where's Dominic, Luke? What about Dominic?"

"He's gone after them." Lucas's voice was soft as he looked up at her and she saw his fear, saw the guilt that he had not been able to stop him. But she knew Dominic better than anyone and she knew that no one could have prevented his going, not even herself. And she remembered the fierce and bitter vengeance he had vowed toward Compton when Hawk lay so desperately ill.

"No," she whispered. "Go downstairs, darling, and tell Nellie to gather some food for us. Where's Tucker?" she asked as she ran down the hall toward her room.

"He's downstairs, too."

"Good," she said. "We'll need him. Have the horses saddled, Lucas—we're leaving in fifteen minutes."

Once on the road, Aimee felt better. The restless energy inside her seemed to dissipate somewhat with each stride of the horse beneath her. They rode hard, not even stopping to eat, until they were no more than an hour from Compton's plantation. And that was when Lucas rode close beside her.

"If I take the trail just ahead, I can get to the Choctaw village, Aimee. I can find Hawk and go through the woods to Compton's house before you get there."

"No, Lucas, it's too dangerous." Her eyes flickered away from the pain and disappointment in his.

"I can do it, Aimee. I'm not a baby anymore. When are you going to treat me like a man?"

A man? Aimee wanted to cry out to him. He wasn't a man; he was just a boy, a sweet, precious boy who she wanted to protect and who she could not bear to lose. How could she let him go on such a dangerous ride alone? Even with Tucker along, she was terribly frightened by what could happen in the wilderness.

Then her mind turned to Jim and how he had died at Compton's place. How he had been alone, just like Dominic, outnumbered and in trouble. And as a result, he'd lost his life.

"No," she whispered aloud. "Not Dominic, too. Please, God, not Dominic." She turned to Lucas, searching his face, searching the intensity of his gaze as he silently pled with her to let him go, to let him help Dominic and prove to her once and for all that he was not a child any longer.

"Oh, God," she said, reaching across to grip his arm. "Go on then, son. Ride as fast as you can and find Hawk. And pray that we're not too late."

A soft smile lit Lucas's eyes and without another word, he wheeled his horse away from her, shouting to Tucker over his shoulder as they went. "Come on, Tucker."

She watched them ride away and felt the fear moving even more intensely in her heart. Somehow, alone, she felt the danger of what was happening even more, and she was terribly afraid that when she found Dominic it would be too late. And she didn't know how she could bear it.

When she neared the drive to Compton's house, she reined her horse into a slow trot and reached down inside one of the saddle bags, drawing out the small pistol she carried. She held the gun in her hand, laying it against her thigh as she nudged the horse's sides.

She saw only one servant on the front porch of the house and she shouted at him.

"Where's Compton? Is he here?"

The old man pointed toward the back of the house and she could see that his eyes were wide with fear. Then she rode around to the back of the house and saw other servants, standing and gazing through the surrounding trees to a clearing just beyond.

"What is it?" she asked. "What's happening?"

They eyed her suspiciously, but one of them recognized her and pointed toward the clearing. "They's havin' a duel," the man muttered. "Mister Compton and the man from your house, Miz Le-Beaux."

"Please," she whispered desperately. "Please . . ."

Pushing her way through the dense vegetation to the clearing, she saw them. Saw Dominic standing tall and erect in the small grassy opening beneath the moss-laden trees. Just behind him, so their backs were almost touching, was Compton, and in his hand, he held a long-barreled dueling pistol.

Within the shelter of the trees, she got down from the horse, still holding the small pistol in her hand. She could see Compton's men all around the clearing, some of them with rifles in their hands, others grinning as if they would make sure what the outcome of the duel would be.

Aimee felt helpless, more helpless than she'd ever felt in her life. She wished she had a rifle, anything except the small pistol that held only two shots.

Aimee held her breath as she heard the count and saw the two men begin to walk away from each other. She gazed around her, feeling her heart being to pound as if in a death knell.

"Where are you, Lucas?" she whispered.

She couldn't bear to watch and yet she couldn't stand to tear her eyes away from the man she loved. How could she live if she had to watch him die? She clutched the pistol in her fist, vowing to kill two men at least if Dominic fell. And the first one would be Compton. She knew now with a hot vengeance how Dominic had felt that night with Hawk. She didn't care that the others would probably kill her; she didn't want to live without Dominic.

"Halt," she heard and she saw Dominic and Compton stop, still with their backs to one another. "Turn . . . and fire at will."

She saw a strange look move just then across the faces of some of Compton's men and as she stared into the dark forest behind them, she saw the Indians who moved silently forward. Compton's men had seen them, too, and those who held rifles, now dropped them to the ground while the others lifted their arms out from their sides away from their weapons.

She saw Lucas, then, and she felt sweet relief. And she saw Hawk, saw the solemn look on his face as he stepped just into the clearing and looked worriedly toward the two men in the center of the meadow.

Compton lifted his weapon and took aim toward Dominic. And in her heart Aimee was crying out, "Shoot, Dominic . . . shoot him."

But Dominic stood his ground with a calm, cold determination while Compton fired first. His shot was hurried and she saw the puff of smoke around the pistol, heard the zing of the bullet as it whined harmlessly through the air and into the forest.

Aimee clasped her hands tightly together, watching Dominic's face as he stood very still and slowly lifted his pistol. She knew he could lower the pistol now and he would still be declared the winner; he could be compassionate and spare Compton's life.

But she saw the look on his face, the pure cold hatred in those black eyes that held such cold purpose. And she shivered, knowing Compton was a dead man.

She could see the man trembling as Dominic took calm steady aim and Compton was forced to stare down the barrel of the pistol, held so steadily in his opponent's hand. She could even see the glisten of sweat on Compton's face.

"This is for Amos, Compton, a poor old Negro who never did anyone any harm. And for my friend, Jim LeBeaux."

The gunshot rang through the forest, loud and jarring, and Aimee felt herself jump.

The bullet struck Compton directly in the heart. Aimee grimaced and closed her eyes as she saw him fall forward like a stone, dead before he ever hit the ground.

She began to run then, oblivious to the men who stool pale faced and disbelieving as they watched their leader die on his own soil. But beneath the watchful eyes of Hawk and his warriors, none of them moved.

She ran across the rough ground, crying and whispering Dominic's name until he turned and saw her.

He threw the pistol on the ground and opened his arms, catching her as she threw herself against him, holding her tightly as he kissed her face and eyes and whispered to her.

"It's all right, love," he said. "I'm all right."

"Oh, Dominic," she cried against his neck. "I was so afraid . . . so afraid."

He looked down to her hand that still held the pistol and he smiled sweetly as he loosened her fingers from the gun and dropped it to the ground.

"I'd hate for you to shoot me in the leg, now that you've rescued me," he said.

"Oh," she said, taking his face in her hands and pelting kisses against his jaw and chin, then his mouth. "Don't ever do this to me again, Dominic

Valcour. Don't you ever scare me like this again. I couldn't live if anything happened to you."

"Never, my love," he whispered against her mouth. "Never. I intend to raise my sons and sit on the veranda at LeBeaux while I watch them play."

"Sons?" she asked, her voice catching in her throat. Aimee found that the thought of having his children made her grow weak with tenderness.

"*Our* sons," he whispered. "Soon."

"Anything," she said. "As many as you want."

He laughed with delight and swung her around until her feet left the ground. He set her back on the ground, and kissed her before they turned to walk away. And he waved toward the Indians at the edge of the meadow and saw Hawk's returning salute. It looked as if they intended to remain until Dominic and Aimee were safely away.

Lucas came running across the clearing and threw himself against Dominic.

"Dom . . ." he said breathlessly. "I've never seen anyone shoot the way you did. Were you scared? When he shot at you, weren't you afraid?"

Dominic patted the boy's shoulder and put his arm around him. He walked between Lucas and Aimee, gazing down from one of them to the other. "Yeah," he said. "I guess I was afraid. But not of dying, Lucas. Only for what I would lose if I let him kill me, son." He bent to kiss Aimee and look into her emerald eyes.

"Only for what I would lose."

412

CLARA WIMBERLY is a native of Cleveland, Tennessee, where she has lived all her life. She has always been fascinated by the history and traditions of the Old South and has taught creative writing and worked for many years for the U.S. government. She is married and has three children—two sons and a daughter. Clara is the author of six Zebra Gothics, and *Tomorrow's Promise,* her first mainstream novel for the To Love Again line.

**FOR THE BEST OF THE WEST, SADDLE UP WITH
PINNACLE AND JACK CUMMINGS . . .**

DEAD MAN'S MEDAL	(664-0, $3.50/$4.50)
THE DESERTER TROOP	(715-9, $3.50/$4.50)
ESCAPE FROM YUMA	(697-7, $3.50/$4.50)
ONCE A LEGEND	(650-0, $3.50/$4.50)
REBELS WEST	(525-3, $3.50/$4.50)
THE ROUGH RIDER	(481-8, $3.50/$4.50)
THE SURROGATE GUN	(607-1, $3.50/$4.50)
TIGER BUTTE	(583-0, $3.50/$4.50)

Available wherever paperbacks are sold, or order direct from the Publisher. Send cover price plus 50¢ per copy for mailing and handling to Pinnacle Books, Dept. 753, 475 Park Avenue South, New York, N.Y. 10016. Residents of New York and Tennessee must include sales tax. DO NOT SEND CASH. For a free Zebra/ Pinnacle catalog please write to the above address.

PINNACLE'S PASSIONATE AUTHOR—

PATRICIA MATTHEWS

EXPERIENCE *LOVE'S* PROMISE

LOVE'S AVENGING HEART   (302-1, $3.95/$4.95)
Red-haired Hannah, sold into servitude as an innkeeper's
barmaiden, must survive the illicit passions of many men,
until love comes to free her questing heart.

LOVE'S BOLD JOURNEY   (421-4, $4.50/$5.50)
Innocent Rachel, orphaned after the Civil War, travels out
West to start a new life, only to meet three bold men—two
she couldn't love and one she couldn't trust.

LOVE'S DARING DREAM   (372-2, $4.50/$5.50)
Proud Maggie must overcome the poverty and shame of
her family's bleak existence, encountering men of wealth,
power, and greed until her impassioned dreams of love are
answered.

LOVE'S GOLDEN DESTINY   (393-5, $4.50/$5.50)
Lovely Belinda Lee follows her gold-seeking father to the
Alaskan Yukon where danger and love are waiting in the
wilderness.

LOVE'S MAGIC MOMENT   (409-5, $4.50/$5.50)
Sensuous Meredith boldly undertakes her father's lifework
to search for a fabled treasure in Mexico, where she must
learn to distinguish between the sweet truth of love and the
seduction of greed and lust.

*Available wherever paperbacks are sold, or order direct from the
Publisher. Send cover price plus 50¢ per copy for mailing and
handling to Pinnacle Books, Dept. 753, 475 Park Avenue South,
New York, N.Y. 10016. Residents of New York and Tennessee
must include sales tax. DO NOT SEND CASH. For a free Zebra/
Pinnacle catalog please write to the above address.*

PINNACLE BOOKS HAS
SOMETHING FOR EVERYONE —

MAGICIANS, EXPLORERS, WITCHES AND CATS

THE HANDYMAN (377-3, $3.95/$4.95)
He is a magician who likes hands. He likes their comfortable
shape and weight and size. He likes the portability of the hands
once they are severed from the rest of the ponderous body. Detec-
tive Lanark must discover who The Handyman is before more
handless bodies appear.

PASSAGE TO EDEN (538-5, $4.95/$5.95)
Set in a world of prehistoric beauty, here is the epic story of a
courageous seafarer whose wanderings lead him to the ends of
the old world — and to the discovery of a new world in the rugged,
untamed wilderness of northwestern America.

BLACK BODY (505-9, $5.95/$6.95)
An extraordinary chronicle, this is the diary of a witch, a journal
of the secrets of her race kept in return for not being burned for
her "sin." It is the story of Alba, that rarest of creatures, a white
witch: beautiful and able to walk in the human world undetected.

THE WHITE PUMA (532-6, $4.95/NCR)
The white puma has recognized the men who deprived him of his
family. Now, like other predators before him, he has become a
man-hater. This story is a fitting tribute to this magnificent animal that stands for all living creatures that have become, through
man's carelessness, close to disappearing forever from the face of
the earth.

*Available wherever paperbacks are sold, or order direct from the
Publisher. Send cover price plus 50¢ per copy for mailing and
handling to Pinnacle Books, Dept. 753, 475 Park Avenue South,
New York, N.Y. 10016. Residents of New York and Tennessee
must include sales tax. DO NOT SEND CASH. For a free Zebra/
Pinnacle catalog please write to the above address.*